CONTACT

Alien Invasion Book Two

AVERY BLAKE

JOHNNY B. TRUANT

STERLING & STONE

To YOU, the reader.
Thank you for taking a chance on us.
Thank you for your support.
Thank you for the emails.
Thank you for the reviews.
Thank you for reading and joining us on this road.

CONTACT

Chapter One

"Did you see anything?" Piper asked. "Anything at all?"

Trevor was slumped on the couch, his NexFlight game system's power cord creating a tripping hazard in the underground bunker. It was supposed to be plugged while charging, but the batteries had dwindled to useless over a month ago. There were vast stores in a cold cellar near the bedrooms, reserved for flashlights and lanterns in case of emergency. Meyer would have a fit if Trevor used them for games. But Meyer wouldn't throw a fit because he was gone. And, Piper felt more certain by the day, was never coming back.

"I didn't look." Trevor's eyes never left the game.

"You didn't look? Go look, Trevor."

Trevor sighed and met Piper's eyes for a split second. Then, as he'd been doing since his teen boy hormones had kicked on months before the ships had arrived, looked moodily away. As if he couldn't face her, or was too cool for a maternal figure — stepmother or not.

"What?"

"What's the point?"

"'*What's the point?*' What if your dad's out there, Trevor?"

"He's not."

"You don't know that."

Trevor shrugged — he didn't have an answer but wasn't ready to obey. The same shrug he'd give his sister, if Lila had asked. But Piper wasn't his sister. And with Heather around, she clearly wasn't his mother. But she was *something*, and dammit, she didn't like being ignored.

"Go on, Trevor. We all have our jobs."

"Why, though? Dad made the place a fortress with everything we'd want or need. You keep *making up* things to do that don't need to be done. 'Check the air filters, Trevor.' 'Check the cameras, Trevor.' 'Bring out more cans, Trevor,' as if anyone can't just grab whatever food they want. And what exactly am I supposed to be looking for with the air filters? What do *I* know about air filters? 'Yep, they still look like big fuzzy accordions.'" Trevor rolled his eyes. "It's like you're just trying to keep us busy."

Piper felt her temper rising. At first, she'd felt nothing but fear. Then Meyer had vanished, and intense worry mingled with her terror. A halfway sense of loss followed a few weeks of missing him, but even the emptiness had been hard to maintain over the past three months as the bunker's day-in, day-out routine composed life's underground ritual.

Wake, chores, kill time, sleep. Rinse and repeat.

Crowds gathered on the grounds above, then swelled to a small colony. They'd stopped being able to go outside, and cabin fever worsened. Resentment was Piper's newest emotion. She had to shoulder this burden herself. She seemed to be the only one willing to do what was needed to keep them together, safe, and sane. It was a responsibility she hadn't asked for and didn't want. Meyer might have saved them, but he'd also left his wife holding the bag when he'd gone … well … wherever it was he'd gone. It wasn't fair.

"Just do it, Trevor," she snapped.

He rolled his eyes again then stalked toward the control room next to the storage pantry. His shoulders were slumped, and she caught his put-upon look. She wanted to shout after him to improve his attitude but couldn't stand the sound of those words from her mouth.

"No sign of Dad on the cameras," Trevor said, emerging a few minutes later. "Though I don't know why *you* couldn't just look."

Piper held her tongue, forcing herself to remember that Trevor was as scared, cooped-up, and angry as she was. It was inconvenient that his method of coping made it harder for Piper, but it was what it was.

The thought softened her mood. She eased onto the ottoman beside the couch as he lay back and resumed his game.

"Trevor. Look at me."

His eyes found Piper's. She saw his angry glare melt into a boy's dark and injured gaze. Then his eyes flicked away, but even a moment of vulnerability was better than nothing.

"I know you think this is stupid. And I guess you don't like me telling you what to do." That last bit had a double meaning. Even back in New York, Piper hadn't told either of the kids what to do. She'd always felt too much like one of them, being only eight years from her teens. But times had changed, and in their new situation, Heather only made jokes. Piper didn't want to be the bunker's only responsible adult, but if she didn't take the helm, nobody would.

"I'm just trying to do what your dad wanted. He built this place to keep us safe. And thank God he did, right?"

Trevor shrugged without looking up.

"But … Trev … it's not enough to *survive*. It's not only just having enough water from the spring — and food, and vitamins, and the UV lamp for Vitamin D, and enough propane to get us through the winters. Yeah, he *did* make this place a fortress, and yeah, he was a smart man who thought ahead and—"

"You mean *is*," Trevor mumbled into his shirt. "He *is* a smart man."

"Of course, honey." Piper put her hand on his arm in what she hoped was a motherly way. Trevor flinched but let her hand remain. At least that was something. "He thought ahead, and that means we have everything we need to survive for a long time."

Piper considered telling Trevor some of the particulars she'd learned from the systems manuals but decided not to. Trevor was barely listening, and he might find the details more daunting than comforting. He didn't need to know about the power redundancies, the satellite hookup, the three levels of water supply, the stockpiled propane, or the weapons that terrified Piper more than reassured her. For Meyer Dempsey, "prepared" and "paranoid" were sisters. There were entire sections of the manuals — the deepest cellars of Meyer's paranoia — that Piper couldn't bear to read. Meyer truly *had* thought of everything, including things nobody should ever have to think about.

"But 'just surviving' is kind of like … like 'barely alive.' We don't want to simply *exist*. We need things to do. To stay normal, you know?"

"That's why we have a TV. And games and books."

Piper sighed. "Yeah, but just being entertained is like being on vacation all the time. Do you know how, at the end of summer vacation, you're almost *eager* for school so you're not just sitting around, doing whatever you want?"

"No."

"I'm not sure I can explain this in a way that'll make sense, but ..." Piper sighed. "Even if the result of our chores don't matter, *doing them does*."

"Mom says they're stupid."

Piper looked toward the doorway, leading into the bunker equivalent of a study. Heather and Lila were in there, mostly out of earshot. Piper would probably win if Heather challenged her authority to tell the kids what to do because Heather was such a wiseass. Piper didn't want to test that theory. Heather, like the kids, seemed determined to deny certain realities. But it wasn't fair to ask the kids to choose between two mother figures. Like parents divorcing, Heather and Piper had to present a unified front rather than using the children as pawns between them.

"She's not thinking about things like this, Trevor. Your mother has her hands full with Lila. She's much better with the whole pregnancy thing, seeing as I've never been pregnant."

Seeming embarrassed, Trevor glanced down at Piper's body then back at his own chest.

"Your mom's good at being a mother, and I'm good at ..." She trailed off. *Nagging* came to mind, but Piper didn't like that at all. She searched for a replacement to describe her pestering duties. Nothing came.

"Look," Piper said. "Think of it this way: do you think it's stupid to keep checking those cameras?"

"Maybe."

"What if tomorrow is the day you check them and see your father?" Piper pointed toward the spiral staircase in the room's corner. "Right up there, at the door by the bathroom, appearing on the kitchen camera. What if he comes back, but we never see it?"

"Can't he just knock?"

The simple question — and the almost hopeless way Trevor had asked — broke Piper's heart. "I don't think he could do anything we'd hear, sweetie. The door is strong, and closed is closed."

Trevor shifted moodily on the couch. "If you wanted him to come back, you shouldn't have closed us in."

"That's not fair, Trevor. We discussed this. All of us, together."

Trevor shook his head. Again, Piper tried to slip inside his mind to see things as he must be seeing them. He wasn't trying to be difficult. He was dealing with their situation in the only way his defenses allowed. They *all* had their defenses. Heather made jokes; Lila got bitchy and blamed it on pregnancy hormones; Raj acted like an obnoxious prima donna, complaining and whining and futilely trying to contact his family on his idiotic little communicator watch. And Piper? She checked manuals and made chore lists.

As Trevor had said: the bunker ran itself so long as power from the windmill stayed on. And yes, that power had been buggy, but it was nothing she needed to worry about. There were redundancies: a rechargeable battery array inside the bunker, plus solar panels on the roof and in a nearby clearing. If redundancies failed, a generator sitting in the utility room with the battery array exhausted to the outside. And if *that* failed (or if its gasoline went bad; she'd read that it only lasted about six months), they had daylight reflected down from concealed skylights to light their way, propane to heat the place, and a lifetime's supply of food. There were plenty of lanterns and LED flashlights, plus a few security lights mounted on the walls. They'd be fine. Her constant policing was just whistling in the dark, and it wasn't fair to blame Trevor because his coping strategies appeared less productive than hers. Fretting was fretting, no matter its form.

"I didn't *want* to close the door, Trevor. But we all agreed that we had to. We left it open as long as we could. It isn't as if we can just leave the thing closed and unlocked. Your dad changed something when we came in the first time, somehow arming the place. Now the only way to get in is for the person on the inside to *let* them in. We would have had to literally prop it open. And how would *that* work once the crowds started showing up?"

Trevor looked toward the ceiling. It was made of reinforced concrete and could probably (knowing Meyer) withstand a bomb blast. But for a moment Trevor seemed to be trying to see or hear through it — to cast accusing eyes on the hundreds of people occupying the house, the grounds, the hills beyond the trees in their tents. The people who'd forced the family to shut the door that might keep his father out.

Power flickered. Piper flinched, looked up, and saw a tear brimming in the corner of Trevor's eye. He noticed it before it could fall and wiped it furiously away.

He looked toward the TV, obviously longing. For the first month and a half, that thin black screen had been their window to the world. They'd obsessively watched. Then, one morning, Lila had turned it on and found nothing. There was still power to the set and satellite receiver, but not a single channel on air. The Internet died the same day. Cell service, spotty from the start, had ceased. They'd used the screen to watch old TV shows stored on the living room juke ever since. They'd been living in a little black box. Their world was the bunker and what the cameras showed them. Beyond that, there might not be any Earth left, for all the Dempseys knew.

"Do you really think he was … you know … *taken?*"

"I don't know," Piper said. But yes, she did think that — same as the many other abductions they'd heard of before the broadcasts stopped. Meyer wouldn't have run off. Not after all he'd done to get them here. And if he'd gone out in the middle of the night and been killed, they would have discovered his body. Despite searching far and wide, they'd found nothing.

"Do you think any more of the people who were taken have been sent home?"

Piper patted his arm. She had no idea. It had been five or six weeks since they'd seen their last news report, but as of that time, abductees had been returning at a rate of about five or ten per week. They simply arrived back at their doorsteps — always dazed and confused, usually strange to loved ones and friends, sometimes paranoid and violent. Even if Meyer returned, he might be different. But still, even after all this time, there was a chance he might come home as he'd been, against all odds. But here and now, Trevor was seeking reassurance rather than fact.

"I'm sure they have been, honey."

"And do you think—"

Trevor didn't finish.

At that moment, the bunker lights began to go out for good.

Chapter Two

"Goddammit," Morgan Matthews said, looking at the lock.

Terrence was behind him, holding his tools. He'd placed the high-powered flashlights, still on and pointed at the nook by the home's bathroom, on the unfinished kitchen countertop. Morgan didn't need to look back at Terrence to imagine his face: smug — very *I told you so.*

Morgan didn't want to turn and confirm. He might kill Terrence if he saw that look on his face. And he needed them all, at least for now.

"I told you," Terrence said.

Morgan clenched his fists, fingernails digging into his palms. He forced himself to take a quiet, sighing breath before turning. He found Terrence's dark features devoid of his smug look, but the fucker had gone ahead and said the words aloud.

"Hack it," Morgan said.

Terrence shook his head. His black skin made him hard to read in the twilit room, and his sunglasses in the

9

dark made Morgan want to punch him. His hair managed to look stylish instead of disheveled. His vest mocked the air's chill in the same way his sunglasses scorned the mostly set sun. His bare, lean arms were painted in tattoos. Morgan never understood why black guys got tattoos. It seemed like a waste of ink since you could barely see them. Morgan's own Irish skin — which had no tattoos — would have made a much better canvas.

Terrence's defiantly cool manner, as he looked back at him now, infuriated Morgan and made him want to shove a gun in his belly. But he'd never enter the concealed basement without Terrence. He forced himself to let the irritation go. Besides, that displeasure was misplaced. He loathed *the closed door*. He merely disliked Terrence and the other four men in his crew in the way Morgan Matthews disliked everyone.

"I can't hack that lock, boss."

"Why not?"

"For one, how am I supposed to get in? The computer controlling the lock is inside the door or behind it. But secondly, I don't know anything about it."

Morgan pulled on the door. It wasn't just closed and locked; its very substance felt solid, as if its core were concrete or solid steel. "But you cut the power."

"This system is solid. Cutting the power isn't enough."

"You cut the *redundant* power, too."

Terrence shrugged again.

Morgan turned toward the approaching footsteps, coming from the kitchen behind him. It was the kid, Cameron. Morgan liked Cameron better than Terrence, despite him being a thug with no special skills. He and Dan, the big mother Cameron had shown up with, seemed like scrappers. Maybe they had a gay thing going on; Morgan didn't know or care.

Cameron had a screw loose, and that was all that mattered. Morgan liked a little crazy in the people he worked with.

Some dumbass from the tents-and-hippies set camping around the house had questioned Morgan's authority to cordon off the estate's west side at the nook where they found the exhaust pipe. The same dumbass had complained when Dan and Vincent dug around the pipe, searching for treasure. Morgan didn't like being questioned. But before he could so much as threaten the dumbass into submission, Cameron had leaped on the guy and beaten him until there were maybe three breaths left in his body. So yeah, Cameron was the coolest of the bunch, in Morgan's mind. A real team player.

"That pipe over on the side of the house is still cold, Morgan," Cameron said, his breath a bit short. That was another thing Morgan liked about Cameron. The kid hustled, even if only from the home's side to the kitchen door.

Terrence turned to face Cameron. Then finally — blessedly — he removed his oversized sunglasses and tucked them into his vest pocket.

"Of course it's cold," he said. "What, did you think the generator was going to kick on?"

Dan and Christopher entered the kitchen behind Cameron. Outside, in the fading light, Morgan could see a few of the gathered hippies watching them enter the kitchen. They'd looked askance at Morgan and his men since their arrival, but those hippies out there wouldn't say dick. Even at the end of the world, tough ideas failed at the finish line. Morgan's gun didn't stop them. Many people in the crowd had guns. But with their pussy attitudes, those guns might as well be sticks. Morgan was willing to *use* his weapons — even for the hell of it. Most people weren't as cool with violence. Morgan was, and those asswipes knew it from watching his walk.

Dan and Christopher traded a glance. They seemed as if they might report the same thing as Cameron: that the exhaust pipe sticking out of the foundation was still cold, and they were surprised that Terrence had been right — that the machine on the other end of that pipe was off and would remain that way.

"I told you, I clipped off the switch," said Terrence. "The generator won't kick on as long as it doesn't realize power from the windmill and solar has been interrupted." He looked at them, annoyed. You didn't question Terrence's technical know-how. Even Morgan, who was otherwise in charge, knew that.

Christopher said, "I'm not even convinced that's a generator on the other end of that pipe."

"*It's a generator,*" said Terrence. "There's a pipe sticking out of the wall."

"Maybe it's a furnace," Christopher said.

"It's not a furnace," Terrence retorted.

"How do you know?"

Terrence rubbed his forehead as if Christopher's stupidity hurt him. "It's not a big enough pipe to be a furnace. It's also not insulated. There's not nearly enough clearance, and it turns a ninety-degree angle within six inches of the foundation. No zoning inspector in the world would okay that, and this is new construction." Terrence gestured toward the unfinished kitchen.

Christopher chewed his lip. "We're wasting our time here."

"How so?" Terrence asked.

"Digging down the side of the house to where the pipe enters the foundation all goddamned day. Jimmying with those wires and junctions." Christopher wiped his nose. "We should be fleecing these fucking hippies. Hell, they *want* to be taken; you hear them serenading the aliens with Kumbaya. Why wait not make it easy on them? We could *take* shit from them right now."

Terrence put a hand on Christopher's arm. Christopher flinched then settled. Terrence glanced at Morgan then gave Christopher his "shut your mouth because I'm trying to save you from getting shot by the boss" look.

"We've searched the house," he said, still watching Christopher's eyes. "There's no basement access inside, and yet there's *clearly* an exhaust pipe coming out of the ground over there. So what did we do, Christopher?"

"We dug."

Terrence nodded. "We dug. And we found out that the pipe goes right into the foundation. Think about that for a minute. What does a pipe going through a house's foundation say to you?"

"Who cares?"

"There are no crawlspace vents around this place. No cellar access on the outside. No basement staircase. And yet still, there's clearly something under the house. Some machine worthy of what's *clearly* an exhaust pipe."

"How do you know that's what it is?" Christopher asked, even though Terrence had just told him.

"Shut up, Christopher," said a new voice.

Morgan looked up to see Vincent enter the kitchen. Vincent was all muscle, with tattoos on dark skin like Terrence. Vincent had run the group before Morgan arrived to show them what a real boss looked like. He usually fell into line under Morgan's orders but bore watching. A big guy like that, clear military background, having been the previous leader? Morgan knew to watch his back. Once they finally breached this bitch of a door, it might be smart to put a bullet in Vincent's face. Just to make a point.

"Got something to say, Vincent?" Christopher asked.

"Just shut your fucking hole." Vincent stepped closer. "Your problems with all of this are duly noted. You still don't think there's a bunker under this place even now, even while staring at a hidden door at the back of a closet with a motherfucking Fort Knox lock? Fine. Go run off and play with someone else. That's one less share to split of whatever's down there."

Christopher exhaled loudly and stepped back. Vincent turned to Terrence, nodding at Morgan as if urging him to continue.

"So the generator doesn't look like it'll kick on now that the main is cut," Morgan said to Terrence, setting aside the twin problems of Christopher and Vincent for another time. "So that means you did it right."

"I told you I had it figured out. What, you don't trust me?"

"You said you couldn't be sure," Morgan said. "Fake wires and all."

"There were a lot of decoys," Terrence said. "The phone box over there's a decoy. Same for the Internet. I don't even think the net here is wired at all, but someone tried to make it look like there's a fiber line running to it. There were two decoy power lines from the windmill, and that's on top of the bullshit wire running up to the pole and then just *stopping*, which flat-out insulted me. But like I said, I got it. There's a legit line buried up to the windmills on the hill and another to the solar — one on the roof and another to the panel farm in the clearing. Then there's the one that goes through the wall. Again, some decoys. But I pinched it off with the inverter and battery, Morgan. That generator in there doesn't realize there's no power coming in." He stopped short of adding, *Just like I fucking told you ten minutes ago, asshole.* Morgan didn't like that. Nobody called Morgan Matthews an asshole.

"So if the power is out, why isn't this door open?" He tapped the big, complicated computer lock on the hatch at the back of the broom closet.

"It's impossible to be sure without going inside, but it could be a few things. They may have a failsafe power supply inside that we can't see. If I were designing a system, that's how I'd have done it: put a self-contained, probably rechargeable short-term power source inside the walls that doesn't rely on anything outside. So it's possible they still *have* power, even with the generator off and the mains cut. Even so, there are still some obvious precautions I'd have taken even if there's no power down there at all, and they're knocking around in the dark."

"Like?"

"A contained power source for the lock itself. A battery inside the mechanism."

"Can you unplug the battery?"

"Not without getting inside."

"What else?"

"There's plain old physical barriers to consider: deadbolts, lock bars — even something jammed behind the door."

"We can break through that kind of shit," Morgan said.

"Maybe." Terrence rapped on the door. "But this? It's a motherfucker. If we want to get inside, we're going to need more than a lock pick."

Morgan eyed his all-purpose electrician, mechanic, and computer hacker. "I assume you're up to the challenge."

Terrence crossed his arms and nodded. "I think so, but it'll be tricky."

"Tell me what you have in mind," said Morgan.

So Terrence did.

Chapter Three

AT FIRST, Lila couldn't see a thing.

She took a shallow breath, her heart beating like a tiny, frightened animal. Somewhere in the back of her mind, she wondered if she might be hyperventilating. Another part of her mind wanted to let it happen if she was. Passing out, with lights gone and danger real, might be a blessing.

Panic's fist gripped her heart and squeezed tight. She was in free fall, maybe trapped, unable to take it.

Seconds ticked, excruciatingly slow, and for the first few moments Lila could barely get from one second to the next.

It's just a power outage, said her reasonable mind. *You've spent three months trapped in this tiny box, pretending it isn't a coffin. But it is, and even if Dad thought to hide the air intakes as well as Piper said he did, those intakes are still the only line you have to fresh breath. You've known that all along. What's happened now is only bringing it front and center.*

Relax, Lila.

It's just fear, with nothing at the root.

You're in the dark, not dead.

But Lila didn't believe it.

As she stumbled in the dark, feeling Mom leave her side in an unmotherly (but very Heather-like) way, Lila imagined herself not in the bunker but in empty space. There were portals in the main room where sunlight reflected down from skylights, but none in the bedrooms. Besides, she was pretty sure it was after dark. There had to be some electronic light down here somewhere; her eyes simply hadn't adjusted.

Or not.

Because as much as Lila's rational mind had to say about sensible power failures and the safe dark in underground bunkers, a larger part thought she might be telling herself what she wanted to hear.

Piper had told them all: there were redundancies on redundancies.

The power shouldn't go out.

Thanks to the strange, flickering visions in her dreams, Lila knew what this *really* was. She knew what was actually happening — and it was more than a simple failure of electricity.

Inside Lila's mind, she saw the tall man in a long overcoat, his hair black, his nose cruel, his voice tinged with a slight accent, British or maybe Irish. A man whose very movements iced her blood the minute her internal vision displayed him, which it had been doing for weeks.

Lila first thought the man in her mind was a paranoid nightmare: the ominous fellow outside like a boogeyman. It even made sense. She was a silly pregnant teenager. The apocalypse hadn't changed that. She had too many hormones. Of *course* she was afraid, and of *course* she'd created a spook to give her fear something to focus on.

But then she'd seen the man on the cameras, same as in her head.

She'd known this would happen. Even now, she could hear five men's voices arguing over the best way to seal their doom.

Cut the power.

That won't open the door, boss.

Just cut it. Do as I say.

Beside Lila, lying back on the bed with pillows stacked against the headboard, Heather had been laughing too hard at a *Three's Company* rerun when the power had gone. Laughing if she were stir-crazy — the only reason her mother would laugh so hard at shows she'd seen hundreds of times, from well before she was born. The only reason she'd ignore the presence of the men outside, hip deep in a hole they'd dug against the foundation, twisting wires and readying clippers.

"Mom?" Lila yelled into the darkness, her voice wavering.

"Right here, Lila."

"Where?" Lila was halfway off the bed. She came the rest of the way and stubbed her toe on something unseen. Her outstretched hands met the closet door before she'd known it was remotely nearby, jamming her wrists and eliciting a cry.

"I'm at the door. Stay on the bed."

But Lila was forward in a second, grabbing at something that did, in fact, turn out to be her mother.

"Dad has guns," Lila said. "Where are the guns? Did you find them? Did Piper?"

Heather laughed.

"*Where are they, Mom?!*"

No answer. Lila could imagine her mother's insulting

look. Then: "Yeah. That sounds like the voice of a person I'd trust with a gun in the dark."

Propped on the bed, watching Jack Tripper stumble awkwardly through yet another misunderstanding with Mr. Roper, Lila had wanted to say something to her mom about what she felt increasingly certain was happening outside — what she'd seen in her dreams and could feel coming like a mass of cold air. But speaking up would only earn her mockery.

Besides, Lila didn't need her mother to tell her she was being ridiculous. It was possible she was just jumping at shadows, even as sure as she felt that her vision was true. They'd all been too long underground, and Lila was surely losing her mind like the rest of them. A pregnant girl with too much estrogen. Heather said as much when Lila had pointed out the man in the overcoat on the monitors days ago and called him frightening. *Just another New-Age hippie dipshit,* Heather had answered. But to Lila, he didn't look New Age at all.

And Lila knew he had a gun, even though she never saw it on the cameras. The gun's presence had been whispered in her ear. It had been shown to her in dreams — where she'd seen it point blank, staring straight down its blue steel muzzle.

"Someone cut the power," Lila said, panting. She felt like she was talking into a box of black velvet. For an insane moment, she was sure her missing mother wouldn't reply because she'd vanished. Lila was alone, in a featureless void.

"It just went out," Heather said. "A loose wire or something. It's been flickering for days."

"Mom, it's not just—"

There was a yell from the other room: either Piper or Raj. Lila wasn't sure, and not being able to tell was embarrassing. For Raj. He hadn't been at his manliest lately. The screech came from the right side of the door as she left the bedroom (Lila thought). But she wasn't sure.

"Heather!" said a voice.

"I'm right here, Piper."

"Are you and Lila okay?"

"We're baking cookies. How about you? How's the family?" Heather replied.

Lila could hear her mother's feet pacing closer, then away. They exited the bedroom and were now in the bunker's central room, which they all thought of as the living room. After three months underground, Lila's ears had attuned to the difference. The larger room held an echo despite the carpet and subtleties of design meant to soften sounds.

Lila still felt lost.

Where had Piper gone? Lila wished she'd reply to her mom's stupid joke, just so she'd be audible. More words from the responsible one — the person who knew where the guns were and had proved she was willing to pull a trigger if needed.

But Piper said nothing. And still, Lila's eyes hadn't adjusted to the dark.

The living room wasn't much brighter than the bedroom. But at least Lila could see shapes, if she focused. It might only have been thirty seconds since the power had gone out. Since it had been *cut* by the tall man and his group — at least five other men determined to get inside. Maybe *exactly* five.

Someone shuffled across the far end of the room. Lila's keyed-up mind imagined a giant insect trundling by unseen. A shiver ran through her.

"Piper!" Lila yelled.

"Lila?"

But it wasn't Piper's voice. Nearby, a shape in the gloom. A male voice: Raj.

Lila wanted to feel comforted or rescued, but she found herself annoyed instead. Raj had never been particularly macho, but bunker living had turned him downright whiny. Right now, he sounded almost pleading. Like he wanted *her* to rescue *him* and tell *him* that everything would be fine rather than the other way around.

Lila's voice came out sounding annoyed more than frightened. "I'm right here, Raj."

"Oh, good. I thought you were Trevor."

"I'm not."

"Why did the lights go off?"

Lila's fear slid further into irritation — a welcome change. "How the hell should I know?"

The room strobed in a series of bright flashes. Lila's breath caught, her instinctive mind interpreting the flashes as an attack. Then she realized the silent flares were the flickering of emergency lights. There was one in each room, mounted near the ceiling. Their glow was bright white, unidirectional, harsh. Glare from the living room light cast everything into sharp-edged shadows and brightly flooded facets of light. The contrast was garish, but better than the dark.

"Thank God," Piper said.

Lila looked over and saw her stepmother on the couch's other side, near Trevor. She was happier to see Piper than she felt comfortable realizing. It was as if she expected Piper to save them all — or thought her dead, and a ghost in the dark.

But she was there: real, corporeal, *welcome*. Piper was the only reluctant killer among them. The only one who'd proved she had what it took to defend the castle now that the man of the house had gone missing.

"Piper," said Lila, her earlier certainty returning. "Someone is trying to get in!"

"It's just an outage."

Lila's mind searched for a way to disprove her. Then she had it. "The cameras! Check the cameras!"

"The power is out," said Trevor. "Duh."

Piper peeked around, fishing a flashlight from a drawer. She turned it on and speared the dark corners.

"What are you looking for?" Heather asked.

"The power is out," said Piper.

"Wow. You really *are* good at this."

"It shouldn't be out."

Heather cackled. "Another brilliant observation."

"She's just trying to help," Raj said.

Heather cocked her head at Raj. "Don't you have some homework to do?"

"There's a generator," said Piper, still searching. "Why didn't the generator come on?"

"Whatever." Heather gestured around the room. "We have light."

"For a while. But the batteries. What about the batteries?"

"Check the junk drawer."

"Piper," Lila said, "*we need to check the cameras.*"

"Take a load off, Lila." Heather gestured toward the couch. "You're sounding awfully pregnant."

"Maybe we *should* check the cameras." Raj looked furtively around, appearing almost as afraid as Lila felt, his brown eyes wide. His head ticked between Heather and Piper, unafraid of being mocked as long as they could all get back to abnormal bunker life.

Lila, watching Piper search for an unknown something, wondered if she should go to Raj. But even more, she thought that maybe *he* should come to *her* instead of peeing his pants.

"I don't mean *flashlight* batteries," Piper said. "I mean, I think there's a battery backup for our power supply, for the whole bunker. I saw it in the books. It's in with the generator. But ... why hasn't the generator kicked on?"

"I can't believe this happened. I can't believe the power went out *now*." Heather slouched onto the couch she'd just offered Lila. "Right in the middle of my favorite episode of *Three's Company*."

"I wonder if I have to switch the batteries or the generator on manually," Piper said to herself. "How would I do that?"

"Hurry up," said Heather, making herself comfortable. "If I don't get my beans and rice, I'm reporting your ass to the manager."

Clicking noises filled the room. The overhead lights came on.

"That's the batteries, then." Piper exhaled with relief, then listened. The room was quiet. "But still no generator." She looked around. "We need to turn stuff off. Conserve the power, at least until morning."

"Who made you Mr. Fix It?" Heather said.

"Mom ..."

Trevor stopped as the sounds of drilling started above, at the bunker's front door.

Chapter Four

TERRENCE STOPPED. The kitchen clamor abated by two thirds as he killed the big drill and set it aside, leaving only the portable generator humming outside. The last time Morgan had fired up the generator, the hippies around the home had come forward, thinking themselves invited to plug in their own appliances, possibly charging their dead (and surely useless) cell phones. That hadn't gone well for the hippies, thanks to Morgan's guns and Cameron's fists. This time, they were all giving the engine a wide berth.

Terrence swore.

"What?" Morgan asked.

"Just kicked on." Terrence pointed at something in the complicated electronic lock on the broom closet's rear door.

"What did?"

"Backup power. Like I figured." He shook his head. "I don't know whether to admire whoever built this place or hate them. Both, I guess."

"But you killed the generator. Cut it off."

Terrence looked up. "I kept it from kicking on automatically, but if the people in there know what they're doing, they can get right back around that and run it manually. But I think we'd hear that, so it's probably not the generator. Must be a battery backup, as I thought."

"You said you could drill through it."

"I'm not talking about the *lock's* backup. I'm talking about something more central. A contained power source."

"But temporary," said Vincent, butting in.

Morgan turned. His hand went to the butt of his gun. Terrence and Vincent had already been together when Morgan had arrived, along with Cameron and the old man, Dan, who acted like Cameron's father. Vincent was a big black man with giant arms who looked like a Marine. Terrence was slightly lighter and a lot leaner, but still strong. He looked like a specialist or an engineer — someone trained to *fight* like a Marine, with the brains for special-ops challenges like disarming bombs and opening doomsday bunker doors. Morgan didn't like that the two were comfortable as a team and could clearly function without him.

"Enough time for them to grab their guns," Terrence said to Vincent, who nodded. "And enough light for them to do it by."

Christopher came to the front of the group. "You don't even know there's anyone in there."

"They're in there, all right," said Terrence, now fussing with the lock, not looking back.

"We should just drive the truck in here." Christopher looked out at the lawn. "Smash it in."

Terrence snickered.

"What?" said Christopher, offended. "Your idea is so much better?"

"First rule of plunder," said Terrence. "Don't destroy what you're trying to plunder."

"We could hook a chain to the door. Pull it off its hinges."

"Those hinges?" said Vincent, pointing.

Morgan looked. The door didn't appear to have any hinges. For some reason this struck Cameron as funny, and he snickered.

"What the fuck you been doing that's so brilliant, then?" said Christopher, glaring at Cameron.

"I'm just yelling and being an asshole. That's my contribution." Cameron looked around the group then back at Christopher. "Oh, no, wait. That's yours."

Christopher surged forward. Vincent stopped him before he could reach Cameron, who smiled while chewing his toothpick.

Morgan turned back to Terrence.

"Can you still get in?"

"I told you the power would probably come back on. It just makes things a little trickier. Did you see that little light —" he pointed at the lock, "—right *there* come on a minute ago?"

"No," Morgan said.

Terrence looked behind Cameron, where Dan was standing quietly. The man really did look like Cameron's father — not in his features but in his behavior. He had curly, going-gray hair where Cameron's was straight and brown. He was broad where Cameron was thin and wiry. But he was always right by the kid when they were in a group, like a burly protector.

"Dan. You hear a clank earlier? When we were around the other side?"

"Hard to hear over the drill."

"The tolerances on this door are almost perfect, but I know I saw pistons top and bottom before when peeking around its edge." Terrence slapped the door then pointed a thin flashlight into the gap. "They're engaged now, but they weren't when I started drilling. I should be able to manually disable the lock in the door, but as long as those pistons are in place, our options are limited. I can't get a saw through that gap even if I could cut through those things, which I doubt." He pointed at the door's bottom then at the doorframe above. "Best I can tell, there are redundant locks top and bottom, probably slid into place by a solenoid. When backup power is on, they're engaged. But when it's off, they open."

"Why?" said Morgan.

Terrence shrugged, pushing his poufy black hair into place above his ear. "Something goes wrong inside the bunker in an emergency, backup-power situation, last thing you want are hard-to-access locks barring your escape. *This* lock here—" he tapped where he'd been drilling, "—stays engaged regardless, and they may even have something simple inside if they want extra protection, like big manual deadbolts. So the place stays secure. But if the power goes out and stays out, there are bigger problems than the door. Air, for example."

"There must be vents."

"Sure. But nothing to push air through them." He shrugged again. "I'm sure there's a workaround. Maybe someone can ride a stationary bike in there to spin a fan; I don't know. All that matters right now is that as long as they have backup electricity in there, there's no way I'm getting this open. That's where part two of the plan comes in."

"So now what?" Morgan asked

"I keep drilling. Take out the main lock, if I can. But as to the rest … ?" He trailed off.

"How long?"

"Maybe half an hour. If I can get through it at all. I've never seen a lock like this."

Morgan nodded and turned to Vincent.

"Head around to the side of the house, and get started," he said.

Then he looked at Terrence, who'd again lifted the drill and pressed it against his in-progress hole in the door's metal.

"Is this going to work, Terrence?" he asked before the drill reclaimed its cacophony. "Or are we just wasting a lot of time?"

Terrence nodded. "Oh, it'll work. If there really are people behind this door, we might be about to kill them all … but we'll get in, all right."

Chapter Five

Piper ran to the control room to check the cameras. The sounds of drilling coming from above were unmistakable.

"What's going on up there?" Raj yelled.

"Shut your curry hole," Heather shouted back.

"I just want to know—"

Heather caught Piper before she reached the control room, stopping her, even though it was the least sensible thing she could possibly do. "Are the cameras going to still work with the power … you know … retarded?"

"I don't know."

"We have to see what's going on! If there are people trying to get in up there, will they—"

"*I don't know, Heather!*"

Resentment washed over Piper in a wave. She shook Heather's hand off and marched into the small control room with the others behind her. She felt like a prisoner who's been put in charge of a prison then blamed by the other inmates for everyone's confinement. But she hadn't built this bunker. She hadn't known the ships were coming as Meyer somehow had. This was her prison, same as theirs.

She calmed herself and thought: *What would Meyer do?*

If Meyer were here, he'd probably laugh at the fact that anyone was trying to break in. What were they, stupid? The bunker was a fortress.

Piper had peeked into the terrifying armory Meyer had left in their care. She wouldn't touch the automatic weapons or boxes of what she feared were grenades and other explosives — a likely reason the armory's door was as thick as a bank vault's. Just being in the room scared her silly. But there were handguns in there, too — plain old automatics and the requisite ammo. Even if their assailants did somehow get in, they'd be able to use *those* weapons just fine.

Relax. Meyer thought of this. Just because someone is trying to get in doesn't mean they'll succeed.

Piper thought of the manuals. How far did Meyer's paranoia extend? If he'd procured assault rifles, gas masks, and God knew what else, had he built a perimeter defense system of some sort? That's what smart guys always did in the movies. Maybe Piper could flip a switch and electrocute whoever was tap-tap-tapping at their door. Maybe she could release a poison gas topside. Maybe she could blow the surface to rubble, leaving only the impenetrable bunker in a smoking crater.

But those thoughts were ridiculous. Flights of fancy. Inventions that only delayed the inevitable.

You're in charge here, Piper. It's all you, girl. You didn't ask for the crown, but Meyer left it on the nightstand when he abandoned you.

"Look," said Piper, sitting, turning back to Heather as the drilling continued above. "The lights are on. So—"

She jabbed a button, and the screens coughed back to life. "There. See? It's all fine."

"So, whatever was wrong with the power is fixed?"

Piper could tell by the lights that nothing was fixed. Too few had come back on, and those that had were far too dim. The whole place was in power-saving mode because their mains were cut and they were on borrowed time.

"I doubt it."

"The generator," said Raj. "You said there was a generator."

"Do you *hear* a generator?" Trevor said.

Raj looked back at Trevor, but Piper only saw the boys measuring their dicks from the corner of her eye. "I think we're on battery power. Enough to run what we want, but …" Piper trailed off. She wasn't an engineer, but it didn't take an engineer to know that the more power they used, the shorter their stores would last. She should tell Heather to run around and kill the lights and anything not strictly necessary, but her breath was stolen by the picture that had flickered to life in one corner of the main security monitor.

"But what?" Heather prompted, urging Piper to go on.

"*Shh!*"

Piper's blood had gone cold. She'd guessed at what they'd find on the monitors, but seeing it was something else entirely. The camera displaying the image was in the kitchen, probably above the island at its center. The view showed the closet alcove near its right edge. Six people clustered around the bunker's front door, a man with a large corded drill as their centerpiece.

She reached for the screen, pulled the image forward, spread her fingers to magnify it.

"They've got a generator." Lila pointed at a cord

running away from the drill. She knew from past nights that the cameras were able to see in absolute darkness, but right now they didn't need to. There were several high-powered lanterns at the screen's corner aimed into the alcove, plus what looked like a shop light clipped on a rack inside the huddle of men, pointing down.

"Oh, sure," said Heather. "*They* have a generator."

Lila ignored her. The group seemed so equipped and prepared. They didn't strike her as mindless UFO nuts who'd decided to riot and storm the castle while waiting for their ride to the stars. They looked like professional burglars: the kind of people who pull bank heists and high-stakes capers. The kind of people who might have figured a way through Meyer's defenses, or were in the process of doing so.

Piper peered at the screen and felt a shiver. She pinched the image back down to size, let it drift to where the software wanted to place it as a thumbnail in the gallery, then turned. Eight eyes watched her.

"What do you think?" said Heather.

"About what?"

"Can they get in?"

"I don't know, Heather."

"But you looked at the video. Is there another angle? Is there a camera in the closet?"

"I don't know."

"How thick is that door?" said Raj.

"I don't know, Raj. Why would I know that?"

"Why are they drilling? Why aren't they just bashing it in?"

"I don't—"

"Do they know we're in here?"

"Hell if I—"

"Is it going to be okay? Can they get in?" Lila's hands

found Piper's arm. She didn't know whether to be more perturbed or touched. It didn't matter. Lila's terrified affection was useless information, same as the rest.

"Lila——" she began.

"But there's a computer on the door, right?" said Heather. "With a really hard code or a scanner or something?"

"Computers don't stop drills," Raj chided.

"Shut up, Princess," Heather said.

"Oh, *that's* helpful. *That* will protect us."

Trevor turned to Raj. "My dad wouldn't build a place like this and then just let people kick in the door." Then, to Piper, he added, "Right?"

"I don't know."

"But the door. The door will hold."

"She *said* it would," Lila told her brother.

"No, she didn't."

"Earlier! You weren't around, Trevor."

"That doesn't mean that——"

Piper stood quickly enough to kick the wheeled chair back into Raj's shins. He yelped. She held up a hand.

"Look," she said, "either they'll get in, or they won't. But we——"

Trevor lost a helpless little inhale, his bravado gone. Piper grabbed his shoulder.

"Dammit, Trevor! Don't lose your shit on me! You're the man of the house now, so act like it!" She shook him until his eyes cleared.

"Hey, I'm two years older than——" Raj began.

"Shut up, Princess," Heather repeated.

Piper began again, locking eyes with each of them. She didn't have time to play nice or coddle them. They wanted a leader? *Fine.* They wanted to be helpless sheep and put all the burden on her shoulders? *Fine.* But she'd be damned if she'd tuck them in and sing them a lullaby.

"Either they'll get in, or they won't," she repeated, speaking slowly. "But *if* they get in, we need to be prepared."

"The guns." Lila looked at her mother, vindicated.

"You're not touching a gun, Lila."

"What did *you* do, with Dad's gun, Mom? You never did tell us how you got out of Las Vegas."

"I said enough."

"*Guns,*" said Lila, nodding to herself. "Okay." She seemed to force a breath. The idea of holding cold steel was apparently comforting.

"I'm not letting you use a gun, Delilah Dempsey."

"I'm taking one, Mom!"

"No, you're not!"

There was a clanking sound from above. The drill stopped as something heavy struck the floor in the home's kitchen. Then the drill resumed.

Lila stared at Heather, her features firm. "*They* have guns, Mom."

"You don't know that."

"Then I guess they just came to say hi? And all they have with them are gift baskets?"

"You don't have any goddamned idea what's really going on, Lila! Shooting first and asking questions later is the kind of thing that—"

"That saves your ass in Las Vegas?" She pointed a finger toward Piper, and Piper felt the jab as if it had struck an open wound. "That saves all of our asses, as long as *someone* is willing to step up and not be a pussy?"

"Watch your mouth, Delilah," Heather said.

"This from the Obscene Queen? How's that mouth that made you famous, Mom?"

"*Look,*" Raj said, interrupting.

Lila stopped. Turned. Looked where Raj was pointing. Piper followed the same finger. Raj had pulled up some sort of diagnostic panel while Lila had been sparring with her mother. Piper saw a readout of some sort: white text on a black screen.

"It says, 'secondary locks engaged,'" Lila read.

"We can read," said Heather, eyeing her daughter before turning to the screen.

A rocket went off in Piper's mind. It felt like salvation.

"Yes!" she said. "*I remember!* If someone tries to force the door, it locks with these giant deadbolts! There's no way to get at them from the outside! There's no way in! There's no way to—"

The drill ceased, surprising Piper into quiet. A new noise grew in the silence. Faint. Like the dragging of metal on metal.

Trevor's head cocked. He stood and left the control room.

Lila threw a final glance at her mother and followed. Piper brought up the rear, leaving Raj behind. In the corner of Piper's eye as she turned, Raj returned to the camera screens, flicking idly, wasting power.

Trevor crossed the large living room, his head still cocked, following the sound toward an interior door opposite the control room, mostly hidden from all but the kitchen side. Now that the drill had either finished or surrendered, the room seemed strangely quiet. The new dragging noise was comparatively loud.

"What *is* that?" Lila asked.

"*Shh,*" Trevor answered, cocking his head, triangulating.

The noise had become brisk, in an on-off-on pattern, over and over. It wasn't constant. It had the rhythm of someone sweeping a floor or moving a broom back and forth. Leaving a pause at the end of each stroke.

Trevor reached the door. It looked like any interior door, but it had subtle rubber seals along all of its edges. It was heavier and thicker, the hinges larger, the kind of door intended to keep something out. The kind of door that means serious business.

"It's the generator," said Heather.

"It's not the generator," Trevor answered.

Raj's voice came from the control room. "Guys?"

Trevor ignored him. He put his hand on the doorknob and pushed. The generator was in the utility room's center, squatting on the bare concrete floor. Behind it to one side was the backup array: shelf after shelf of what looked like ordinary car batteries strung together with wires.

The metallic dragging stopped. There was a pinging sound, then more rattling, this time less metallic. A gurgling sound followed, echoing in the space.

Raj again: *"Guys!"*

Lila turned suddenly white. She grabbed her brother's wrist.

"Close the door, Trevor."

"Is something dripping?" Trevor was looking at a small pool of liquid beneath the exhaust pipe's ninety-degree bend. He leaned forward, sniffing. A harsh smell assaulted Piper's nostrils.

"Close it, Trevor. Close the door."

Piper looked at Lila, then at the puddle. Her mind found a match for the earlier sounds — the ones that had come after the drill's riot had ceased.

A back-and-forth metallic dragging, like a saw.

The gurgling, and now a forming puddle of gasoline.

All at once, Piper understood.

She shouldered Trevor aside. Slammed the door. Raj

came sprinting from the control room, his dark skin blushed and eyes wide.

"There's another guy by the side of the house!" he stammered. "In a little hole they dug by the foundation! And I think he's—"

Raj's report was severed by the soft *fwump* of fire, followed by an explosion.

Chapter Six

HEATHER, behind her children, shouldered her way forward, obeying an impulse she didn't entirely understand. But a place deep within her *did*. Something was about to happen.

She'd seen it in a dream.

She's walking with Meyer. Somewhere ancient, somewhere uniquely shamanistic. It's a thing Heather has no interest in, and Meyer normally wouldn't either. But she's with him, even now, after he's vanished, because this place — this place of dream walking — is timeless. And Meyer says …

But he doesn't *say it, because they're in another place now, a dark place. A sleepy hum buzzes like high-tension wires. The air smells like ozone. Meyer is here too, oblivious to where they just were and what he almost said. Now feels like a second chance. But the space is too small, like a concrete cell. Meyer has his hand on some sort of an engine, and inside what seems to be a steel box is more fuel for the engine. Meyer looks at it and says, "I put it in a fireproof box in case it spills. Because fire would use all our oxygen."*

In the dream, Heather wants to ask Meyer where he went after he vanished. Where he's been. If he's alive and safe. Meyer smiles and

39

laughs — laughs and smiles being more natural to Meyer in here, in dreams.

"It's you we have to worry about," he says.

But the dream never finishes. The fire begins even inside the dream as it begins to peel back into real things. She watches him burn, and …

The second explosive clap hurled Heather back to reality, blinking, catching sight of Lila beside her. She felt divided, her mind in two places at once. Heather hadn't merely been daydreaming. It was something else.

Something is about to happen. You've seen this in a dream.

The heavy door kept whatever had blown inside the room, but the seals around it were already melting. The edges bubbled with heat. Then she saw nothing because—

And now the power goes out.

— because at that moment lights died as fire consumed the backup power source inside the room, melting the wires, perhaps cracking the batteries. Soon the door itself would give way. Heather knew it would happen. She'd seen it. And Meyer had explained it — not with words, but with some sort of mind-speak in her persistent dreams:

They built the door to withstand force, Heather — even fire. But the man outside, he dropped a cherry bomb down the pipe. Then the fire has all the oxygen it needs to burn, flowing from the outside like a supply line.

And oxygen —

And fire —

Heather pushed against the two soft lumps she found behind her in the dark, her children, driving them across the room, shoving their protesting forms into what she suspected was the corner behind the couch. It was impossible to be sure where they were or even that she was shepherding Trevor and Lila instead of Piper and Raj. Then she heard voices, and the first of the emergency lights ticked back on. The room became a carnival of hard, contrasting edges: the light's bright-white knife lines of black shadow. She saw her children below her, could sense Piper somewhere behind, maybe above.

"Mom ..."

"Fire, Lila. It's burning."

"*Mom!*"

Heather rolled and looked over her shoulder to where her daughter was staring with terrified eyes. There was a monster crawling along the ceiling, its body made of churning, boiling black smoke.

"Gas masks! *Piper*! You said there are gas masks!"

"Will gas masks help with smoke?"

"Stay on the floor, Trevor. We're in some serious shit right now."

Heather bounded up, knowing she'd displayed terrible bedside manner but not remotely caring. The generator room door had buckled and was spilling smoke around its edges. It had been built to keep the machinery in and the people safely out. It was meant to withstand some sort of internal failure — maybe even a fire that could kill their last power supply. But it should only need to hold for a few scorching minutes because *nobody* — not even Meyer — had anticipated this. But Heather knew from her dreams.

They'd cut the generator's exhaust pipe with a hacksaw.

They'd stuck a funnel in its top, then filled it with gas.

There had been an old but effective firecracker.

And a match.

With the ruptured exhaust pipe feeding from outside, the fire had plenty of what it needed to burn.

Fuel.

Oxygen.

Meyer, his voice as clear as if he was standing beside

her: *I put the gasoline in a fireproof box in case it spills. Because fire would use all our oxygen.*

But he hadn't fireproofed the gas poured through a funnel, through the cut-off pipe — a new air source opened wide with a cherry bomb.

Fire would use all our oxygen.

The door wouldn't last forever. And although there was oxygen in the generator room, there was much more in the bunker. And with the electricity dead, fans wouldn't do the job of bringing new air in, or clearing out the smoke.

Something hit Heather in the chest: three gas masks, one for each. The person above her, who'd thrown the masks, was already wearing one. Raj, wearing it like a nightmare.

But the things were merely masks without tanks. How would *these* help them breathe?

Heather had no idea. Meyer had babbled on and on about his survivalist bullshit, and that's exactly how Heather had taken it when they'd lain on warm sheets in post-coital haze: *as bullshit.* Did you have to turn a gas mask on? Did it somehow feed you air? Or did it *clean* the air? Heather had no idea.

She only knew her heart was hammering like a drum. And that the bunker, which had always felt plenty large, suddenly felt much too small.

They would suffocate and die.

Raj handed her something else. This he didn't throw. A blue steel handgun. He held one of his own in his other hand.

"*Guns?* Now?"

"Put those masks on!"

Did Raj know something she didn't? Heather had been making merciless fun of her daughter's baby-daddy the entire time they'd been shut in together. He pouted, he complained, he fiddled with that stupid fucking watch. The phones had been out for six weeks. Did he really think he could reach home on his secret agent wrist communicator?

But here he was now, crouched while she was prone, masked while she was bare-faced, armed while she tried to refuse the weapon. Maybe he'd be breathing after she'd choked and died. Or maybe he was clueless and had only ensured that he'd die looking like an idiot.

A gushing sound came from the mostly closed generator room.

The sprinklers had kicked on. Was that even a good idea? Couldn't fire burn on top of water? It's not like the room was filled with wood. There should really be—

The halon system, Heather. When it happens — when the fire breaks out — the halon system will do the job faster than the sprinklers.

Piper ran past. She was keeping low; black gasoline smoke was filling the upside-down pool of the ceiling from the top down. The air felt heavy and hot. The living room sprinklers would go off soon too, once it was hot enough to melt the wax plugs. If they went off too early, as a false alarm, everything would be ruined. It's not like they could run to Walmart for more supplies, which was why Meyer had installed the—

Halons

—the halon system in the first place. *Halons*, not water sprinklers. But it had to be manually activated. Pulled like a school fire alarm. The switch to activate them, he'd shown her, was accessible in three places: the foot of the stairs, the master bedroom, and—

"Hang on!" Piper yelled. She was headed for the—

—the control room, where she could pull the red lever and smother the fire, disrupting combustion at the molecular level without suffocating them. It was the perfect fire suppression system. It had to be activated manually because the system's designers assumed a fire bad enough to warrant full-home suppression was the kind you'd want to *run* from, particularly if you were trapped in an underground bunker, and hence you'd—

"*When it happens,*" Meyer had told her in her seemingly prescient dream, "*use the sprinklers and the extinguishers on the walls, but don't touch the—*"

Heather bolted to her feet, making her children's still-unmasked, prone bodies jump in surprise below her.

"*Piper, don't activate the—!*" Heather began.

But she was too late. The air filled with hissing halon gas. The crackling fire sounds in the generator room abated.

And then from above — from the door at the top of the stairs — something clanked as the secondary locks disengaged, leaving only the drilled-through primary locks between their bunker and the outside.

The sound of a door slamming open.

Rushing feet on metal stairs.

Heather gripped her gun, suddenly glad for its cold comfort.

Chapter Seven

TREVOR GLANCED at the gas mask in his lap, completely ignoring it. He turned to Lila, who looked absolutely terrified. He felt it was his responsibility to worry about her (she was his sister, after all), but right now he needed to take action. He'd been useless and stir-crazy so far, but shit was hitting the fan. He finally had a chance to prove he was the man his father had been — and *still was*, somewhere.

Trevor stood and plucked the pistol from his mother's shaking hands.

"Hey!"

"I got it, Mom."

"Give me—!"

Everything was happening too fast. His mother was in plain sight, an ideal target for the men whose boots were now tromping down the spiral staircase. Trevor blocked her body with his. She protested again, but he'd be damned if he'd lie down and cry. People were breaking into their home? He'd live or die on his feet.

Piper, disoriented, peeked out of the control room. She'd gone in to activate the fire extinguishers. Suddenly, the place was under siege, and Piper didn't seem to be following whatever had happened. Her huge blue eyes were wide with shock. She was unarmed, as big a target as his mother.

"*Get back in there!*" Trevor shouted.

Piper retreated, thankfully obeying.

Maybe ten seconds had passed. Trevor had felt the world's shortest burst of adrenaline. He still felt keyed up and ready to kick ass, but realized now just how far his heart had climbed into his throat. His breath was quick and too shallow; he felt as if the fire had done its job and robbed the room of air. He couldn't focus. He could barely see Raj across the room, wearing that stupid fucking gas mask, holding a gun with the safety clearly still on.

"*Raj!*"

Feet rushed down the stairs. Trevor raised his weapon and, realizing the safety gaffe himself, flicked a small lever on the gun's side. A red dot appeared beneath the lever, and Trevor remembered something his father had taught him: *Red means dead.*

He ducked, realizing too late that despite being low he was still entirely exposed to the boots now halfway down the staircase. His only chance was to get the first shot and take them by surprise. A bullet through the ankle of the lead man would do plenty. One would be hobbled, and the others would tumble down over him, making for a mix of target practice and Twister.

He raised the gun and sighted. Tried and failed to calm his breath. Blinked. And fired.

The bullet struck the concrete ceiling a full six feet from the staircase. Dust sifted down.

"*Gun!*" yelled one of the intruders.

"Vincent, get your ass down there!" another shouted.

Trevor swallowed, feeling his large, shocked eyes

unable to close. He looked at the gun in his hands, confused by its betrayal. He didn't have to cock it to fire again, did he? No, the slide ejected the empty and chambered a new round, cocking the pistol at the same time. His father had taught him that, too.

He raised the weapon again, but one of the men on the stairs ducked low and bared his own firearm first. The shooter's black, muscle-covered arms were as steady as granite. A half-second beat, then the man fired.

For a second, Trevor thought he might be dead, but the man had merely shot out the emergency light across the room and plunged them in shadow.

Light spilled from the other rooms, but the main area had become a confused gray. Trevor wanted to run, but his feet — like his gun — betrayed him. The men came forward, rushing with a sureness Trevor had to envy, spreading in a precision assault, each barely seen shadow seeming to know exactly where to go. They ran from room to room, and more lights went out. At one point, Trevor felt the gun plucked from his hand, his body unceremoniously cuffed to the ground.

"*Clear!*" one of the men shouted.

"*Clear!*" another echoed.

"*Clear!*"

The room quieted. Trevor didn't dare move. He was under the distinct impression that although he could see little, the invaders could see everything.

Night vision goggles, his mind told him.

But who wore night vision goggles? Who brought generators and powered drills to an apocalypse bunker, scavenging for scraps?

Military maybe? A special-ops team gone rogue?

It was as if the group had come here specifically to take the bunker. As if they'd known exactly what would be required … and, curiously, how to take over without killing a soul. Not a shot had been fired after the first man, squatting low, had killed the lights.

A new set of footsteps paced casually down from above then moved to the middle of the now-quiet room.

"Get a light."

The voice chilled Trevor's spine. The newcomer who'd said those words spoke like someone giving a lecture, not someone who'd spent less than a minute masterminding a flawless raid. The man had a slight accent, but rather than it making him sound distinguished to Trevor's ears, it made him sound somehow broken.

A lantern lit. Trevor recognized it as the one Piper kept in the middle of the coffee table "just in case." The glow was weak for the large room, but enough for Trevor to see the raiders.

There were six of them. The man who'd spoken last was in the center, wearing a black overcoat, newly arrived only after the dirty shooting work had been completed. Trevor watched all six men remove night vision goggles, his heart pounding. His eyes caught Lila, with their mother, to one side, staring at the lead man in abject horror. As if she recognized him and sensed something horrible seconds away.

"Well then," the tall man said. "What a fine little place you have here."

The man was roughly in the room's center, a few feet from the lantern. His proximity to the only light source threw a huge shadow opposite, across Raj, who'd been knocked to the ground, guarded by a thick-looking man with curly hair and bad skin. Heather and Lila were clasping each other nearby.

Piper was still at the control room door, but now her arm was held fast by the big black man who'd shot out the lights. She looked frail and beautiful, out of place amid this violence. She looked at Trevor, seeming suddenly helpless. All the strength she'd gained over the past months had vanished in an instant, stolen by this band of marauders.

Trevor gave Piper a blinking nod that he hoped seemed reassuring. He looked around at the others, seeing how completely and easily they'd taken the bunker. The man above Raj was holding Raj's gun. The others trained hand-guns around the room — casually, as if they thought their prisoners offered no threat.

"What do you want?" Trevor tried to puff himself up despite his position on the floor.

The man looked down, surprised. Piper was tossing Trevor glances with a clear meaning: *Shut up, and play dead.*

But Trevor had shut up and played dead enough. He'd let his father save them from the bad men who'd occupied the house when they'd arrived. He'd got himself nabbed by Garth and had to be rescued by *Piper* of all people — the woman he had regular daydreams and normal dreams about saving. He'd spent many hours over the past months thinking about Piper. They were flights of fancy he'd never act upon, but the facts were clear: *her man was gone, she was lonely and sad, and there was only one unencumbered male left in their corner of the world.*

"I should think what I want would be obvious," said the tall man, his slight accent unplaceable. He paced, looking into each of the bunker's rooms. "Not a bad place to hide, is it? And anyone who'd build such a place, we'd guessed, would have plenty of goodies to share." He reached the armory's open door and peered inside. He turned back and spoke again, sounding genuinely shocked. "*Many* goodies."

"This place is *ours*," Trevor said.

The tall man jerked his head at the man above Trevor.

"Allow him to stand." Then, to Trevor: "What's your name, son?"

"Trevor."

"I'm Morgan." He smiled then pointed around at the others as if they were at a tea party. "This is Dan, Vincent, and Christopher. Terrence is the other, around here somewhere. Were you the one who shot at us, coming in?"

Trevor swallowed. Morgan's full attention was like being X-rayed. He nodded, trying to hide his nervousness.

Morgan nodded back. He looked at Raj, still on the floor, not trying to stand tall. "I guess it wasn't this one, eh?" He looked at Piper and smiled in a way that Trevor *definitely* didn't like. "And not that one either, though that would have been … interesting." He turned back to Trevor, reached into the small of his back, and pulled out a semiautomatic pistol. To Trevor, it looked like a cop's.

"Then if you *are* the man in charge, I have a question for you: In my shoes, what would you *do* with a young man who declared himself in charge — and tried, even, to kill your team?"

The man watched Trevor. His gaze was intense, his eyes a haunting shade of green.

"I don't know," Trevor said.

Morgan smirked. "Indecision is the worst trait a leader can have." Then he leaned in and whispered, "You must always cut off a group's head if you want the body to follow."

Trevor thought to ask what that meant, but before he could Morgan rolled the gun in his grip, turning the butt to face Trevor.

Morgan struck him very hard. Trevor thought he felt something shift and break in his nose, but there was no time to think before consciousness was gone and his unprotesting body fell to the floor.

Chapter Eight

MORGAN WATCHED THE BOY COLLAPSE. Then he let the two women — one older and one younger, both pretty — go to him. Once they had gone, four eyes glared up as Morgan slipped the gun back into his belt. He looked away from their stares, uncaring.

Lights flicked on overhead. Morgan blinked up, pleased with Terrence's timing.

"Let me explain how this will work," he said, looking around at the group. "This is *my* home now. It seems you can accommodate guests, given all your space and supplies. We had a rough time getting in, so I feel we've earned our welcome. But we have a problem."

The younger of the women — the one with brown hair — stood from her crouch and came toward Morgan.

"You win," she said. "Just let us go."

"Well, that's the problem. For one, the kind part of me doesn't *want* you to go out there, for your own good. The lawn is full of hippie campers who will drag you into sing-alongs. Beyond that, there are alien ships in the skies. Not here now, but there's no way of knowing when they'll return."

"'*Return*'?" said the woman.

"You don't know?" Morgan laughed. "You've been visited. I've heard many stories. That's the reason these people are here: ships have come, and they want to be taken along for the next joyride if they ever come again."

The women exchanged looks. Not far away, the teenage girl — possibly the daughter of the other; they looked alike — stared at Morgan with the breed of terrified awe that always made him feel happy to see.

"But if I just toss you out," Morgan went on, "those ships might come back. They might take more of you."

The woman blinked. After a moment, she hesitantly asked, "What do you mean, *more of us?*"

Morgan looked at Cameron.

"She doesn't know," Cameron said.

Morgan studied the woman. "You *must* know. Who *was* he? Your father?"

"Who was *who?*" She looked baffled.

They couldn't be this clueless; they must know that one of their own had been taken.

"The man who was taken."

She swallowed. "He's my husband."

"*Him?* With *you?*" Morgan laughed. The hippies outside had shown them pictures when they'd still been pretending to be friendly, and the abducted man had been much older than this exotic flower. He sighed. "Well, it is what it is."

"What's his name?" the woman asked. "The man you're talking about?"

Morgan looked at Cameron. He didn't remember. Cameron knew a lot about the abducted, being a stone's throw from a UFO freak himself. Morgan didn't care. There had been a crowd here, and crowds meant opportunity. They'd learned of the bunker, and from that point on their needs had become clear. Beyond that, he could care less whose property they'd just seized or what had become of him.

Cameron's eyes ticked up. Was he nervous? The situation was under control. Morgan turned to see Christopher behind him, but the boy had no answers either.

"Meyer Dempsey," Cameron said. "*The* Meyer Dempsey."

The dark-haired woman stood. "Do you know who *I* am?"

Cameron paused then nodded when Morgan's eyes gave him a go-ahead. What did Morgan care? Cameron and Dan had studied this place, but guns and drills were all the research Morgan really needed.

"You're Heather Hawthorne."

"*How* do you know me?"

"Everyone knows you."

The brown-haired woman spoke up again, looking at Cameron. "What makes you say Meyer was taken? It wasn't on the news that we saw. Or the Internet, before ours went out. So how——?"

"Word gets around." Cameron's eyes flicked to Morgan then again to Christopher. Why did he seem so nervous? Nobody here cared how Cameron had come upon his information. They were much more frightened about being killed. Justifiably so, Morgan thought.

"But your fame does raise a problem," Morgan said. "Because people *do* know you. A few of you anyway. We kick you into the crowd, they might go to you even if you're good little boys and girls——" Morgan looked around the group, "And say nothing to them about us and what happened here after our drill went silent and we vanished into a closet."

He looked up at the sound of Terrence descending the stairs.

"*This* fellow—" he pointed at Terrence, speaking to the woman, "—can lock us back in. I'm not worried about others trying to get inside. They left us alone while we were up there, and they'll definitely leave us alone down here. And, as I said, that's assuming they know what we did or where we went. They may think we were just breaking into a safe — an impression we intend to drive home later, when we walk out in plain sight hauling goods … then sneak back after dark. With luck, we'll be able to hide down here as you have, mostly unseen, no matter how many new pilgrims follow the stars or the spiritual energy or whatever and tromp all over our new lawn above."

He nodded toward the young woman, annoyed that Cameron hadn't provided her name.

"But you, Mrs. Dempsey," he said, compromising. "And *you*, Ms. Hawthorne. *You* might tell on us. And worse — because you are known and maybe even famous, certain authorities might listen if *you* show up and start talking."

Heather shook her head. "We won't tell anyone you're here."

Morgan shrugged, resettling his overcoat. This had always been the most unpleasant part of this endeavor. You could *take* something easily. You could even — if you had trained men like Vincent and Dan — take what you wanted without making a mess or unnecessary noise. But it was harder to settle in and play house with what you'd taken without trimming loose ends.

"I'll be honest with you," he said. "You're too big a liability to let go."

The younger woman shifted nervously, seeming to weigh

her chances. Morgan was struck by her beauty. She had poise beyond her years — some haunting shadow that lurked behind her eyes. Something that gave her edges where a simpler woman would have none. She looked almost wild enough to try something rash, but the other men still had their guns ready, the two boys were clearly still out of commission, and the famous woman and her probable daughter looked too frightened to even think. But not this woman.

"Let the others go," she said.

Morgan blinked. "Maybe you didn't hear me."

"I heard you fine." She swallowed then looked around at the others. "These three are just kids. Heather, she's …" She looked at Heather, who said nothing. "Well, the kids need her. Especially Lila." The woman pointed at the teen girl, and Morgan thought she might be trying to humanize her in his eyes — to give her a name and a personality so she'd be harder to think of as chattel. That kind of thing didn't work on Morgan Matthews, but he admired her trying.

"And who are you, other than this man's wife?"

"Piper. Piper Dempsey." Then she went on. "Lila is pregnant. Just three months along. She's going to have to have a baby six months from now, when who knows what might be happening. That's Raj, her boyfriend. Her baby's father."

Morgan watched Piper Dempsey's big, blue liquid eyes.

"But me?" She seemed to blink back fear. "I can stay if you need insurance."

Morgan shook his head. "No deal."

"The others won't say anything to get you in trouble. Not if I'm here." She looked at Heather again, but instead of protesting, the older woman held the girl to her chest.

Whether she was being practical or a coward, Morgan couldn't decide.

"You're a liability," Morgan told her.

Piper looked at the boy, finally sitting up, his face painted in blood. He wiped it away. His eyes were hard as he listened to their sordid negotiation, but he didn't seem quite dumb enough to try anything.

"Maybe I'm not a liability." She came forward and, seeming to summon intense will, reached up to straighten Morgan's lapel. "Maybe, if you let them go, I can make it worth your while."

Morgan watched Piper's big, blue eyes. She was gorgeous but not soft. Hard and determined. Fiercer, perhaps, than she herself realized. She might intend to honor her words. But she also might take it upon herself, if he agreed, to do something rash and deadly.

He watched her, weighing his options.

If she stayed, there would be seven people in their group: himself, five other men, and this woman. He was willing to share, but they'd have to keep her restrained like an animal. It was fine; the alternative was death. But whenever she was out, they'd need to watch themselves. Watch their guns. Watch their *backs*. She might try anything.

But it could work. Maybe.

He'd already planned to thin their numbers anyway. Vincent clearly had to go. Maybe Dan, too. Accidents could be arranged. Duly trimmed, after things eventually got messy topside, their little group would be well positioned. *Oh, yes.* He who owns the guns owns the land. He who owns the land controls the people. And he who controls the people can have whatever he wants.

And what's more, the bunker had plenty of weapons. Not just handguns. Some of what he'd seen in the armory appeared to be well beyond what an ordinary citizen was permitted to have. Assault rifles, full-auto machine guns, grenades, maybe even fucking *C-4* if his eyes hadn't deceived him. Plenty of muscle. Plenty of security. Plenty of all they'd ever need to -

Chapter Nine

Piper's ears echoed with the gunshot's ringing blast. Gore was suddenly everywhere.

Lila was covered in blood, screaming so shrilly that Piper almost wanted to plug her ears to stop the noise. Her face was dripping, her shirt red and spattered like a Rorschach.

Piper, not far from Lila, was battling shock, fighting ringing ears that nearly muted the girl's shrieks. But even in her shock Piper thought that Lila looked like Carrie, the girl from that old movie Meyer liked so much. The girl who'd finally had enough, and decided to fight back.

Morgan's body fell to the ground and slumped without ceremony. He didn't bend his knees or announce his reasons. He simply folded and hit the carpet like meat, a golf ball-sized hole raining red from his forehead.

Behind the body — at just enough of an angle for the bullet to miss Piper on its way out — was the young man Morgan had called Christopher, holding a gun with its barrel smoking.

Piper looked down, finding herself more gore soaked

than Lila. Her entire front had been painted as if by a harried modern artist. Lumps of matter clotted the goo. She looked down and a snot-like clump of something fell to the floor. She didn't hear it land. Her ears were baffled by the gunshot in the concrete bunker, and Lila was still holding her hands up and screaming.

Piper was startled to realize that she was screaming too.

"Calm down," Christopher said.

His gun was still up, but he was no longer pointing it. His wrist had bent, the smoking barrel now aimed at the ceiling. His other hand was out, palm toward Piper, pacifying. But she could only look down at her bare arms and hands, at the collapsed corpse at her feet. Morgan had rolled on landing and was now looking up at her, seeming to ask why this had happened. With one eye anyway. Most of the other was elsewhere — maybe in her hair.

Piper screamed. Looked around. Screamed some more.

Part of her expected Morgan's other men to swarm, but they were slipping their own weapons into holsters or under waistbands. One of them — the big-armed black man — was helping Trevor to his feet. Trevor looked confounded and angry (an interesting blend) but took the man's assistance without protest. He held himself at arm's length, looking up at Christopher, looking at Piper, looking at Lila.

The big man reached into his pocket and pulled out a tissue and handed it to Trevor. He looked at the tissue as if he'd never seen one before.

Raj was up much faster, pedaling backward, his gas mask still on despite the takedown. The back of his calves struck an end table, and he tripped sideways, his hip catching the corner and knocking an errant deck of cards to the floor. He crab-shuffled away, and the man with the curly hair moved toward him, hands empty and out, seeming to offer help. But Raj was kicking, looking like a ninja knocked flat on his ass.

Heather was still with Lila, not screaming and somehow seeming above it. She must have seen what was coming and flinched — or had used Lila as a shield, which was possible — because she showed only a few specks of blood. Now, trying to comfort Lila and not knowing how, Heather looked split: she could let Lila keep screaming, or she could embrace her and have to touch all those wet pieces of Morgan's brains.

"It's okay," said Christopher, focusing on Piper, side-stepping to match her as her knees unhinged. He held Piper's eyes. His were brown. His hair was black and short under a stocking cap, and he had a square jaw adorned with a jet-black goatee. It occurred to Piper that if he hadn't just blown someone's head off, she'd probably be attracted to him.

"I told you, no hollow points!" said a voice.

Piper felt her mouth open, wondered if she was still screaming, and decided she wasn't. She closed her mouth, tasting unwanted moisture, wondering if she was swallowing Morgan in a different way than she'd so recently offered. She managed to turn and saw the kid — the one with the long hair on top that swung in his face. He wasn't really a kid, she realized. He might be around her age. And now that he wasn't affecting his earlier vacant, crazy expression, he looked more seasoned, less insane.

"It's fine," Christopher told him.

"Jesus *Christ*, Christopher. You're cleaning this up since you insisted on fucking hollow points. You hear me? Every fucking drop. *And* you're dragging his ass outside."

Christopher looked over. "Bullshit! I kill him, you guys haul him! That was the deal!"

"If you'd used a normal slug maybe! Half his fucking head is gone, Christopher! You think I want that shit all over me?"

"Look," Christopher continued in an eminently reasonable tone of voice, "I'll clean up the blood. But I'm *not* dragging the body."

"You're doing it all!"

"How is *that* fair, Cameron?"

"How is you *using fucking hollow points* fair, Christopher?"

"That's just what I had!"

"Nobody just *has* those!"

"Well, I did," Christopher said, crossing his arms.

Across the room, Lila slipped in a puddle of blood and almost struck the ground. The big-armed man caught her. Raj came at him, apparently meaning to protect his woman, but the big man cuffed him away. He set Lila down and turned toward Raj instantly, apologizing, mumbling that the strike had been force of habit.

"Okay, everyone. *Calm down!*" Cameron said, raising his arms.

Lila was ranting and screaming, not hearing at all. Heather was mumbling.

Cameron put his fingers in his mouth and loudly whistled. Lila shrieked one last time and fell silent. All eyes turned to the group's new leader.

"It's over," Cameron said. "*Over.* Okay?"

He looked around the room to make sure everyone planned to remain quiet then continued.

"I'm sorry to have put you through that little bit of drama and violence, but it's over now, okay? It was an unfortunate consequence of how we found things when we arrived."

Piper found her speech. It was, apparently, right where she'd left it: under her terror.

"Who *are* you?" she asked.

Cameron put his right hand on his chest, fingers splayed.

"My name is Cameron Bannister." He pointed around the room at each of the new arrivals in turn. "And as Morgan kindly informed you before losing his mind, that's Vincent, Terrence, Christopher, and Dan."

Piper blinked. Her eyes wanted to water, but at least she'd stopped screaming.

"It's okay," said Cameron, giving her a too-big smile. "We're the good guys."

Chapter Ten

THE DEMPSEYS WERE UPSET. Cameron could understand.

Until a few months ago, he'd never seen a dead body — not even at a funeral, because he'd assiduously avoided them. He always gave spiritual excuses ("we should celebrate her life, not remember her earthly remains") that hid his own fear of death. Until two months ago, he'd never seen a body in plain sight, discarded like litter. Even during the first weeks of occupation, Cameron had stayed in America's guts, keeping to the little villages where drinking and music made people forget the skies, despite the ships. It had been easier to find those places than he'd thought. At first, there had been nothing but fear. And after a few weeks of nothing, burgs with only clouds above almost seemed to forget.

No ships. No abductions. Might as well get back to our business.

In retrospect, Cameron supposed he'd been rationalizing. The bands of people he'd found those first weeks — those who sometimes knew his music and always enjoyed it once he started to play — were more huddles than towns.

And really, those who "got back to business" did so by living in their houses and settling into daily routines. Living and shopping, even if so many of the stores became free-for-alls. But at the time, it had seemed to Cameron that he'd found a way to stay normal. To rise above it all. To see the ships in the sky and pretend they didn't mean what they did.

And as he'd continued his backwater tour during those first weeks — never playing the venues Dan had booked him into but finding a park or a garage where people wanted to hear him play acoustic — Cameron told himself he was living life on his terms, refusing to be defined by events that didn't touch him. Then he'd realized that just because there were no ships above Shepherd's Bend, Iowa, that didn't mean the people there weren't vulnerable to global events. It definitely didn't mean that Cameron Bannister was immune.

He was human, same as anyone. And he had his own cross to bear — most of it back in Utah, from where he'd been diverted to come here — same as the Dempseys.

Cameron looked around the room as the family settled. The teen girl — that would be Lila; she looked just like the photos in his mobile folio, taken at her father's side — was covered in spatter. Piper (she looked much *better* than the photos Cameron had found) looked almost as bad. That was unfortunate. Even after traveling with Vincent, Dan, and Terrence, he himself was still new to gore. If he'd been painted with another man's brains, he'd find it hard to trust, too. But he supposed he should take it easy on Christopher. The original plan had called for *Cameron* to kill Morgan, and he still wasn't entirely sure he could have done it. Just too damn human, apparently.

"Will ..." Piper swallowed, then tried again. "Will *you* let us go?"

Cameron held up a hand. "You misunderstand. You're not captives. Not anymore."

"So we *can* go." She looked at the others: Lila, Meyer's son, Trevor, and … he didn't know who the Indian kid was, but he'd find out soon enough. And, yes, the slippery son of a bitch really had brought his ex-wife to share the bunker with his current one. There was no question that was Heather Hawthorne in the corner. And to think: he'd laughed when Benjamin had said Cameron and his crew might run into her. Apparently, Meyer had giant balls outside the boardroom, too.

"Of course. But there's no need to. This is your house, not ours."

Piper blinked. He may as well have been speaking Chinese.

Cameron sighed. "Christopher, give her a wet towel or something. Lila too."

Christopher, duly chastised, entered the kitchen. The faucet ran. Good news; if the water was running as hard as it sounded, that meant the pump was probably running. Maybe there really *hadn't* been too much damage. He hadn't been entirely comfortable with the "gasoline and cherry bomb" plan, but Terrence had assured him that any bunker worth its salt would have a door between a gas generator and its supply and the rest of the living space … and that because it was so critical, it would have a good fire suppression system that would run even with the power on reserve. Cameron hadn't been in a position to argue. He'd been pretending to be a crazy, violent kid for Morgan's benefit — Morgan, who'd already staked his claim on the place and made himself feared prior to Cameron's arrival.

Christopher returned with two towels. He handed one to Piper and the other to Lila, who snatched hers like a nervous animal. Piper accepted hers with a smile and a grateful nod. If not for all the Morgan-gore on her face, neck, and clothes, she would have looked adorably shy.

"How do you know our names?" Piper asked.

"Have a seat. Please." Cameron gestured toward the couch and looked around at his crew. "And you guys — put the guns down and take five. You look like a goon squad."

Vincent shrugged then sat. Under his impressive body and demeanor, the small wooden chair looked miniature. Christopher didn't seem willing to go far enough to grab a chair and half sat on a cabinet against the wall. Dan remained standing because Dan — though Cameron loved him like a father — was a son of a bitch. Terrence had already crossed his arms and leaned back, doing his best James Dean.

Piper waited for Cameron to sit in the living room's least comfortable chair before nodding an okay to the others. The kids flanked her, staring hard at Cameron. Heather sat on the couch's arm. The Indian kid seemed put-out as he came to the couch and found himself excluded. Pouting, he sat on the love seat alone.

"I know your names because we came here to find you. Morgan ..." Cameron stopped, looking down at the floor's bleeding meat, wondering if they could all ignore it for now or if someone should drag it away — or at least put down a few paper towels. "Morgan was here to take the bunker, and he'd already established himself when we showed up, so it was either fight him outright or pretend to ally with him and double-cross him later. We took the coward's way out, but the one least likely to get anyone killed — other than Morgan anyway. But he wasn't here because of Meyer or because of you. He wanted what was in the bunker, and you were in the way."

"How did you even know it was here?" Piper asked.

"Me? I assumed there had to be something below ground. Well ..." Cameron shifted. That wasn't actually true. "I was *told*," he corrected, "because *someone else* assumed. We found the house empty, and it didn't make sense that Meyer would have come alone then lived in an open house without even boarding windows. But you didn't fool Morgan for a second. He knew right away that there was more to this house than others were seeing. This house had no basement, no crawlspace ... but it did have all sorts of strange, survivalist preparations in place. Windmills on the hill. A solar farm. He had everyone out there scared of him."

"Not everyone," Christopher said.

Cameron scratched his cheek, nodding in agreement.

"Christopher was with Morgan when we arrived, but *he* came to Vincent. Said he didn't trust Morgan. They joined up on the road, but then Morgan started to get crazier. Threatening."

"You were looking for us," Piper said.

Cameron nodded.

"And that's supposed to make us trust you. To *not* think you might be worth being afraid of."

"We don't want to hurt you."

"But you know all about us. You know who this house belonged to. You knew enough about Meyer that you 'assumed' there'd be a bunker here. You didn't come to take what we had, but still the best way to get in was to team up with ... with *him*." Piper looked at Morgan's body, clearly disgusted.

"I understand that this has been rough." Whether Cameron meant today's events or the totality of their stay in the bunker, he wasn't sure.

"All I know," Piper said, "is that you broke through my

front door. That you blew up our generator and started a fire. And that I'm supposed to *trust* you just because you shot a man in the middle of my living room."

Cameron looked helplessly up at Dan.

"Tell her about The Nine," Dan suggested.

Chapter Eleven

TREVOR WATCHED the man who'd killed the group's leader: *Christopher*. Even wedged between his mother and Piper (and holy shit was *that* uncomfortable; her boob was pressed into his arm to the nipple, and even after a siege he'd managed to pop a boner), Trevor was weighing his chances. If needed, could he squeeze himself out of his tit-pressed position, leap for someone's gun, and gain an advantage?

Probably not. But he didn't trust these men any more than Piper seemed to. It was awesome how obviously she wasn't buying into a word of their bullshit. Maybe they really *were* the good guys, and maybe they weren't. But after seeing one man's brains darken the far wall, it was the kind of claim anyone would be stupid to take on faith.

"Morgan was right. Your husband was taken into one of the ships," Cameron said.

"But how could you possibly know that?" Piper asked.

He sighed as if deciding to omit a complicated piece of the story. "I know people who have studied this stuff all their lives. There's a lab I'll tell you about later, still very operational. And they have … well … *resources*." Cameron looked again at the broad man with the curly hair and bad skin: *Dan*. "Anyway, you know about the big wave of abductions that came right after the ships arrived, right?"

"That was our favorite TV show," interrupted Trevor's mother, her wiseass quips still intact after the quarrel. "Except for the part where they fucked up Moscow. That was clearly the network suits interfering with the artistry to please viewers."

Cameron turned from Piper. "Heather, right?"

"Dickhead, right?" Heather answered.

"Mom …" Trevor said.

"We know there were abductions," Cameron turned to Piper, ignoring Trevor and his mother. "At first, they were just rumors, then they — the people I mentioned — started to receive footage from all over the world from a network of sources. But they never knew for sure about Meyer."

"We figure he'll be back any minute," Heather said. "He ran out for some smokes."

Cameron gave Trevor's mother more of a smiling acknowledgement than she probably deserved then spoke to Piper.

"According to our stats, there have been just shy of twenty thousand worldwide abductions. Some of that is government information accessed through leaked channels, some is NASA, again through leaked channels. Plenty is via an informal network of nerds that have managed to keep a primitive version of their own private Internet up and running. But there's good reason to believe the figures are accurate, down to the person, excepting very recent activity and unreported or unobserved phenomena. But that last bit is hard to say because communications have been spotty at best, and even harder to keep an eye on since we joined Morgan and had to start playing our parts. It's been weeks since I've managed to raise anything reliable about the overall state of the nation."

"'Raise'?" Piper said.

Cameron nodded. "There are still a few open communication frequencies. I can't take credit for that; Terrence found them." He tipped his head toward the cool black man still leaning against the wall.

"The open frequencies are mostly noise," Cameron went on, "but we've also heard what sounds like military chatter."

"Military!" Trevor didn't like drawing attention to himself, but the word left him almost involuntarily. He'd forgotten about the military. In movies (even a few of his father's films, come to think of it), the army always managed to shoot down the big, bad alien ships. The fact that they were still around and scheming felt strangely encouraging.

Cameron nodded. "It's highly encoded. I can't even guess at the encryption or what they're saying. Might not even *be* military. Point is, the specificity of the open frequencies tells us it's probably intentional. The fact that most frequencies are blocked and only a few are open, I mean."

"'Blocked'?" said Piper.

"By the ships," said Terrence. Trevor looked him over. The man was dressed in fitting jeans, boots, and a black leather vest.

"But why would a few channels be open?"

"If I had to guess," said Terrence in his deep, syrupy voice, "it's to create a bottleneck. A way to force communication into a few channels so they can easily monitor it."

"The government?"

"The other guys," Terrence corrected, pointing up.

Cameron looked at the TV. "When did your news stop broadcasting here?"

"About six weeks ago," Piper said.

Cameron nodded. "Black Tuesday. It happened everywhere on the same day. But at that time, people who'd been taken were being returned, right?"

Trevor remembered that quite plainly. That had given them hope. There had always been the possibility that Dad had walked away, that he'd fallen into a hole and died, or that he'd been killed by bandits. But there was an equal possibility that he'd been taken, and when the first abductees had begun appearing back at home — altered somehow, strange, maybe a little frightening — that had made them all think Dad might return.

"Yes," Piper said.

"What you may not know is that abductee returns have slowed over time. At first, it was thousands of people coming back per week, worldwide. Then hundreds then dozens. Finally, just single digits. As far as we can tell, it slowed further after Black Tuesday. Kind of like listening for your microwave popcorn to finish popping."

Trevor said, "What's a microwave?"

Heather rolled her eyes. "Kids these days."

"My dad had one." Cameron smiled at Trevor, and Trevor had to remind himself that these men had yet to prove they could be trusted. "They used to be a popular way to cook food. We used to make popcorn in ours, before we watched movies. You'd put this flat bag in and set the timer for a minute. At first, the popcorn kernels would pop really fast, but eventually they'd slow down, and you'd hear a cluster of new pops, then just one or two every other second. The returning abductees were like that. Right up until three weeks ago."

"What happened three weeks ago?" said Piper.

"Three weeks ago, I was on my way to Moab, Utah. Me and Dan. To the facility I told you about. A lab. I had one of the communication channels open to Moab — well, not '*to Moab*'; you can't connect point to point anymore, so far as we can tell — but we'd agreed to use the same public frequency, knowing everyone could hear us and being careful what we said. I got this message, telling me to meet up with Vincent and Terrence and come here, to a private residence in Vail instead."

"But the abductions …"

"That's when they stopped. That's why I came here."

Piper shook her head. "I don't understand."

"Mrs. Dempsey—"

"Piper."

"*Piper*," Cameron said, "it's been three weeks since the last abductee was returned. But as it turns out, it's not just *most* of them who've come home. As of the day I'm talking about — and this is still true today, unless something has changed in the last handful of hours — *all* of them had been returned. All but nine."

Trevor looked from Cameron to Piper. He said, "*Nine?*"

Cameron nodded. "Nine of out twenty thousand abductees remain missing, and have been for more than a month. Meyer — your husband, your father — is one of them. And my friends in Moab feel that the missing are somehow significant, not just oversights or loose ends. They *matter*, Piper. Trevor. And so in our circles, we call them 'The Nine.'"

Again, Trevor looked at Piper before focusing on Cameron, who now had every nugget of the room's attention. "What's so 'significant' about these nine people?" he asked.

"That," said Cameron, "is what we're here to find out."

Chapter Twelve

"I don't like it," Raj said.

Lila was sitting at the kitchen table. It was a nice polished wood, surrounded by typical kitchen chairs. It seemed to have been modeled after the home they'd had a dozen years earlier, after her father had made his wealth but before he'd fully extricated himself from mediocrity. Just one more way her father had planned ahead to stave off the madness of confinement: a nice kitchen that was more familiar than luxurious. If Lila ignored the blood-stained floor and the complete lack of windows, she could almost imagine they were in that old house when they'd all been a family together.

She looked at Raj. He was eating toast. Among the supplies had been a freezer full of bread — which, it turned out, thawed and toasted just fine. "What don't you like?"

"The way your mom and Piper have just accepted these people."

Lila craned back in her chair and looked out into the living room. It wasn't from the same house as the kitchen's model, but it had become plenty familiar over her months spent living here. There were times she hated not being able to go outside, but she must have moved past anger and into acceptance, or however that stepwise grieving process was supposed to work. Life wasn't all bad. Despite being pregnant, she was actively encouraged to lie in the tanning bed for a few minutes each day to make Vitamin D. What the hell; it was better than school.

Trevor was out there, clustered around a folding card table with their erstwhile home invaders. Vincent had rescued the table from some storage closet. The bunker had an endless supply of lockers filled with twenty garage sales' worth of miscellany. It wasn't hoarding, exactly, but Lila supposed the only difference was that they kept finding uses for the hoard. She'd found Mad Libs in a box in one closet with no idea where it had come from, and the only person awake when she'd found it had been Christopher. They'd filled in the absurd (and often obscene) blanks for over an hour, playing with hands over mouths to dim the sound of their laughter.

"Oh, relax," Lila said.

Raj shook his head. "These people drilled through the door. They poured gas into the generator exhaust and blew it up. Then they stormed in with guns and started shooting. Trevor got his nose broken. I nearly snapped my ankle."

Lila rolled her eyes. They'd been through this, but Raj wouldn't let it go. Trevor's nose had been broken by Morgan — the man whom Christopher had handily removed from the picture and the corpse that Vincent and Dan had later dragged up the stairs, once the cameras showed a clear path, to bury in the woods. And Raj's "nearly snapped ankle"? It had been a sprain at the most, and he'd done it to himself by tripping over that end table. Sometimes she wanted to offer to put a Big Bird Band-Aid on it and kiss the boo-boo to make it all better, which it clearly had been for days — though Raj was still affecting a limp, just to show them all how much he'd been wronged.

"What were they supposed to do? They needed to find out about Dad."

"And this is how they did it."

"If they hadn't taken care of Morgan, we would have had to! Or maybe we wouldn't have been able to. Maybe he'd have come in, killed us all, and that would have been the end of it."

"He never would have made it inside without their help." Raj set his toast down then walked quietly forward to peer into the living room, trying not to get caught. He lowered his voice to a whisper. "And Christopher? Who can just casually blow someone's brains out like that? You were screaming your head off, totally covered in blood and—"

"He did what he had to do!"

"But not by hitting him, right? He had to *shoot* him. In the head. Point blank. *With hollow point bullets,* Lila!"

Lila rolled her eyes again, making sure he saw her this time, then took her plate and set it in the sink. The bunker even had a dishwasher. Discharge from the toilets had to go somewhere, so why not put dishwasher water into the leach bed, too? They got their water from a spring and their heat from renewable electricity. There was no reason not to live like royalty. *Mole people* royalty anyway.

"Look," Raj said, following her, "they're here. Okay, whatever. And maybe they're fine. But it's been … what … a week since they barged in here? And already, look at your brother. Do you think we should get them all matching tattoos?"

At that exact moment, she heard a voice that sounded

like Christopher's, though she couldn't hear what he'd said. Then Trevor laughed very loud. Her brother was a bit overenthusiastic and might want to dial it down, but Lila could hardly fault him. He was managing happiness while buried in the dirt. Good for him.

"It's sending the wrong message," Raj said. "They bust in here then say, 'Oh, our bad! We're actually awesome, and this was all a misunderstanding. Sorry about the fire, by the way. The fire *we* set, not Morgan. And yeah, that was our idea and not his, but we *had* to get in. Not that we looked for cameras or tried to talk to you first. We figured we'd shoot our way in, knowing you'd understand.' And then we all slap our knees and go, 'Ha ha! You're right; that *was* hilarious. Remember when Christopher sprayed everyone with brains? *Classic*. Ah, memories.'"

"Raj . . ."

"And what does Cameron spend his days doing? Piper's just like, 'Oh, sure, Cameron. *Definitely* go through all of Meyer's computer records. Building permits? Stored blueprints? All good. What about defenses? Weaknesses? Say, how many big weapons are in that room of death, and do you mind if I browse through it? Cool. Thanks.'"

Lila spun. Her hands were wet, and Raj was closer than she'd realized. She left wet spatters on his shirt.

"That's *enough!*"

Raj gave her a second then shrugged in a way that suggested surrender — it was her own stupid, bitchy, hormonal funeral. "Just seems like we're too forgiving, too fast."

"So we should hold a grudge. For no reason. With someone who *might* — and yes, I know I'm 'dumb and naive' to believe this; I got that — be able to help us find Dad? I don't want to have to be the one to tell you, Raj, but there's an apocalypse afoot. Things are different now.

Maybe you'd better stop holding onto all those prejudices from your youth. You know — from, like, four months ago?"

"'*Apocalypse,*'" he said, scoffing. "Everyone acts like cities are burning."

"Mom said Vegas was burning."

"Sure, Vegas. What do you expect from Vegas? But what did we see when the news was on? Just that one thing in Moscow."

"Moscow? Oh. I guess you're referring to that *insignificant little tiff* they had over there. You know, when the entire city was obliterated."

"But where else has that happened? And besides, they fired first!"

"Then it's all good. The aliens are our friends. That's why they took twenty thousand people. That's why they took my *dad*."

"I'm not saying that's not bad, but they did return *most* of those people."

Lila turned and met Raj's eyes for a disbelieving moment. She slowly shook her head, mouth unhinged. It was one thing for him to be a shit to the five new people in the bunker — people who had all behaved like perfect gentlemen, even deferring to their own supplies rather than eating bunker food. But this was just bitchy.

"You are *unbelievable*." She turned away, headed for the living room.

"I'm just being prudent," Raj said, still following her. Lila wanted to swat him away like a fly. "That's your dad's personal shit that Piper and Heather are letting Cameron paw through."

Lila shook her head, not looking back or giving him the satisfaction of her response.

"Do you think, if he were here, he'd want them looking

through all that stuff? You're betraying him. All of you. He might as well be dead for all the—"

Lila turned. Her tongue found the corner of her cheek and she felt her eyes harden. Raj clearly hadn't expected another confrontation, but this time he'd gone too far.

"Why are you here, Raj?" A loaded question. Lila knew how she wanted him to answer, just so she could react in anger. She felt her heart rate increase, heavy in her chest.

She wanted to claw his face. How *dare* he talk about her father? If Dad were here, she'd have to spend most of her time keeping him from ripping Raj's head from his shoulders. He'd left before discovering her little baby secret, but the boy who'd knocked up his daughter wouldn't have had such an easy life if he'd known.

Her mind drifted back to their cross-country escape. Meyer had tolerated Raj, but she'd always felt his grace would only last as long as Raj remained neutral. Dad was willing to let him ride along, but he'd have dropped him without remorse the second he'd become a liability — and never had that cold fact been clearer than the freeway exit outside of Chicago, when Raj had tried to play the racist card to take them where he thought they should go.

"I'm ..." But Raj seemed unsure of how to answer. The fire had left him the minute he'd been challenged. Just like a coward. Meyer Dempsey had been a *man*, and he'd raised his daughter to be ... well, not a *man*, but a *woman*, and to respect those who possessed all those very male traits: decisiveness. Determination. Even arrogance and stubbornness, when he knew he was right. But Raj, unlike the new guys, could only whine and complain.

"It's a real question, Raj," Lila sniped, feeling as if her father's spirit had occupied her bones. She could be like him. She was the daughter of an industry titan and a sarcastic bitch. "*Why are you here?*"

"What do you mean?"

"I don't mean literally. We all know 'you're here' because you hopped into the car with Piper and Trevor in Central Park. And we know that 'you're here' beyond that because we didn't have time to detour and drop you off. I suppose you could have stayed in Jersey, but we know 'you're here' because my father — who, I'll remind you, I know better than you do — apparently decided to extend his well-prepared mercy instead of forcing you to *try* and make it on your own."

"Now hold on, Lila."

"And really, that all boils down to the fact that 'you're here' because I wanted you to be. But even that's not what I'm talking about."

Lila heard how she sounded but pushed on anyway. Like father, like daughter. She could run a boardroom with an iron fist, too, when the time came.

"The door's open. Why don't you ask Vincent or Terrence to unlock it for you then just get the fuck out if you have a problem with the way things are going down?"

Raj looked stunned. "I don't ... I mean ... I'm just saying that they're taking a lot of liberties with—"

"With my father's house? With the house and supplies that *he* decided to let *you* share?"

"Look, I didn't want to fight about it or anything, I'm just saying that—"

"You're the only one, Raj. The *only one* who has any problem with what's happening here. So either we're all idiots and we need you to protect us, or *you're* the asshole. And maybe we *are* idiots! But listen to me: For the fiftieth time, *we trust them.* We even *like them.* And one more? We think they're an *asset,* that we're actually *better off* with an engineer, a big, strong military man, two guys who are good with guns, and one guy who seems to know a whole hell of a lot more about what's going on with the aliens than any of us do."

She took a breath.

"Now, maybe I'm wrong. Maybe that's stupid. It sure doesn't *sound* wrong to me, but maybe you're right, and it is somehow. But I'm tired of arguing. Do you hear me? *I'm tired of having this argument with you.* Your objections have been noted. But this is how it is — and honestly, it's *none of your fucking business.* This isn't your family, and this isn't your house! So you can stay here with us, as our guest, or you can *leave!*"

Lila's chest was heaving, as if she could feel her baby's heart pumping double time along with hers.

Watching Raj's face fall, her first instinct was to apologize. A lot of what she'd said — about why he was here anyway — was untrue and clearly unfair. She'd wanted Raj with her. And he was part of the family now, bound to the Dempsey clan by unborn blood for better or worse. But he wouldn't listen. He'd raised the same arguments day in, day out for the week their new visitors had been in the bunker. Every innocuous moment, Raj had been warning her of doing wrong, of not seeing the truth, of turning a blind eye to the ill intentions of others.

But they didn't have any ill intentions. Raj had been having crises the entire time they'd been in here. This was about *him*, not anyone else. He was maybe jealous, maybe feeling inadequate. But the truth was that Meyer would have accepted the attitudes and ethos of the new men much more easily than he'd accepted Raj ... and they both knew it.

Still, she thought Raj might retort. He might even run off and pout. But he surprised her. His jaw hardened and he said, "Fine. You're right. I'll keep my opinions to myself."

Cameron entered the kitchen then looked at Lila and Raj. They must have looked like two fighters preparing to square off. "Everyone got a minute?" he said.

Lila turned toward Cameron. Past him, she saw that the living room had filtered into a group, as if to prepare for an announcement. Had they heard her rant? Probably some. She felt a blush but held it in.

"What's going on?" Lila asked.

"It's time for me to head out," he said, "to try and find your father."

Chapter Thirteen

IMAGES ROLL past Heather's line of sight.

She understands and doesn't understand at all.

Meyer is beside her, but they, the two of them, are nowhere in particular.

Like many times when they were together in this place, space doesn't matter. There were times when they lay on couch cushions and pillows on Heather's floor — in what was once their house — and times when they met the shaman in other places. It never mattered.

For Meyer, it was about the depth of his dream.

The dream showed him understanding.

Like Heather almost has now.

"It's a beacon," Meyer says. "But at the same time, it's an inductive charge. A way of providing power without requiring them to keep that power source aboard."

He's pointing. Heather sees the pyramid — common enough imagery for her in these dreams, which most of her mind is aware enough to know is floating through a haze of artificial reality — but this time something is different.

She usually goes where he leads her, but for Heather it's always been like taking a tour with Meyer as the guide. For her, it has always been about a shared experience. She'd never say it in their usual version of reality, but in the ayahuasca dreams she used to feel that the places they went — or the places he went, while she tagged along — didn't matter as long as they traveled as one. It's a curiously vulnerable idea for the wakened Heather, but her defenses always soften in this place.

Except that she shouldn't be here. Meyer is gone. And Heather — the corporeal Heather, in a bed in a room — has taken none of the medicine.

She's about to ask what Meyer means about beacons and power sources, but then she sees it. They've often visited symbolic places, her higher self somehow was aware that Meyer was traveling and she was only seeing what he wanted her to see.

But now the image is in her.

She's never been to Egypt, and has no interest in the ancients or the structure of their monolithic buildings. But now she understands that there are two main passageways inside the structure itself, fluted up at an angle like vast vents, converging on a place at its heart called the Queen's Chamber. Looking at the pyramid now, she sees the beacon Meyer means: a thin line of light emanating from one of the ascending passageways, lancing the atmosphere. Beyond it, at the beam's end, she sees the moon. Only it isn't a moon. It's a large sphere, tied to the beacon, receiving the power generated in the earth-bound building.

Other images shuffle past before she can wonder.

A hole in the ground, going down forever, booby trapped and unreachable.

Lines of stones. Monoliths. Perfect precision from supposedly imperfect instruments.

Primitive networks. Nodes.

And points of power — nine of them — where dormant secrets lie hidden.

Meyer is still beside her as the images flit past. "Do you understand?"

Heather does not, and says so.

"But you do. You do."

She turns to him. None of this matters. And none of this is real.

The days when they would lock themselves in a room with Juha and purge into buckets then travel for hours are long gone. The days of facing their darknesses before finding this place, this togetherness, this space — long gone. She's dimly aware that she is only dreaming. But the dream is so real, so deep in its understanding. Unlike any dream she's ever had.

"I miss you," she says.

Their surroundings change in an instant, as if a switch has been flipped. There are no more scenes of spiritual cliché. No pyramids, no Sphinx, no Incan ruins, no supposition, on the part of the dream, that she should imbue the old places with meaning. Now the background is hard and metallic. Lights. Panels and tables and wires.

"Then protect it for me, Heather," he says. "Protect what will allow me to return."

Chapter Fourteen

HEATHER AWOKE TO A GENTLE SHAKING. Her eyes blinked away sleep's haze, her mind slowly coming around to the realization that she'd been dreaming. She was suddenly sure that the dream was important, and she rushed to hold it close, but it was already slipping away. She'd dreamed of Meyer and a very important task he'd assigned her. But as seconds ticked by, her certainty faded. Why couldn't it just have been a dream?

"Mom."

She rolled halfway over beneath the sheets. What time was it? Living underground had shifted her perception of day and night. Clocks no longer mattered. Daytime bled through the skylights and reflectors, but the way it filtered down, never direct, made it feel like just another bulb. Lila and Trevor seemed to be settling into a circadian rhythm that was just under twenty-four hours whereas she (and Piper, Heather guessed, and who the fuck cared about Raj?) wanted to stretch hers to twenty-five or more. If any of them had been sealed away alone, time would probably pass slower for Heather than for her daughter, and in a few weeks they'd disagree on how many days (how many cycles of sleep and awake) had passed. But because they were all trapped together, their schedules blended. Heather was tired more often than she had been topside, and had solved the mismatch by joining her children's schedules and taking naps. Like the one, she now realized, she was rousing from.

Lila was above her.

"Hey, baby," Heather said.

"Cameron needs to go."

"Oh. Well, goodbye, Cameron."

"I thought you might want to hear what he had to say."

"Is it different from goodbye?"

Lila smiled down at her mother. She wasn't a little girl anymore. She'd been knocked up, and despite that being a bad thing by Old World standards, this was the New World, and the pregnancy gave Lila and Heather something to bond over — while, interestingly, caring for Lila had given Heather and *Piper* something to bond over. So that was nice. But on the other hand, she'd been knocked up *by Raj*, about which Heather was less enthusiastic. He was probably a catch by most mothers' standards, but Heather wasn't most mothers.

"Come on, Mom."

"I'm really tired. I had a hard day of sitting around underground and watching episodes of *ALF*."

"Mom."

"Why didn't Alf ever eat that fucking cat he wanted so badly? It was *right there*, and it's not like Alf had much self-restraint. I've never understood that."

"I've never understood why you like that old show."

"I'm fascinated by the complex character work."

"Come on." Lila tugged at her. Heather protested. But

hey, she had this coming. Back when they'd all lived together, Heather had tried to drag Lila out of bed in exactly the same way every school day. Now the tables were turned, so there.

Lila finally dropped Heather's arm and stood. She was thin, and Heather wondered if she was imagining the tiniest of baby bumps. Probably. They were all getting fat down here. Obese at the end of the world. And to think: there were starving children in Africa. And starving crowds of looting murderer-rapists everywhere, including their front lawn.

"Okay," Lila said. "I tried. We'll fill you in later."

"She coming?" yelled a voice. It sounded like Cameron.

Heather yelled back: "No. You interrupted me before I could."

Cameron laughed. "Then by all means, finish."

Lila rolled her eyes. Heather ignored her.

Heather liked Cameron. He was Piper's age but had the seasoned feel of a much older man. He'd told them how he'd traveled with his father in the past, hitting a world's worth of obscure destinations — and, once older, how he'd traveled to dozens more places with his band. They didn't make much money playing obscure backwaters, but Cameron always chose experience over profit. And Dan, bless his heart, went right along. As Cameron's agent, he worked on commission. But somehow Cameron was allowed to play all the low-paying gigs he wanted.

"'Night, Mom."

"No, no, hang on. Just let me wash my face." She shouted past Lila, through the door, into the living room. "If you're playing Twister, wait for me!"

"Right foot green," said Christopher's voice.

Heather rolled out of bed, wondering if she was

netting sleep with these naps. She'd never been a napper back before the ships' arrival had made life socially awkward. She'd stayed up until 3 a.m., never bothering to break the pattern because she needed it for those nights she had comedy shows. Many times, she'd need to be awake earlier than eleven or noon and would eke through the morning on fumes, drinking cup after cup of highly cream-and-sugared coffee. But even on those nights of little rest, Heather refused to nap. It upset her sense of night and day enough to fatigue her. Little had changed. Naps still tricked her body into thinking day was night, and she still woke feeling like she was wearing a one-ton cloak. But what else was there to do around here besides watch old TV recordings and walk on one of the gravity treadmills?

The two larger bedrooms shared a master bathroom. Heather entered, turned on the light, and thought for a moment of how thankful she was for all of Meyer's preparations. He hadn't just built them a haven for what might be the end days. He'd given them a sanctuary with two full bathrooms and a Jacuzzi. If things really went to hell, that Jacuzzi might become a cistern and the bathroom a dark cave in which to store scavenged metal from topside, but for now the wind and sun continued to give them all the electricity required to run the pump. The spring or aquifer or whatever gave them water to fill the tub. So why the hell *not* have a hot, bubbly soak while the alien invasion went about its business outside? Meyer had been practical like that. He could afford anything, so he bought everything.

And what's more, he'd done all of it well in advance of knowing what was coming. Damn near psychic of him, everyone agreed. It was enough to make the bunker's residents believe in the positive power of paranoia. Although Heather, for her part, was beginning to believe Meyer hadn't been operating as blind as it seemed at first. Nobody else had Heather's intimate knowledge of Meyer Dempsey. Not even Piper knew him deep to the core, because she never journeyed with him, high on what he called healing. Heather even thought he might've had some sort of trippy vision during a few of their ayahuasca sessions that led him to—

She stopped, her hands on the sink's edge. The mirror was in front of her, as nice as the one in her home (her *old* home, by now) back in LA. There was a Heather in that reflection, but for a scant moment she seemed to see right through her.

What *about* those sessions?

Something with her dream. She'd dreamt something important. Not just about Meyer, but something with him that seemed to have meaning.

But it was gone.

Still she blinked and ran water in the sink slowly, delicately, feeling something on the tip of her mind's tongue. The dream was mostly gone, but one of its delicate gossamer threads seemed to still cling. If she was careful, she might not break it. If Heather kept her mind defocused — paying attention to the departing dream while not watching it closely enough to scare it away — it might yet come. If she refused to wake fully. If she let herself settle into the heavy fugue of recent sleep.

She blinked at her reflection. *Nothing.*

Heather sighed, turned on the water, and was about to cup some to splash her face when she stopped, watching the water swirl down the drain.

Plug the hole.

She'd just wanted a splash, needed to wet her hands, and slap the sleep from her head. She didn't need to plug the sink to do any of that. Yet the compulsion felt heavy for some reason, so she pulled up the stopper. She watched the basin fill a few inches, then turned off the water.

Whatever you do, protect it, Heather.

That mental voice had sounded like Meyer. Like he was right beside her in this empty bathroom.

Suddenly, intensely, Heather needed to *un*plug the hole. To unstopper it. To make sure it was never, *ever* plugged again. The new compulsion was so much heavier than the deep need to stopper the sink, which in itself had been bizarre. It was almost as if she'd plugged it just to see how obviously *wrong* plugging it was, how the faucet should *always* be allowed to run as it wished without encumbrance, and how if anyone *ever* blocked the damn thing, they'd all be fucked.

Still, the compulsion was so strange and so powerful that Heather forced herself to wait a beat, desperate to understand it, rather than allowing it to master her.

Then, another beat.

But … there was nothing.

Trevor's voice: "Hurry up, Mom!"

She looked up into the mirror and told her reflection, "You're going crazy down here."

Heather pushed the plunger down, uncorking the drain. Water swirled away, its rotation ticking off days and minutes and hours like a timepiece. But even the sink looked wrong now, turning her sarcastic self assessment into something with barbs. Why the hell was she staring at the sink? Why was she wary of her own reflection? Why had she been so compelled to stopper the sink then drain it, as if pushed from outside? Maybe she really was going mad. Maybe they all were.

Heather splashed her face, then used one of the towels to dry off. She felt the soft terrycloth against her skin with her eyes closed, wondering how much that one towel had cost. And to think: people were killing each other for scraps above them.

She pulled the towel from her face, but when she did she saw that the towel looked as wrong as the sink had. It was brown, but it had been smudged and blotted with a more intense color in the strange bathroom light: red, like paint.

Heather looked down at the sink, then fell two steps back, covering her mouth to hold in a scream.

The bowl in front of her was filled with blood. Viscous red liquid swirled down the drain, painting the basin walls behind in a murder scene.

She shut her eyes, feeling her mind unhinging.

A few terrifying seconds passed.

With effort, Heather opened her eyes.

The sinks contained only water. Plain old water. The final half inch of clear liquid drained away. The sink itself was clean and unmarred.

Trevor called again, louder.

Heather blinked. But there was nothing wrong with the sink or the towel. There *had never been* anything wrong. Everything was fine, and always would be.

She sighed, then hung the clean towel on the bar beside the sink.

"All right, all right," she called back to Trevor, flipping off the light.

But as Heather left the bathroom and headed in with the others, she couldn't help but feel herself still in the dream, and that what she'd seen with Meyer — whatever it had been — was her true reality, long forgotten.

Chapter Fifteen

"I NEED TO GO," Cameron told the group. "I can't do what I need to do if I stay here."

He was speaking to everyone, but mainly addressing Piper — announcing his intentions as if asking permission. Piper couldn't help but feel flattered. For months, she'd been the bunker's default leader, but it had been a chore without gratitude. She'd been responsible for everyone, yet nobody thanked her. The simple, acknowledging looks this new man had given her in the week she'd known him almost made up for it. She saw respect in those glances. Appreciation — not for himself, but for what she'd done for the others.

"Okay," Heather said. "Bon voyage."

Heather's hair was wet and plastered to her forehead, as if she'd just washed her face. She looked bleary but fresher than Piper felt right now — than, really, Piper *ever* felt anymore. Heather had plunked down on the sofa beside Lila. Piper didn't want to feel jealous and wasn't, but still there was that small, selfish pang. *She'd* taken care of Lila over the last few years and had, in a way, kept her alive over the past months. Heather had done nothing. She was an absentee mother, even now that Lila was pregnant. Piper had always felt like a friend rather than a mother figure to the kids, but that feeling had flipped. Now Heather was the buddy, and Piper was the nag Heather had never needed to be.

"I'm not an expert on this stuff," Cameron continued. "We came here to answer a question about Meyer, but it's too big and too sprawling. I don't even know where to start. There's simply too much I don't know."

"Hmm," Heather added.

Piper looked at Heather. She was phoning it in, present for the departure only because Lila had dragged her from a nap. Clearly, she couldn't care less, slouched in her chair like a teenager. Almost a generation older than Piper yet a full generation less interested in giving a shit.

"You said you thought you could get him back," Piper said. It was a hope she'd been holding onto far tighter than she dared admit, even to herself. She was surrounded by people but felt like the planet's last occupant. Meyer had cheated on her with Heather, but he'd also saved her life. Sometimes, the prospect of his return felt like the only thing that could keep her going.

"No." Cameron shook his head emphatically. "I didn't say that. I said I thought we could find out what happened to him. That's different."

Piper kept her face neutral, hiding her disappointment.

"The ships have kept The Nine far longer than the others. The questions are why, what these people mean to them, and what the aliens are planning to do with them as part of their grand plan, if they have one. That's the big puzzle, and it makes everyone nervous. Everywhere we know of that communication has been attempted with the ships has experienced a violent result. They showed up and hung in our skies, but it's as if they just want to be left alone now that they're here. But the people at the Moab facility think this — this period of *waiting* — is a lull before contact is finally made. But if we wait until it's obvious what those nine people mean, their fear is that it might be too late."

"Too late in what way?" said Lila, fear in her voice.

"No way to be sure," Cameron said kindly.

"But why do you need to leave?" Piper asked.

"We've done what we can here. Now it's time to take what we've learned to smarter people who can look at the information about Meyer and the others and try to find patterns."

Piper said, "Why would there be patterns?"

"There are *always* patterns." Cameron looked away then sighed as if with heart-weary regret. "I didn't always believe that was true, but turns out it usually is. See, Benjamin, the guy I mentioned runs the lab in Moab? He just so happens to be my dad. He dragged me everywhere as a kid, searching for evidence to support this fringe nutball theory called 'Ancient Astronauts.' It basically says that aliens have been here in the past, doing things like helping humans build pyramids and putting the big stone heads on Easter Island. I played along for a while, thinking it all seemed very exciting to explore and solve mysteries. But as I got a bit older, I decided it was stupid. Because the truth is, if you look long enough with the desire to find something, well, sure enough, you'll find it."

"Like what?"

"Like the pyramids of the Giza Plateau maybe. The Ancient Astronauts people say those three pyramids, seen from above, are lined up just like the stars in Orion's belt. 'It's too perfect to be coincidence!' they'll say. And then they'll point out that in the constellation of Orion, the belt draws a line right to Sirius, the brightest star in the sky. And they'll say, 'The Giza pyramids line up to point directly at the ancient city of Heliopolis!' And on and on. Over and over again, people find three ancient things that line up 'just like Orion's belt' and point at 'something very important.' But I always thought, 'They're *only three things*. You can find collections of three things anywhere.'"

His eyes ticked toward the wall, where spatters of Morgan Matthews's blood still stained the paint. He shouted, "Look! Those three smudges are like the stars in Orion's belt! And hark: they're pointing directly at the corner, which is the most important part of the wall! That proves aliens have been here!'"

Cameron laughed then shook his head. This was much more information than any of them needed, and Piper saw his verbal meanderings for what they were: something in his past that had meaning — apparently *defining* meaning — to him. Watching Cameron, Piper couldn't help her curiosity. There had been nothing but time for talking over the past week, and still they knew precious little about the group's quietly insightful leader. Cameron had convinced Morgan he was a crazy kid, but clearly he was much more.

"But as it turns out, all that bullshit might be true. The aliens have been here before, and it's all very obvious once you see the patterns. Aliens and humans, recorded in trails of evidence. In a loop through time, over and over again."

"This is fascinating," said Heather.

Heather's dry voice seemed to snap Cameron out of his reverie. He scratched at his chair's fabric.

"The problem is I don't know enough to see patterns about The Nine — or about a lot of it, really. My dad took me all over the world chasing flying saucers, but I was just a kid. All I have are vague memories, some surface knowledge, and a lot of what ended up being ill-informed resentment. I can't form a pattern without knowing a lot more, and I can't form a pattern with only one data point for reference — with only Meyer."

"Okay," said Piper, knowing there was more.

Cameron nodded and looked toward the office. "I'd like your permission to copy those files and take them with me to Moab, where it might actually mean something."

"So you're all going to leave us." Lila's eyes flicked from Cameron to Christopher and the others. "Just like that."

"Fine," said Raj. Lila glared at him.

"Actually," Cameron said, "I can move faster if I go to Moab alone. I've traveled a lot, including into some crazy little backwaters around the world, and am damned good at disappearing when I need to. Keeping a low profile. So —" he looked at Raj, "—this depends on you, but if you'd like — if you're comfortable and want to do it this way — I was thinking the guys could stay here with you."

Heather's exhale was audible. It was disturbing to think how much they'd come to emotionally rely on their houseguests in the past week. These men had been frightening when they'd come in pretending for Morgan's benefit, and they'd been frightening right up through his death. But since that time — since they'd become the people they were instead of the characters they'd been playing — they'd become friends. Terrence had already fixed a few things around the place that Piper had given up on, including the security on the bunker's door and the induction oven. As predictable as it was, Vincent's formidable bulk turned out to be much-needed muscle — for lifting, yes, but also for peace of mind should someone break in. Dan turned out to be a fine storyteller, having traveled far and wide with Cameron. And Christopher, just twenty-one years old, had practically become the kids' best buddy. He chummed around with Trevor and joked with Lila. They were part of the family now, for better or worse. Only Raj didn't seem to like the newcomers, but lately Piper had begun to feel as Heather did about Raj: he could live with what they'd decided to give him or hit the road.

"So you like that idea," said Cameron, looking at Heather.

"I like it," she said, relief permeating her tone.

"Then I'll head out tomorrow. Just before first light. That way, I can sneak out without the people up top seeing me."

"It's a long walk to Utah," Lila said.

"I can find a vehicle of some sort somewhere along the way. I'll just need to be careful. The military controls the main roads. The back roads?" Cameron shrugged. "Well, everyone wants to be a kingpin and lay claim to their own piece of land these days. I don't know how long it will take, but I'll have a radio, and Terrence will show you how to use yours. Even the open channels are intermittent, but that way we'll be able to stay in touch at least some of the time. I can't share what I might learn on air, you understand — but if I learn anything about your father, I'll do my best to come back and tell you in person."

"I want to go with you," Trevor blurted.

Heather glared at her son. Trevor's suggestion was the height of stupidity. They were all safest in the bunker with their protectors. They'd nearly died trying to reach Vail. Heather wouldn't let Trevor or Lila set a toe outside until the world ended or the ships left. And on that point, at least, Heather and Piper were in agreement.

"No, you *won't* go with him," Piper said.

Trevor's head hung. He knew that had been coming.

Piper looked around the group, then back at Cameron. "But I will."

Chapter Sixteen

It was 1 a.m.

A strange afternoon acquiesced to an even stranger evening. Trevor was awake, lying on a cot in his mother's room, hands under his head, elbows out. It was strange not being in his normal room, but Cameron's announcement — coinciding with the realization that Vincent, Christopher, Terrence, and Dan would be staying a while — had prompted a shuffling of roles. Cameron and his crew had been bunking in the middle of the main room, some on the floor and some on cots. That had felt fine for a while, and they assured the bunker's original inhabitants that they didn't mind at all.

But now that it seemed they were at least semipermanent, Trevor's mother had launched into an uncharacteristic nesting frenzy, eager to make their underground house a proper home. She'd seemed so relieved to learn the others were staying (she'd muttered about it often enough during the past days, lamenting the idea of being "alone and vulnerable again" weighing heavy) that she was going out of her way to make them welcome. It was very un-

Heather Hawthorne. She didn't snip; she didn't crack wise; she didn't even make fun of Raj as he rolled his eyes over the affair. She made beds like a proper matron, washing sheets as Trevor had never really seen her do, pointing here and there assigning quarters.

In the end, Cameron's pack had been stocked and set near the spiral staircase. Piper's (regrettably, to Trevor's mind) was beside it. Cameron had fought her on the issue, but Piper had won. She knew Meyer Dempsey far better than those files knew him, and was hence a valuable asset for the people at the Moab facility. Trevor's heart broke a little — okay, a *lot* — at the thought of her leaving, but Piper was right, and Cameron couldn't argue. It was what it was, and it's not like he could profess his love to keep her from going.

The others had found themselves in new rooms. Trevor and Lila were with their mother as if they were five years old. Everything was settled. The only rearrangement left to make would be for Piper's soon-to-be-vacant master bedroom. She was where she'd been for one more night. Tomorrow, the room would be taken by Vincent and Terrence, who'd split Piper's mattress and box springs with each sleeping on one of them because, as Vincent said, "I'm not sharing sheets with this fag" before Terrence punched him.

For now, things were as they'd been in the next room: the last modicum of normality left in their abnormal situation. Trevor was glad the others would be staying — especially Christopher, who felt like the cool older brother he'd always wanted — but the thought of Piper leaving was — as things always were for him with Piper — strangely entangled. He felt something deep and longing, along with something more primal. Between the time his dad had left and the others' arrival, Piper had been the family's leader.

She'd kept things running. In a way, she'd kept them safe. She'd made the decisions his mother wouldn't. Her departure left him unbalanced, without a rudder.

He sat up on the cot, setting his feet on the carpeted floor. Sleep wasn't coming. He wondered if anyone else was awake or if he was alone. He had limited options. He couldn't turn on the TV, and he shouldn't go into the living room because Raj was on the couch. Vincent and Terrence, without a room for one more night, were on the floor.

Maybe he could read. His Vellum was in the main room, but if that was all he went out there for, he could be quiet.

Trevor stood then walked into the bathroom. The room was long and wide — larger, probably, than your normal bunker bathroom, which was probably a coffee can that required emptying outside. But the size was perhaps justifiable because it was shared by two bedrooms.

Trevor didn't turn on the lights — that was the surest way to wake the others. But the bathroom was lit by small, glowing azure night lights. Necessities of underground living, where there was no star or moonlight. And, of course, for safety. These lights, dim as they were, would stay lit if the power went out. Even if the other emergency lights failed, they'd at least keep everyone from stumbling blind.

Rather than going right to the toilet, he bent over the counter, in front of the sink, and peered into the mirror's dark depths. As a kid, he'd heard the sleepover legend of Bloody Mary, and how if you said her name three times into a dark mirror she'd appear behind you. For years, he'd avoided mirrors in rooms filled with black. But now it felt safe, thanks to the world's more immediate horrors.

Trevor watched his pupils.

Lila had come to him earlier. She'd seemed embarrassed and hadn't agreed to tell him anything — even though *she* had come to *him* — until he'd promised not to laugh. Trevor agreed too readily. His big sister had been his best friend for a long time and (though he'd never admit it) a kind of role model. The recent awkwardness between them and the distance it came with (Trevor's fault; he was the one who was into his stepmother) had bothered him, and he welcomed a chance to share secrets again. But then she'd asked him a strange thing.

Trevor … do you ever … you know … hear things?

I hear a lot of things.

Like … in your head.

He'd looked at her funny, and she'd backpedaled immediately.

Maybe things that just seem *to be in your head. Maybe moving outside. Or … talking outside.*

You're hearing talking outside? Through the ground?

Talking or singing. Never mind. It's nothing.

Wait … singing?

That had made her look hopeful. He'd merely been confused.

Like … you'll get a bit of a song stuck in your head. I've had something stuck in my head, like I've heard it before.

What?

"Plug the hole."

Trevor almost laughed. It sounded like porn. But Lila was barely telling him this as it was, so he just shrugged.

Never heard of it. But he had to give her something. Lila was out on a limb, and he needed to do the same or lose her trust. Her confidence. *I think about Dad a lot. I guess sometimes it's like I hear his voice.*

You hear Dad?

Trevor shrugged. The answer was no. He *thought* about him. But whatever made her feel better.

Do you ever … you know … dream about him?

Dunno. I guess.

She'd really paused hard there, as if trying to steel herself. Finally, she'd broken.

I keep dreaming of him in a big, metal room. Like … She hesitated again. *You know, like the inside of a ship. And sometimes …* Lila's eyes were wide, almost frightened. *Sometimes, it's like I'm actually awake, and I'll look in a mirror and see the same room behind myself, just for a second, with him standing behind me.*

Hmm.

Have you ever had that dream?

Trevor shrugged again.

I'm not crazy, if that's what you're thinking, she'd said, watching his eyes. *It's just a dream.*

Weird.

She'd watched him for another long while. Then, abruptly, she'd said, *Never mind* then went straight to bed. When he'd come in an hour later, she'd been sleeping, possibly deep in haunting dreams of their father.

Looking into the mirror, Trevor saw nothing. No metal room. No Dad. No Bloody Mary. Just the same bunker he'd lived in for a season and counting. The bunker, he sometimes thought, where he'd die.

There was a sound from the other end of the bathroom. A sliver of light appeared, lancing the darkness in a long, vertical slice. The sound had been a switch clicking on, lighting the other room adjoining the bathroom: *Piper's.*

Trevor crept forward. The door was barely ajar. Holding his breath, he put his eye to the slit.

He saw Piper. She hadn't been asleep after all. She must have gone into the living room while he'd been staring at the ceiling, also unable to sleep. But it was 1 a.m., and she was setting out on a long and dangerous trip in the morning. She had to get some rest.

Through the crack, he watched her walk back to the bedroom door and push it closed. That was strange. They all slept with their doors open. It just felt safer, under the circumstances, to not close themselves off.

Trevor's heart hammered hard enough to hear. She'd closed the door because she was going to change for bed.

He should go. This was well past wrong. Trevor had crossed "wrong" almost a year ago, when he'd seen the liquid beauty of Piper's eyes and the way light summer dresses clung to her body, and the strap of a messenger bag pressed her shirt against her chest, enhancing the natural swells.

If Trevor stayed where he was, he'd see them for real. Bare. Without a shirt or a bra between his eyes and her skin.

Casually, as if unaware of her display, Piper reached down, grabbed the bottom of her shirt, and pulled it over her head. There was no ceremony or strip show splendor. A practical motion that said *No big deal* — and *No big deal*, consequently, for what came next.

There was a creaking from behind him, in the other bedroom. Trevor glanced back, saw that the door was, of course, still closed. He'd come in here to pee. You didn't leave the door open when you peed.

He returned his eye to the crack.

In the brightly lit room, Piper unzipped and stepped out of her jeans. Her legs were long and lean. Bleached of their usual color by confinement, yes, but her complexion was pale anyway, and she seemed to have used the tanning bed like the rest of them.

Trevor's heart beat harder.

He swallowed.

He held his breath, afraid that exhalation would betray him.

Her panties stayed on. She stepped into a pair of loose shorts then bent her arms behind her back to unfasten her bra.

He should go.

Of *course* he should go.

And of course he wouldn't.

Piper pulled the garment away, and Trevor nearly fell into the doorframe. It was one thing to fantasize but another thing to see her breasts for real. There were no tan lines. She took her Vitamin D topless.

Somehow that was too much.

Piper glanced at herself in the mirror for a moment, seeming to assess her figure (*Perfect*, Trevor wanted to tell her), then pulled on a T-shirt. She dug her hands behind her neck and fluffed her hair out from under the collar, then applied something to her lips (lipstick? No, Chapstick) and slipped beneath the sheets. She reached for the end table and clicked off the lamp.

Trevor was alone in the dark again, his incestuous sin committed.

Despite his shame, a few extra minutes in the bathroom were required.

He left the bathroom, sure that at any moment Lila and his mother would wake and see what he'd done, clear on his face like a brand. But they didn't stir.

He wouldn't be able to sleep, so without pausing at the cot, he crossed to the door.

He'd find his Vellum in the front room then come back and read by its internal light. In time, he'd have read enough to forget. But soon enough he'd remember what he'd seen of Piper — before he willingly recalled the memory — and would feel that conflict again.

He found the light on in the kitchen. Vincent, Terrence, and Raj were sleeping where he'd expected them, but Christopher was at the kitchen table, reading a paper book by the overhead light.

He looked up. "Can't sleep, bro?"

"No."

"Then have a seat, my friend, and let's have ourselves a midnight jam."

Chapter Seventeen

THEY SET out just before first light, as planned.

Piper was more nervous than she'd expected. She'd been living in a vaguely apocalyptic world for over three months now (a calm apocalypse; as far as she could tell, if humanity had been able to ignore the ships and waning abductions, life could have gone on the same as ever), but she'd spent it mostly in a bunker.

New York felt a lifetime ago, and the Chicago freeway melee years distant. Even their fight to take over Meyer's Axis Mundi seemed to be someone else's memory. The bunker was Piper's reality. Safe. Comfortable. They couldn't go outside, but so what? Ignore the missing father figure, and it's another mixed family living out the American dream underground.

The thought of opening the door and leaving willingly chilled her blood. She almost called the whole thing off. Piper had barely slept and rose hours early, finding Cameron eating his predawn breakfast. She'd joined him with a hushed good morning, and they'd eaten in silence. She'd had to bite her lip several times to trap her cowardly change of mind. It would be so easy. But if she let Cameron go off alone, he might never return. That thought barred the words from her lips. If she could make at least half of the trip (the outbound half), she'd learn what the others knew about Meyer. If one or both of them were killed on the return trip, at least she'd die knowing what there was to know.

Cameron stole glances at her through the meal. He, too, seemed to be holding something back. Perhaps he was going to suggest she stay where it was safe to await his return. Thank God, he didn't. Piper might have stayed.

She *had* to go, for everyone's sake. Cameron knew that. His protests were gallantry. He was a thoughtful, perhaps overly polite man — opposite Meyer in many of his failings but very like her husband when it came to his strengths. Both wanted to protect them and would do as they promised, or die trying. But Cameron also wanted to do the right thing. To apologize. To ask for permission. And to keep ladies from heading out into the wild, wild West.

But he knew the truth. Meyer's tax receipts and email and memos to employees wouldn't paint a complete picture. So much of what made Meyer unique was holistic, not recorded in any document. Piper knew Meyer could be sweet, though he never let the world see that side. You'd think, seeing Meyer on so many magazines covers through the years, that he enjoyed publicity. And he did when it advanced his business. But Meyer himself was (*is*, Piper corrected herself) a private, almost shy person. When his ambition and reserve butted heads, ambition always won. Without her there to guide the Moab facility's investigation, the people there might never find their answer. And if Cameron was to be believed, the world might need it.

There was another reason Piper held her tongue. She

was a vital, irreplaceable "Meyer data" archive, yes — but she was also alone. Lila had Raj, Trevor had Lila, Heather had Lila and Trevor. Piper was a mother in name, but at the end of the world, children clung more firmly to blood. Lila's connection to Heather had deepened since she'd announced her pregnancy, and that was something Piper (try as she might) couldn't relate to. And Trevor? She'd hoped confinement would heal whatever had broken between them, but it had only seemed to make things worse. He looked at her in the strangest ways and avoided her even more fervently than during the cross-country trip. The looks could have meant anything, but to Piper, they seemed to say, *You aren't needed anymore.*

It broke her heart.

And now that Cameron's men were here, she *really* wasn't needed. She'd kept the bunker running, but now Terrence had it handled. She'd done the dirty chores, but the men with their disciplined military backgrounds were happy to help. The men pulled their weight so well, in fact, that they pulled the slack left by the others. There was now officially more help than chores required. She was just another body. A loose end without a purpose and without the man she loved, taking up space.

And there was more.

She'd thought a lot about the life she'd ended. Garth had been a threat, no question. She had to stop him, no doubt. But couldn't she have hit him with something? Couldn't she have shot him in his arm or leg? But Meyer's admonition had been loud in her ears: *Don't hesitate.* She hadn't, and it had all worked out fine. But Meyer hadn't warned her about the nightmares. About the second-guessing and the questions. And it's not like anyone wanted to talk to her about it. To them, Garth had been another of the bad guys — same as the bad guys Meyer himself had dispatched. Did anyone even really remember that Piper had pulled the trigger last? Or had they grouped the incident into a collection in their minds, attributed to the man of the house?

She was a murderer. For better or worse, justified or not, Piper was a killer. If she had to stay in the bunker as a useless murderer (and she'd thought this in a logical, calculating way, not in despair), she might just kill herself.

Better to go with Cameron, who — due to his play-acting with Morgan and the journey he'd made — was maybe a murderer too. Piper lifted right out.

After breakfast, before climbing the stairs, Cameron came up behind her with a long-sleeved T-shirt, dirty ripped jeans, and a baseball cap.

"Wear this."

Piper looked at the clothing then up at Cameron.

"They're mine. I don't mean this as that male thing where I'm implying you'll fit into man clothes, and I'll ask you to please not comment on the fact that I can provide clothes to a lady."

Piper looked at Cameron. He had a young face with longish hair parted in the middle. She'd never thought of him as small because his personality was so bold and confident, but he was barely bigger than she was, and slight of bones. He really would be able to vanish. Like a wily rodent hiding in debris rather than a clunky fat cat, like Vincent.

"Please." He held the clothes out to Piper.

"Why?"

"You need to look like a boy."

"I need to—" But she stopped, understanding.

"We both look young. With any luck, we can come off like a couple of gutter punks." He pointed to his filthy face. She'd assumed that packing made him dirty — scavenging in the burned generator room, perhaps — but his grime was apparently intentional. "But it won't work unless you tie up your hair and wear something loose and unflattering."

"'Unflattering,'" she repeated.

He shrugged. "You're too pretty. Do you think you can be uglier?"

The question was disarming, sarcastic, just the tension breaker she needed. "I'll try. But … you know." And she batted her long lashes.

"Do you have sunglasses?"

"I hear Terrence has a pair or two."

"Yes, but they all look like he's about to accept his Grammy."

"I have a pair that have been rolling around in my purse without a case. They're so scratched, they're useless."

"Perfect."

Piper carried the clothes into her bedroom to change. On the way, Trevor — up early like the rest of them, to say goodbye — followed her with his eyes. Like he hated her and was glad she was leaving.

Piper emerged, and Cameron declared her transformed. She'd pinned her hair back, managing to squeeze the cap atop it in a way that didn't look odd, though she did have to pin the hat in place, too. She'd put on her tightest sports bra then donned the shirt. The clothing was loose with a masculine cut that hid her gender. She had the sunglasses to bury her big, blue eyes and a pair of Meyer's reading glasses for use when the sun wasn't shining. When they were outside, she could roll in the dirt. And Cameron promised to give her a few "man tips," because she still had a feminine gait.

But still, he smiled through his assessment, and for the

first time in a long while Piper felt purpose. Uglying herself had been like a makeover in reverse, and it pleased Cameron plenty. Soon she might be able to help the cause against the aliens … if it turned out there was a reason to oppose their silent, still-mostly quiet presence around the planet.

And as thin as the hope felt, Piper might see her Meyer again.

They said their farewells, keeping them brief and choosing "see you soon" over "goodbye." Cameron said it was about 250 miles to Moab. He joked that once they found a Corvette as their chariot, they could be there in three hours.

After the door had closed behind them and they'd made it to the trees without attracting undue notice, Piper told Cameron that she needed to pee. He made a joke about learning to pee like a man then gave her privacy. He told Piper to keep the gun in her hand, safety off.

Out of sight, she leaned against a tree and let herself cry.

Just for a few minutes.

Because Piper was a man now, and real men don't cry.

Chapter Eighteen

THEY RAN into the roadblock an hour after sunset, and the dead cop sixty seconds later.

The roadblock had the look of something official — orange-and-white crowd-control barriers alongside a few big orange-and-white rain barrels. Stacked sandbags created a semipermanent blockage. There was a pair of cop cars behind them, parked opposite so the drivers' windows would line up. But there were no cops in the cars. The officers, it turned out, were all in the ditch.

Cameron saw the first body a few seconds before Piper but didn't try to hide it. He held hands up to stop her then put a finger in front of his lips and pointed. It was a disturbing/kind gesture that covered both *disturbing* and *kind* at once, like how a cat will bring its owners mouse organs as a gift. He was showing her bodies, yes — but he hadn't insulted Piper by implying she couldn't handle it. They were out in the real world now. No need to play coy.

Despite that, her first instinct was to gape. Not to scream, but gape. She held her lips shut. She'd seen this before. She'd even *done* this before, right down to dealing death.

Cameron patted the air, squatting in the ditch. Piper mimicked him, lowering her body and keeping her eyes on his. He pointed toward the barricade, now above their line of sight.

Piper shrugged, not understanding.

"There's someone behind the car," he whispered.

"I didn't see anyone," she whispered back.

"Just one person. Go ahead and look. Do it slowly."

She looked at him for confirmation. Did he really want her to raise her head and look? Did he think she might not trust him? Meyer would never say such a thing if it were him with her instead of Cameron. Meyer loved and trusted Piper and wanted her to feel empowered, but in times of crisis he was in charge, and she — along with anyone else who came for the ride — needed to do as they were told, no questions asked.

After a moment, she rose slightly, very aware of her hat, thinking it might give her away before her eyes were high enough to see what was coming. Still, she saw nothing.

"Look at the wheels," Cameron whispered.

Piper did. Under the car's body, visible past exhaust pipes and struts and springs, she saw someone's lower half, sitting on the road, back to the car. She squatted again.

"Did you see him?"

"How do you know it's a man?" Piper asked.

"Okay, I don't. Did you see *her?*"

In spite of the situation, Piper smiled. "I saw her."

"I don't think it's really a woman," Cameron said.

"You don't, huh?"

"No. I know this is an unfair and sexist generalization, but women don't kill cops nearly as often as men do." He pointed at the first corpse. There were another two farther down. How had she missed them?

"How do you know that person killed them?"

"There's blood all over his pants."

Piper would have to take Cameron's word for it. She hadn't noticed. How had he? They'd barely seen a flash, and the car was a good fifty feet away. His eyes were sharp, and he had, apparently, been paying greater attention.

Piper made to stand again, wanting to see what else she'd missed, lollygagging along while he'd been watching for snakes in the grass. "Are there …" She paused, curiosity pressing. "Are there more?"

"I don't know. I didn't see any. And maybe I'm wrong on my read. Maybe that person didn't kill these guys. Maybe they were already dead when he showed up. But I'd bet he dragged them away, at least. And now he's camping up there. Hanging out." He made his voice lower than it already was. "Best to assume guilty until proved innocent."

Piper touched her gun, pre-congratulating herself on having what it took to survive in this cruel new world. Cameron shook his head and pointed back the way they'd come.

Staying low, they headed past the roadblock, staying in the trees until Piper could see the full side of the person who either killed at least three policemen or feng shui'd their arrangement. She turned every few seconds, wondering when they might make their move.

"What do you keep looking at?"

"Just seeing if our cop killer is far enough back yet."

"Far enough back for what?"

"To sneak up on him."

"Why would we sneak up on him?" Cameron asked.

Piper realized they weren't walking around the roadblock to get a better angle. They just needed to *get around the roadblock.*

Cameron gave her a smile that was just short of patronizing. Pitying maybe. Piper didn't like it. Not because of anything Cameron was doing, but because it made her feel like a liability. He'd said he wanted to travel alone because he could move quickly and stay out of sight. That was already becoming easy to believe. It would be a lot harder if he was dragging a klutz behind him.

"What's the first rule of survival?" Cameron said.

"'Trust no one'? 'Don't do your business too near where you eat'?"

Cameron shook his head. "'Survive.' That's it. That's all you need to keep in mind. Don't think about specific survival tactics. Always see if you can step back and veer right to the big questions: 'How do I survive this situation?' 'How do I get to where I need to be without getting harmed?' 'How do I find enough food?'" He pointed at the roadblock. "'How do I get past something that might be dangerous?' Did you assume we'd fight?"

Piper nodded sheepishly. It was stupid. The road was wide open, and the culvert and woods were seemingly empty. The idea that she'd seen that single person as someone they'd need to "go through" was idiotic, but she'd thought it, all right. She'd been so focused on doing what was necessary (fighting as needed) that she'd missed the obvious way out (simply going around). That kind of thinking would get them killed.

"We need to get from here to Moab. Any way works." Cameron looked around: up at the sky, at the open mountain road to the woods' side, and at the mountains all around them. "It's hard to believe there's anything threatening out here. But Vincent, Terrence, Dan, and I ran into some sticky situations on our way to your place. Nobody seems to know what to do. It's worse because nobody knows what's *been done*."

He tapped the small radio fixed to his belt. "Even if we believe everything we hear on the open frequencies, which we shouldn't, we have to assume it's being monitored and that people might be talking in code or doublespeak. Best treat it all as rumor. The people who have returned after being abducted?" He looked a bit uncomfortable, as if just remembering why Piper was here. "They're … strange, some of them. They come back spouting warnings. Really cuckoo stuff, about the ships being on some sort of countdown to the end of the world. Others are vacant, like they've lost something. There are a few, I guess, who are coherent, and I've heard one or two spouting off on what passes for drive time radio shows these days."

He laughed. Apparently, it was hardly an apt comparison.

"Those people describe almost a kind of summit with the aliens, saying they're here to urge us forward as a species. They go gray on specifics, and some people think they're hiding a plan that they think most people won't be okay with, but that they're somehow 'high minded' enough to understand. But everyone seems to know about a few 'incidents,' say, where fringe nut groups have shot at the shuttles or motherships or tried to approach them in helicopters or small planes. The ships don't refuse. They just incinerate. And sometimes, they'll decimate the land below. Then the confusion brings out all the crazies — *maybe* crazies; there's no way to tell if their reports are accurate or the same old bullshit — and you'll hear about classic stuff: bright lights zooming around in people's houses like ghosts or probes; beams of light in the night; all sorts of close encounters; cattle mutilations and things like that."

Piper felt cold. It was bright out, and the air was barely

chill, but Cameron's story made her feel like a little girl cowering in bed, waiting for the boogeyman to come out of the closet.

"People are scared," Cameron said. "Maybe they're scared of real things, like someone being taken from their house or fearing being taken themselves — unlike those nuts around your place, who *want* to be taken and think shuttles will return just because they've gone there a few times before."

Piper almost interrupted him. *A few times before?* She'd thought there had just been the one shuttle, come to take Meyer. The idea that there had been other alien visitations during their time underground was unsettling, as if the very ground might not hold her.

"And maybe," Cameron continued, "the things they're scared of aren't real at all. But it doesn't matter. Fear is fear, and it's contagious. No matter how peaceful things may seem out here sometimes, no one's our friend. It would probably be better for everyone if the alien ships went ahead and attacked us if they're going to, rather than waiting and hovering first. Everyone's afraid, but nobody knows what they're afraid *of*. Which means they're scared of everything, just to be safe. Afraid of *us*, for instance. Like bees. My dad used to say, when I was terrified of being stung, that the bee was more scared of me than I was of it. But see, that didn't mean it wouldn't sting me, even if it didn't want to. *Because* it was afraid."

Cameron nodded toward the man leaning against the police car, still visible behind them. "It's always better to run than to confront. It's always better to avoid people than engage them."

"What if someone we see might be able to help us?"

"*Always* better to avoid people than engage them. The more we're alone, the safer we are. And there's no such thing as cowardice or fighting dirty. If we get into a bad situation, we run. We turn our yellow tails and haul ass, courage be damned. You need to kick someone in the balls, you do it. Eye jabbing, hair pulling, backstabbing? All fine. The goal is only to *survive*, nothing fancier than that. I learned that all the hard way growing up."

It was a curious statement. She'd learned nothing substantive about Cameron's past in the previous week other than that his father had hauled him around the planet on an alien scavenger hunt. Had he lived on the street during one of their stops? Had he been in a gang back home? Piper knew he was worldly and that he'd seen much more of the globe than he had at the foot of his father. Nothing more, though she was curious.

"How did you — ?" she began.

That's when the screaming started.

Chapter Nineteen

LILA GRIPPED HER ABDOMEN, clenched her teeth, and held her breath for a long, frightening moment. Then the pain in her gut finally subsided for long enough to exhale. She did, then sat where she'd plopped: on the toilet, its lid closed. She didn't have any business in here now, but with the shared bedrooms, the can was literally the only private place.

Her pain had mostly receded, but still she waited through cycles of breath, her hands still almost superstitiously over her stomach. She lifted her shirt a few inches and looked down at her belly, as if her unborn fetus might tell her all was well. Everything down there was still pretty flat. She'd been told she had a good body, and for now it still was.

Lila stood, moving slowly as if she might re-upset whatever had just gone (temporarily) wrong. But there was nothing, same as before. Except for what felt like an intense gas pain. Maybe it *had* been a gas pain. It wasn't like she'd done this pregnancy thing before. And it wasn't like she'd thought to download a copy of *What to Expect When You're*

Expecting. Her mother would have, had Lila confessed before the Internet fizzled. Or rather, *Piper* would have. Her mother probably would have downloaded *101 Jokes About Pregnant Women's Vaginas* or something.

Lila crossed to the sink and splashed water on her face.

She wished Piper hadn't left.

Lila was seventeen, and Piper was twenty-nine. The age difference was enough to make them a perfect hybrid of mother/daughter and sister/sister. Piper hadn't ever been pregnant, but she'd lived enough life to have adult perspective (and the perspective of a *really cool* adult, too; Piper's clothing line had been a hit before Dad announced their engagement, and Lila had been over the moon to inherit such a hip stepmom), yet not so much life that she'd forgotten what it was like to be a kid. She'd helped Lila and Trevor with schoolwork when they'd asked, but always with rolled eyes as if to say, *Yeah, school sucks.*

If the world hadn't gone wacky, Lila had always imagined Piper would have been the first person she'd tell about the baby. She'd have told Piper before Raj if it wouldn't have been so wrong to do so. Piper would have seen the joy and downplayed the rough times ahead because that's how Piper was. How Piper *is*, Lila corrected.

Maybe she should tell her mother about the pains she'd been having.

The idea felt awful. Her mother loved her, but Heather Hawthorne was also (and there was no easy way to put this) an asshole. If Mom found the pains troublesome, she'd fret and demand that everyone lay down their lives to head out and summon a doctor or at least some books that Meyer hadn't thought to stock. Or if, on the other hand, Mom found the pains to be nothing, Lila would have to endure jokes for weeks.

Ordinarily, Lila and Trevor only spent a few weeks a

year with their mother. Right around the time in each visit when Heather's quirkiness soured toward obnoxious, it was time to hop on a plane. But since they'd been in the bunker, everyone was approaching an overdose. It was like getting an X-ray. One or two were fine, but nobody set up an X-ray machine in the corner of their living room and left it on.

Lila, is that sausage giving you gas?

And then she'd point to Raj's crotch.

Lila, you look uncomfortable. Is your stomach still bothering you? Did you swallow something spicy and ethnic that disagreed with you?

And then she'd point to Raj's crotch.

And Raj — in her mental theater now but in reality as well — just kept taking the abuse. Only now was it dawning on Lila how strange that was. Raj wasn't supposed to come on this cross-country errand, but he'd been in the right place at the right time, and Lila had insisted they not leave him behind. Since then, a normal family would have accepted him. It had been over a month since she'd told her mothers about the baby, and the shock had passed fairly quickly. It was hard to stay mad at a girl for getting knocked up when only a concrete wall separated you from crazies and an armada of alien ships. But as easily as her family had accepted the baby, it still hadn't accepted Raj.

That made Lila feel bad. She suddenly wanted to do something nice for Raj. She'd apologized for the incident in the kitchen, taking care to *not* apologize for her line-in-the-sand insistence that he stop bitching and accept their collective decisions. After that, they'd returned to quasi-normal, and in the few moments they could manage — in the middle of the night, quietly and quickly in the bathroom — they'd remained occasionally intimate. But something had changed. Not just between her and Raj, but in the bunker as a whole.

The arrival of the new group and the departure of Cameron and Piper had, she supposed, made everyone realize there was still an accessible outside world. For the past months, they'd grown used to the idea that the rest of their planet was a poisoned, unreachable place. But now, staying felt like a decision. And after all this time underground, Lila wanted to decide something different.

She felt pent up, claustrophobic, restless. She'd watched enough old shows on the juke. She'd even watched her father's shows — even stored episodes of the web series he liked so much, about the super-Internet of the future. She'd played cards, read books (both paper and on Vellum), done puzzles, run on the treadmill, lain in the UV bed for a few minutes even though she suspected that might be a terrible idea for a pregnant girl, stacked cans in the pantry, arranged cups from smallest to largest, and counted the kitchen floor tiles. In a way, the addition of new bunker mates made things palatable (Christopher felt like any of her and Trevor's friends despite the murder), but in another way it made things harder to know they *could* go outside … but shouldn't.

Maybe Cameron really would be able to work out her father's riddle. Maybe, together with Piper, they could bring Daddy home. She was a bit nervous about how he might be changed after his experience but desperately longed for him back either way. She didn't want to hope. But it was something to consider — a possible light at the end of the tunnel, even if distant and probably unlikely.

And that was good because if Lila didn't focus on something, she might go crazy.

Really, she was headed there already.

It wasn't fair. She had these issues with the baby to contend with

(you could tell your mother)

but on top of all of that,

(you should, because something's wrong, not with me but with the air, this place, what's coming)

confinement was giving her crazy dreams. Snippets of something (dialogue from a movie? Lyrics of a song? Something someone had once told her?) kept getting lodged in Lila's head, and she couldn't place it. If they'd still had the web, she'd have Googled *plug the hole* and a few other choice phrases,

(network nodes brains)

but she didn't. So she had to be content not knowing where she'd heard those things before, why she kept hearing them now, or if she'd maybe never heard them at all and was just losing her fucking mind.

A cavern, deep in the ground, with a platform broken away along the walls every ten feet down, deeper than anyone had ever been. Rising water. A hidden place, a secret left behind.

It all mingled with something Lila knew she'd seen somewhere before — an image from a paper book in a used bookstore, showing cave explorers kneeling around a rather ordinary patch of wet rock, looking at the camera with expressions that were more weary than jubilant. The photo, apparently, showed the "bottom of the world" — the deepest navigable cave in existence. The idea had intrigued her, and she'd thumbed through the pages, skimming the story. Apparently, the journey to reach the world's bottom had been incredibly dangerous and terrifying. So why had the explorers risked their lives to reach it? For the same reason mountain climbers climbed in the opposite direction: because it's there.

And that's sort of where they were, or what it felt like,

sitting on the bottom of the world. Maybe they were safe from the ships (although they'd managed to get Dad anyway), but this place was its own kind of death. Its own sort of torture. First, she'd clearly seen Morgan Matthews in her mind and anticipated his arrival. Then, in a flash before it had happened for real, she'd imagined Christopher putting a bullet in Morgan's head. Now she kept thinking about Piper and Cameron, picturing them not alone, but with three new companions. Why was she so sure that those things had happened, whatever they were? None of it was real. They'd managed a brief chat with Cameron on the radio just an hour ago, and he'd said nothing of others or strange barriers. The signal came and went, leaving them with no idea when they might chat again.

Morgan, outside, trying to enter.

Endless rows of stones.

Piper and Cameron, plus three.

The bottom of the world — both recollection in pictures and something else, something she'd never seen. The book's descriptions of spelunking had made Lila feel boxed in just reading them, but the dream/thought/vision of the wet hole with its broken platforms every ten feet was worse. It didn't feel like a deep pit, whatever it was. It felt like a descent into Hell, with something unthinkable hidden at the bottom, stored since

(the last time)

forever.

Lila looked up into the mirror. She was okay. For now anyway. If the pains came back, she'd tell her mother. If they didn't, then no big deal. And while she was at it, maybe she could ask Mom about —

Lila's hands flew to her abdomen. She couldn't breathe. Everything was tight, constricting, muscle tugging bone hard enough to snap it. She fell to one knee then the other. She saw her own shocked expression in the mirror for a second before she fell to the ground, rolling backward, racking her head against the tile floor. Her eyes squeezed shut. This pain was so much worse. So much *harder*. So much —

It stopped as quickly as it had started.

It's all beginning.

Hearing the voice — more feeling than actual words — Lila looked down. Her clenching hands had opened, no longer holding her midsection. Her palms were on her sides, fingers now standing straight out like a jazz hands parody of surrender.

But she'd noticed something. Something that chilled her, as obvious as it suddenly was.

In the pain's aftermath, it now seemed clear where those hints and whispers and visions and mental voices were coming from.

Not from her head.

From her stomach.

Chapter Twenty

THE SCREAMER WAS A WOMAN.

Piper chased the sound without thinking. Years of running in Central Park made it easy to cross the distance and leave Cameron in the dust.

Years of running in Central Park had also (and this occurred to Piper once she heard a new volley of screams and knew she was close) bred a specific reaction to screaming. The sound elicited alarm, yes, but sympathy was Piper's stronger response. She'd never witnessed a mugging or a rape in progress, but she'd heard enough warnings (and was human enough) to recognize one when she heard it.

There were two basic ways to answer something like that. You could call the police on your cell, sure, but how long would it take for the cops to arrive? People screamed to draw attention. To get help. And help, if it was worth anything, didn't stand idly by waiting for the men and women in blue.

Piper stopped when she saw them. There were six people in the clearing: three men, two women, and a small boy, maybe four years old. If there was any chance of inaction, it vanished the second she saw the kid. Free to run, he went nowhere. The kid sat at the struggling group's edge, canted down on one knee. He was crying, watching in horror as three assailants — two men and a woman — pummeled what had to be his parents with a series of strikes and punches.

"Let's go," Cameron said, arriving beside her.

She could hear his shallow breath and see him in the corner of her eye without turning from the melee. The attackers had guns, hanging uselessly from straps or, in the case of the rough-looking woman, tucked into waistbands. They were using their fists and what looked like a board to do their work, and the work itself was sadistic. If they wanted to rob people, why not point their guns and demand they hand over what they had? Although they must already have done it; there were two extra packs near the crying child. Why didn't they go?

"We have to help," Piper said.

"There are three of them."

She turned to look at Cameron, anger flaring. "I can count."

"The idea is to *avoid* conflict."

Piper gave him a hard look then reached for her gun. Staring him straight in the eye, she raised it overhead. And fired.

Activity in the clearing froze as if someone pressed pause. Piper lowered her gun and leveled it at the others.

"Jesus, Piper," Cameron muttered. He had a rifle and a handgun, but it was the rifle he reluctantly raised, taking aim. Then, seeing that they were already hip deep and might as well power through, shouted to the others below. "*Get away from them!*"

Both men raised their hands, stepping back. But the

woman didn't hesitate. She reached for her own weapon and fired almost blindly. The shot struck the dirt a dozen feet below their position on a small rise. Her aim was to shock, and Piper, as brave as she'd felt a half second earlier, felt herself collapse. She was a crumpled heap in plain sight. Cameron had ducked behind a tree.

"Run!" he yelled at her. "Back the way we came!"

That got her moving. Piper came up far enough to raise her gun, aware that she was presenting a rather large and obvious target. The weapon's weight bothered her. She'd fired a gun twice in her life, once point blank. She had no idea how to hit her target.

But she fired anyway, knowing that Cameron's alternative was both more survival oriented and, to her, reprehensible. Sure, they could escape. But then she'd have to avoid mirrors for the rest of her life; facing herself would be impossible, knowing she'd left a family to die.

The shot went predictably wide. Piper had no idea where it landed, but her slug didn't hit any of the six people below. She'd have to be more careful and make sure she didn't hit any innocents.

Cameron racked off another two shots. He also hit nothing, but Piper suspected he wasn't trying. One of the men had circled around to where the kid was but hadn't — as she'd feared — snatched the boy to use as a hostage or shield. Instead, he'd taken the two backpacks and was already moving toward the others, away from Piper and Cameron. They had what they needed and were apparently content to call it a draw. All three assailants ran, one of the men turning to fire one last time, for cover.

Then it was over.

"Let's go." Cameron looked at Piper, annoyed.

But the woman was already running up the hill toward them, her face a mess of tears. The man seemed shocked.

He'd taken a worse beating and, from a distance, seemed bloody. They'd roughed him up. Maybe because they'd had intentions with the woman and hadn't wanted to damage the merchandise. Even in her jeans and filthy T-shirt she looked pretty.

"Thank you!" She fell at Piper's feet. Either they were hurt or exhausted. Or maybe she'd been overcome with fear and adrenaline. Looking down at the woman, watching her cry and paw her way back up, Piper felt something bruise inside. Her eyes traveled to the man below, gathering the wailing child into his arms, and that bruised spot broke open.

"Are you all right?" Piper asked.

She sniffed. "Thank you! Oh my God, if you hadn't been there, they'd have …" She looked back at the man then traded glances between Piper and Cameron and the rest of her family until all five of them were huddled together at the rise's top. The clearing below was littered with scraps and refuse, as if they'd been attacked mid-picnic.

"Thank you," said the man, more composed. His face was bloody indeed, but it wasn't as bad as it had looked from above. They must have hit him near the forehead — maybe with the board or branch or whatever it was — and lacerated the capillary-dense area that made wounds seem worse than they were. A little cleanup, and that part of him would be fine. But he was also heavily bruised, and his nose was askew enough that Piper wondered if he'd been born that way, or if it had just been broken.

"What happened?" Piper asked.

"They surprised us," said the man. "Like an ambush. Must've seen us coming, then hid around that little area and waited. They had guns, so we all just raised our hands and said they could take what they wanted."

"Did you have guns?" said Cameron.

The man shook his head. "I'm not a fan of guns." Then he laughed, despite his obvious pain. "At least, I wasn't. I became a convert after we learned about the ships. But I didn't own any, and the stores were all stripped straight away. We ran across …" He lowered his voice, as if to keep his next words from the boy, who he handed off to his mother. "We ran across some bodies. Pretty early. They had guns, so we took them. But later we ran into some other people and …" He shrugged, as if to say, *Easy come, easy go*.

"Have you just been out here walking?" Cameron asked. "Where are you trying to go?"

"We've been staying at my mother's. She has a ski lodge." He reset. "*Had* a ski lodge. We live in Denver." He swallowed, and the shambling, pained way his throat moved made Piper cringe. "Used to anyway. But Denver …" He inhaled as if steeling himself.

"We came from New York." Piper nodded. Of course Denver would have been a zoo, and anyone with a nearby ski lodge would want to get away.

The man nodded then looked at Cameron. "Did you drive?"

"Just me," said Piper. "Me and my family."

The man looked at Cameron, seeming to decide not to ask how they were traveling together if they hadn't started off that way. Cameron didn't answer or volunteer his place of origin. His body language was closed and stiff. Piper did most of the talking. Cameron, it seemed, wanted to keep moving.

"Anyway," the man said, "we came up here. It wasn't a bad trip. Problem was, everyone else in Denver had the same idea."

Piper looked at Cameron. She and Meyer hadn't

noticed many people headed into the mountains from Denver unless she counted the roadblock that had freed them of the car they, in turn, had stolen from the man bunkered in the dealership. Again: *easy come, easy go.*

The man shrugged again. "I was able to hold down the homestead for a while, but we were finally 'evicted' three days ago. We heard there's a community up this way."

"A 'community'?" said Piper.

"Almost like a commune. A wanderer — one of the few who didn't want to attack us and take the supplies we managed to get away with — told us he heard about it on the radio. And I know how that sounds, but—"

"There are still broadcasts on some frequencies."

Piper noticed the way Cameron actively hid the radio on his belt when he said it, and that he didn't volunteer the obvious: that the "commune" he and this wanderer had heard about was almost certainly her home.

The man seemed to realize something then wiped his hand on his pants. He stuck it out toward Cameron. "I'm Mike. Mike Nelson."

Cameron shook it. "Cameron."

The hand jabbed at Piper. She shook it. "Piper."

"This is my wife, Rachel." He smiled a kindergarten smile, as if they were meeting casually and he hadn't been robbed and beaten nearly to death. "And this is Charlie. Say hi, Charlie."

"Hi," the boy squeaked, hiding his face against his mother's side.

"Well," Cameron said, nodding. "Good luck, Mike."

Piper shot him a look.

Cameron pointed. "The place you're looking for is that way."

Piper grabbed his arm and whispered, "We can't just leave them."

Cameron looked at the family. Their faces had fallen. "They don't have any supplies."

"It's only a few hours. They'll make it."

"They don't have any guns."

"Excuse me?" said Mike.

They turned.

"I don't mean to impose, but I was kind of hoping we could stay with you. At least until we figure out where we're going."

Cameron pointed again. "Follow the setting sun."

"But I'm not exactly an outdoorsman," Mike protested. "I figured I could get us there, but we're kind of …" He looked helplessly at his wife.

Rachel came forward, Charlie hiding behind her legs. "They took everything we had. Food, water …"

"It's not far," Cameron said.

" … and if they come back …"

"I don't think they'll come back."

Piper's eyes stayed on the boy. She kept seeing the way they'd found him, on one knee as if knocked down or fallen, crying, branded with the image of his family's beating, probably minutes from enduring the sight of his father's murder and his mother's rape.

"We have to help them," Piper said.

"We can't spare the supplies."

"We'll find a way to get our own. There's a stream back there." Mike pointed. "And if we don't have far to go, we won't need food just yet."

"Then how are we supposed to help y—"

"Please. You have guns." Rachel looked toward where the bandits had fled, giving a shiver. "At least let us walk with you for a bit."

"We're going in the opposite direction."

"We'll go that way, then," Mike said. "Maybe those

people left my mom's place. Probably did, actually; I heard them say they were headed somewhere else, somewhere east. There will be stores left. Mom was a hoarder."

"I'm sorry," said Cameron.

"We won't slow you down," Mike said.

"They won't slow us down," Piper echoed, holding Cameron's sleeve.

"They will," he whispered. "A family with a kid? We'll be a huge target. What's the first rule of survival, Piper?"

"Please?" Rachel said.

"Please … Cameron," Mike said.

"*Pweese*," said Charlie, the kid.

Piper put her hand on Cameron's shoulder. "Just a day or two. Same course. We go where we were going anyway, and they follow or find another way."

Cameron took a long, slow inhale then exhaled. "Fine. They can follow us along Route 24, but we lose them when we start following 70 West. I want to see if we can get a car at some point, and we aren't getting one with a baby seat." He glanced back at the family then at Piper. "Agreed?"

Piper nodded.

"But I don't like this at all. *At all.*"

"Noted." Piper tried to bat her eyes at Cameron to smooth his edges, but her battered sunglasses muffled her charms.

"If they get us killed, it's on you."

But Piper didn't think that would happen.

Almost certainly not.

Chapter Twenty-One

"KID," said Vincent, still laughing and clapping Trevor on the back. "You've got a lot to learn about playing cards. He stood, and Trevor could've sworn he heard the chair breathe a sigh of relief. They'd been playing cards for three hours, and Trevor felt like he knew less than when he started.

"Sorry," Trevor said.

Christopher shook his head. "You fucker."

Trevor looked across the table. He liked the casual way the guys swore around him. Nobody would think a man Trevor's age didn't know those words, but it was different when others assumed he did and treated him like an equal instead of a kid. He'd been getting annoyed looks from his mother and sister for what felt like months, and those looks clearly painted him as a moody teenager with delusions of persecution. Well, the shoe was on the other foot now. No longer was he a lone man around a bunch of girls (Raj didn't count). Trevor finally had guys to treat him like one of their own.

He could accept Christopher's jab as genuine, or he

could be a man and say something pointlessly vulgar. Because that's how this crew worked. Insults were good. They bonded people.

Instead of demurring or apologizing again for losing his team the card game, Trevor said the wisest thing he could think of: "Fucked your mom."

Christopher threw a dish towel.

Trevor, smiling, gathered the cards.

Christopher said, "Hey," and Trevor looked up.

Christopher tossed his chin toward Raj, reading on the couch.

"He doesn't like me, I don't think."

Trevor shrugged. "He doesn't like any of you."

"And?"

"Whatever," said Trevor. "That's his problem."

Christopher looked from Raj to Lila sitting on the over-stuffed chair at the far side of the living room. Trevor followed his gaze. Lila looked tired. *Very* tired. Her eyes were dark circles. She'd been staying in the room later and later in the mornings. But judging by the movements he heard through the door in the mornings, he didn't think she was sleeping any more during the day than at night.

Lila was quieter, too. She'd stopped talking to Trevor almost entirely, and a small part of him felt positive it was because she knew he'd watched Piper changing her clothes and was disgusted with him. That seemed impossible, but no other explanation made sense. She'd vanished into the bedroom for several hours just this morning, this time with their mother. Trevor hadn't liked that. He'd made eye contact with Lila as she'd been pulling Mom aside, and he'd made eye contact with them both when they'd emerged from the bedroom much later. Nobody said anything, but Trevor knew accusation when he saw it. They were probably deciding what to do with him.

Was ogling your stepmother grounds for being kicked out of the bunker? Probably not, but Trevor's gut clenched at the thought that Lila might know and doubly at the notion that she'd spent the morning discussing his deviance with their mother. Was Mom working up the courage to confront him? She wasn't in the living room now. Was that even something Heather was capable of doing — talking to her son about inappropriate, incestuous boobs? What would that conversation be like? It would either be hard because she'd be disappointed and chiding … or it'd be even harder because she'd be inappropriate and flip about the whole thing. She might joke about whether or not he'd want to see *her* naked, his biological mother. Or she might draw comparisons and gross analogies suitable for her crass standup act. For instance: *Just because you didn't come out of a pussy doesn't mean it's okay to want to enter it now.*

But Christopher knew none of this. And honestly, maybe *Lila and Mom* didn't know about it either. In fact, they *probably* didn't. How could they know he'd peeped that night, with the door having been closed? How could they know that he thought about what he'd seen all the time, when he spent a bit too long in the bathroom and came out relaxed?

"I'm not sure I understand them as a couple," said Christopher.

Trevor shrugged.

"I mean, he's … I guess he's fine, when he'll talk to me. Seems like a nice enough guy. And smart. Maybe as smart as Terrence. If he'd stop being so …" Christopher trailed off. "Sorry."

"What?" Trevor asked.

"We're guests here."

"Well, so is Raj."

"But I mean, he was here before us."

"It's cool, Chris. You can say Raj is kind of an ass sometimes." Trevor smiled.

"I don't mean it like that. Your sister just seems … well, it's hard for me to see them together."

Trevor looked back. They really were an odd couple. Before the world had gone to shit, he'd wondered at things Lila said about Raj. She couched everything and played like nothing was a big deal, but she was Trevor's sister, and they'd once been close enough for Lila to shamefully admit to having made a buck or two pirating her own father's films in advance of their release. Trevor could read her and knew she was a bit gaga over Raj — or had been, at least, before they'd all been locked in the madhouse together. And Trevor, accordingly, had tried to imagine them married, with Raj as a brother-in-law. It was okay, he supposed. But there were way cooler brothers-in-law than Raj.

"It's hard," Trevor agreed.

Christopher chewed the inside of his cheek.

"Do you think he misses them?"

Trevor didn't understand. But when he followed Christopher's gaze, he saw Raj fiddling with his watch phone thing. He seemed to think that if he fiddled enough, he'd be able to call home. If home still existed.

"His family?" Trevor asked.

"Yeah."

"Dunno."

"You're lucky to have yours."

Trevor shrugged. He supposed so.

"I lost mine. I guess that's why I ended up with Morgan for a bit. Not that I was ever really *in* with him. You know. Just … kind of … needed someone. Or whatever." Christopher seemed embarrassed. But it was true that he was tight with Vincent and Terrence and Dan. He'd seemed tight with Cameron, too. Like a brother.

Maybe there was some hurt there, but he didn't ask Christopher for more. His family might have been killed, or he might have literally *lost* them, like Raj had lost track of his. He might have a mother and father still out there somewhere. Maybe a wife. He was young to be married and didn't wear a ring, but stranger things had happened. Trevor didn't want to know. This was all kind of a bummer.

"You like her, don't you?" Trevor asked.

"Who?"

"Lila."

"No." But yeah, he clearly did.

"You know she's pregnant. With Raj's kid."

"Yeah, of course," Christopher said. "So?"

"I'm just saying."

Before Christopher could respond to Trevor's just-saying, a muted thud banged from above. Christopher stopped with his mouth about to open, and his eyes ticked around. Following them, Trevor realized that everyone had stopped to trade glances. Except Vincent, who seemed not to have noticed.

Terrence's head poked out of the control room. He was wearing another pair of large sunglasses. Again, Trevor wondered how he could see what he was doing.

"Vincent!" he shouted. "Get your ass in here!"

Vincent was poking around in the storage pantry. "Just a minute," he said.

"Not in a minute. You need to see this. *Now!*"

Chapter Twenty-Two

CAMERON WOKE FROM A DREAMLESS SLEEP.

The previous night, he'd tossed and turned. They'd needed to wake early enough to be out the door before dawn, and time to prepare before that. He'd set his alarm for 4 a.m., and his body had seemed unable to settle in light of the early deadline.

This must have been his body making up for the shortfall. There had been no tossing and turning. No waking, not even to take a leak. He'd felt secure as they'd nodded off, and that had probably helped. Piper had proposed someone staying up to guard, but it seemed unnecessary. By the time they stumbled upon the barn, they hadn't seen anyone for hours. Animals were still inside — six horses they might pick from and try to ride in the morning. They'd been obviously hungry and a bit malnourished, which told Cameron that nobody had been tending to them for maybe a week. The house had been freshly burned, the tang of smoke still clinging to the nearby brush. The barn, he had to assume, had been abandoned.

Nobody would bother them. The world hadn't turned entirely upside down. As far as Benjamin and Charlie (Charlie *Cook*, not four-year-old Charlie Nelson) had told him and as far as he'd heard on the airwaves, there were entire sections of the country that had returned to civility. Few cities had stayed in riots or disorder. Many towns had normal power and were still playing by the rules. They probably even stopped at crosswalks in those places. Maybe Scouts still helped old ladies cross the street.

They were in the mountains. Yes, there were a few marauding gangs. But what barrel didn't have its bad apples? Cameron had certainly been in worse places. Americans acting like a single roving gang was cause for alarm — reason for ceasing life and holing up with your guns permanently drawn. But Cameron had wandered Mexico, South America, Israel, the Balkans, and the Middle East. Kingpins and warlords had controlled land even before the ships had come. Sometimes, people got killed. Sometimes, it happened often. And yet life, for most, simply went on.

They'd slept without a guard, and well.

The barn was quiet. He was the first one up. He'd thought he might be. If Piper and the Nelsons could *get* to sleep, odds were they'd *stay* there. Piper had suffered as fitful a previous night as Cameron and would be coming off an adrenaline spike. Mike, Rachel, and little Charlie had lived through something traumatic. The adults should sleep like the dead, in desperate need of recovery.

But Charlie surprised him. Some kids could sleep through anything, but others would be understandably nervous with an unstable life as described by Mike and Rachel. Cameron hadn't wanted to talk to any of them, but once the die had been cast, his distance had seemed overly rude. He'd made it clear they'd part ways tomorrow or the next day, and Mike kept assuring them — almost preemptively — that they'd be splitting off before nearing the highway. Fine. A day's compassion might not hurt them after all.

Rolling over on his ratty horse blanket, Cameron found himself tangled in his rifle strap. He'd slept with it on because flouting caution would be stupid. Reminding him of the same point, Cameron felt a crick in his back. Because dammit, he must've slept on his damned pistol, too.

He pulled the gun from his waistband, thinking *that* was stupid, and that rounds in the chamber or not, spending a night atop your firearm was asking for a bad back in the morning.

Piper was beside him, on her own blanket, curled into a comma with her back to Cameron. Her pistol was in her pants too, but at least right now she wasn't sleeping on it. Maybe only one of them had learned a lesson.

He sat up and stretched. Damn, was he stiff. He'd been in a bed or cot (he'd hit both, plus the couch, in rotation) for too long. On the way to Meyer's compound, they'd slept on just about everything. He was out of practice after just a week. Soft. Even when they'd been playacting their way into Morgan's graces as hoods, taking Christopher's temperature to find his loyalties, they'd slept on the ground, padded with coats stolen from the other people camping under the stars around the house, yes ... but ground nonetheless.

He smacked his parched lips, needing to take a leak.

One thing at a time. It was rare for Cameron to sleep so soundly, rarer still to sleep like the dead with a goddamned gun under his back and around his shoulders.

His body was used to drinking and peeing at least once per night, trading old moisture for new.

He reached for his backpack in the dimly lit barn and struck hay.

He reached again. Grabbed hay.

He turned. Rummaging in shadow, his searching hands discovering nothing. Given that his eyes had been closed, they were as adjusted as they were going to get. He swore inside his head. What he wouldn't give for a lamp or a switch to flick.

Without bothering to unclip it, Cameron found the small metal flashlight on his belt and turned its end. A tiny flood of bright white light washed the hay.

Just hay. His backpack was gone.

Piper must have woken in the middle of the night and moved it, wanting to fish out a water bottle without waking him.

He knelt tall then shined the flashlight momentarily on Piper, taking a guilty moment to appreciate her sleeping face and form. She was definitely ballsy. Ballsier, in fact, than she probably gave herself credit for. He'd been mad when she'd run toward the scream, for sure. He'd been even angrier (and not a little unnerved) when she'd fired that shot into the air to break up the one-sided fight in the clearing below. And he'd been absolutely furious when she'd bullied him into allowing the man, woman, and child to glom onto their group. Cameron was all about saving people, but dammit, that could get them both killed.

But the same things that were infuriating and stubborn made Piper noble. Attractive even. Cameron liked strong women. And her strength, too, was surprising. Benjamin and Charlie (again: not *little* Charlie, he thought with a smile) had given Cameron a full profile of Meyer Dempsey. The man was arrogant, pushy, narcissistic to an almost clinical degree — a force to be reckoned with both in business and life. He'd studied all the public, still-accessible information the facility and world still had to offer about Meyer. At least as much as they'd been able to send to his cell before the network's most protected data channels had died. Heather Hawthorne made sense with Meyer. She was brash but damaged, meaning they'd butt heads, even though behind the scenes she'd always submit to his way of doing things. Their inevitable divorce made even more sense, as did the fact that he'd dominated his way into custody of the kids.

But Piper? Little was known about Meyer's second wife — and of that little, Moab had sent him almost nothing. He'd gone in blind on the younger Mrs. Dempsey. He'd formed his own guesses about who she'd be. She'd have to be much more submissive than Heather. To put it mildly, such a woman — meeting Meyer after he'd achieved megalithic status, being groomed through his own companies and support — would have to be a dishrag. A pretty, obedient doormat.

But Piper wasn't like that at all.

Cameron moved the flashlight past her to shine on the hay beyond and saw something that filled him with terror and rage.

His teeth gritted. His heart thrummed. His fists clenched.

"Piper," he said, barely containing his fury. "Wake up."

She blinked her big eyes. Her big, innocent, naive, accidentally sabotaging eyes.

"Good morning."

Her smile vanished when she saw Cameron's expression.

"What?" She rolled, finding something amiss, patting

the empty hay beside her, still flattened by the impression of a horse blanket.

"Where are Mike, Rachel, and Charlie?"

"They're gone, Piper," Cameron said, trying hard to keep himself from shouting, "and they stole everything we had."

Chapter Twenty-Three

Terrence called for Vincent, but everyone came.

Lila hadn't heard the whole story of how the troupe had come together, but she'd gathered that Vincent and Terrence had been in the military together — in what capacity or branch she didn't know. But it didn't take a story to see that Vincent and Terrence were their own thing. Of the four men in the bunker, Terrence and Vincent paired off most often, always with an unspoken understanding between them and plans brewing under the surface. If they ever had to fight their way out of here, the battle would follow a clear order: Terrence would tell them what to do; Vincent would take the lead and make sure it got done. Dan was big but clearly not military. And Christopher? He was almost out of place. He must've had a rough past and struck Lila as a lost soul. He'd do what he was told, or what felt right.

But despite only calling for his right-hand man, Terrence's urgency had summoned half the bunker's occupants before Lila so much as rose from the couch. The little control room was overpacked — spilling into the living room's corner like a popular bakery at opening.

Heather looked over. She seemed almost as tired as Lila felt.

"Don't get up," she said.

But Lila had already risen and was moving forward. Heather rose behind her, following like a woman in a trance.

Inside her head — more a fearful echo than anything present — Lila could still hear the voice that had come after she'd doubled up in the bathroom. She didn't want to look down. Voices came from other people. If you were creative, voices might come from inside your mind. And if you were crazy, they could come from everywhere. But under no circumstances did voices come from your stomach. That didn't make sense, stir-crazy or not.

And still she heard it.

A suggestion, like a command:

Plug the hole.

And a promise:

It's all beginning.

But *which* hole should she plug? *Where?* The need to know was urgent. Lila felt sure that if she didn't do what the voice seemed to be telling her, something awful was going to happen. And *what* was beginning?

Too many questions to ponder, each making Lila feel more unhinged than the one before it. She didn't even want to think about it. In order to consider the notion that she'd seen this coming (the way she'd seen Morgan Matthews), Lila would have to admit she was seeing visions and hearing voices. She'd have to admit that the more she considered it, the thinker, dreamer, and speaker of those thoughts and voices wasn't Lila herself. No. Ever since coming out of the bathroom feeling as weak as she must have looked (judging by her mother's reaction), she'd started to entertain the idea that there was actually someone else talking to her. And that someone was …

No. That was too insane. Too ready for the rubber room.

She might as well say that she'd been getting personal messages from Jesus, or hanging out with Shakespeare's ghost. Forget what anyone else might think. If *she* started believing things like that, Lila herself would think she was crazy. Supposedly, if you *worried* that you were nuts, that meant you couldn't be. But it wasn't a rule of thumb Lila was willing to test.

She could barely see through the clutch of taller bodies. Terrence and Vincent were at the front, pointing at the monitoring screen and talking low, pinching and swiping to magnify and swap views. She couldn't hear all of what they were saying from back here, but snippets came to Lila like scraps of sheared-away fabric:

" … camera six, on the utility pole, if you can …"

" … a fire? Maybe one of them spilled …"

" … not a fire. You felt it. Well, *the rest of us* felt it, and …"

" … back there, though — isn't there a way to see …"

" … all of them, and what the hell would …"

Trevor appeared at Lila's side looking downright insulted. She'd seen him rush into the room just behind Vincent, but he'd been squeezed backward and out. Now the four original members of Cameron's group were front and center, making a scrum, mumbling and pointing. Raj was somehow up there, too. The room wasn't much more than a closet; it barely fit three comfortably, and they'd jammed five tight like sardines. Trevor had been ejected, and they probably didn't even know they'd pushed him out.

"What's going on up there, Trevor?" Lila's mother asked from behind them. She'd wanted to ask the same thing, but speaking had been hard for the last few hours. She'd barely had the strength to tell Mom about the abdominal pains and hadn't told her the rest. It scared her to say the words, in the way it would scare her to ask a doctor about a new lump in her breast. People got diseases all the time. Could they get mental diseases, too? If the bunker still had the Internet, she would've already spent way too much time on WebMD, deciding just how terribly ill she was.

Hearing voices? Check.

Feeling paranoia? Check.

Disorientation? Confusion? Increasing difficulty separating reality from fantasy? Triple check.

Well, then, congratulations, Delilah Dempsey — our diagnosis is that you're shit out of your mind.

"Something on the cameras."

A lump rose in her throat. What felt like a bubble popped in the back of her mouth; she practically gasped. "Is it Dad?"

"I don't think so."

Heather grabbed Trevor's arm. "You're saying it might be?"

"Why would Dad make the walls shake like that?"

"Trevor!"

"Look … *ow!* I don't know, Mom. Let go! That hurts."

Lila kept hold of Trevor's arm. She watched her, seeing the same stupid, vacant-eyed optimism in her mother's eyes that Lila had to admit she felt in her own. Who was this woman? She was never serious, never *not* making crass jokes and talking about penises. But right now she looked frazzled and lost. Like Lila felt.

"Is it Meyer?" Heather shouted.

Vincent turned back. "Everyone sit down."

"Answer me!"

"I don't know."

It was the same answer as Trevor's. But that didn't make sense. Saying he didn't know while looking right at the monitor (after Terrence had called him over, urgent and perhaps even panicked) made less sense than seeing just about anything. Of course he knew. She wished he'd just say something outright absurd instead of pretending he didn't know.

The sun just set in the middle of the day, Lila. Everyone topside has stripped naked and painted themselves blue, Lila. Fetuses can talk, Lila.

But he wasn't going to budge. He turned back to the monitor. Lila was about to object when her mother stuck her outstretched arms between Trevor and Dan then pushed. She wasn't subtle. She would either get through or squeeze herself to death, so Dan rolled out of the room, and Heather rolled in. Lila followed, staying in her mother's wake like a race car drafting off the leader's slipstream.

Lila glanced back and saw that the others were all out in the living room, including Raj, whom she almost wanted to wave apologetically to. They were letting Lila and Heather stay where they wanted. Because all men knew to stay away from crazy women.

"Is it Meyer?"

This time, Terrence turned, his face unreadable. "I don't think so, Ms. Hawthorne."

"How can you not know?"

He tapped the monitor, stepping aside and reaching to allow the women to see. Lila saw the front lawn from maybe twenty feet up, angled down, where the hippies had made their shanty town. The shanties were still there, but there were no people at all.

Terrence narrated, his voice like a mission commander delivering a brief.

"You're seeing the east lawn. There's not much to do down here, so I've counted their tents and bivouacs a few times. In this shot alone, there's almost forty. And there's more here—" He changed the shot with a finger: more camping setups but again no people. He touched the screen a few more times, scrolling through empty views. "And here and here and here. All told, guessing at an average of two people per setup, I guess we have maybe four hundred campers up top. But now look at this."

He touched the screen again. This time it showed a multiview — the topside cameras all visible at once, as thumbnails. He found the one he wanted and tapped it to expand. The new view filled the monitor — the first he'd pulled up so far with anyone in it — perhaps a dozen people apparently at the rear of a larger crowd, on one side of the screen, jockeying for position in the same way Heather and Lila had jockeyed inside the control room.

"So what?" said Heather.

"What are they looking at?" Lila asked.

Terrence nodded at Lila and ignored her mother. "That's the question."

"You don't know?"

Terrence shook his head. "A minute ago. Did you feel that thud?"

Lila nodded.

"Right after it happened, people on the monitors started running. Actually *running*. Not walking but stopping what they were doing and hauling ass toward … toward whatever it is. But there are no cameras over there."

"Why not?"

"It's off the property. There's a small open area to the side of the lake. See here?"

It took her a minute to reorient. After he'd shown her the shanties, Lila assumed she was looking at something right around the house. But this was down by the lake, maybe forty or fifty yards away. And the ground had shaken in here? It had felt like a boulder tipping and falling.

"Why are there no cameras out there?"

Lila looked over at her. It was strange how seeing her mother lose it made Lila feel better about her own sanity.

"It's too far, Mom."

She reached forward anyway, jabbing and swiping at the screen. Images changed more rapidly than anyone — including the woman supposedly looking for something in them — could follow.

"Heather …" said Vincent.

"We have to go out there."

"What?" Vincent shook his head. "No way."

"What if he's come home?"

"If he has, he'll come this way. We'll see him."

"What if he's hurt?"

"Mom," Lila said.

Heather turned to Terrence. She looked almost panicked, hysterical. "Why are all these people here? You guys seem to have all the answers. So why the fuck has everyone camped on our front lawn?"

"I don't have a cl—"

"Oh, but you knew right where the fucking flying saucers had gone, didn't you? Knew exactly who they'd picked up. And they just kept coming back, didn't they? You've got your radios and someone's telling you shit, and you come in here like some sort of assault force and—"

Vincent held up his hands. "Cameron told you all we know."

"But how? How do you know?" Heather jabbed her accusing finger at the screen. "And how can you not know what's going on out there?"

"There are no cameras that show—"

"How can you not *want* to know? You're the big, bad men, here to protect us with your guns!"

"It's not that simple. After Morgan and the rest of our group 'left' and never came back, they've been rotating through shifts in the house. A regular commune. Right there in the kitchen, there's a—"

"It might be him! We have to see!"

Heather was having none of it. They'd been down here for more than a quarter year, and day by day nothing changed. Safe but trapped. To Lila, it felt like the joke might be on them. The hundreds-strong community above wasn't fighting and killing and stealing from each other. Meyer had nicknamed this place something reminiscent of a spiritual oasis, and that's the way everyone topside was treating it. Lila and Heather had chatted often, wondering at what point staying in the bunker made sense. The ships might hover forever. They might be stuck here, like in that old alien ghetto movie about South Africa her dad had liked so much. And if the world paused where it was, never getting better or worse, did it make sense to hide forever?

This felt like the final straw. Mom had been keyed up for a few days. She seemed almost desperate to leave the bunker. She also seemed afraid — worried that something here was vulnerable and that if they weren't careful, whatever it was might be taken or harmed. How those two things went together, Lila had no idea. Heather hadn't liked hearing about her strange pains either and seemed to sense something troubling Lila's mind even if she hadn't admitted to the craziest of her crazy feelings.

She said that Lila needed a doctor and that they had to get out and go. Lila's baby couldn't be born in the bunker. *Not in this fucked-up place*, were her exact words.

Vincent watched her, his expression neutral.

Heather's face twisted and she pushed her way out of the control room, marching toward the spiral staircase.

"Heather!" Dan shouted after her.

She didn't turn. "You don't want to go? Fine. But I'm going, and my kids are going with me. *We're going!*"

"Mom!" Trevor yelled. Lila watched her younger brother with jealousy as he shuffled after her. Trevor was at home here — more now, in fact, than at the beginning. Unless he was hiding it well, he wasn't suffering any of what Lila or their mother was. No visions. No hallucinations. No overheard snippets of conversation or song. No growing certainty that something was off — and that they weren't on solid bedrock as it sometimes felt but were somehow suspended above a pit like a distressed damsel in a classic film.

She was up the stairs in a determined flash. Lila was below, looking up, seeing her mother through the metal lattice staircase.

Terrence came to Lila's side. "Ms. Hawthorne …"

"Open it. Open the door, and let me out."

"Come down, Heather," Vincent said.

"Come on down, Mom," Trevor echoed.

Heather banged on the door with her fists. "Open the goddamned door, Terrence!"

"It's too dangerous," Vincent said.

"*I don't give a shit if you think it's dangerous! Let me out!* We can't just assume it's nothing when the entire goddamned fucking shit-ass hippie colony ran down there the second something happened by the lake, and instead just sit here with our thumbs up our asses watching TV and—"

There was another thud.

And another.

And another.

"*What the fuck is going on out there?*" She screeched from above. But now — unbelievably, for the caustic Heather Hawthorne — Lila thought she could hear tears in her mother's voice.

"It's all beginning," someone said.

It took Lila a minute to realize the voice was hers.

Chapter Twenty-Four

Morning broke behind them, painting Cameron's back and his horses's rear in an amber spotlight. Piper followed behind on her mount, westbound with the highway distantly visible to the north, obediently mute. She'd need to let Cameron cool down. Only then should she attempt conversation again. Until then, he'd only shout. Not that she could blame him.

He'd been furious after realizing their gear was missing. Piper had been furious too, but she hadn't been allowed to indulge her rage before Cameron started stalking around the barn, ranting and kicking hay. She found herself pinned between the worst of both worlds: angry and made to feel stupid on one hand, the butt of impotent anger on the other. She was betrayer and betrayed, caught in the middle, unable to move.

Cameron — twenty yards ahead, his back seeming to scowl — was sulking. The worst thing was Piper thought he had a right. He hadn't wanted to bring the family along with them, but she'd insisted. Because they were people, and people had to stick together. They were a mother, a father, and a small boy. And what was more, Piper and Cameron had saved their lives. How could they be any harm? How could allowing them to tag along for an afternoon possibly cause any problems?

She'd thought Cameron was being callous, rude, uncaring. Of course they had to help. They had supplies, and the family had none. How could Cameron argue? He'd watched their backpacks get carried off with his own eyes. He'd shot at the bandits himself. They weren't being asked to take these people on their word, swallowing a story of high risk on the mountain trail. *They'd been there.*

The old saying was that the life you saved was your responsibility forever. Piper wasn't willing to go that far, but she'd surely felt they could give the Nelsons twenty-four hours.

That simple act of mercy had cost them too much. Maybe everything.

All of their water.

All of their food.

All of their extra clothes.

And a bunch of gear that Cameron and his men had relied on to reach Vail in the first place. Right down to compasses, cooking gear, a pair of the night vision goggles they'd used when claiming the bunker, matches, a water purification kit … *everything.*

Cameron had wanted to leave the family to their own devices, and that had struck Piper as so, *so* wrong. But in the end, he'd been right. They'd woken in the middle of the night and stolen both backpacks, leaving them less than the Nelsons themselves would have had if they'd walked away as Cameron had wanted. They were left with what was in their pockets or on their bodies, including their guns.

Piper had been thinking about that last bit while

saddling two of the barn's horses and riding away from the rising sun. If one of the guns had been in the packs or laid to the side, would Mike and Rachel have left them sleeping? Or would they have covered their tracks further — and more permanently — just in case the two looted travelers decided to track their robbers and retrieve what they'd stolen?

Surely not. But if this morning had proved anything to Piper, it was that everything really had changed. Maybe there were towns out there where business had returned to normal in the absence of alien activity. But now you could be robbed by anyone. Piper didn't want to find out if the same was true of being shot in the back.

It was all her fault.

She rode behind him for miles, doing her time in her moving dunce corner. He slowed as the sun climbed. Piper slowed to stay behind, embarrassed and ashamed. Finally, he stopped entirely, turning in his seat to face her for the first time since they'd set off that morning.

"Are you getting thirsty?"

At first, she didn't answer. It sounded like mockery. They had no water. The nice family they'd saved from rape and death had stolen every drop.

"Are you?" he repeated.

Maybe it was a serious question. "Yes."

"I hear something this way. Come on."

Piper looked back through the trees, watching the highway vanish as they headed farther south. She didn't want to ask Cameron what he had in mind, but after a while she heard it too: the muffled babble of a stream.

When they reached the small waterway, Cameron dismounted and looked around.

"What are you looking for?"

"A way to tie my horse."

"You don't think she'll stick around?"

"I'd rather not leave it to chance." He was still looking, slapping his hands on his thighs. His medium-length brown hair kept falling in his face. He didn't look nearly as young as she'd first taken him to be, back when she'd thought him one of Morgan's bad guys. He had to be midtwenties, maybe late twenties. How had he made himself seem barely eighteen? It had been something surprisingly convincing in his manner. She wanted to ask him if he'd ever taken acting classes but was still too gun shy about her mistake, and the question felt too familiar.

"Guess we should have brought some ropes." Piper fished into the dusty canvas shopping bag she'd found in the barn and tied to her saddle, pulled out a blue and white rope with a clip on the end, and handed it to Cameron.

He met her eyes. A small smile turned up the corner of his mouth. And just like that, Piper realized it was over. She was forgiven. He took the rope, secured his horse, then held out his hand to help Piper dismount and secured her horse to the same tree as his with a second rope. Both animals were close enough to drink the water.

"What else you have in there?" He nodded toward the bag. They weren't speaking when she'd loaded it.

"Some treats."

"Anything that's not for the horses?"

"I tried the water spigot, but it wasn't working."

"Probably had city water. I don't know that I'd trust it anyway." Cameron knelt beside the stream.

"You trust that?"

He smiled up at her. "It's literally a mountain stream."

"But …" She gestured. "Dirt. Rocks. Moss and stuff."

"The moss is on the bank. The water is moving too quickly to stagnate. You'll get some dirt, I'm sure." He scooped up a double handful. "But think about it. This is what Coors brags about using for their beer." He took a sip.

"What if you get parasites?"

"Good enough for them." Cameron nodded toward the drinking horses. "Besides, whatever's in here," he took another sip, "is better than dying of thirst."

Piper knelt, dipped her cupped hands into the water, and lifted them to her lips. She drank. It was cool and fresh, different than the water she was used to. She was a nature girl now. Soon she'd be milking cows and drinking raw milk from the teat.

"I guess we'll find out," she said.

After they'd had their fill, Cameron stood and tipped his chin toward the west.

"I've been thinking." He patted his horse's side. "We have two great rides right here. Maybe we don't need a car after all."

"You want to ride the whole way?"

He nodded. "I didn't want to say so earlier because it seemed depressing while we were on foot, but I'd thought that from the beginning. We had a car — 'we' meaning me, Dan, Vincent, and Terrence — on our way to your place, coming down from the Dakotas. Sometime after we diverted away from Moab and toward Vail, we started running into military blockades. Kind of like that one we saw yesterday morning but much bigger. At first, it was just one, and we turned around and retraced our steps. But then we hit another and detoured again. It became apparent pretty quickly that they had a method to their madness, and sure enough we started to pick up what sounded like military chatter on one of the open frequencies. They were using some sort of a code, and as good as we are, none of us are able to crack military codes, but to me it confirmed what we'd been seeing."

"What?"

"Cordoning off. Maybe even quarantining, though I doubt it's that. Likely just making a bigger effort to control the roads."

"Control or block?" Piper asked.

"We were carrying a bunch of weapons and didn't want to find out. Besides, there was no real guarantee that any of them were military. Another thing we'd heard a lot about and run into a time or two were … how to put it? 'Land grabs,' I guess. The real estate version of looting. Vincent and Terrence are good with maps and hiding. Dan and I are good at following directions—"

"So you aren't in charge? I thought you were the leader."

"It's complicated," said Cameron, moving on. "We never got stopped, but we saw a lot of people in Jeeps and pickups with a lot more guns than we had, on patrol. Fewer pro blockades. One guy had strung up razor wire. Regardless, between the military and … 'people staking their claims,' I suppose … we started to realize the roads were no longer a smart place to be. But we were close enough by then, so we ditched the car and walked the rest of the way."

"I thought we'd be driving. 'In Moab by nightfall' and all that."

"It was a possibility. But not one I ever really liked. Best-case scenario might have been motorcycles because they can get around most of the roadblocks, so if they're unmanned it's easy. Problem is, once you get past one barrier, you might have just gone *into* something. Like into someone's land, in the middle of a circle of roadblocks. So really, if we're wishing, I'd say ATVs would have topped my Christmas list for this trip. So we could cut through the brush."

"ATVs," Piper echoed.

"Or even snowmobiles, which will run on dirt in a pinch if you don't mind destroying the works with sticks and stuff. I'll bet a lot of these places up in the mountains have snowmobiles." He looked around, but there were no houses to be seen, then patted the horse again. "But even ATVs and snowmobiles don't have a horse's advantage."

"They're quiet."

"They're also good on uneven terrain and don't require gas." Cameron patted the horse's neck then looked toward its rump. "Though they do tend to *emit* gas."

He untied his line then mounted the horse and coiled the rope around the saddle horn. Piper, following his lead, did the same.

She looked west then turned to ask what was on his mind. Cameron answered as if he'd known the question was coming.

"I'd guess it'll take us a week."

"A week."

He nodded. "Best get started." He nudged the animal's side, and the horse started walking.

Piper's mind drifted with the animal's motion. She kept thinking of Lila, Trevor, Raj, and Heather. She'd left them alone with Cameron's men. Even if everything went perfectly, a there-and-back trip would take half a month. That assumed they didn't run into delays or problems, and it didn't account for the time they spent at the lab Cameron kept mentioning but hadn't yet fully described. She might be gone a month, and she'd led them to believe it would only be days.

Maybe that was fine. Maybe that made it easier to go — and really, she did need to. The men would know it wouldn't be a few days. Cameron's explanation sounded thought out, and he'd spent a lot of time talking to Vincent and Terrence before they'd left, poring over maps that were now in the Nelsons' possession. They'd know. Maybe they'd already broken the news, telling the others not to expect their return for a lot longer than anticipated.

Cameron still had the radio. She might even be able to tell them herself, if they could manage to secure a signal and squeeze a few words into the crowded common frequencies.

Still, Piper couldn't help but wonder if it mattered. In that missing month, Trevor would do fine, judging by the cold shoulder he'd been giving her for forever. Lila would cross into her second trimester. Maybe she'd be showing when Piper returned. She'd like that. It would let her pretend she'd have some sort of a role in the family, even though Meyer's absence made that connection more tenuous than it already was.

Cameron stopped his horse. Piper, after a minute, stopped hers.

"Do you hear something?" she said, thinking of the tales he'd told of land grabs and controlled territories. She waited, listening for the crack of a stepped-on twig.

"No," he said. "But I *see* something."

He pointed.

And she saw.

Chapter Twenty-Five

Lila was sitting in the control room, flipping between views, pinching in and out to magnify one unhelpful scene after another. After the banging had stopped and her mother finally exhausted herself yelling at Vincent, banging on his muscled chest before stomping off to bed, the whole bunker settled into quiet. Now it was dark.

"See anything?"

Lila turned. Raj was behind her, holding his telephone watch in one hand.

"Almost. I found a shot from the kitchen where you could see out the window and there was … something. But it got dark, and nobody seems to be down there with lanterns." Lila nodded at his watch. "Any luck on your end?"

Raj shrugged and re-strapped the watch to his wrist. "Thing is useless. Maybe I should just get used to the fact that I'm here with you forever."

Lila noticed two things Raj didn't mention. The first was that for all Raj's certainty that the watch was useless and that he'd never be able to use it to reach his family, he still put it back on. The second was that "I'm here with you forever" sounded resigned rather than cheery. Perhaps the alien invasion had plucked the bloom from their rose.

"You want to sit down?" she said.

"I was thinking I'd go to bed."

"It'd be nice if we could spend some time together." Lila wasn't sure if she meant it. He'd been the apple of her eyes before this all started, but she wasn't as in love with the man he'd proved himself to be. Raj had his moments of bravado, like when he'd slapped on a gas mask and prepared to battle their home invaders, but it was always misplaced and ended so poorly. Mostly, Raj complained. He'd been doing a lot less since Lila yelled at him, but hadn't stopped. And Lila didn't feel as bad about having shouted at him as she supposed she should, especially considering his baby inside her.

"Maybe you could come in, and we could spend some time together in the room."

Lila looked up at him. He couldn't possibly be thinking what she thought he was. But he was staring with a double meaning on his face, eyebrows slightly raised.

"What do you think?"

Yep. He really *was* thinking that.

"You're kidding."

"Why would I be kidding?"

"Because I share a room with my mom. And you share a room with Dan. And both are already asleep."

"Exactly. Your mom is *out*." He ticked his head toward the staircase as if to add, *exhausted after her crazy little tantrum.* He might even be right; she'd gone in looking defeated and drugged. If only HBO could see their great comedienne now.

"I'm not having sex with you in a cot beside my sleeping mother."

"The shower then."

Lila rolled her eyes. "Good night, Raj."

He watched her for a minute then his face fell and he walked out, sulking. A moment later, his bedroom door slammed too loudly.

Lila returned her attention to the screen. It was pointless; if Terrence with all his tech knowledge hadn't been able to pull a decent image from the surveillance feeds, she sure wouldn't be able to. But the thudding noises had been loud enough that it seemed impossible to believe whatever had made them wasn't visible *somewhere*. But no, she couldn't see a thing. They'd watched the people topside scramble like ants until the light faded.

The cameras only showed evidence of people headed toward something out of sight. If they wanted to see what those people saw, they'd have to exit the bunker. But Terrence and Vincent wouldn't let them. It was something Raj had, earlier in the day, seemed dangerously close to bitching about. He was holding it in, and probably thought he deserved sex for being a good boy and doing as she'd asked.

There was a knock behind her.

"Go to bed! I'm not going to scr—"

But it was Christopher, not Raj.

"You're not going to what?"

Lila had been about to say she wasn't going to screw him in the shower. She turned away, feeling her cheeks burn. "Nothing. I thought you were Raj."

Christopher sat with a mischievous smile — all teeth and charming green eyes. "Okay. What aren't you going to do with Raj?"

"Nothing."

Christopher made a *tsk-tsk* sound. "Well. Isn't dating you full of perks?"

"Shut up, Christopher."

"The guys usually call me Christopher. I kind of like it when you call me Chris."

They'd been through this before. He was flirty. It was inappropriate, but he seemed to delight in her squirming. The only way to face him was head on.

"Fine, *Chris*."

He swiveled in the chair. "What did you mean, before, about how it's 'all beginning'?"

"I wasn't thinking straight. I don't know."

"When there were all those big booming noises. You said, 'It's all beginning,' and it was like you knew something."

"Well, I don't." And boy didn't she. Lila didn't know all sorts of things. Like, for instance, whether or not she was losing her mind.

"Did you have that talk with Vincent?"

"Forget it." Christopher shook his head. "He says no one leaves the bunker."

"Did you tell him that this is my dad's house?"

"I did. He said your dad turned over control to Piper, and that Piper gave her blessing for Vincent to be in charge while she's gone. He said you're welcome to fight him for the leader role."

"That's not funny. He can't tell us what to do."

"You're right." Christopher nodded. "And if you really, really force it, he'll cave. I know he will. Right now, he thinks he's saving you from yourself. Your mom, too. He thinks you're being emotional, not thinking straight. Get a good night's sleep, get the crazy out of your eyes, and talk to him tomorrow. If you still really, truly want to risk going up there and getting us all killed, he may step out of the way, no problem."

"How does it get us all killed?"

Christopher nodded toward the screen. The monitors had resumed their normal rotation, and now showed the sleepy, lantern-lit shantytown. The lanterns would die soon enough. There were only so many batteries left in the world, and Lila kind of doubted that Energizer and Duracell were cranking them out the same way they had half a year ago.

"They seem pretty quiet, don't they?"

Lila shrugged.

"They were when we were with Morgan. A big, old vegetarian convention. But they're all waiting for something. And I'd bet they're afraid. Maybe some of them are getting cold feet. A lot of them have guns. And if they see that the door off the kitchen isn't just a safe but that there's actually a bunker down here filled with food and water and electricity and—"

"You don't know they'd force their way in."

"I don't know they'll try to force their way in," Christopher agreed. "But I *do* know that you can't be sure they won't."

Lila sighed and shook her head at the screen. "It could be something about Dad."

"How?"

"I don't know. Cameron said this place was special, but he didn't know why. Or whoever he talked to didn't know. He also said that Dad was special. And that the ships came here. Don't you think *he'd* want to know?"

"Call him. Tell him to come back and look."

She'd already tried. But Lila didn't feel like telling Christopher. She felt unhinged. Dad was still missing and didn't know he had a grandchild on the way. Raj was no help. If Mom kept unraveling, Lila might end up raising this child by herself. She didn't know the first thing about babies and had no way to find out what she needed to know. She'd have to deliver here, without a doctor. And worse, she was having phantom pains she'd only told her mother about (her crazy mother, maybe) and suspected — and yes, she knew how nuts it sounded — that her baby was somehow communicating with her. Warning her that something needed to be done … or undone. Showing her the future or what might someday be.

Lila buried her face in her hands.

"Hey …" Christopher planted his hand on her shoulder.

"Do you know what today is?"

"I could get a cal—"

"It's my birthday." Lila looked up, her vision blurred. She tried on a wry smile. "Not exactly the way I saw spending my eighteenth: underground, afraid, alone."

"You're not alone."

"I'm more alone than you think."

Christopher put his hand on Lila's.

"Well. I'm here anyway."

Lila tried to laugh, but it came out as a half sob. She corrected, snorted, wiped her nose with the back of her hand. She was such a disgusting mess.

"Where's my birthday present?" she said, hoping to waste seconds. She wished he'd go away — not because she wanted Christopher gone, but because she needed to be alone.

But why was she asking questions if she wanted him to leave?

"If it weren't so late, I'd bake you a cake."

Lila laughed again. "Hardly seems like a cake-baking world anymore. Maybe you should give me a gun. Maybe for your present, you could shoot your way through the crowd to get me outside."

She looked up. Maybe that hadn't been funny.

"I killed the bad guy for you. Does that count?"

The terrible thing was, it kind of did. Lila remembered screaming with Piper. The spatter of blood — one more threat leaving the world. Christopher behind the trigger. It was more than anyone else had done, other than her father and Piper. Certainly more than Raj.

Lila nodded. Christopher leaned closer. She answered his sarcasm, her voice stupidly serious, almost quiet. "That *was* very romantic."

He reached out with his foot and closed the control room door. Lila found she didn't mind. There was, it turned out, one place in here where two people could be alone.

His hands on hers felt strong. Safe. She just wanted it all to be over. She wanted to stop worrying. To stop being pulled in a dozen directions. To stop feeling so constantly unsure. She wanted someone else to make her decisions for a while. To make the ground stop shaking beneath her, both literally and figuratively. To give her some solidity and substance. To be her rock, at least for a little while.

For just a *little* while.

"Happy birthday, Delilah Dempsey."

And for a little while, Lila forgot all her troubles, all her worries.

Chapter Twenty-Six

CAMERON STOPPED his horse shy of the first huge gray mass. To Piper, he looked afraid.

They'd been on the edge of a large clearing when they'd stopped to take their drink. Once back atop their horses, it had been easy to see down the gently sloping hill and into the clearing.

First they'd seen one stone. Then another, maybe twenty feet past it.

And after moving past a few intervening trees, they'd seen the rest: two long lines of huge stones bisecting the clearing. The lines were parallel with fifty feet or so between them. The stones themselves were taller than broad — rock fingers, not squat round boulders.

"I've never seen anything like it," Piper said.

"I have."

Cameron hopped off his horse. He uncoiled the braided rope and tied his mount to one of the last trees before woods gave way to grass and slowly walked forward, as if in a trance.

Piper had lost a lot of her bearings but thought the

freeway was still somewhere to her right and they were facing west, directly through this clearing. They'd just stopped, and if they were truly facing a week of travel, she wanted to keep moving. But fascinating geology was apparently, for Cameron, worth stopping for. Maybe he'd take their picture to share online if the network ever returned.

Piper reluctantly hopped down, tied off, and came to Cameron's side.

"Should we keep moving?"

"Have you ever been here?" he asked, not looking toward her. "Meyer's house isn't that far, but it's not like there are any roads. Did you ever hike through this area?"

"I'd never been to Colorado at all before we came to the ranch."

Cameron moved slowly forward. He ran his hand along the surface of one rock then knelt at its base. He dragged his fingers along the dirt at its foot where the ground was buckled, like a bunched-up carpet. Grass bulged in odd lumps in a rough circle around all of the stones' bases as far as Piper could see.

"Why?" she asked, watching him.

"I was wondering if it's always been here."

"There are all sorts of weird rock things around here."

Cameron continued to play in the dirt. Looking at the wavelike rings of raised grass at the bottom.

"These were placed here recently." He stood. "All of them."

"Okay."

"It doesn't bother you?"

"A bunch of rocks? No. They don't bother me."

Cameron ran his hand along the stone. "This is granite. It's probably three hundred tons."

"You know a lot about rock weights."

"I've seen them before, I told you." He backed away

then looked up at Piper. "We need to go around."

"Around?" She looked to the right and left, watching the line of rocks stretch to the clearing's edge and beyond. The line of stone went as far as she could see. "Don't be silly. It's clear here, and you can walk right between them."

Shaking his head, Cameron pointed to the rippled ground. "You see that? They'd tip over if they weren't half buried, so there's as much stone below ground as above. But there's no loose dirt, and the ground looks almost broken. Like … well, like they were just *pounded in*."

Piper wasn't buying it. Maybe there was a fault line here or something. She vaguely remembered hearing that just as some faults in the Earth's crust made big cracks, other overlaps of the tectonic plates made mountains. They were in the mountains, places where rock erupted upward. It was much easier to believe that these rocks had risen like jagged teeth than that someone had dragged them here, into the middle of the woods, where there wasn't much room for cranes or heavy equipment. Strange-looking for sure, but nature was full of logic-defying crap.

"Fascinating," said Piper. "Ready to move on?"

"We need to go around. Come on." Cameron remounted his horse and began moving parallel to the stones. The clearing was large, but he nudged his horse to a canter and made it in under a minute. Piper followed, and they found themselves where the trees resumed. But the rock lines didn't stop. They continued into the woods, now wedged between trees, their positioning precise in the clearing, but their newness now obvious. Tree roots, driven down by the stone's force, erupted around their edges, creating giant, gaping soil caves around a few.

"Come on," said Cameron, continuing to ride parallel

to the stones.

Now that they were inside the woods, the air was cooler and darker, the rising sun dampened by the leaves above. Piper felt her skin crawling and felt stupid. Cameron's mood and the stone formation's oddity blended to give her the creeps. But that wasn't reasonable. Someone had wedged a bunch of enormous stone spears into the dirt, driving through tree roots as big around as her thighs … and, in at least one case, directly through a fallen tree, splintering the trunk into a mess of pale-brown splinters around the planted stone. So what?

"Dead end." Cameron pointed to where the path descended into a treacherous valley. They wouldn't be going down there. But, Piper saw, the stones did. Evenly spaced in twin rows all the way down and back up the other side, out of sight. He nodded. "We'll have to try the other way."

"This is ridiculous, Cameron. Let's just …"

Piper moved to steer her horse between the stones.

Cameron raised his hand to protest and opened his mouth to yell — the way a parent might shout at a child about to run headlong into a busy street. But Cameron barely managed a yelp, because her horse balked before he could yell, whinnying and rearing onto her hind legs. It wasn't much more than a frightened hop, and Piper managed to stay on, but the horse continued to whine and protest even after she'd bent forward and clutched the animal's neck. She watched its big, brown eyes dart toward the stones, terrified.

"Easy, girl!" Piper ran her hand along the horse's neck as it pranced back from the stones.

The danger passed, Cameron lowered his hands.

"The other way," he repeated.

Piper turned the horse with some difficulty; her mount

only moved after she allowed enough distance from the stones. Cameron followed.

"When I was a kid," he said, "my dad dragged me all over the world. All these crazy places where there were all sorts of funny things to look at. Like Göbekli Tepe in Turkey, where a shepherd found a rock sticking out of the dirt one day and decided to dig and ended up unearthing the first corner of some sort of huge underground city that appears to have been deliberately buried: stone megaliths much fancier than these and elaborate sculptures of animals, all precisely carved something like twelve thousand years ago. Twice as long ago as we'd previously believed human civilization existed. But there were so many more places like that. That's where I spent my childhood: trotting the globe, looking at rocks."

Piper turned to the massive stones. Now that they were back in the sun, they just seemed like rocks. But she couldn't help recall the horse's panicked eye, the animal's obvious terror.

"There are stone circles everywhere — 'stone henges' all over Europe in addition to the famous Stonehenge in England. Sacsayhuamán in Peru, where enormous stones are arranged like Tetris blocks, so precisely fitted, without mortar to hold them together, that you couldn't slide a piece of paper between them. But what this makes me think of most," Cameron pointed at the rocks as they rode past, "is Carnac, in France."

"Carnac," Piper repeated, with no idea what he meant.

"Enormous granite megaliths, just like these. Several hundred tons each, standing upright in long rows. They're dated between 4,500 and 2,500 BC, toward the end of the Stone Age, so we're talking about cavemen doing the work."

"So they lined up rocks. Terrifying."

"Not terrifying," said Cameron, refusing the bait, "but strange. First, how did they move stones that large? They'd be hard to move today. Local legend says that giants built it. Beings with strength enough that moving the stones was easy. But that's not even the most amazing part. The stones seem to be placed randomly, but they're not. The rows are all exactly 2,860 meters long, and 1,430 meters across the whole formation at the end. A one-to-two ratio, in a right triangle. When you see it from above, it's obvious. Understanding of the Pythagorean theorem thousands of years before Pythagorus was born. And also, it's one of the only man-made sites that can be seen from space."

"Convenient." With part of Piper's mind, she thought it ironic that her skepticism about some sort of "aliens did it" theory was intact even after aliens had invaded the planet and stolen her husband. Maybe it was repression. It almost had to be. There was no question the rocks beside her hadn't been placed by nature. And there was no question they hadn't been placed recently from above, with enormous force.

Cameron nodded. "That's what I used to think. The problem with so much of the stuff I was dragged around the planet to see is that nobody started with the evidence. They started with the theory to explain the evidence. That's not the way science is supposed to work. You're supposed to make a hypothesis then try to disprove the theory. You're not supposed to decide on something you want to believe then search for substantiation. Because you can find patterns in everything."

"Like Orion's belt," said Piper, remembering what he'd said back in the bunker.

"Right." He nodded forward. "This way."

They reentered the woods, this time on the opposite

end of the clearing. But after a few minutes, they confronted an impassable valley — probably the same one, curving around from side to side like a horseshoe.

Cameron swore.

"Finding another way around will cost us *hours*."

"They're just rocks," Piper said. "The horses may be afraid of rocks, but I'm not. We can blindfold them and lead them through."

"But that's just it. I don't think they *are* just rocks anymore."

"*Anymore?*" Piper wasn't sure what she was hearing. If the huge gray slabs beside them weren't rocks, what were they? Sock puppets?

Cameron moved his mount toward Piper then clipped a line to the horse's bridle and tossed it to her.

"Hold this for a sec." He hopped down then stood beside Piper and her horse, not approaching.

"People who visit Carnac," he said, "say they can feel energy there. You know, like crystal weirdos who say that vibrations in the crystals heal them and stuff. But at Carnac, it almost seems legit. The Earth has its own magnetic field — a good thing, since that's what keeps the solar wind from blowing our atmosphere away like it supposedly did on Mars — and that field is caused by our spinning metallic core. Metal." He walked forward and slapped his hand against the closest stone. "Like the metals that make up these stone megaliths."

Cameron looked back at Piper. "Anything containing a ferromagnetic metal — iron, nickel, cobalt, even lodestone —can be magnetized to some degree. There's a discernible magnetic field at Carnac. You can measure it. It's as if something long ago polarized then froze them that way. It's subtle but there. And that's probably what tourists claim they can feel. But my dad's lab in Moab? One of their theories is that aliens have — and have always had — plans for our planet that span the globe. Meaning they see Earth as one giant entity. If you wanted to do that, you'd need a way to mark certain spots — the same way surgeons draw lines on patients with marker before making the first cuts. One of the ways aliens might mark those spots — as well as gathering all sorts of unseen information, right down to — maybe — thoughts and bioenergy … well, let's just say that electromagnetism is a much, much stronger force than we usually give it credit for, and a hell of a lot stronger than gravity."

"But you said there are natural magnets all over the place."

"Look at your zipper."

Piper was wearing a pullover with a zipper down the center. The zipper tab wasn't lying down like it was supposed to. It was standing straight up, pointing at the line of rocks.

Cameron reached to his side, pulled out his knife concealed in a leg sheath, and touched it to the stone's surface. He let go. The knife, which had a heavy wooden-inlay handle, hung where he'd placed it. Then he tugged with substantial effort and restowed the blade.

"They're as strong as industrial magnets," he said. "The kind that will erase your credit cards if you hold them too close."

"We're not credit cards. They won't do anything to us."

Cameron's eyes followed the line of stones to the right and left, their demarcation possibly heading off into infinity. They had to go west, and there might not be any practical way to get around in the time they had.

"I hope you're right," he said, "because it looks like we're about to find out."

Chapter Twenty-Seven

HEATHER STOOD in a field surrounded by a wide ring of trees, her feet bare on wet grass. She hadn't been here a moment ago and realized without surprise that she was dreaming.

But this wasn't like her normal dreams. Normally, Heather's dreams were hazy and indistinct, with obvious plots and storylines but no true clarity. She never stopped in dreams to decide whether or not they made sense (they didn't), and she never experienced any senses other than sight and sound. But the sensation of the grass between her bare toes was distinct. She thought, *I've missed this.* She'd lived in Los Angeles for most of her life, more concrete than grass. She'd never been much of a barefoot girl. But three months in an underground bunker could change a person, make them long for things they'd never cared about before.

In front of her, barely meriting notice in the bizarre "of course" way of dreams, was a double line of enormous gray stones.

"They crossed a line today," Meyer said.

Heather took Meyer's hand as he stood beside her. He clasped it for a second then let it drop. It wasn't a rebuke or rude, but his meaning was clear. He wasn't here for affection. Probably because the "they" he was referring to, visible just ahead, included Piper. His current wife, whereas Heather — always special to him, a great friend and fellow psychedelic voyager — was his wife in the past.

Heather watched Piper and Cameron step between the stones. They had horses for some reason, and they'd both taken off overshirts and wrapped them over the horses' eyes to blind them. They were leading their mounts along between the stones as well, but not without difficulty.

Heather turned to look at Meyer. He was the same man as always, but that in itself was strange. He'd left presumably in his pajamas, but he was beside her in one of his finer suits. Looking down, she saw that his feet were also bare.

"Am I dreaming?"

"Would you like a mirror, so you can make fun of yourself for asking?"

"I have to ask."

"Why? Because this makes sense otherwise?"

Well, yes, she thought. It was perfectly realistic so long as Heather ignored the fact that nothing within it was possible. She distinctly remembered going to bed exhausted, realizing that for once she wasn't going to get her way. She knew the door had been super-locked somehow (a necessary alteration to the mechanism since the main lock had been destroyed when their new visitors drilled their way in) and that she couldn't leave without Terrence's help. She also didn't know where she was. It wasn't the house. If this vision was true (and that itself didn't make sense), Piper and Cameron had to be halfway to Utah by now, but here she was with them. Apparently invisible.

"It's not like when I normally dream of you."

Meyer laughed. "I think we both know those weren't dreams."

"I meant before now. Even before you were …" Heather didn't want to offend him, even in a dream or whatever this was. But she didn't know another way to say it. " … *taken*."

"'Taken' is different from 'went,'" he said, watching the spot where Piper and Cameron had vanished. He sighed. "Now they can see them."

"Who?"

Meyer turned to face Heather, handsome as always. It had been a long time since she'd been with him. A long, stressful time with no release save her occasional interlude with the shower massager.

"Even back then, they weren't dreams. We traveled."

Heather laughed. Meyer always said such stupid shit. They'd lay on the floor after drinking Juha's medicine and purging, and she always saw the worst things for a while thereafter — her soul purging its evil along with her body, according to Juha. But afterward it was a trip. Kinda groovy but nothing otherworldly. Meyer, for all his normal, businesslike stoicism, claimed his experience was different. Metaphysical in a way readers of his *Forbes* magazine profiles would mock. Meyer always said he went other places. Heather played along, mocking him only lightly, because she'd never really stopped loving him, even after she'd learned to hate the parts of him that lived on the abrasive surface.

"You never believed it. But you didn't need to, for it to do its job."

Heather didn't feel like having this conversation. It wasn't fun without the drugs.

"Is this real?" Then, remembering she'd recently asked

if this was a dream, Heather clarified: "Did this really happen? Am I tripping on a journey right now?"

"How could you travel without the medicine?"

"I'm seeing you, aren't I?" Heather narrowed her eyes. Everything was so detailed. She was having to work hard to remind herself that she was dreaming, strange as everything felt. She'd felt connected to Meyer since he'd left, and she'd seen him in the same trippy ayahuasca she remembered. But this was different. When Heather woke up, she'd probably feel the same sense of fractured reality.

"You've seen me plenty of times before." Meyer's voice was almost mocking. She was being tested, led, encouraged to say what he wanted to hear.

Meyer surprised her.

"Talk to Lila," he said, now taking her hands. "Talk to our daughter."

"Talk to Lila?"

"She's in trouble."

"She's pregnant."

"That's not what I meant."

"She told me today. Some sort of pains. If I can get her out and take her to a doctor, maybe—"

"That's not what I meant either."

"You're not the only one who's being led." That made Heather think of Lila's heavy, tired eyes. The way she'd looked desperately soul weary and unhappy. The way Heather had felt quite sure that Lila, despite her candor about the problems she'd felt with her baby, was holding something back. Keeping secrets.

"Is something wrong with her baby?"

"You're not safe here," Meyer said.

"It's this place. Something is wrong with this place." She meant the bunker, not the field where they found themselves. But Meyer would understand. Because this had to be a dream, and he was part of her.

"That's the way it seems. But it's not."

"The drain—"

"You'll want to try to stop what's coming — to block their way to what's below," he said, "but you shouldn't. You must protect it. Make sure the way remains *open*, not closed."

Heather was about to ask Meyer what he meant, but Piper and Cameron surfaced on the far side of the stones, safe and sound. Of course they were safe and sound. All they'd done was to walk between some giant rocks, no different from stepping between buildings on the streets of New York.

"Now they can see them." Meyer turned his serious eyes on Heather. "Same as they'll be able to see Lila. Same as they've been able to see you and me all along."

"What do you — ?"

But Meyer was gone.

The field in front of Heather began to fragment and split, its stark reality suddenly falling apart, cracking as if the whole thing had been a backdrop. Chunks crumbled and dropped away as if into a black pit beyond.

Heather bolted upright in bed, sure that something was wrong even before the cacophony hit her ears.

Some sort of alarm in the bunker was braying loud enough to wake the dead.

Chapter Twenty-Eight

PIPER STOPPED. Cameron instantly followed. They were back on their horses, pulling back on the reins with such perfect synchronicity, they were practically limbs sharing a body.

"Why did you stop?"

"Why did *you* stop?"

"I just got a feeling," Cameron said.

Piper looked to the north, toward what she assumed was Route 70 snaking westward into Utah. They hadn't had a compass since last night, but even during the middle of the day she'd felt a better-than-usual sense of direction. Maybe they were way off course and she was oblivious. She'd find out soon enough. Either the sun, now past its apex, would continue to set toward what she thought was west, or they'd end up having looped back to the double line of monoliths.

Piper hoped not. It would mean they'd gone the wrong way, yes, but that wasn't why she didn't want to see them again. Maybe it was Cameron's sense of doom infecting her, but she'd felt far more uneasy passing between those big rocks than she'd had any right to. They were only boulders — but she'd sworn she could feel something between their rows, pressing inward like a force field. The horses, even blindfolded, hadn't wanted to pass.

He'd had a *feeling*. Ridiculous. If their positions were reversed, he'd already be laughing at her. But they'd both stopped, and neither seemed to know why.

"Let's cut south," Cameron said.

So they did. Piper kept looking back over her shoulder, feeling like they might be followed. But they hadn't neared a road in a while, and they hadn't seen or heard people for much longer. The terrain was mountainous, turning their trusty mounts into surprisingly adept trail guides. It would be hard for anyone to approach them unseen.

They reached a ravine. The trail wanted to nudge them west again, so far as Piper could tell. They curved and followed it. After a few minutes, as the ravine fell to their left, the trail drifted from true west toward northeast, the sun looking like it wanted to slip down in front of Piper's left shoulder rather than straight ahead.

There were three trees to the path's side. Piper stopped, watching them.

"What?"

"Something's wrong."

Cameron looked like he might contradict her but then turned forward.

"Something with those trees. I can't tell what. Just … something." He turned to Piper. "They're just trees. How can something be wrong with trees?"

Piper didn't know, but there was definitely something wrong. It wasn't dark. There were few shadows. Even the most talented storyteller couldn't spin a yarn about this haunted forest and the monsters lurking in its nooks and crannies, because it didn't look haunted in the least. It seemed charming, beautiful, peaceful. Their surroundings were open and inviting. Well lit and welcoming. Yet Piper couldn't shake the feeling that something was impossibly wrong.

"Go up and check," Piper said.

Cameron didn't move. He was watching the trees as if waiting for them to spring. But they weren't even old and gnarled. No splintered branches or knots like strange faces. They were straight, smooth, young, intact. Their branches didn't weave into frightening shapes.

"You can feel it, too."

Cameron nodded. "Same as before."

"What is it? What's wrong?"

"I don't know.

Piper only knew that she wanted to back away. She didn't want to look at those trees anymore. Or have them behind her. It was as if she could see someone nailed to the trunks, their body bleeding and twisted. There should be something macabre ahead to justify this creeping dread — the feeling Cameron shared, judging by his face — but there simply wasn't.

"Did you see someone hiding behind them?" Cameron asked.

"There's nowhere to hide."

"Did we see them earlier? Maybe we made a loop by mistake."

"Do you think you'd forget that ravine?" Piper gestured. But he already knew they hadn't seen the trees before. Because again: *They were just trees.* Not an enemy's hiding place or an altar of human sacrifice. Just ordinary trees she'd have felt foolish to fear passing … if Cameron didn't clearly feel the same irrational way.

"We could go down there." He nodded toward the ravine. Its sides were sloped but not terribly steep. Still, a stupid choice with a perfectly good path straight ahead. Piper was glad he'd made the suggestion. She would have insisted if he hadn't.

"Okay."

Cameron dismounted. He led the horse, walking slowly downward, choosing his footing. Piper carefully followed. It took them ten minutes to reach the bottom, and the only place to stand and walk, once down, was in the middle of a shallow stream running through the ravine's beating heart.

Cameron looked up. "That was stupid."

"Do you want to go back up?"

He shook his head. "You?"

"No." Piper looked up. Chill still filled her. "I don't know what that was all about. Have you ever had anything like that happen?"

"Yeah. A half hour earlier, when we turned south in the first place."

Piper nodded slowly. "I guess we'd better hurry to your Utah ranch. Before we both go crazy."

Cameron tried to laugh but barely managed.

They walked the creekbed floored in stone.

"Cameron," said Piper.

Cameron looked over.

"Does the word 'Andreus' mean anything to you?"

"I feel like it does." He shook his head. "Can't place it. What is it?"

"I was hoping you'd know."

Cameron smiled. "I guess it's too late on that whole 'before we both go crazy' thing."

"No, no. I heard it in a movie or something. I can even sort of picture the scene. It was ..." She struggled to grasp the slippery image, wondering why it had been jarred loose now of all times. But once noticed, Piper realized that the word and scene had been playing in her mind for a while, like barely heard background music. " … something kind of … macabre? … I feel like it was one of those scenes that Meyer would have thought was cool, but I'd have hidden my face in my hands. Something gross. Like torture porn." She tilted her head, still chasing the memory. "Why would I have watched something like that?"

"I've seen it too. And I don't watch many movies."

"Did you see it in a theater, do you think?"

"I don't know. Probably not."

"I wonder if it was one of Meyer's movies. His studio's, I mean. But they don't go into stuff like that. Not that I've seen?" Every thought wanted to end in a question mark. Piper couldn't figure it out. And she didn't know why it was bothering her — especially now, of all times.

Cameron said, "There was a man with a cowboy hat. A hat too small for his head, like a stupid little thing. I remember being afraid of that guy."

"So you were a kid."

"I don't know." He scratched his head. "I watched even fewer movies growing up. Maybe it was something I saw or that my dad told me about? It feels very 'warlord.' Like some powerful guy torturing and … sacrificing? We went to a lot of places where they still do stuff like that."

"But then why would I remember it?" Piper furrowed her brow.

The picture was coming clearer. She remembered the man with the hat, too. A dumb look — it should have been laughable. But she hadn't wanted to laugh at this man whenever she'd seen him. In a movie. Although now she was getting goose bumps and could see the scene with a memory's clarity. As if it were something she'd witnessed. Something that scared her. The man with his hat. Who'd carried a machete on his hip. Who told a group of stern-faced guards what to do. The guards were worse than the man. She distinctly remembered a scene *(memory)* wherein one of the hat-man's dissenters or enemies had earned his wrath, and the guards had tied a rope to each of that man's arms and legs. The other ends of the ropes had been fastened to the backs of plow horses, and the horses had been whipped in four different directions.

Piper remembered that part *very* vividly now that the memory of what she'd seen on screen *(witnessed in person)* was getting clearer. The man's arms had come off first. Then he'd bled out and died, ruining all the hat-man's fun.

"I remember something really hideous," Cameron said, seeming to think. "About someone being … drawn and quartered? And you're right, there were people chanting that word. *'Andreus.'* Like a cheer. Or an anthem." He shook his head, disgusted. "I've never seen a movie like that. I never *would* see—"

A gunshot crashed through the quiet.

Piper and Cameron looked up, halting in their tracks. The stream had its own music, and the horses' footsteps had vanished into its flow. But they'd been talking. The ravine wasn't all that deep. Ground level was maybe five feet above their heads.

"*Get down!*" Cameron whispered.

Heart beating hard, Piper dismounted. Cameron led his horse toward the steeper embankment. He leaned back, trying to stay out of sight. More gunshots echoed above.

Piper heard two sets. Someone near the bank above and a second round of reports, farther off. Two people in a gunfight. Piper's head swam, suddenly sure that whoever was above would be interested in knowing there were a pair of people below, hearing everything. Being where they shouldn't be, nearly seeing what they shouldn't see.

She heard a great, inarticulate cry. A sound like

animals stampeding — with human voices. The far-off shooter fired twice more in rapid succession, but Piper could sense their panic. He or she was being chased by a horde, and there weren't enough bullets to end them all.

Cameron's eyes were on Piper's. The sound of water combined with the shouting above would drown anything out. But his eyes were wide and round, flicking between Piper and the ravine. His lips didn't move. Yet distinctly, she heard him say, *We'd have walked right into that.*

There was no question. If they'd stayed on their current path, they'd have ended up in the melee. They couldn't have hidden if they'd wanted to. Their horses were too big to miss.

There are hundreds of them, Piper thought. Not only because she could hear the tumult of shouts as the large group chased the runner, but because she'd seen this before. Quite clearly. In something like a memory.

Cameron nodded.

From above, there were more shots. More struggle. Whoever was being chased

(Simon, his name is Simon, and he should have kept his mouth shut)

(traitor liar greedy little shit, get back here)

(go around. I should run around to the far side, but then what if they think I'm running too)

(HAIL Andreus!)

Piper closed her eyes. Tilted her head down. Put her fingers to her temples. Words and high emotions were now a live show instead of a movie. She could sense Cameron beside her, probably watching with concern, but he wouldn't ask what was wrong because

(oh my God, we'd have walked right into that what if we'd done that. I'd have been responsible, all my fault)

because he surely had his own problems. And because

she was sure he knew damned well what was wrong with her; no need to waste breath, risk drawing attention.

The sounds came closer, the runner driven back around, funneled along the ravine's lip and back into his pursuers like draining water. There was no easy way down into the ravine

(*unless he jumps*)

(*Simon, you shit, you'd better not jump, you coward, you greedy fucker*)

but he wouldn't jump because it was still a good fifteen-foot drop with rocks at the bottom, and if he broke his leg and they fell on him, he'd be done.

Piper squeezed her eyes tighter shut. She was having problems keeping her bearings and remembering where she was. Was she running from the others? Was she chasing Simon?

No, she was down here, in the ravine, praying they'd stay hidden.

A single gunshot almost *directly* above preceded a voice: "I surrender. Take me back to the stockade."

Then: "I'll go quietly."

Then: "Donna. Help me out, Donna."

Donna, whoever she was, didn't or couldn't help.

Piper gasped at the sound then again when something struck the stream behind them.

A head. *Just* a head, no body attached.

A new voice above: "You two. Drag the body."

Then: "You. Go get the head."

Loose rock spilled down twenty tense seconds later. Maybe two dozen yards back, where the slope into the ravine was shallower. A tangle of roots gnarled behind Piper and Cameron, but not enough to shield two people and their horses.

Cameron climbed into his saddle so fast he nearly

spilled over. He didn't need to tell Piper to do the same. "Go!" he hissed.

The group was headed away, apparently dragging a headless body. The sound of the stream, if they were lucky, might drown their hoofbeats.

Still, Piper saw the man descending the bank before she turned forward and kicked her mount. She saw his head turn and heard him shout.

Chapter Twenty-Nine

"GODDAMMIT, TURN THAT OFF!"

"I'm trying. Hang on."

"FASTER, TERRENCE!"

"Almost. Almost."

"JESUS FUCKING—"

Vincent stopped midsentence. Trevor, watching, thought he looked almost comical. Vincent slept in boxers and a sleeveless white tee. He didn't have a hair on his head, and his frame was intimidating. Yet he managed to look like a flustered old man with his hair in tousles, wearing a flapping white nightgown: utterly baffled, standing in the room's center with his legs wide as if bracing for something. His eyes were wide, his hands out. His last words had come out after the alarm had ceased its blaring, and in the quiet, they were shockingly loud.

"Is it off?"

"Do you hear it, Vincent?" Terrence asked.

"*Permanently* off."

"I silenced it. But don't worry; I'll keep an eye on it."

"'Keep an eye on it?'"

"In case it wants to go off again," Terrence explained.

Dan emerged from the bedroom, rubbing his face with his palm. Dan had the old man thing going on even more than Vincent. He was probably in his fifties, by Trevor's estimation, and his hair was going gray at the temples, curly and too long, sticking up like a rat's nest.

"The fuck was that about?"

"Environmental alarm," Terrence said.

"Environmental? What, did someone forget to recycle?"

"Why would it go off again?" Vincent demanded.

"It won't. I'm watching it."

"But if you didn't watch it."

"Well, sure."

"Sure *what?*" Vincent sounded stressed and furious. They'd all been woken from a dead sleep. All but Lila. She was already in the control room, wedged up against one wall. It looked like she'd stepped aside to let Terrence in. He stood scrolling through menus and checking monitors in the small space. Why had she been out here so late? She looked almost guilty. Maybe she'd caused the alarm. She or Christopher, who was outside the room but looked like he'd fucked something up as well. Trevor looked toward him, but his eyes flicked away.

"It'll go off again if I don't watch it," Terrence said matter-of-factly, as if this had been no big, loud, panic-inducing deal.

"What *happened?*" Dan said.

Heather sprinted from her room. Trevor had come out the moment the alarm began to blare but had cast sidelong glances at the bed and other cot beforehand. His mom had been sleeping, twitching, seeming to miss the whole thing. Lila's cot had been empty.

"What's going on?" she demanded.

"Get in line if you want *that* question answered," Dan mumbled.

"It was an *environmental alarm*," said Terrence, his voice patient.

"Where did it go off?"

"Where the fuck do you *think* it went off, Vincent?" Terrence answered.

"*Topside!* Did it go off in the house?"

"I have no—" Terrence stopped midsentence and turned back to the controls, tapping screens, scrolling frantically.

"What's the big deal if it went off in the house?" Terrence was talking to Christopher, but Christopher was looking at Raj, who, ironically, seemed the most composed.

"He's thinking it gave us away," Raj said.

"Won't they just assume it's a house alarm?"

"Maybe." Raj shrugged. "But then again, the house has been open for months. And supposedly, the house doesn't have any power."

"Wouldn't an alarm have batteries?"

"It was only down here," Terrence said to Vincent.

"Yes, it would have batteries," Raj told Trevor, rubbing his face and yawning. "But Vincent hasn't figured out that the alarm not going off in the house is a bad thing."

Vincent's head snapped toward Raj. He looked like he was about to say something, but Terrence seemed to get whatever Raj was saying immediately. He was staring at the monitor feeds, tapping and zooming.

"Shit."

"What?" Vincent said.

"Shit. Shit mother*fucker*."

"*What?*"

"They heard it."

"What did they hear?"

Terrence swallowed. "The vents. The skylights."

"What the hell are you talking about?"

Terrence pointed at the monitoring screen. Vincent crowded in to look. Trevor pressed in behind him, Heather at his side. They were packed enough that he noticed his mother shivering. How could she be cold?

The screen was expanded to show the east lawn. The people camping there were moving slowly forward. Trevor was reminded of encroaching zombies.

"What are they looking at?" Heather asked.

"They heard it!" Vincent snapped. "The alarm. The goddamned alarm!"

"You said it didn't go off up top," Christopher said.

"Exactly." All heads turned toward Raj, and he took a half second before speaking to bask in his earned attention. "An alarm going off up there might be strange, but whatever. There's no power. An alarm would have a battery. Going off somewhere else, just loud enough to be heard from an unknown place? That's *much* more interesting."

"Where is this shot?" said Vincent.

"East."

He reached forward and flicked through screens. "They're all looking. Every camera. So they can't tell where it came from."

"Maybe they'll figure it out," Raj said.

Vincent ignored him. "The door is concealed. Locked. They can't get in."

"But now, maybe, they know there's something here. Another place, with an alarm."

"We knew there was a bunker," Vincent said.

"But you were also trying to get in here alone, while keeping the others at arm's distance. What did you suggest you were doing, if not breaking into a bunker hidden under the house? Did you let them think you were cracking a safe?"

"Nobody's getting in here."

"I'm not so sure." Raj pointed at the screen. Some of the people were getting closer to the cameras in their various locations, looking up, pointing. "They must all be hungry. They're clearly scared. They used to wander around, but now they're clustered. Since those big thumps, they've seemed scared shitless to me. Desperate maybe."

Lila shook her head. "You're not helping, Raj."

"Maybe we should go up," he said. "Plant something. Even if it's just a rumor.

"How exactly would *that* work?" Christopher asked.

"Got it," said Terrence, who'd been tapping around on another screen. "Auxiliary vent, south. Where is that?"

Trevor pointed. "That's south."

"I meant the vent."

"Hey, Terrence, how about you just explain what the shit you're talking about?" Vincent waved around. "Tell this fine group what's going on, before everyone loses it?"

Terrence sighed then looked around the group, Trevor first. "Okay. Look. We're in a sealed room. Sealed by design; that's what it's here for — to keep the outside out and the inside in. But we need air. I'll bet your dad has some liquid oxygen around here somewhere, based on the diversity of crazy shit he has stowed in that back room. Emergency use only, and very, *very* flammable. Dangerous if it's used wrong, for sure. We're all breathing outside air. Of course. Nothing wrong out there. So there's vents. A bunch of them; I'd need to study the schematics to have any idea where they all come up. And they're designed for redundancy. But we can't just sit down here and let gravity bring us air, because we're also filling this place with carbon dioxide.

Slowly, but we're doing it sure as anything. CO2 is as toxic as oxygen."

"Oxygen is toxic?" said Trevor.

"Corrosive, actually. That's where rust comes from. But again: *whatever*. This isn't a space mission; we're just underground. We need recirculating air. Like a furnace, even if it's not heating or cooling, though I'm sure the getup here is doing that, too. Problem is, you block too many inputs or outputs from that system, and it loses efficiency. We could choke to death on our exhales."

Lila looked white, hand near her mouth.

"No worries, little girl," said Terrence, using an expression only he could have pulled off. "There are failsafes aplenty. Your daddy thought of everything. Or his designers did anyway. We suggested blocking your vents to Morgan as a way to force you out — don't worry; we wouldn't have done it; just needed him to think we would — but there were problems. First, you all dying didn't help. We needed you to work with us, whether you wanted to or not. But the second reason was simpler: we couldn't find them all."

"So ..." Lila said.

"I doubt anyone's going to do enough damage to us without trying — or even *with* trying — to make us suffocate. But they can do shit like this." He tapped one of the screens, which showed a collection of tents like anywhere else on the grounds. Seeing it, Trevor thought of how, if these were the last days, the hippies had somehow managed to be the only ones able to mind their manners.

"See that big red tent there?" Terrence said.

Lila nodded.

"See that shed it's up against?"

She nodded again.

"Okay. Now look closely."

Lila did. After a moment, Terrence pointed at part of the screen as a hint.

"The tent material is sticking to the shed?"

Terrence nodded. "I'd guess that's Auxiliary Vent South. He's blocked it. No big deal, ordinarily, but shit, look at this place." He tapped another of the thumbnails, and they saw the house from above, presumably from a camera in a tree farther up one of the hills, looking down onto the grounds. The lawn was packed, almost edge to edge. A few curious pilgrims coming to Meyer Dempsey's Axis Mundi in hopes of being taken or meeting their celestial comrades had turned into a city, clotting the place and, apparently, taxing the bunker's breathing.

"There's no way they've blocked even half of the ins and outs," Terrence went on. "If I'd designed this place, I'd have put a few up high — especially outvents, where the breeze would draft gasses out without a fan. I'd have put ins on the most typically windward walls. Stuff like that. There's probably a few out in the woods, hidden under shit. So no worries for us. But the alarm, which is watching things more closely, feels different." He tapped the console.

Dan looked at Terrence, Heather, Vincent. "So the alarm went off because, what, the pressure got too low or high or something?"

Terrence nodded.

Trevor pushed closer. On the screens, many of the people who'd come forward at the screaming alarm were wandering away.

"They're letting it go."

"Yeah," said Vincent, turning toward Trevor. "But they'll keep wondering. I'll bet we get some more curious explorations in the next few days. Especially now that they seem to be avoiding the alcove near the lake. Whatever's over there makes them uncomfortable. And I'll bet they like the idea of being safe and protected a lot more than they used to."

"And," Terrence added, "the vents are still blocked. Give them time, and they'll block more, and I'll have to practically sit on the alarm to keep it from going off every ten minutes."

Trevor waited for more, but the room had gone quiet. A proposition seemed to have been set on the table, but Trevor wasn't catching it.

"So what do we do?" Lila finally asked.

"We go up," said Vincent. "And clear the decks."

Chapter Thirty

SHIT.

Cameron remembered the danger as if from a long-forgotten movie, never seen. The knowledge was simply there. He knew it in the way he knew his head was on his shoulders.

Footing in the creekbed was unsure. Cameron didn't have much experience with horses, but movies and books said you shot them when they broke legs. Stakes were higher now; if the horses faltered, they'd *all* be shot — two people and two mounts. Maybe the horses could gallop full-ass over the slippery wet rocks, but Cameron wasn't willing to risk it.

They were trapped. It would take time for the Andreus warriors to run back and inform Nicholas that there were intruders on their land who hadn't paid tolls in chattel or blood. It would be tricky to get ATVs and maybe even motorcycles down the slope into the ravine. But if they'd managed to descend on horses, the warriors would follow fine. Then, when they came from behind with their superior speed — driven to their quarry as if sliding down a funnel — the warriors would easily overtake them.

Cameron looked at Piper. A thought — clearly hers, inflected with her voice — hit him.

We have to leave the horses. We have to run.

A vision, as if from his own imagination: dismounting, grabbing their bags and gear from the horses' packs, then climbing the dirt walls, clinging to rocks and roots. Maybe, if they needed a boost, standing atop a horse's back if the animal could be made to stand still. The two of them running, now on flat land, maybe making for the highway. Flagging down a car. Finding a savior. Watching as the sun was eclipsed from above, looking up, seeing the enormous form of one of the alien motherships, hearing it talking, watching it —

It wouldn't work. He shoved aside the paranoia, focused on reality.

There weren't any motherships around here, but there were plenty of folks like those behind them. Cameron and the others had run into a few land posses on their way to Vail, but he'd had Vincent with him then. Vincent was a little crazy. A *lot* crazy. He had a way of turning impossible situations into wins simply because he was too stubborn for failure. He fought like an idiot. His remorseless tactics were cold, logical, almost perfect.

Even if they found the road, they probably wouldn't find a car. The roads were controlled. That's why they were sticking to the woods, following their shadows but never the roads themselves. Cameron had seen the folly of sticking to known paths in a dozen war-torn lands visited with his father, and the experience was reinforced shortly after the ships appeared on the Astral app.

They surely couldn't climb up and out, crossing the flat land on foot. If their pursuers had half a mind, they'd split into two groups. One would follow them into the crevasse like water down a river. The other would stay high, riding along and barring escape. They'd be much slower on foot — as easy to catch as Runaway Simon.

It won't work.

"Why can't we climb out and run?"

Even with his mount at a nervous canter, Cameron's heart tripping a rhythm almost as fast as the hooves, he paused at the question, thinking it odd. It was how he'd respond, if he'd done it aloud. Piper wouldn't be asking if they weren't somehow sharing thoughts — if she hadn't heard him say her idea wouldn't work. But that was impossible, so she'd included the supposition in the question, in case she was as crazy as Cameron.

"They'll see the horses. They'll know right where we stopped."

Now that she'd spoken, going back inside his head felt wrong. Not just illogical but ridiculous. *Of course* they hadn't been hearing each other speak without words. *Of course* they hadn't seen and heard through the eyes and ears of the Andreus warriors above. And *of course* they hadn't detoured — twice — before seeing that severed head, as if they'd known the future.

"The horses will keep going!" Piper shouted back. Beneath her, the horse slipped and nearly spilled, causing her to grasp its neck for balance. The animal stayed upright and recovered, delaying their decision another few seconds.

"They're exhausted! They'll stop, and those people will know right where we—"

Piper's head snapped back. She rode looking the wrong way, hands turning white as she gripped the reins too hard.

"They're down here now. With us," she said.

"And up top."

"Their own horses."

"Four-wheelers."

"And a truck up top, filled with—"

"You have a gun too!" She seemed to realize something and reached back. "And so do I!"

Two guns against dozens. Cameron and Piper weren't Vincent. They'd be turned to pulp. Decapitated. Their heads would probably be mounted on pikes as a warning: this land was spoken for, and none may enter.

He shook his head. *No.* They could defend themselves with guns, but only in the way honeybees used their stingers as a final defense: a last resort to do some damage before their inevitable deaths.

They couldn't go up.

They couldn't keep going straight.

And given the fact that they were already at the ravine floor, they sure as hell couldn't consider the final direction and go dow—

Or maybe they could.

They're close, Piper said inside his mind.

And then, frighteningly, seeing through the minds of those behind them: *We're close.*

But could their pursuers hear Cameron's and Piper's thoughts, as impossible as that was? His plan wouldn't work for a second if so. If they kept running through the ravine, they'd be caught. If they climbed to the right, they'd be caught. If they climbed to the left, they might buy themselves a minute or two. But in all likelihood, the Republic of Andreus would have sentries on that side as well.

It might work, and it might not. But they were running out of seconds to try.

A clock ran down inside Cameron's mind, its second

hand too fast, its sweep too urgent. They had to do it *now*. And there were still the horses to consider — the horses which, left to their own devices, would rather rest than continue to run.

"I'm sorry, girl," he whispered down the horse's neck, "but they'll take it out when they catch you." And maybe, if there was any justice in the world, get themselves kicked in the process.

Cameron kept a few things in his pockets at all times. And despite the fact that he hadn't been home for nearly half a year, old habits died hard. He reached into his pocket and pulled out the small key ring to his Chicago apartment: thumb lock and deadbolt. And a small mailbox key, for mail he was never in one place for long enough to receive.

He removed a key from the ring, gripping with his legs and trying desperately not to fall off as his mount moved beneath him. He reached back and shoved the key between the saddle and the horse's back, point down.

The horse whinnied, bucked, tossed its head.

Piper didn't need to be told what to do. She held her hand out to catch Cameron's keys. She did the same, seating the key far enough underneath the saddle so it wouldn't slip out or flip down flat.

Go. Now!

A nearly synchronous jump. Piper spun to one side and dropped, but Cameron was too hurried; he fell as much backward as sideways and caught a hoof to the chest as the horses ran on, kicking up, fighting the strange new pain under their saddles. Riderless, they might turn and run back the way they'd come, but Cameron didn't think so. The ravine was narrow. The only way to run from the spikes was forward.

Reeling, his breath kicked from his chest, Cameron still

managed to drag himself to the small creek's side. Piper was already there as he wheezed forward, trying not to clutch his chest and what might be a broken rib so he could dig. Piper was already shredding the root-strewn embankment, dragging autumn's leaves and spring's moss down in giant disgusting handfuls.

They didn't speak. Time was gone.

With the loose detritus cleared away, they made themselves tiny, tucking legs and arms, retracting their necks like turtles. They dragged the filth back atop themselves, becoming one with the fetid earth.

It took too long. Precious seconds. Cameron could hear his own heartbeat in his ears. He dragged in painful fits of breath, feeling suffocated as he melted into his blanket of moist leaves. Then it was done, and they waited. And waited.

The sound of engines. ATVs shambling through the creekbed.

The engines grew louder.

They couldn't run now if they wanted to. They'd never reach their guns, pressed against the embankment as they were.

Waiting was all they had.

Chapter Thirty-One

LILA HADN'T BEEN SLEEPING WELL. She woke from a dream of Piper barely rested, feeling as if she'd been running for hours at Piper's side instead of sleeping in the middle of …

… but who cared what time it was? Who cared if it was day or night? Who cared if the bunker was real or if that pleasure belonged to her visions? She knew all the answers but didn't care. Maybe it was all real. Maybe none of it was. Lila wasn't the only one coming apart. Her mother seemed just as threadbare. Jumping at the same shadows.

Trevor had finally grown himself a pair, but he'd become a different person since Piper's departure. Almost as if he'd been waiting for the cat to go so the mice could play. He spent all his time with Cameron's men (if they were, indeed, still *Cameron's* men; Lila couldn't remember if her dream showed Cameron dying or if he'd lived … or if it mattered since that was fake and the bunker was real), playing cards and shooting the shit. Sometimes, Lila wanted to point out that he wasn't a rough and tough commando but was still a teenage boy.

Lila rolled onto her side, head throbbing through a moment of vertigo.

Lila tried to find her center.

You're in a concrete box.

You're almost halfway through a pregnancy.

With some sort of demon baby maybe.

You're hearing and seeing things. Oh, and feeling deadly abdominal cramps.

Your baby-daddy has been a drama queen and asshole since he got here.

And Christopher …

Oh, right.

Lila really shouldn't have done that. She was eighteen now — officially an adult, old enough to know better. But that, too, was a joke. Her mother still let hormones pull her strings. Their parents didn't think Trevor or Lila knew they were still hooking up despite Piper, but neither was stupid. Dad talks to Mom on the phone all the time? Dad plans his trips around Mom's time in LA? Mom seems to know a lot more about this place — about Dad's so-called Axis Mundi — than an *ex*-wife should? Check, check, and double check. Lila, if she'd been forbidden to see Raj, could have covered her tracks better.

But despite being eighteen — despite knowing better — she'd done it anyway. Not *it*, exactly. Not that. The broom closet wasn't exactly the most romantic spot for that kind of encounter. But they'd made out plenty, and she'd had her top half off with her somewhat-enlarged boobs practically kissing the open air. Anyone could have come in and seen … and when that alarm had gone off, Vincent damned well almost had. She'd still been finagling her bra into place through her shirt by the time Vincent stormed into the living room, then toward the control room. Her nipples ached throughout most of the ensuing discussion.

It was odd and inappropriate, and Lila had felt sure she was responding poorly to the situation. She should have been focusing on their air intake problem and whatever Vincent had in mind to "clear the decks." Maybe she could have managed to be either excited or afraid at the prospect of heading up top, doing exactly what her mother had wanted ever since the ground thumping started.

But all she'd been able to think of was how she was still tingling — having some sort of boobs-and-body version of what Raj described as blue balls, when he'd been trying to guilt her into relieving his pressure with "at least a handjob."

Raj.

Yeah, that was a problem times two. First, Raj himself had become a fifth wheel. If they were topside, she'd probably have broken up with him by now. It would be fine; she'd thought she'd loved him, but unity had a way of driving people apart. Maybe it wasn't a fair test, but three months trapped in a post-apocalyptic bunker had brought out everything about Raj she'd only had a peek at before. He sulked. He complained. He was stubborn to the point of idiocy, like how he obsessed over futilely trying to contact his parents. He was a drama queen and a prima donna. And although Lila knew it was a sexist thought (or maybe a reverse-sexist thought?), she suspected her biggest problem with Raj was simply that he wouldn't *man up*.

Look at Trevor. Her brother had manned up so much, it was almost embarrassing in the other direction. He practically walked bowlegged now, to allow room for his enormous balls.

Vincent, Dan, Terrence, Christopher — those four had come through hell without blinking. And what's more, they sorta came through it *to save the Dempseys*. It was easy to be impressed.

Lila shouldn't have hooked up with Christopher. But she was pregnant. Her hormones were out of control, and her boyfriend was whining around in prissy little circles. It was hard to blame herself, no matter how guilty she felt.

Lila sat up on the cot, specifically avoiding a glance at the clock because buying into "surface time" would only raise her hopes. She hadn't paid attention to the last few attempts to contact Cameron and Piper for the same reason, and would plug her ears and say *LA-LA-LA* this morning if anyone tried. The dream was still too fresh. Probably more of that whole "going crazy" thing. The dream probably didn't mean she was seeing real things from Piper's yesterday. The fact that she'd woken around the time Piper and Cameron had—

(Got out of a car? Off horses? It was something like that.)

Whatever they'd done anyway. But seeing things didn't make them real. It wasn't like Lila could see the future, or already had. *Lucky guesses.*

And her baby was *not* talking to her. That was some rubber room shit right there.

With the last thought circling her mind, Lila looked defiantly down at her midsection, curling her back to properly stare. Lila had been a terror to her mother from time to time, and she supposed her baby would, once it graduated from uterus to diapers to mouthing off, be a terror to Lila. But that was years away, and she'd be damned if this kid would disobey her before it was even born.

There were no pains. No strange thoughts. Maybe those things would stay away if she kept her eye on the ball. If they did, Lila thought she might take back what she'd told Mom about the pains. She'd shared out of fear — but rather than getting her some much-needed motherly support, the news frightened Mom, too. Now she was afraid of the pains and terrified that her mother would lose her head and do something stupid, like charging upstairs and demanding to be let outside. *Like she'd already done.*

Lila rubbed her belly. Yes. Maybe things would be quiet. And if they were, maybe she could forget about it. Maybe it had been gas. Or false contractions. She'd heard that could happen.

And the voices? The visions? The way she'd felt all caught up and blurted something about "it's all beginning" without meaning to? The snippets of sound and songs? The expressions she'd never heard that ran around inside her head regardless? The seemingly psychic dreams — especially the one where she was descending a fathomless pit, underwater, headed toward some glowing, warbling light? That one came plenty during daytime.

Well, all of those things were signs of being stir-crazy. Perfectly understandable.

Lila stood, wondering if she was rationalizing.

Probably. But it might be better to rationalize and deny than admit she was nuts. They needed to get out of the bunker. And maybe, given what Vincent had said *(Yesterday? Earlier today? Before she'd slept anyway)*, they finally would.

Lila entered the living room, her feet plodding like a zombie, and saw Raj. He seemed more chipper than he'd been in days. He turned and gave her his old smile — the one he had before all this started. The smile that had made Lila fall in love. Now, it hurt to see. She'd only gone to second base with Christopher, but she'd have gone further. Worse: as her eyes flicked to Christopher, she found that she very much wanted to.

She smiled back at Raj as best she could, avoiding Christopher's gaze on her second sweep of the room, trying to find something else to feign interest in.

It wasn't difficult. Not once she turned her head and saw what was happening in the kitchen. Lila approached the table, eliciting welcoming nods from Terrence, Dan, and her brother, who was basically one of the Big Boys now.

Lila looked down at what Terrence was sketching on a sheet of paper then at the objects on the table. But she had to be seeing this ill-conceived plan all wrong. *Had* to be.

"You're kidding," she said.

"This is the best way." Terrence shrugged. "We need a distraction."

Chapter Thirty-Two

HER EYES COVERED by muck from the embankment, Piper's world was a curtain of confusing internal images. She seemed to hear more, see more, and lose herself in the unreal desolation.

She could see her own memories.

She could see other memories, from people other than herself.

And she could see what *they* saw, but only in bursts.

Piper was blind, and yet it seemed her eyes were open, seeing things she shouldn't be able to see, ears ringing with things they shouldn't be able to hear.

Wet soil pressed against the back of her shirt. It had taken a few minutes to soak through, but one minute split into two then expanded to five, and just as the engine noises were almost atop them, she began to feel the press of wetness all the way down to her skin. The leaves and gunk they'd spread on their fronts weren't as insistent in their filth; Piper really only wanted to cringe from the leaves that touched her face, certain for some reason that it was crawling with maggots and worms.

But she'd take maggots and worms from morning to night if this worked.

Engines came in bursts. The uneven terrain was strewn with rocks, branches, and other obstacles that the horses were able to surmount at a trot or canter. The ATVs, though (Piper was sure they were on ATVs; she kept seeing flashes from one driver's point of view, looking down at hands that weren't hers) weren't as nimble. They had to throttle up then back off. The going was faster than on foot, but not at full rip.

That thought made her wonder if they'd made the right decision. Maybe the horses were faster than the ATVs, given that brains were better than engines; feet could be picked up, but wheels had to roll. Maybe they'd have been able to outrun their pursuers after all.

Cameron's thoughts came at her, strung together in one long, unbroken, runon jumble: *if they see us i'll run the second they do maybe they'll chase me not see her they'll come after me if i just keep running and she can get away yeah that could work we won't both make it but at least one of us can and anyway it's fine i'm ready i'm ready i'm ready ...*

Piper tried to return a thought, but this was all so strange. First of all, she couldn't be sure any of it was happening. She'd never had an ounce of psychic inkling. She'd even taken one of those ESP tests once because a college friend had picked up a deck of testing cards somewhere. She'd managed to get fewer correct than dumb luck would have allowed, which led to jokes about how Piper must be psychic after all, to so perfectly avoid the right answers.

What she managed — fighting her thumping heart, as sure as Cameron that their minutes were numbered — felt more like a daydream. She had to think in a way that seemed "open" and hope he'd pick it up. He did, and she could feel it.

They won't even look at us. They'll follow the horses.

That much seemed true. She'd glanced back while Cameron had clawed his way to the bank, gasping for air. Hoof prints where the horses had stomped outside the creekbed were deep and plain. Piper doubted their pursers were watching the banks. They'd have their eyes forward, fixed on the prize. But knowing didn't make her feel better, and the wetness at her back felt like the cool hand of coming death.

But if they hear us … came his next thought.

We're not making any noise.

I hear you fine, said Cameron inside her head.

Piper doubted he'd ever been psychic either. Something had changed. They'd both heard the Andreus warriors before they spoke, and seen their thoughts. They'd wanted to turn from their normal trail not once but twice. As clear as it all was to Piper, it was hard to imagine that the warriors on their ATVs wouldn't home in on the two buried people without considering the horses.

The engine noises would stop as if they'd meant to park in front of them all along. And then, probably without even seeing their murderers coming, Piper would feel the blade. Or maybe she'd hear Cameron die first, before her own heart was stopped.

I'll run.

Don't run.

We shouldn't both die.

DON'T RUN.

The engines came closer. *Closer.* Now close enough to see, around the bend, if her face hadn't been covered in filth. It was maddening to know the men and women of the Andreus Republic (whatever *that* was; she only had their own thoughts to explain it) could see their hiding place, if they'd left any clothing visible, or if the leaves and gunk weren't as opaque as she'd thought.

Piper was suddenly sure that they'd been stupid to try this. They'd had minutes more than they'd thought. There had been more time to dig deeper, to cover themselves better. But they hadn't, and now the warriors were surely staring right at them like an indulgent parent might stare at the obvious form of a child hiding under her covers.

What's this big lump on my bed? There's clearly not a child here.

What are those two big lumps under the leaves and dirt on the south side of the creekbed? Har-har, those two kids sure are cute, running from us, thinking they could hide under nature's muck.

The engines came closer. A pulse then a break. Piper could hear at least three distinct sets of revs and releases. Three ATVs. That's all they'd sent? It didn't seem like enough. The rest must be on foot. Probably running behind or walking. Taking their time. Looking for what the ATV party might miss. But who could miss this? Two people-shaped humps in plain sight?

And oh shit, Piper hadn't even considered the way they'd *disturbed* the muck. It wasn't enough to be covered by leaves and grit. They'd had to rake the crap over themselves, upsetting the bank's set-in appearance. This had been stupid, stupid, stupid. Even if they were adequately covered, followers would see their position as clearly as a freshly dug grave in an otherwise packed-down field.

I'll run. They've seen us. Wait for them to chase me. They might not stop for you. Wait for them to go then climb up as planned. Go south. They might not have anyone that way, if you're lucky.

But the engines were winding down. Decreasing in pitch.

They were past. They'd gone by without seeing or

hearing them. Without sensing their thoughts, in the way they were sensing each other's.

But they couldn't surface even after the engines were sixty seconds distant, likely around the westerly bend in the ravine. They couldn't even peek. Not yet. Piper stayed rigid, and felt Cameron's mind intending the same. Because there might be more, perhaps a rear party ... or maybe those on the ATVs had seen them after all, but wanted to return slowly, stealthy enough to take them by surprise.

Piper was suddenly sure that's exactly what they were doing. Being cruel. Killing them quickly, in an obvious way, was too easy. Not as fun as piking heads.

A minute might have passed. Piper wasn't sure. Then maybe another.

Three minutes. Five?

Time stretched. Her heartbeat: insanity. Piper had no idea how long they'd been here, silent, waiting for nothing. She couldn't hear Cameron.

Cameron? she thought/said.

Piper didn't know if she was doing it right.

Maybe his throat had been silently slit by assailants.

She'd heard him until now. Something was missing. Wrong.

Cameron?

The engines seemed to have faded more quickly than they'd arrived. She tried to separate the sounds, but they were too far off to tell.

Maybe one had stopped.

The sound of water was hard to separate from other noises. Like approaching footsteps.

Cameron? Are you still there?

He wouldn't have been able to scream if the man who'd stopped his ATV and crept over on foot had pierced his larynx. But still, she'd have heard him struggle. She'd have heard the strike as the machete bit his neck. If the man who'd stopped had killed Cameron by slitting his throat, surely he'd have thrashed before dying.

Yes. She'd have heard that. Piper was blind, not deaf. If there was someone leaning over her — which there might be; her skin prickled in anticipation — it would have been hard for him to kill Cameron without alerting her. She must be imagining all of this. Getting paranoid. Fussing for nothing, winding herself up, driving herself crazy.

It was all in her head. The ATVs had all gone on. They were safe.

Cameron was fine; he was staying still, same as her.

So why couldn't she hear his mind anymore?

Because he's dead, that's why. Hard to hear a mind that's no longer working. And it'll be hard to hear anything at all when the man in front of you raises his blade again and—

Something struck Piper's shoulder.

Or grabbed. Something *grabbed* her shoulder.

A hand. A rough hand. The lone man who'd stayed behind, meaning to drag her out before killing her, to have some fun, now that they were alone.

Piper's thoughts turned crimson. She wouldn't scream. *She would fight.* She wouldn't just take it. She would —

The filth shook away, and Piper found herself looking into a man's hard stare.

Cameron's hard stare.

"I didn't … I couldn't …" she stammered. Then: "I thought you were …"

The ravine was empty. Piper was still mostly in her pocket of leaves and moss and mud. Cameron was in front of her, intermittently clutching his chest where the horse had kicked him, his face streaked with browns and yellows and grays.

They were alone.

He ticked his head up. This time, he had to speak aloud before she could hear him.

"Climb," he said. "Hurry. Before they come back."

Piper shook herself off, turned, and climbed the embankment, hearing the alteration in pitch as the distant engines changed direction.

Chapter Thirty-Three

"We make a fire," Terrence said.

"Oh, sure." Heather shrugged.

"In the air shaft," Terrence continued.

"Of course."

Trevor sat back in his kitchen chair. He was trying to be cool, to act like this was all very *of course* and *what must be done will be done*. But deep down, he wasn't feeling it. He was a fifteen-year-old kid, not yet legal to drive the caravan out of this post-apocalyptic hell. Though exceptions would probably be made. Alien invasion and all.

"Forgive me for asking," said Heather, "but isn't the air shaft where … oh, I don't know … where our air comes from?"

"Astute." Raj had already voiced his objections. Lila had argued with him for a while, which Trevor had found surprising. First of all, Raj wanted to go up top to scope the situation, and this was a way to do it. And second, Lila and Raj had been bickering a lot. Lila was, really, being kind of a bitch. She seemed to take sides against Raj just to do it. Trevor suspected she did it even when she kind of agreed with him.

She must be having her period. Except, wait. No, she wasn't having that. But other things were surely afoot, making her crazier than usual. Raj wasn't the only manifestation of Lila's new attitudes. Trevor worried about her more than he wanted to.

"It's the exhaust." Terrence looked at Heather. "If we set the fire far enough in, it should draft out."

"If," Raj said.

Lila shook her head, looking at her mother and Raj. "What's wrong with you two? I thought you wanted to go outside."

"I do." Heather said, although she'd surrendered much of her urgency over the last day. She wasn't ranting about how the thumping might herald Meyer Dempsey's return.

"This is the way," Terrence said.

"Setting a fire. Maybe you don't remember the fire we had before. The one that almost killed us? Oh, wait. No, of course you don't. Because you were outside, having set it."

"That was always controlled," Terrence said. "We knew the smoke would vent, and that it wouldn't burn long because the halon fire-suppression system would—"

"Oh yes." Heather touched her chin in mock thought. "That's how you planned to burst in here. By tricking us into trying to save ourselves *after* almost burning us to death."

"We're fine, Mom," said Lila, looking at Christopher.

"So you think this is a *good* idea?"

"I think it's the only way."

Raj said, "Because you have such an extensive engineering background?"

"I don't need engineering to understand how fire works, Raj!"

"Look," Vincent said. "We can't go out the front door anymore. There are too many people up there. And I don't care how much of Meyer's artillery we take — I'm *not* willing to go up top just to shoot our way through the crowds. I'm not too big on killing people who don't deserve it. But asking them nicely won't keep people from shoving their way down here when they realize what's under the house, and while I'm a hospitable guy, I don't think any of us want to share with huddled masses that might number half a thousand."

He looked around the group, waiting to see if anyone would argue. Nobody did. They'd discussed this at length. There was no way to pop the door and walk out, even in the dead of night. That had worked a few weeks ago and had worked to dispose of Morgan's body and create a false "the bad guys left" trail. But it wouldn't work now. Topside growth had been exponential. It was as if everyone was telling their friends, and their friends were telling friends. What they were all coming for or waiting on, Trevor didn't understand. His father's assertion that the place was his center in the world shouldn't make it magical for anyone else, and it didn't seem likely that the alien ships were going to keep returning on repeat. To Trevor, the hippies' mood above was a kind of group psychosis, not unlike the emperor's new clothes.

"So there's only one option, and that's to create a distraction," Vincent continued. "But it's kind of a Catch-22. We can't go up there to create a distraction because that means going through the same door they need to be distracted from."

Raj raised his hand. "I have a question."

Reluctantly, seeming to know he was taking bait, Vincent said, "Yes?"

"Can anyone explain why a man paranoid enough to

stockpile fucking *gas masks* and *plastic explosives*," he pointed at the heavy door to the arsenal, "wouldn't think to give his hidey hole a second entrance? Isn't that the first rule in the paranoid rulebook: Never get backed into a corner?"

"Nice way to talk about the guy who saved your ass," Heather said.

Raj ignored her and raised his eyebrows at Vincent.

Terrence answered. "The second exit *is* the air shaft. It's six-six in height and comes out in a little toolshed on the far edge of the property, back into the woods a bit. But they've clustered around its end, too. If we eliminate the grates and go out that way, we'll be seen just the same. And from what I can tell, it'll be a bitch to carry stuff out that way. You have to climb rungs set into the sides of a vertical shaft. We have that option in an emergency, but right now we need a distraction."

"And a fire is how we do it," Heather said.

"Yes." Vincent crossed his big arms and nodded slowly. "There's no fire suppression in the vent itself. We can set the fire far into it, keep the fuel wet to make it smolder more than burn. We'll make smoke. The fire will produce smoke that the corridor's natural outdraft will waft up the chute, through the shed, without flowing back into the bunker — as long as it doesn't burn too hot. We can put a few fans in the shaft, to increase the draft."

"As a bonus," Terrence said, tapping his sketch, "if we cut into the vent *here*, that should give us access to reach the ducts above that feed into the house. We build the fire here," again he tapped the schematic, "and the smoke should vent up into the house as well as to the shed."

"I thought we wanted it to *look* like the shed's on fire," Trevor said. "To draw attention?"

Terrence nodded, eyes buried behind his giant sunglasses. "Right. We want them going to check out the big column of smoke. And they will, because that's what people do. Fire is dangerous, but everyone wants to watch it burn. Routing some of the smoke into the house should set off the smoke alarms. Combine some smoke in one place with smoke and alarms in another. They should make the connection and leave."

"But won't they just go right back after they realize there's no fire? And won't the smoke give us away when they notice nothing in the house has burned? How will we get back? If we're out there for even an hour, people will go back inside, won't they?"

These were the tips of Trevor's questions. They also had no idea what they'd find when they surfaced, and Vincent had been mum on what exactly qualified as "clearing the deck." They needed the bivouac shantytown to disperse so they'd stop clogging the bunker's air intakes (and allow its occupants to occasionally go outside), but right now the plan was about sneaking and hiding. What came next?

But one issue at a time.

"We go down the shaft," Vincent answered.

"You mean the shaft with all the smoke?" Heather asked.

"After we're up, Dan will douse the fire," Terrence said. "The people camped around the shed will have found another place to hang out because all their shit will smell like smoke. We won't be able to get back in through the house without being seen, but we should be able to sneak back in through the vent. We'll be lighter, so the ladder won't be a problem."

"What exactly are you planning to carry in the first place?" Raj sounded as if he might already know.

"It's no problem," Vincent answered. "Christopher and I will carry it."

"That's not what I asked."

"All told, the risk is low," Terrence said, ignoring Raj. "We already know the shaft drafts pretty well, and fans in front of and behind the fire will make it draft even better. The outvents are surely concealed — we know that because no one's come down here. The schematics show a rather large trapdoor on that end, concealed and locked with a system like the one on the main entrance. If I'm reading the plans right, air drafts out through something like two dozen smaller vents concealed to look like a primitive sort of baseboard heat system in the shed, and the chimney. It should look plenty on fire. And like I said, we can always put it out."

"I have a question." Again, Raj raised his hand. "What are you planning to do when you're up there?"

Vincent didn't look over at Raj.

"Let's get started," he said.

Chapter Thirty-Four

CAMERON SLEPT FEARFULLY THAT NIGHT. He didn't show his fright to Piper, so she fell asleep beside him, exhausted more than peaceful.

They'd avoided the highway throughout the rest of the day just as before, but this time they both seemed to agree without speaking that they should avoid all other traces of humanity. Doing so was easy. The mountains and woods seemed to sprawl forever. As long as they didn't cross Route 70 and followed the setting sun, they were heading in the right approximate direction. Cameron wasn't worried about getting lost. He'd traveled many nameless roads in the world's corners both with his father and alone — places where GPS was worthless and maps were suspect. When attempting a return to his father, after the networks fell silent, he'd had to revisit those skills.

A person soon learned that the adage was true: Whatever didn't kill you made you stronger. Literally: It seemed to take something maliciously trying to *kill* you to knock most people down. Those new to "surviving" as a bare-bones standard often fretted over food and clothing and small comforts like toilet paper. They'd sweat predators, infection, exposure. Those things were worth minding, of course, but in Cameron's experience, the biggest threats were more obvious. Far more black and white.

Today, if he had to guess, most people were finding shelter and living a stripped-down version of their old lives — perhaps a *very* stripped-down version, where "survival" ended up being enough. Others were living high, building their own little groups like the Andreus Republic, scavenging what they could. Maybe a bunch were still in cities, going about their business as if little had changed — because when you got right down to brass tacks, not much had, except for the families of abductees.

What was being done to the world today was mankind's doing, not the aliens'.

They'd managed to evade their pursuers, who seemed to have given up after losing the trail. Those people hadn't managed to kill them as they'd killed the runner, Simon. So now he and Piper were stronger. They were alive. Little else mattered. They'd head west, then follow 70 close enough to reach Moab. Cameron knew the way from there.

Their eschewing of all human contact had left them light on supplies and needing shelter, but the air wasn't overly frigid, and they'd found a spring for water. They'd survive. He'd be cold if he'd made this trip alone — burying himself under whatever he could find, but cold nonetheless. Fortunately, he'd brought a heater: Piper. And she had him for a heater as well.

They slept without dreams.

Cameron woke before dawn. He'd passed the night in fits, unable to get comfortable even with Piper wrapped around him. The woods were filled with sounds, but still things seemed too quiet. Whatever strange connection they'd shared, it was gone. Cameron found he missed hearing her thoughts. They'd been a warm hand, soothing scars he didn't dare show.

Piper blinked then slowly sat up.

"Morning," he said.

"*Is* it morning?"

Cameron pointed at the eastern horizon, which bore the barest blush of violet. In the otherwise black sky, that smear of color was almost bright.

"That's not morning. Wake me when the coffee is ready."

Cameron sighed. "We're going to need to find transportation today."

"I hope you brought a bus schedule."

"I miss the horses. They're faster than we are and don't force us to eat as much to sustain our energy. And they consumed a naturally renewing source of food."

Piper blinked around, fighting sleep. Cameron repressed an inappropriate flash of attraction as he watched her, telling himself that it was their tight situation causing it, rather than anything genuine.

"Can we find other horses?"

"I'm sure we could. I just can't help but feel we should pick up the pace."

"Why?"

"Just a feeling."

Piper nodded. Cameron didn't need to explain. During the previous day's odd mental acrobatics, they'd both sensed something as indistinct as the foreboding felt while looking at the cluster of three trees. A sense of being watched — of something unseen ducked out of sight milliseconds before they spun their heads to catch its eyes upon them. During the worst of their pursuit, the sensation had been too much in the background to mind. But once in the clear, their connection had broken. It felt pressing, causing them to look back. Especially up, as if their watchers might be arriving from above.

"We could get a car."

"No roads." Cameron shook his head. "Who would drive a car right now? Haven't you ever seen any disaster movies? Everything bad happens when people try to drive."

"Meyer drove us from New York," Piper said sheepishly.

Cameron looked away. "Well. I'm sure it made sense at the time." And hey, maybe it did. "Before panic, roads were fine."

"What then?"

"Those ATVs were pretty nifty. Where do you think we can get one?"

"You aren't worried about the noise?"

"Actually," Cameron said, "I was wondering where we'd find one. But now that you bring it up, yes, I'm worried about the noise. Also, I don't suppose you know where we can find a glider plane?"

Piper shrugged. A cute gesture — sarcastic without being pandering.

But he should stop this.

Their banter was annoying. If two other people had been doing it and he'd been watching, he'd have told them to knock it off. No flirting with the big man's wife. Because that's what Meyer Dempsey was, even if nothing else: a big man. An *important* man. Cameron knew Benjamin was right when he saw the throngs flocking to the place of Dempsey's abduction. Meyer wasn't the only one who'd sensed something about that place, and even if no one in Moab knew what he'd sensed, it didn't change the fact that he had, and had built a home there. His abduction wasn't coincidental. The sooner they found out *how* or *why* Meyer and Vail were important, the better.

Cameron picked up his rifle and slung it back over his shoulder, rubbing the spot on his chest that seemed to be a bruise rather than a broken rib.

"Horses then."

Piper looked up. "What? You want to go now?"

"Do you want to stay for the continental breakfast?"

"But it's barely light."

Cameron peeked at the bandless watch he kept in his pocket — his great-grandfather's timepiece still ran, though he'd never bothered to make it suitable for his wrist. Before the networks fell, it always made more sense to check his phone for the time. Well, the joke was on the world. Granddaddy's watch still had a purpose other than sentimentality after all.

"We've slept nine hours."

"Nine hours!" Piper stretched. "I don't believe you."

Cameron found himself wanting to banter back as she smiled playfully at him in the scant predawn light, but he forced himself to look away, now snugging the rifle.

As if on cue, Piper's stomach grumbled.

"I guess I don't need to remind you we don't have any food. We could go scavenging for mushrooms, but I think it's worth following a surface road a bit and looking for a farm. If we can find an abandoned one that had horses, they'll probably still be in the barn. Two birds, one stone. We need transportation either way, so we can look for any leftover supplies while we're daring to approach a man-made building. And if there's no food in the pantry, maybe they'll have cows. I'll milk them to get us some calories if I have to." Cameron shrugged. "Way I figure it, when people abandon a place, they probably don't think much about their chores."

"Why would you abandon a perfectly good farm?"

Cameron didn't want to answer. The chances that a farmer would simply leave seemed slim, but the odds that the farmer could have been killed or dragged away were plenty robust. And besides, when people panicked, many moved around. If he didn't know better, Cameron would have thought the same about Meyer rushing his family across the country when the ships had appeared on Astral. Why not stay where he was? It made no sense. But that was humankind for you, always looking for greener grass.

"Let's just see what we can find," Cameron said.

It took them until the sun was fully up to come across the first farm's back fence: an obvious no-go. They stayed low, Cameron wishing he had the binoculars that had been in his backpack with the rest of his gear. But even from this far they could see a pair of armed sentries. They moved on, stomachs grumbling.

The rest of the morning passed without luck. There were other houses in a cluster near the farm, but it was obvious that either the same group controlled the entire area or homeowners had held their claims. There were a few abandoned places without barns or leftover food or supplies worth taking, and a few that seemed to be out in the middle of nowhere — ancillary barns to a larger claim, perhaps. Two of these contained tractors, but Cameron laughed at the idea of taking them. Speed or stealth, tractors served neither goal. But one barn did net them a dusty old backpack and a few discarded, empty water bottles for carrying sustenance once they found it. They each also took a machete from the walls, neither commenting on the irony that they'd nearly been killed with machetes not even twenty-four hours earlier.

On and off, Cameron pulled out his radio. The batteries would only last so long, but it turned out that power, at least for the moment, wasn't the problem. He'd programmed the radio with open frequencies, but communication with Vail had thus far proved impossible. They could hear chatter. Ninety percent was military. But in dead spaces, Cameron tried raising the bunker, using the call signs and codes he'd worked out with Vincent before leaving, trusting Terrence's antenna modifications in Vail to do its job. But there had been almost nothing.

"Any luck?" Piper asked as he returned the radio to his belt.

"Lots. But I still can't raise them. It's strange."

"Do you think they're okay?"

Cameron hadn't a clue. And considering the care they'd taken to ensure they'd be able to communicate, the lack of response made "they're not okay at all" the most reasonable explanation for the silence. But he kept quiet. It could be anything: sunspots, maybe even that double line of Carnac stones they'd crossed that had scrambled their thoughts so completely. Maybe they were fine. And they'd stay that way, with Vincent and Terrence in charge. Even Dan would give his life for them. He'd damned near given his life for Cameron enough times before they'd rendezvoused with Vincent and Terrence.

"Of course," Cameron replied with a smile he didn't entirely feel.

At one point, they passed a winding mountain road, looking around and ducking past at a section without traffic or residences. In the far distance was a roadblock. Piper said there was a tank among the blockade's mess, but Cameron hadn't been able to tell and wasn't about to head in for a closer look.

When the sun was high, they finally found what they were looking for. A small farm tucked back on a spur — an off-jut of a road that was itself a rutted, dirt-covered off-jut. The porch was covered with cats, and the house empty. To Cameron, it felt *left* rather than *raided*. There were no signs of intrusion. They themselves had barely found it, tucked behind two hills as it was.

No, whoever had lived here had gone somewhere else — to find Grandma in Utah, to meet up at a bigger farm with lots of supplies, protection, and company. There was no way to tell, and Cameron didn't care. There was mold-covered bread in the pantry. Boxes of cereal had been split open and littered the kitchen: the work of rodents, who in turn were keeping the porch cats fat and happy.

Anything perishable had long since rotted, but there were plenty of cans, a hand-operated can opener, and even some unaffected dry goods. It was enough food that it hurt to leave, but there was only so much two people could carry. They found a pair of good backpacks and raided the house for anything portable and necessary. They drank from a spigot in the yard and filled their bottles. There was nothing in the way of survival gear, but Cameron counted them lucky, happy to at least not starve for a while.

Once packed, they returned to the barn, where they found three horses and a goat. The goat seemed to have escaped and dragged a bag of feed to almost within the horses' reach. The horses didn't need it; the farmer had left them in the pasture with enough grass and water from low spots and puddles. But they'd eaten all they could reach anyway.

Piper helped Cameron saddle two of the horses. They mounted and prepared to ride.

At the door, Cameron, feeling a strange pang of something unarticulated, looked back at the lone horse. They'd opened the gate to let it leave, but it wasn't going anywhere.

"It's stupid," Cameron said to Piper, "but I feel bad taking two of them and leaving that horse all alone."

Piper shrugged. "He's got the goat."

Cameron looked at the goat and then the horse.

"Horses like goats," Piper explained.

The goat bleated.

"Then I guess this is a win," Cameron said.

They left the barn and headed true west, checking the position of Route 70 first to reorient themselves before heading out in earnest, double time.

Cameron couldn't shake the feeling that the clock — now more than ever — was ticking.

And he couldn't shake the sense that they were being watched by unseen eyes, attached to strange hands with unknown intentions.

AVA GLASS, DOMINIC TRAIN

Chapter Thirty-Five

LILA WATCHED, feeling tired, while Terrence, Vincent, and Dan moved aside a large freestanding shelf at the far end of the living room and pried at what turned out to be an enormous grate. She hadn't noticed it before, but that had surely been the intention. Her father was equal parts practical and aesthetically minded. He wore bespoke suits and bought the best things he could afford chiefly because he could afford them. It made sense that, even needing a back door to his bunker, he'd hidden it with grace. The shelf unit did a good job of hiding the vent because they were made of the same shiny silver metal, and the vent simply looked like the unit's back. But the shelves were barely stocked, so the air flow wasn't blocked. Form and function, perfectly married.

But with the unit out of the way, the vent came off easily using only Vincent's fingers. There were no bolts holding the thing in place — presumably because if you needed to flee through the vent, you wouldn't want to be held up just because you hadn't thought to grab a screwdriver.

The vent's interior looked like three-quarters of an oven's inside. The floor was concrete, probably because the bunker itself was a big concrete shell. The walls, however, were bright, reflective silver metal, like the air ducts in her grandmother's basement. It was tall enough for Vincent (the group's tallest) to stand without ducking, and slightly narrower in width.

Christopher was sitting across from Lila. It had seemed okay to sit with him because when she'd first sat, Raj had been at the table too. She'd merely wanted to get some food in her before whatever happened happened. But then Raj had left, and she'd found herself alone with Christopher, their hands almost near enough to touch.

"Should you be helping?"

Christopher shrugged. "They've got it."

Lila looked. Vincent had already sliced a hole in the roof of the thin metal twenty feet or so down the corridor-like vent and was now standing on a stepladder with his head and arms above the ceiling, his top half invisible.

Lila's eyes ticked toward Raj's room. It didn't make sense for him to be in there now, so he'd be coming back out. She was just sitting at the same table where he'd left her, but she couldn't shake an awkward feeling at the thought of Raj seeing them alone.

"You know," said Christopher, "I can tell this is making you nervous."

"Oh?"

"I just want to make you feel better."

"Thanks," she said. But truth be told, Lila wasn't feeling it. Things had been hot and heavy with Christopher for a while there, and the way they'd been broken up had left her hungry for more. For half a day afterward, he'd been tossing her looks that — again — accelerated her heart and constricted her jeans in a way that had nothing to do with a slowly growing belly.

But now she felt conflicted.

Between Vincent and Terrence's explaining and implementing their plan, Lila had lain on the couch, and Raj had brought her two pillows: one for her head and another to prop between her legs if she chose to lie on her side. It was the simplest, nothing kind of gesture, but his offer and delivery had been somehow touching. For once, he hadn't struck her as self-pitying. The way he'd slunk away had seemed defeated instead, and it dawned on her all at once that she'd been as big of a bitch as he'd been an asshole. She'd called him back, and he'd sat on the floor in front of her, guilt churning her gut as she'd run her hands through his dark, coarse hair, like she used to do when the world had been different.

"Can I get you anything?" Christopher asked.

"No. Thank you."

"Anything to drink?"

"I'm good."

He watched her for a second, his green eyes magnetic and smile charming. There was an innocence in his gaze that was hard to turn from. He'd done nothing wrong. Lila had. And worse, she kind of wanted to do it again. *More than kind of.*

"How are you feeling?" he asked.

"I'm fine."

"Your ..." He nodded toward her stomach. "You know. How's your ... how's he or she doing?"

"You know?"

But then really, how could he *not* know? Her mother knew; Trevor knew; Piper had known. Trevor must have said something. They were all buddy-buddy, so that seemed logical. Still, Lila felt violated. She wasn't showing much yet, and it should be her choice to tell others matters of her own body not her brother's. Especially when the person in question had already explored some of her body, and she'd spent time in the shower imagining him exploring the rest.

"Yeah. Is that okay?"

"Of course," she lied.

"So?"

"Fine, I guess."

"Because you seem tired."

"Tired how?"

Christopher shrugged. "Just tired."

"Bad tired?"

"No, no." He smiled. "*Beautiful* tired."

Lila tried to smile back.

"Look," she said. "About the other day."

Christopher smiled wider. "What about it?"

Lila wanted to say that it wasn't a good idea but couldn't. If she said it, he'd probably stop trying to get into her pants. She hadn't wanted Raj in her pants lately, despite the four-month package he'd deposited there, and sometimes that felt like a stubborn shortcoming, especially when thinking about Christopher. But they were all trapped here together, and it was probably a bad idea to mix business and pleasure, if that's what it was. On the flip side: Was it really her fault that aliens had come and forced her and her boyfriend to live together? She might have dumped him by now, and could play with Christopher all she wanted. It wasn't fair.

"Nothing," she said.

Lila remembered the way Raj had brought her the pillows. The sad way he'd slunk off. The way she'd called him back. The feel of his hair between her fingers. The girlish dreams she'd had a lifetime ago, of how they'd live happily ever after with their accidental child, and damn her father's judgments.

"You okay?" His eyes flicked toward where Raj had vanished, then dared to lift Lila's chin and meet her eyes. Another check of the room, and then he let her chin drop.

"I'm fine."

"You're sure?"

"Jesus, Chris, do you really think I'm this fragile?" she snapped.

Christopher blinked.

"I'm sorry." But she wasn't. Lila was Meyer Dempsey's daughter. She was strong. She didn't need boys — *any* boys — to hold her upright and keep her from fainting. Or possibly swooning.

"It's totally fine. No worries."

Dan passed, walking toward the vent with an armful of cloth. He looked over, nodded to his burden, and said, "Rags and shit. You don't mind, do you?"

"Why would I mind?" Lila pulled away from Christopher. She registered a small hurt look; he'd been reaching for her hand, and she'd yanked it away. She hadn't broken anything off with him, if there was anything to break off, but Christopher wasn't stupid. He'd seen her moment with Raj. He couldn't be this bad at reading emotion.

He knew what she was thinking. And as unfair as it seemed in the moment, Lila felt another layer of guilt descend upon her.

"They're *your* rags and shit," said Dan.

"I don't mind."

"There's also some wood we want to use. Happens to be a broken stretcher from a painting. I rolled the painting up and left it in the storage room. I assume that's okay too?"

"What was the painting of?"

"Landscape."

Lila shrugged. She didn't care. Why her father had stocked his bunker with paintings in the first place was a mystery. But that was Daddy again: form always married to function. If he was going to have a place to spend the end times, it would have to be posh.

"But the frame thing is already broken."

"Yeah."

"So you're asking me if I care about a pile of wood shards."

"Yeah."

Lila waited to see if Dan was kidding. He kept watching her.

"I don't care."

"Thanks," he said, heading for the vent.

Christopher rose. He did a fair job of making the motion look casual, but Lila could tell he'd grown uncomfortable.

"I should go help."

"Sure," Lila said.

Watching him go, Lila realized she still had no idea if she wanted to be with him or break it off. Regardless, she couldn't stifle concern.

Christopher was going up with the others while she stayed down here, and for some strange reason, Lila couldn't shake the feeling that after he went through the door into the house above, she'd never see him again.

Chapter Thirty-Six

CHRISTOPHER SNUGGED his backpack straps and nodded up to Vincent standing at the top of the spiral staircase, his hand on the manual latch Terrence had installed after they'd drilled through the door's original defenses.

After getting the fire going with a splash of generator gas (stored away from the room they'd burned coming in; Meyer Dempsey thought of everything), Dan had laid a few of the dampened rags in the flames, being careful not to smother it. That had smoked like crazy. It smelled like old laundry … because, Christopher supposed, that's exactly what it was.

The fire had been going for fifteen minutes. It had only taken ten for the smoke to build to epic proportions on the surveillance screens — enough to catch the eye of the first weirdo up top and get him shouting to the others. Terrence had been right that some people had set their wacky shanties around the shed, but they all seemed to gather on the lawn with the others during the days. What they all did to pass the time while waiting for the second coming of

E.T. Jesus, Christopher couldn't imagine. Sing "Kumbaya," probably. Shake maracas. Bang tambourines. Wear tie-dye headbands. Shit like that.

Once the hippies had seen the smoke, the crowds had moved off the lawn and toward the rising column.

At that point, Terrence had removed the metal flap covering the hole Vincent had cut in the vent's ceiling, allowing a line of smoke to plume inside the home. They'd watched that happen onscreen, too. Watching on the monitors had felt to Christopher like watching a practical joke in process: knowing the hammer was on its way before the victim fell into the trap.

Alarms screamed. People in the house looked up, saw the smoke, and ran. In the bunker, they'd laughed at the topsiders' comic flight. Now that the house was empty and the commune had moved out to watch the shed fake-burn (and what they'd think of the lack of flame, Christopher could only wonder), phase one was green-light-go. Time for phase two.

He caught Lila's eye. She gave him a little smile. Then Christopher caught Raj's eye, and got a flash of stink-eye. Raj hadn't trusted any of them from the start. Or rather, he just hadn't liked them. Maybe because Raj had once fancied himself the man of the house — although really, *that* was hard to believe. Piper had been the man of the house. In her absence, Heather was probably the leader, or maybe Trevor. Not Raj. Christopher knew his type. He was the kind of guy with lots of opinions and no action.

Raj sure hadn't "acted" when Christopher fondled his girlfriend's tits.

That wasn't *exactly* fair. Raj didn't know he was a cuckold. Nor was he to blame. The kid was who he was, just as Christopher was who he was. Just like Lila was who *she* was. It was hard to fault Raj for falling apart in a crisis or for having his doubts.

At the same time, it was hard to fault Lila for the conflict she seemed to feel about their budding relationship. Because really, Christopher thought, if Lila *didn't* have doubts and conflict, he wouldn't want to be with her. She wasn't a skank. Lila was trying to do the right thing, especially considering the jilted party was her baby's father. Christopher couldn't blame Lila — or resent the way she'd seemed to lean on the issue a moment ago, hurtful as the moment had felt.

She'd come around in time.

"Let's go," Vincent said. Then, without waiting, he pushed the door open.

Feeling the home's open air after their time underground was strange. It made Christopher feel sort of buoyant despite the phase two task at hand. He could only imagine what it would be like for Lila, Trevor, Heather, and Raj, who'd been in that hole for nearly four months. Probably feel damned near euphoric. Trevor, for one, had practically begged for a mission. He couldn't come up just yet, but that was why they were here — to pave the way for Trevor and the others *later* — after phase two was finished.

Christopher slipped the pistol from behind his back and held it at his side. Not pointed but ready.

"No gunfire." Vincent didn't whisper because the smoke alarm was too loud.

"I'm just keeping it ready," Christopher said.

Vincent looked at Terrence then nodded. The two of them didn't have to go over any of this. They'd worked together for years and had a quasi-psychic thing going on. Maybe a bit of a *gay* thing going on, Christopher sometimes thought. Regardless, they both seemed to feel the need to tell Christopher things that the others took for granted. Same with Dan, and Cameron when he'd been around. Only Christopher got extra instructions, extra warnings, extra reminders of things everyone else was assumed to get without being told. It was a little annoying. But again: They'd been together when he'd met them, so it made sense even if it was obnoxious. They knew he hadn't really been a full-on member of Morgan's gang, but that didn't change the fact that they'd *found* him with Morgan. Their interpersonal cues simply weren't as developed yet.

"Okay," Vincent said. "But remember, the idea is to stay invisible. Reconnaissance and setting up, that's all. Any of us discharges a weapon, we'll draw attention, and that changes everything. It makes it harder to get back inside. People who hear it will be on edge — not just now, but from here on out. And we all know that would be a problem. Cool?"

Again: *Cool?* on the end. Without the "cool," it was merely a mission reminder. The reminder would have been for Terrence as well — but the little "cool?" addendum had been Vincent checking in one more time. Making sure Christopher wouldn't screw up.

But had he screwed up yet? No, of course not. Not once.

"Cool," Christopher agreed.

Vincent left the kitchen, moving onto the porch, staying low. It was a calculated risk to surface in daylight, but one Christopher had agreed with from the moment the four of them had started planning, and something about which he'd toed the company line in the public version recited to the family. Without daylight, it would be easier to hide … but without daylight, the smoke would be invisible. No distraction, no mission. So daylight it was.

There were a few idiot looky-loos from inside the house who'd gone out to watch the house "burn" instead of moving to the shed. Christopher and the others moved around to the home's rear, then sneaked away and were at the tree line seconds later.

Things got easier from here. No one would know they'd come out of the house even if they got caught. That was half the battle. Heading back in through the shed should be easy, especially if they waited for nightfall. Even if they were spotted, they could pretend to be anyone — newcomers even. Or maybe they could don gray suits and pretend to be aliens. These stupid people would believe anything.

But they were also moving away from the human clot, and that made things easier, too.

They skirted the lake to the off-screen alcove where they'd seen everyone gather after that initial THUMP. The way they'd all run down here that day, it was as if Jesus (again, E.T. Jesus) had jumped down here and demanded worship. That hadn't lasted long. Shortly afterward, the hippies had moved from interest in whatever was here to active avoidance. Just like they would with the fire: they'd run to it, knowing it could hurt them, like lemmings. Then they'd leave, and steer clear of the reeking smoke.

The alcove was like that: first interesting, now deserted.

"Start recording," Vincent said as they neared it, still unable to see what waited behind the trees.

Terrence touched the device mounted above his sunglasses, finally useful out here in the sun. "Recording."

"You give a verbal time index?"

"There's a time index on the file sixty times each second, Vincent."

"Manually."

"Why would I do it manually?"

"To index it, asshole."

"The *file* indexes it, Vincent."

"Jesus, Terrence. Just say the time, and make me happy."

"Okay. 'Fourteen twenty-seven p.m.'"

"What day?"

"Tuesday, I think."

"Day of the *year*."

Terrence was rolling his eyes, so Christopher stepped in front of his face, front and center on the camera above his sunglasses. "Hi, everyone, thanks for tuning in today. I'm Christopher Green, and I'll be your host for the reveal of whatever the fuck the frightened villagers saw. It's Tuesday at two twenty-seven PM, and—"

"Fourteen twenty-eight now," Terrence corrected.

Fourteen twenty-*eight*, and —"

"Shut up, Christopher. Terrence, start a new file. Delete that one."

"That's not how it works," Terrence said.

"You can't delete and start again?"

"It's repurposed surplus. I figured I'd just cut it up when we got back inside."

"Well, shit."

"Who exactly are you trying to impress with this dramatic footage, Vince?"

Vincent looked at Christopher. Possibly because he didn't like being called 'Vince' and possibly because the question was valid. This footage wasn't for posterity. It was for the people in the bunker since the trio hadn't allowed them to come topside in person. Posturing as if they were doing the moon landing was stupid and self-important — two things Vincent was usually bigger than.

"Okay, fine. Let's go."

They moved forward through the trees. When they reached the clearing, Christopher felt his breath stop. He couldn't say why, but it caught in his throat nonetheless.

He fell back a step, staring at the titanic stone finger pointing straight into the sky.

Chapter Thirty-Seven

"WHAT IS THIS?" Christopher said.

"It's a rock." Vincent shrugged, unimpressed. "I figured we'd find a weapon or something. *This* is what they were so worked up about?"

But Terrence, at least, seemed to respect the thing. He moved forward and touched its surface. With, Christopher thought, something like reverence.

"Quartz. Feldspar," he said.

"Bless you."

"It's granite."

"So what?" Vincent shrugged.

"What's it doing here? It has to weigh hundreds of tons."

"That's fantastic. Let's make countertops."

Terrence had made a half circle around the stone, looking up, letting his mounted camera take it all in. He reached the stone's side and jumped as if goosed.

"What?" Vincent's hand flinched toward his gun.

Terrence turned and pointed. "Check it out."

Behind him, partially concealed by the trees, was a

second massive stone, and he'd jumped when moving between them, as if shocked.

Christopher didn't want to stand between the granite fingers as Terrence had. Vincent stood farther back, avoiding them even more. The straightest path toward the second stone was directly between them, but Vincent and Christopher were hugging trees rather than using it.

"You getting all this, Terrence?" Christopher asked.

"Getting it."

"Fascinating footage," Vincent said, thick with sarcasm.

"You don't think so?"

"Rocks. I've seen rocks before."

"Look at the ground, Vincent." Terrence pointed. The soil and spare grass looked like a bunched-up rug at the thing's foot. "These were dropped here. Or *stuck* here, or something. Like Cameron said, about the pyramids and stuff."

"I like Cameron fine. Anyone who's right with Benjamin is right with me. But … *the pyramids?*"

"You're questioning *Cameron* talking about that stuff and then citing *Ben* as your frame of reference? Do you remember when everyone thought Ben was crazy, before all this happened?"

"Motherfucker, I *still* think Ben is crazy."

"What are you guys talking about?" Christopher asked.

Vincent waved the question away. "Before you hooked up with us. It's nothing."

"Except that it's *not* nothing." Terrence turned to Vincent. "It's the reason we were sent here in the first place."

"No, it's not," Vincent argued. "We came to get what Cameron needed to know about Meyer Dempsey."

"Who is special *because* ..." Terrence made *come on now* gestures with his hands. Christopher assumed he was trying to get Vincent to admit that aliens were real — something he seemed reticent to do based on the stones. As if he'd forgotten that Earth had already welcomed an alien fleet.

"Okay, fine." Vincent looked up. "Aliens dropped big rocks down here. Despite not being anywhere around."

"Just because there's no ships in the sky now doesn't mean they weren't when these stones were placed."

"There was nothing on the cameras."

"The cameras don't show much sky," Christopher said.

Terrence gestured at Christopher for Vincent's benefit, declaring a valid argument made.

"No wonder you like Cameron," said Vincent, rolling his eyes.

"Look." Terrence pointed.

Christopher looked. He did not, however, step forward. Neither did Vincent. They watched Terrence move a few steps farther away, trading a single glance. *I won't mock you for being chickenshit about walking between those things if you don't mock me for the same thing,* he seemed to say.

There was a third stone buried a few feet into the trees at the clearing's edge. It seemed to have broken some branches on its way down, but they'd missed it in the shadow at first.

"Three of them?" Christopher was more nervous than rocks should merit. It almost made him want to abort phase two.

Terrence pointed. He almost seemed excited. "Four."

The four stones formed a perfect square, with Terrence in the center. Christopher couldn't say why, but he wanted to grab Terrence and drag him out of there.

"Okay, people," Vincent said with an air of command.

"We came up for two reasons, and figuring out what happened here was only one. It's not Dempsey, returned in carbonite. So let's go back to the house and get this over with. I'm hungry."

"It's only two twenty-eight." Christopher smiled at Terrence, hoping he'd give him the updated time, but Terrence was moving farther into the trees, exiting the box of stones at the far side, practically running. Vincent and Christopher shuffled down to join him.

"Six of them?" Vincent said.

Terrence shook his head and pointed past the two new stones, one of which had knocked a moderately sized tree flat. More pocked the distance. Trees intervened, but the pattern was clear: a double line of stones curving through the woods, arcing around the house. "More than six. It's a whole row. *Two* rows."

And you're standing right between them, Christopher thought. For some reason, the thought gave him goose bumps.

"How many thumps did we hear?" Terrence asked.

Vincent shrugged. Christopher didn't know either. A bunch for sure, but maybe a bunch more beyond that. Not all sounds traveled down into the bunker, and there had been times he'd woken in the middle of the night, sure that something had just happened.

Terrence, usually too cool, was looking down the double line of stones in both directions, almost excited. It was strange but amusing. "They're circling the property." He pointed, drawing an imaginary ring. "All the way around."

"Maybe," said Vincent. "Okay, come on. Let's go. We have shit to plant."

Terrence wasn't moving. His eyes were on the blue sky, its clarity marred by the line of smoke billowing toward the utility shed. He looked over, his delight departed, replaced by what looked somewhat like terror.

"Did you guys feel that?"

"What?" Christopher asked.

"I felt something."

"Come on, Terrence. Let's go. This backpack's getting heavy."

"Something just feels off." He looked toward the lake then pointed. "Down there. I think it's down there. Do you see it?"

"See *what?*"

"I don't know. Something's different. Is it the float? Was there always a float in the lake?"

"I think so," Christopher said.

"Yes," Vincent agreed.

"You're sure?"

"No, you're right. Someone must have run down there and put it in just now. Just to fuck with us."

"I'm serious."

"Clearly," said Vincent, reading the puzzled way Terrence was staring across the clearing. "What I don't understand is why."

"Something's different."

"Go down and look if it's bothering you so fucking much." Vincent rolled his eyes.

Terrence's cool slipped another notch. He stared at the lake as if it had slapped him. "No way. I don't like it."

"You don't like the *lake?*"

"I feel like we're being watched," Terrence said, now looking around in all directions.

"Terrence …"

Terrence's head ticked toward Christopher as if he had shouted. "You're not serious."

Christopher hadn't said anything. "Serious about what?"

"She's Meyer's *daughter*."

"Who is?"

"Lila."

Vincent was impatient to proceed with the mission and get back inside, but also with Terrence's sudden baffling bullshit. "Let's go, guys."

"What about Lila?" Christopher said. "Why are you bringing up Lila?"

"You're the one who brought it up."

"I didn't say anything!" Christopher felt strangely defensive. He hadn't said a word, but Terrence was looking at him like he'd caught Christopher pissing in the orange juice.

"If you two don't get the fuck over here so we can get this done," Vincent said, "I'm going to revoke my 'no gunfire' rule and shoot you both in the dick."

"I can't believe you can't feel it," said Terrence. "Can we check with Dan? I feel like they've all left the shed and are watching us from the trees."

"In the *dick*," Vincent repeated.

"Come on, Terrence," Christopher said.

Terrence looked up again then came forward. The flash of oddity on his face seemed to be waning. Once back with the others, his cool slowly returned. Still, Christopher could see a bit of his eyes' whites through the sunglasses, and they kept ticking around, as if he felt a mysterious stare upon him. Upon *them*. It was stupid, but infectious. Christopher was catching his paranoia, wanting more than ever to hurry.

They walked away from the stones, approaching the house, keeping to the shadows and out of sight. They stopped behind the garage, at the end of the house opposite the kitchen and porch.

Vincent removed the first brick of C-4 from his pack. "You got your shit together enough to do this, T?"

Terrence nodded. "Yeah. But let's be quick."

"I don't want to be out here anymore than you do." Vincent looked toward the trees, where the lawn was flattest and the hippies had built their shantytown. There were tents scattered through the trees and a handful on each of the home's sides, but most were on the roadside. There was no way to be sure that they'd all left their tents and shacks to watch the shed burn, and that surety would decrease by the minute. Curiosity only lasted so long. The plan to get back inside assumed the people around the house would eventually lose interest — leaving the shed unattended so they could get back into the bunker through the secured trap door.

They'd planned to leave explosives along the lake side — enough to mostly level the house. No house, no site to flock to. Vincent figured a blast at the right time (with another distraction to get the hippies out of the way) would scare off the current refugees. The lack of any structure would deter the remainders. But Christopher wasn't so sure. He'd even tried to raise Cameron on the radio, sure that the boss would agree and countermand Vincent's plan, but Cameron had been unreachable.

Christopher didn't really think the hippies were flocking to the house and figured any idea that they were was stupid. Meyer Dempsey's place wasn't on some sort of tour. They weren't being drawn by the idea of camping around a mountain villa. They were here because ships had come. Because the place supposedly had an energy. Christopher hadn't felt anything, but it was hard to deny that the hippies did.

Leveling the house would merely expose the bunker's concrete top, at the bottom of a smoking crater. Then the hippies would camp right on top of them.

Terrence was working fast. He already had the first brick mostly wired to the remote trigger. "You sure this shit won't just blow up the bunker?"

"You ever been in the military, Chris?" Vincent asked.

"No."

"Weapons technology has changed a lot since C-4 was basically a glorified construction explosive." He patted the brick. "In the Corps, we called this shit C-5. Because it's more than C-4, get it? No matter what they call it on the box."

"What box?"

"It's an expression," said Terrence, his eye still flicking around whenever he looked up from his work.

"Set right, it's pretty directional," Vincent said. "The bunker is reinforced not just with rebar, but solid fucking iron plating. It's meant to withstand nukes as long as they're not dropped right on top of it. But even if it turns out to be shitty construction, which it won't, 90 percent or so of the explosive force will go forward, not down."

"You're sure?" said Christopher.

"You're welcome to come stand in front of it when it goes off," said Vincent.

"One in," said Terrence. "Move down. I want—"

Christopher didn't find out what Terrence wanted because Terrence stopped cold, probably when he saw movement from the corner of his eye. Christopher had been looking out at the mountains while Vincent was talking so he saw it come. He saw how *fast* it came.

"Shit," Vincent said.

"Get the backpack, Vincent."

"Shit."

Christopher stood from his crouch, back to the home's siding. He couldn't move his eyes from the sphere hovering fifty feet away. He'd never seen one up close, and as much as he felt he might be close to shitting his pants, he couldn't turn away. The motherships had an indented ring around their middles and various protrusions on their surfaces — but the shuttles, it turned out, were polished and perfect like giant ball bearings. The thing had shot up from somewhere behind the peaks on the western horizon, screamed forward over the lake then stopped on a dime to hover without a sound. If he'd blinked, he'd have missed its approach entirely.

Beside Christopher, unseen, Vincent said, "Back up."

"I don't think we're going to outrun it, Vincent."

"Back up," he repeated. Christopher glanced over and saw Vincent carefully zipping and securing his backpack, never moving his eyes from the sphere. Terrence was already halfway down the home's length, walking backward.

"Come on, Christopher."

"I'm coming."

"Slowly."

He backed up, almost tripping on Vincent. The sphere stayed where it was, silent and still as a hole in the air.

"To the woods. Get to the woods."

"It knows what we were doing." Christopher looked at the lone brick of explosive they'd left behind. So much for blowing up the house. They could remodel the garage, but that was about it.

"It can't know what C-4 is," Vincent said.

But that wasn't what Christopher meant. He was thinking of Terrence, and how he'd said he felt watched. Terrence, who'd gone between those big, strangely forbidding stones. He didn't mean that the ship, now that it had arrived purely by coincidence, would see the brick and cast judgment. The ship had arrived *because* of what they'd been doing.

The ship slowly glided as if on rails. No vibration, its motion smooth and perfectly soundless.

"You see on the news," said Christopher, "about how they've leveled houses and cities with those death rays or whatever?"

"When people mess with them," Vincent said from behind him.

"You're right." Christopher eyed the approaching, featureless sphere. "Clearly, it doesn't have a problem with us."

There was a shout. *Many* shouts. Followed by the tromping of what sounded like thousands of feet in stampede.

"More are coming!" Vincent shouted.

They'd reached the tree line. They'd also reached Terrence, who was halfway behind a tree, waiting with his sunglasses still on.

"It's not more ships," he said. "It's *them*."

"*Go!*" Vincent shouted.

They turned and sprinted. Into the woods, arcing around the forward-surging hippies making for the newly arrived ship. They were shouting, running, stomping, dying to be among the first to get taken. But Christopher was sure the sphere had other plans.

The thicket of people was near. The ship moved closer, pushing through and breaking branches to follow. Christopher glanced back, almost causing a tumble. The thing was fifteen or twenty feet above ground and still coming. Even with no front, Christopher felt as if it was watching them. Hunting them.

They burst into the shed, Terrence in the lead. Christopher fell to the floor, pounding on the concealed door.

"Dan! Open up!"

Vincent was still outside. Christopher looked up, saw Vincent guarding the window they'd leaped through. Watching. Waiting for the onslaught of people approaching the ship, toward them. Protecting and ensuring their safe and undetected entry.

The sphere was visible, nearing, breaking branches.

"Vincent, hurry and — !" Terrence yelled.

Something changed, something Christopher could smell before it happened. The ship seemed to open. There was a blast of heat. A flash of light. Then Christopher saw Vincent's large form crumble into a scree of small black rocks, flash-crystallized like cauterized wood.

Christopher turned back to the door, no time for shock. His fists struck wood backed by hidden metal.

"Motherfucker, let us in right fucking now!"

Dan, audible through the concealed vents: "Working as fast as I can!"

The shack was still smoky from their distraction. As the ship powered up to strike again, the air took on the scent of burned meat. Christopher pulled his shirt over his nose.

"Open this goddamned door! Open it, Dan! Motherfucker, you let us in right this—"

A clicking sound then a ratcheting noise: metal sliding against metal.

There was a pop, and a previously concealed handle snapped up from the floor.

Christopher wrenched the door open. A huge glut of smoke billowed upward, covering them. Terrence, taking charge, shooed Christopher into the pit. He dropped in then dragged the door shut.

Dan met them at the secondary grate, now removed, holding his shirt over his face beside the now-extinguished fire. "Where's Vincent?"

Christopher couldn't answer.

"*Where's Vincent?*" Dan repeated.

Dan's eyes flicked behind Christopher to Terrence, ready to ask again. Trevor appeared at the vent's end before he could, his eyes panicked. He'd probably come from the control room, where he'd been watching the monitors.

"Vincent," Christopher said, finally finding breath. "He's ... *gone.*"

A sound like lightning crashing. All four looked up.

"That ship's still up there," Trevor said. "And it's *pissed.*"

Chapter Thirty-Eight

THE INTENSE PSYCHIC bond between Piper and Cameron had essentially vanished, but she still found herself receiving stray images and snippets. She said nothing. Telling Cameron felt stupid and somehow wrong, like admitting to believing in ghosts. He'd been there when they'd sensed the Andreus Republic before they could see or hear them, and he'd been there when they'd talked each other through the end of that particular dicey encounter. But the subject had a tinge of unbelievability — the way even the most terrifying nightmares feel foolish at dawn.

And, strangely, there was a twinge of shame.

Piper realized, a full day after the fact, that she knew things about Cameron that she had no logical way of knowing. It felt intrusive, like peeking in on him sleeping naked.

She knew that at age thirteen, he'd fallen off his bike when the front wheel, which had a quick release, had popped off the axle. He'd landed awkwardly on the gravel and scraped a quilt patch of skin from his face. Cameron marveled that he didn't have much of a scar, but hated the small amount he had — a blemish that Piper, looking with her real-world eyes, couldn't even see.

She knew that at fifteen, he'd traveled to Egypt, Peru, and somewhere she couldn't place in Central America. There had been someone with him during those trips — a man with a beard she assumed was Benjamin, Cameron's father. His favorite thing from that trip had been the colossal stone Olmec heads. Piper, for her part, didn't know what Olmec meant, but still found herself cherishing the memory, the way she knew Cameron did.

She knew that at eighteen, something bad had happened with Cameron's father. A sort of breaking of ties, or estrangement. The division, in Piper's mental field of view, was a strip with black on one side and white on the other. Cameron's father had been his hero before whatever had happened. Afterward, things turned rancid. But strangely, Piper also knew that when Cameron thought of that turning, he felt ashamed and regretful.

He caught her looking at him when they stopped to refill their water bottles in a well spigot in the outback of a farm field.

"What?"

"Nothing."

"*What,* Piper?"

She wondered if he got the flashes too. Did he know about Meyer's infidelity, seen through Piper's denying eyes? Did he know how she felt about it? Had he seen her intimate moments? The thought made her blush. Maybe his psychic remainders were more generalized. Piper had caught images that felt like Lila (something to do with her baby?), Heather (bad dreams?), and Trevor. Trevor's were at once intrusive and bothersome. If she was really catching his thoughts — and it felt like she was, as stupid as it sounded — then there was something Trevor was keeping from even himself, the way he'd withhold a secret from someone else. Something dark and buried — so troubling even to Trevor that he'd pushed it all the way down: a vision of a shadow-draped person, maybe female, hidden in a cloud. Invisible when he was controlled, yet always threatening to fester like a sore. And there were random thoughts, too, more or less useless. Flitting images through other people's eyes: a man who'd been lost, a newborn baby, a shiny gold object hidden in a closet. It was like tuning an old radio, picking up transmissions too distant to clearly hear.

"Seriously," she said, smiling slyly. "Nothing."

"Fine. Don't tell me."

Piper smiled again. She might also have batted her eyelashes but hoped she was above something like that. She was a grown woman, for God's sake.

She stooped to fill her water bottle. She was directing a controlled stream into the bottle's mouth when a noise at her rear surprised her.

Cameron's radio.

" ... hear me, Cameron?"

Cameron ripped the radio from his belt. They hadn't heard from the bunker in days. Something — possibly the alien ships, who knew — seemed to be blocking the signal.

"It's them," said Cameron.

"How do you know?"

"Because I didn't turn it on. This is a *radio*. If I want to scan for the open frequencies, I have to tune in."

"So, what ... it's a ghost radio?"

His finger had been hovering over the talk button, about to respond, but he paused to answer Piper first. "It's multipurpose. It works as an open-frequency radio, like citizen's band or if you flat-out just wanted to listen to music, but it also works point to point. Like a phone."

"But phone service is out."

" … hear me …?"

The radio belched static, just a few words at a time seeping through.

Cameron put the radio to his mouth and depressed the talk button. "Dan? Is that you?"

More static. "Yes!"

He looked at Piper, visibly excited. Speaking into the radio, he said, "How the hell are you calling me?" Then without the talk button depressed, to Piper: "This shouldn't be possible. Or at least, it wasn't last I checked, but maybe they opened the airwaves again for some reason, who knows. But this isn't going out on the air. Whatever's been blocking the signal, if that's the problem, won't affect point-to-point, but point-to-point shouldn't be available. This is cellular, like a phone."

" … Terrence. He was able to … watch."

"'Watch'?"

"Raj's watch," said Piper. "It works like a phone. Could Terrence have—"

"Terrence can do anything." Cameron's smile was broad, genuine, bright with life. A smile from a world where none of this was happening.

"Can you hear me okay?" he asked the radio.

" … stal clear. Can you … me?"

"There's a lot of static."

Static? Piper had never heard static on a cell phone, if this was cellular.

The next time Dan spoke, the sound was perfect. "Is this better?"

"Wow, yes. Perfect."

"Where are you guys?"

Cameron sighed. "Not as far as I'd like. But getting there."

"We thought you might be dead. We've been trying to reach you forever, but you never answer."

"Same here," said Cameron.

"We can't get any air signals. Once Terrence realized that, he knew it was us, not you. Something was messing up the signal. Has to do with magnets or whatever."

Terrence's voice, very dim, in the distance: "*Magnetism. Not magnets.*"

"Whatever. So we figured we were fucked. But he got around it with the watch thing Raj is always screwing with."

"How?"

"I guess there are still analog cellular repeaters out there. Do you remember analog cellular?"

Cameron paused. Thanks to the speaker, Piper was hearing all of this, but she didn't seem to know what Dan was talking about either.

"Fucking kids," said Dan's voice. "I'm not *that* old, am I?" Then: "Anyway, he did the MacGyver thing, got Raj's watch to work with the analog signal somehow, something I guess they didn't think to block, and—"

"What's a MacGyver?"

"Fucking kids," Dan mumbled.

"Are you okay there?"

"Well, yeah, I guess." He paused, as if with gravity. "We got a visit, though."

Piper didn't like the sound of that. She looked at Cameron.

"What kind of visit?"

"Vincent, Terrence, and Christopher went topside to … well, that part's not important. Point is, while they were out there, one of *them* … a ship … it showed up out of nowhere."

Piper put her hand over her mouth, big eyes wide.

Dan sighed. "It chased the guys back inside. But before they all got in, it ..." He trailed off, leaving the sentence hanging.

"It *what?*"

Before Dan could answer, the radio beeped. Whatever Terrence had done to make the call, it didn't appear to be permanent. The beep and accompanying display icon were prelude to a fading signal.

"I'm about to lose you, Dan."

"Yeah, we thought that might happen. They seem to be watching us now."

"What do you mean?"

"Look. Call drops, we'll call you back. Not right away, though. I don't understand it, but I've learned to believe this dodgy motherfucker about computers and stuff. Terrence says it's like poking holes. Eventually, someone can spot the signal and shut it down, but then, if he watches, he can jab another hole. Just doesn't know when or for how long it'll be before that happens. And we have to call you; you can't call us. So if we—"

"DAN?"

"No, I'm still here. Sorry. Raj was asking for his watch back. You believe it?" Then, apparently to Raj: "Yeah, I'm talking to you, Chuckles." Then back to Cameron: "Raj is on Terrence to try and call his folks. But it doesn't work like that, like with normal phones. Radio/radio, over analog cellular ... shit, I don't know or care."

"What did the ship do?"

"Pardon?"

"You said that before they all got back inside, it did something."

Heavy sigh. "It got Vincent, kiddo."

Piper's hand returned to her mouth.

"What do you mean it 'got' him, Dan?"

"I mean he's dead, kiddo. It got him. It just … well, let's just say he's gone. A bunch of those people camping up top, too. Did this big ray thing. Not the kind of thing you can get out of your head. I'd guess maybe a dozen people dead, burned a bunch of their shit. Like it was trying to make a point or was mad or something."

"Is anyone else h — ?" The radio beeped again. Twice, this time. "Signal's going, Dan."

Dan sighed again. The mood there must be terrible. Piper hadn't been close with Vincent, but she found herself wanting to cry. "If it cuts out, we'll call you back in a bit," he said.

"Is anyone else hurt?" Cameron repeated.

"No, kiddo. The rest of us are okay. Scared shitless, but okay."

The radio beeped twice more.

"It's really going now. I'll keep the radio on me."

"Yeah, and with batteries. But here's the thing, Cam. Have you seen any of those ships while you've been on the trail? Big or little?"

The spigot was at the corner of a field. The field was wide open. Piper looked up, feeling exposed, suddenly sure she'd see an approaching armada.

"No. Nothing."

"Well you watch your ass, okay, kiddo? Stay under trees if you can." Then he swallowed audibly. "You know how the movie aliens always say, 'We come in peace'?"

"Yeah?"

"Well, these ones don't."

Cameron looked at Piper then at the radio.

Piper whispered, "Ask about Lila."

"Dan?"

"Yeah."

"How's Lila? How's she doing, with her baby and all? Piper wants to know."

"Oh, right," said Dan. "Shit, *really* glad you asked. I almost forgot. Tell Piper that—"

Dan stopped midsentence. Cameron held the radio to his ear then shook it. He slapped it like a busted TV set.

The signal was gone, and they were alone.

Chapter Thirty-Nine

THE RADIO DIDN'T CRACKLE AGAIN for days.

Piper's nerves, which had been soothed by Dan's report, were now more jangled than ever. Before that first call had come through, a part of her mind had thought the bunker might have been decimated and everyone dead, but a much larger, more sensible part of her mind knew the idea was paranoid lunacy. Meyer had seemed to predict the alien invasion somehow, so it made sense that his bunker would be built well enough to hide them. And besides, she'd been getting snippets of thought from Lila, Heather, and maybe Trevor, thanks presumably to their encounter with the massive magnetic stones. The part of her mind that accepted those flashes knew the truth.

But now, days distant from the line of stone monoliths, the psychic bolus she'd felt had mostly disappeared. Piper could still occasionally gather Cameron's thoughts but only the loudest, and presumably because he was right there beside her. Random visions from people she didn't know were either gone or had faded into the background miasma of ordinary thoughts. There was nothing clear from Lila, Heather, Trevor, or anyone else.

She didn't like the way Dan had been cut off midsentence, even though they'd known the signal could fail at any second. She didn't like his hanging thought: "Tell Piper that—" Tell her what? He'd said that right after Cameron had asked about Lila and her baby. Was there a connection, or had Dan's memory simply been jogged about something else?

Tell Piper that Lila says hello.

Tell Piper that Lila lost the baby.

Tell Piper that Lila got prepartum depression and killed herself.

She fretted whenever their traveling twosome fell silent — which was often, since they had days of travel and only so much to talk about. Strangely, Cameron was still guarded. Despite all that time, she still didn't know much of his history. He hadn't yet hit on any of the memories she'd pulled from his mind, especially those of his father. Did he know Piper had seen all those thoughts? Or did he think that by saying nothing, he was hiding them well?

When they stopped talking, Piper thought of the bunker.

When they stopped for the first night after Dan's call, she thought of it more.

The second night, she couldn't stop thinking about it at all.

And by the third night, when Dan or Terrence still hadn't called, she birthed new worries. They kept Piper from sleep and cast the stirring woods in menacing chatter.

She was already fretting over whatever might have been happening with Lila. Now she worried for them all. Dan had said Terrence would be able to call back. "We'll call you back — not right away, though," he'd said ... and that seemed to imply the process was difficult or random.

But *three days?* She'd thought it might take hours. A day maybe.

But by the morning of the fourth day, there was nothing.

They crossed into Utah.

Her companion was unperturbed. Piper had kept her bothered thoughts to herself, and Cameron, if he was anything like her, could no longer reach into the heads of others. She kept her face impassive, and when they spoke, she didn't let her voice or tone betray her. Piper was probably being stupid. If Cameron wasn't fretting about Vail, then she shouldn't either. He'd been out in the big, scary world — not just on his way to the bunker to join and betray Morgan Matthews but throughout his life. He'd been to places that made Piper uneasy, sure she was just another coddled and xenophobic American: China, India, Central and South America, the Balkans, the Middle East. If he wasn't showing concern, maybe she was being stupid. *Maybe.*

Although if a ship had arrived and killed a bunch of people above the bunker, her fears weren't exactly unreasonable.

She'd seen what the mothership had done to Moscow before the TV signals and Internet died. She'd also seen — again on the news — reports of smaller destructions, with deaths numbering "only" in the single digits. She'd heard rumors of other alien attacks, and the ships seeming impervious to anything the world's governments tried hurling their way.

If Terrence hadn't made them a new connection despite the way Dan seemed sure that he could, maybe that meant the ships had returned to Vail and killed more than just Vincent.

A fourth night passed.

Then a fifth.

On the morning of the sixth day following Dan's call — the seventh or eighth total since they'd left the others behind (maybe to die), Cameron stopped his horse at the top of a slowly rising hill made of red rock. The last days had been warmer, and they'd made them mostly without cover, nothing but empty blue sky above. Utah was different from Colorado. Mountains had given way to craggy rocks, sculpted, wind-eroded outcroppings that looked like precariously balanced art. Piper hadn't liked traveling in the open, but there was no other way. They'd been a cowboy and a cowgirl on the range, with nothing stretching from one horizon to the next.

But for the past two hours they'd been following a valley. It reminded Piper uncomfortably of the ravine in which they'd evaded and then hid from the Andreus Republic, only far deeper, far steeper, and with walls of red stone rather than soil. They'd been following a road, but it looked seldom used and forgotten, more clay than pavement. It seemed the middle of nowhere to Piper, as they followed the canyon's meanderings. But Cameron seemed to know where he was going, and by the time he stopped, she knew they must be near — even as out in the middle of nowhere as she felt.

"This is it," he said.

Piper looked around. There was nothing but dust, road, canyon walls, and what seemed to be a dried-up riverbed. The sky above, visible as a strip between the walls, was pure blue.

"Nice place."

"Okay, not literally. It's around that bend." Cameron pointed, but the canyon curved ahead, and Piper saw nothing.

"Then let's go. And please tell me they have food. I'm sick of beans."

Cameron paused. "Just … just remember why we're here, okay? To find Meyer. To find a way to get him back."

"Of course."

He looked at his horse but didn't urge her forward.

"Cameron, what is it?"

"The people here. They're professionals. They know things. Just keep that in mind."

"Cameron, *what?*"

He said nothing. Just sighed again then nudged the horse with his heel to get her moving.

As they neared the bend, Piper realized that the path was rising, moving them slowly out of the canyon. It wound up and around, the walls shorter with each passing step.

The lab Cameron had told her about entered their view. It was the strangest building she'd ever seen. By the time Piper could fully see it, the canyon walls had shortened to the height of a two-story building, maybe one and a half. Set into the wall directly in front of them was a brick facade with a door in the middle, as if someone had walled off the front of a cave and built the lab right inside it.

But the lab's appearance wasn't what stole Piper's breath: It was the mothership hovering in the newly revealed sky.

"They think he's in there, Piper," Cameron said, nodding at the mammoth sphere floating above the cliff. "The people here? They believe Meyer's inside that ship."

THREE MONTHS LATER

PIPER WOKE, lying on her side, a soft pillow under her head. One arm was beneath her, sticking straight out. The warm arm draped over her other side, however, wasn't hers.

She rolled back and met Cameron's gaze. He was already awake.

"I had a dream," she said.

"Was it about racial equality in the 1960s?"

She rolled fully to face him. "No."

Something in her expression must have registered. Cameron sat up and propped himself on one elbow.

"About Meyer?"

No, it hadn't been about Meyer. She wished he hadn't said it — and wished even more that she'd just told him the dream's contents rather than making him play this guessing game. She was split exactly down the middle on the topic of Meyer. When they'd arrived at the Moab ranch three months ago, Meyer had been all she'd wanted to discuss. She'd pestered Cameron's father unceasingly, asking question after question, pursuing avenues that

Benjamin had already traveled but that Piper's desperation forced him to revisit anew. When Benjamin grew exhausted, she'd pestered his right-hand man, Charlie. He was less patient than Benjamin; he'd told her to sit down and let the professionals do their work.

But after those first six weeks in Utah — five weeks longer, at the time, than she'd been told they'd stay — the idea of Meyer had begun to feel like the concept of God. She still believed both were out there somewhere but not in any reachable way — and the impression of Meyer's distance had only increased in the time since. Eventually, she'd stopped denying her feelings for Cameron, and his for her. But despite her justifications, Piper felt plenty guilty when her mind turned to her missing husband.

"It was a dream about Lila," she said.

"What *about* Lila? Was it an ordinary dream, or …"

A voice in Piper's head ran atop Cameron's words:

(dream prescient vision prophecy)

" … or something else?"

"I don't know. But I can …"

(hear you see you feel you)

Piper didn't finish her sentence. She didn't have to. Cameron nodded.

"Can you, too?" Piper didn't need to explain what *that* meant either.

(can you hear me too)

"I've had dreams," he said.

"Just dreams?"

"It's hard to say. Lila … in your dream. Was she … was she okay?"

Piper closed her eyes, trying to chase the vision as it fled her awareness. But it was already gone, like water swirling down a drain. She spent an extra few seconds trying to recall the dream, knowing it was pointless. She could remember the mood, but none of its contents. Ominous and tense. Not exactly a big help, considering the way she'd been fretting over Lila's well-being — *all* of their well-beings, actually, but Lila's most of all, since the signal's death three long months ago.

How's Lila? How's she doing, with her baby and all?

Tell Piper that —

She'd filled in that particular blank thousands of times. She'd spun on a chair in Benjamin's office, hoping to puzzle out what Dan was in the middle of relaying when the radio died. She'd sat on the deck of the old ranch house on the lab's property that she and Cameron had taken as their own and considered it. Doors to the cliff-bunkered lab and the ranch house nearby were always double locked at night, but she'd contemplated going out into the dark to walk and think.

"I don't know if she was okay. And I don't know if it was a … vision or whatever. I just know I had a dream."

Cameron sat up, already pulling on a shirt.

"We should tell Charlie."

Piper rolled her eyes. "I don't want to tell Charlie. He makes me feel guilty for everything. And I do mean everything. The other day, I walked over to the lab with my coffee, and I said, 'Good morning, Charlie.' He looked at me with those bug eyes of his and said, 'Good *morning?*' I almost apologized."

"It's just how he is. How he's always been." Cameron laughed. "He's been my dad's research partner since before there was really any research. You know how most people show off their vacation photos? Dad would show Charlie photos from the vacations Benjamin and I took together, and he'd bustle off to analyze them. You should have seen the way he descended on King Pacal's sarcophagus."

"King Pacal?"

"Mayan king of Palenque, famous carving on his sarcophagus showing him in a space capsule?" Cameron shook it away like Piper might shake away a pleasant memory of walking the beach with her mother. "Not relevant. You don't want to tell Charlie, we tell Benjamin. But Dad's just going to turn around and ask Charlie. And you know it'll be worse if you don't say anything and he finds out later."

Morning light was already clearing cobwebs from Piper's mind. In the seconds after she'd woken, the dream's meaning had seemed full blown and urgent. Now it felt gossamer thin, like a belief in fairies. The day would be warm, and the ranch had almost no shade from the desert sun except for the few hours it touched the ship's shadow. The house had bare-bones utilities. They'd only find AC across the red clay in the lab building. But here in bed, it felt warm and pleasant. Hard to believe this place was one of North America's most feared.

"I changed my mind. It was just a dream. Really."

Cameron dragged on his pants and ran hands through his messy dark-brown hair.

"Come on. Let's go."

"I want to stay in bed."

But then a whispered voice inside her mind:

(It's all beginning)

Piper blinked then sat up. She didn't remember details of the dream and no longer could be positive that Lila had been in it. She'd been afraid for Lila quite a while during the radio blackout. Anything could have happened to her family in Vail, but for some reason, Lila — for Piper, at least — felt like the center. She didn't worry about Trevor as much as she worried about his sister. They might all be dead. Maybe even *likely*, given the last things Dan had said about the killer alien shuttle. But she'd been living under a mothership for a while now and was still alive, somewhat used to its only sometimes-ominous presence. She no longer sprinted and looked up when crossing from house to lab. Maybe that's how it was in Vail.

But that phrase. She remembered that phrase: *It's all beginning.* Not that it was an unusual phrase; you could say it before the start of a movie. But something about the whisper and Lila set gooseflesh on the back of Piper's neck.

She looked at Cameron.

"Cam."

He looked over.

"Do you remember the story your father told me yesterday, about the first time you played guitar?"

Cameron nodded.

"I've been trying to remember the name of the company on the pick he showed me yesterday. Your first guitar pick, that he'd saved."

"Oh. Gibson."

"You weren't around when he told me that story. And Ben said you didn't know he'd saved that pick."

"I just ..." Cameron's brow furrowed, as if trying to remember something, looking unsure.

"I can hear your thoughts again too. Like I could after we first crossed that line of stones."

"He must have told me." Cameron chewed on his bottom lip. "And I've always played Gibsons, always."

She shook her head, now seeing the pieces fall into place. "What Charlie told us might happen?" Piper swallowed. "I think it's starting."

Chapter Forty-One

"Mom."

Heather looked up, seeming totally normal. This, more than anything, bothered Lila once she stepped back enough to see it. By her old standards, she didn't look "normal" at all. By pre-invasion standards, Lila's mother looked ragged, tired, baggy-eyed, haggard, old. She'd always tried to look casual onstage, doing her shows in T-shirts, jeans, and sneakers as if she didn't give a shit. But Lila had been in the dressing room to witness the careful orchestration of that casual look. Heather Hawthorne came off as a woman who paid no mind to trends or beauty, but was plenty vain in her way and never wanted to look or seem old. Especially after Dad had married Piper, who was a decade and a half younger.

"What?"

"I need to talk to you."

"Is it about Raj? Because I don't want to hear about Raj."

Lila would have rolled her eyes in the old days, but now that felt like too much of an on-the-nose teenager thing to do. She no longer felt like a teenager and hadn't for a while. Lila felt approximately a billion years old. The six-month-old fetus in her belly that seemed to be streaming unwanted thoughts into her consciousness wasn't helping.

"No. It's not about Raj."

"Good." Something seemed to strike her. "But oh. There's one exception. If he ever stops wanting to have sex with you just because you're—"

"Mom, *gross.*"

"I agree. There are so many less-gross men around. But *you* chose him."

"No, I mean—" Lila stopped, and this time she did roll her eyes. The simple motion felt shockingly good. Like stretching after a long time in one position. There was something so *ordinary* about mother-daughter baiting. Ordinary felt good. As awful as it sounded, mocking Raj with her mother was the most comforting thing Lila did these days because it was so predictable. The kind of thing that had happened before living underground like a mole person, before getting knocked up with a spooky baby, before her father had been abducted by aliens.

And before Christopher. That was its own nest of poisonous snakes.

An alarm screamed from the front room. Lila's heart took its customary leap, but then Terrence was running through the living room, past the open bedroom door, shouting, "*Air vent, just an air vent!*"

Lila relaxed.

"There was a day when I didn't live like this," Heather said, looking at the ceiling.

Lila could sympathize. There had been better days for her, too. Days when she wasn't scared two out of every three waking hours. Days when she hadn't feared for her sanity. Days when she hadn't been keeping at least two hideous secrets. Days when love had been simple, and she hadn't felt blackmailed by her affection. Days when she hadn't been splitting her time between two boys, enjoying her time with neither.

"I … I have to tell you something," Lila said, ignoring her.

"Is it about Raj's throbbing curry stick or his sticky mustard seed?"

"Oh my *God*, Mom. Can you just be serious for a minute?"

No. Of course she couldn't be.

"Okay, okay," she said, looking put-out. "I'll be good."

"Because you're the only one I can talk to." Lila eyed her mother seriously, knowing it was a risk to lay herself bare at the foot of Heather Hawthorne's mockery.

But who else was there? Piper was gone. She was betraying Raj and couldn't meet his eyes for long (which is why they usually made love with him behind; she said it was more comfortable with her belly, but secretly she couldn't face him). Christopher had once seemed like a good substitute boyfriend — maybe even a replacement — but somehow she'd ended up feeling more manipulated than loved.

"Fine. Okay. I'm sorry. I'll be good. What's up?"

Good question. She'd come in here to talk to her mother about the baby. But even in her mind, that sounded crazy.

Heather surprised her. "Is it about your dad?"

She blinked. No, that hadn't been on her mind at all. For long periods of time, Lila forgot the life in which she'd once had a father. Like she forgot a life in which the idea of going outside didn't fill her with terror. Even three months ago, when she'd wanted to go topside for air, seemed a lifetime away. Now she was trapped. Going up top sounded horrifying. Staying here was awful and claustrophobic. There was no way to win, every day held its own unique agony.

"Why would you think I wanted to talk about Dad?"

"Oh. No reason."

"*Mom?*"

"No reason," she repeated. "I just … there's not a lot to think about down here." She forced a laugh, but to Lila, it sounded like insanity. And these days, she knew what insanity sounded like just fine. And she knew what it looked like in the mirror. "It was either that or Raj's spicy meat stick."

"Mom. Please."

Heather sighed.

"Okay. Fine." Another sigh. "I guess your dad's been on *my* mind."

The idea that Lila's mother was pining for her father? Surprising. Her parents had remained somewhat acrimonious friends, but clearly they'd remained lovers. Still, the idea that there remained genuine affection between them — especially from her mother's side — was so strange as to be unnerving. But really, it was sweet. And now that Lila's attention was shifting to match Heather's, it felt nostalgic, too. An old memory of her hand in her father's, a sense that all would be well because he was there to protect her.

"Do you think he'll come back?"

There was a tiny moment where Lila thought she might make a joke, but then it skittered by, and Heather answered honestly. Vulnerably.

"I don't know. And you've heard what Dan and Terrence say about the people who've come home."

"Those were the early people. If Dad is still with the … the aliens …"

" … then he'll be worse? *More* out of his mind, *more* on

edge, *more* frightening to us, like the other people who came back and frightened their families?" She closed her eyes and exhaled slowly. "I'm sorry. I shouldn't say that. I guess I've never been very good at the mom stuff."

The ventilation alarm had ceased in the living room — surely caused by more hippies blocking intakes. Lila was already used to the sound, seeing as it went off so often and Terrence couldn't figure a way to permanently disarm it.

She sat on the bed beside her mother, almost sitting on her feet.

"Sometimes," Lila said slowly, watching her mother to survey her response, "I *dream* about Dad."

"Me too," her mother said.

Still watching Heather's face. "The dreams I have are really *weird*."

"Weird how?"

"Like … he's almost talking to me."

Her mother was nodding slowly. "Hmm."

"You ever have dreams like that?"

Heather watched Lila's eyes. It felt like a standoff. Each knew something, but neither was willing to expose their mind first. Lila had felt for a while that her mother was sensing some of the same things as her. Or rather, a sense of very, *very* strong intuition coming from the neighborhood of her uterus.

"Maybe. But dreams are always kind of funny."

"Yeah," Lila said.

"Not like 'hilarious.' Like … 'strange.'"

"I know this might sound … *strange*," Lila said, using her mother's word, "but since we've been here, I've had some really whacked-out dreams."

Heather nodded slowly. "Me, too."

Oh, just go for it, something told her. Whether that was

her own voice, the voice from below, or the voice of intuition, Lila hadn't a clue.

"Mom?"

Heather raised her eyebrows.

"You've done drugs, right?"

Heather seemed to edge a knee-jerk reaction but then sighed and said, "I've experimented."

"With Dad?"

"With … ?" Her aborted sentence wasn't a no. But Lila saw confusion. Lila had never thought her father was into drugs at all. He was too straight-laced, too hard and logical, too ruthless and strong. Drugs were about a loss of control, as far as Lila's dash of experimentation had shown. Meyer Dempsey, on the other hand, had both hands firmly on the wheel of any situation at all times.

"I just got a … a feeling."

Actually, she'd seen it in detail. She'd had dreams, but the vision was also accessible like a memory. Maybe her baby was somehow sending her psychic messages, or maybe she was as crazy as the notion made her feel. Either way, she'd clearly seen her father and mother lying somewhere on the floor with vacant faces and far-off minds. At first, Lila had wondered why … *something* … had felt the vision important enough to impress so firmly upon her mind. But then she'd realized it was somehow connected to all that was happening. That the drugs, somehow, had mattered.

They were connected to her father's preparation.

Connected to her father's disappearance.

Connected to her mother's odd state — her way of jumping at shadows.

And, Lila thought, connected to a truth: that Heather Hawthorne knew more about what was going on now and in the near future than she let on … or that she even realized she knew.

"And I got a feeling," Lila continued, "that when you did them together, Dad felt like he wasn't just seeing visions, but was, in fact … well … *going somewhere else.*"

Images she'd been shown but didn't understand, some literal and some in metaphor: *a door. A hole in the ground, going down into forever. A plug in a socket, a connection made. Nine pillars of fire. Nine contacts on a conductive wire. Gods of the past. Gods of the future. A sense that as much as life crept forward, they were all really on the backside of a loop, replaying songs that had been played before.*

"And somehow, I just get this idea that you and Dad," Lila swallowed, knowing she might be lining herself up for hours of mockery at the hands of a master, "somehow *connected* to each other when you did that stuff, and maybe are still, you know … *connected* now. Like in your dreams."

A voice inside, whispering that Lila wasn't the only person in the bunker clutching a bouquet of possible answers.

Heather nodded slowly then looked at Lila's six-months-pregnant belly.

"I've had feelings about you too," she said.

Chapter Forty-Two

CAMERON FOUND Benjamin in his office. He nodded hello, standing beside Piper, thinking of how even after three months in Moab, he still defaulted to calling this man "Benjamin" instead of "Dad." It was old, leftover distance he'd once built between himself and the crazy UFO nut who'd embarrassed him into leaving home all those years ago. But Benjamin — *his father* — had been right all along. And so Cameron kept trying, now that they were finally reunited, to have a true father again.

"Well," he said, looking up at Cameron and Piper's arrival. "Good morning!"

"Is Charlie around?" Piper asked.

"*Good morning*, Piper," Benjamin repeated, smiling slightly behind his dark, messy beard.

"Good morning, Ben." Pause. "Is Charlie around?"

Benjamin twirled his chair in a circle like a kid playing, deliberately wasting a few seconds to slow Piper down. "Nobody ever asks for Charlie," he finally said. "Charlie's insufferable."

A thin man approached, a curly gray-and-brown beard

on his face, walking like a robot or a person with a stick up his butt. Benjamin rotated his chair halfway, a *Boy am I in trouble now* look on his face.

"Who's insufferable?"

"You," Benjamin replied.

Charlie turned to Piper and Cameron. "What are you doing here?"

"He says good morning," Benjamin translated.

"Good morning. What are you doing here?"

Cameron swallowed his retort. Charlie wasn't rude so much as incredibly efficient. When he asked why they were there, he meant it literally. There was little point to pleasantries. They'd come directly into the lab earlier than usual then asked for Charlie. Benjamin was right; nobody asked for Charlie unless they had to. Cameron sometimes thought Charlie was like a vulture. He wasn't fun to be around at all, but his function at the lab was essential, and you'd want him on your side when dying time came.

"Piper wanted to talk to you."

Charlie's head snapped toward Piper. "What?"

"Can we sit?"

"I have," he looked down at his watch, "three minutes left on an enzymatic reaction on my bench. Come with me if you want to talk for longer than that."

Piper was looking at the chair beside Benjamin with a sense of longing. Cameron had learned, after all the time they'd spent together, that she wasn't her best in the mornings. She preferred easing into them as she would a hot bath. She'd want to sit, get a cup of coffee, and shake off the last of her sleep with light banter before delving into anything heavy. Charlie was the opposite. He didn't yawn for fear of wasted oxygen.

"Go finish what you've got, and come back, Charlie," Benjamin said.

Charlie's head snapped toward Piper, Cameron, then the elevated gantry where the incubators were stored — "Charlie's Nest" Benjamin sometimes called it — before he bustled away.

"Not used to him yet, are you, Piper?" said Benjamin.

"No." She sat.

Cameron pulled a wooden chair from beneath a second desk and sat beside her. "It's okay. I've known him my whole life, and I'm still not used to him."

"And I've known him for five years longer than that." Benjamin reached for a Mr. Coffee and an empty cup then poured Piper her morning routine. "It's actually a great endorsement. You know how Smuckers jelly used to have that slogan, 'With a name like Smuckers, it's gotta be good'? Well, that's how it is with Charlie. With a personality like that, my working with him this long must mean he's outstanding at what he does."

Piper smiled and accepted Benjamin's coffee, soothed by his manner in the exact opposite way she was bristled by Charlie's. Cameron had seen it before. He'd traveled the world with this man, granted access to the most forbidden and sacred of places in the unfriendliest nations, bought by that charm. When Cameron had finally grown sick of all the crazy Ancient Astronauts/UFO conspiracy bullshit and left to make his fortune with a guitar on his back, it had been hard to break away. He'd felt like he was wounding someone who couldn't defend himself, hurting a man who loved him. But *enough*, teenage Cameron had thought, *was enough*. And hadn't his face been red when the ships had come to prove Dad's wacko theories true?

"So," said Benjamin. "Not to use Charlie's expression, but why *are* you here? So early, I mean. Usually, you take your walk, I thought. And believe me, it's so much nicer now that you don't run across as many cattle mutilations and spectral green lights. Although there is the giant floating ball." He pointed upward and smiled again.

Cameron watched Piper squirm, unsure how to start.

Still too early. Still too crazy a thing to say.

"What's Charlie working on?" he said, diverting the conversation.

Benjamin waved a hand. "Oh, I don't know. Something extremely competent but vaguely annoying, I'm sure. Charlie can't help but pick at loose ends."

Cameron raised his eyebrows. His father loved nothing more than to discuss his work, but these days Cameron had to goad him. A bit gun shy, probably, considering the way that fringe work had bulldozed one marriage, many friendships, and a fatherhood in his past.

"Still looking for evidence of panspermia," Benjamin said.

"Any luck?"

"The problem with the whole panspermia theory is that it's a chicken-and-egg situation. Did aliens seed life throughout the galaxy, including here on Earth? Maybe. There's certainly evidence. But at the same time, life on Earth is what it is, and we don't exactly have a lot of other life, away from this planet, to compare it to so we can say, 'A-ha! This life is like that life! Therefore, aliens did it!'" Benjamin shrugged. "Now, with the appearance of these monolith lines everywhere—"

Piper raised a hand. "Everywhere?"

Benjamin nodded, wiping a stray drip of coffee from his upper lip after setting down his mug. "Mmm-hmm. Our sources under the government's skin are sending us evidence of more and more. There seem to be two basic configurations. There are lines, like the ones you walked through. Then there are henges." He waved the jargon away and elaborated. "Circles. Like Stonehenge: stone *henge*, stone *circle*. Get it? Well, anyway. Large circles. Charlie's still working on the scraping you brought us, but we've had others too. Seems like normal moss and lichens to me, probably because they're Earth rocks. But Charlie's relentless, as you might have noticed."

"Might," said Cameron.

"I'm much more interested in the network," Benjamin said.

"Network?" Piper asked.

Benjamin rotated his monitor. He zoomed out of the displayed map of Utah to show the entire American West. They'd discussed this before — keeping it from Piper until the right moment, which apparently was now.

Benjamin looked over at Piper then continued using his screen as a visual aid.

"This is the line you crossed." He pointed at a horizontal white line superimposed on the map, east of the Utah/Colorado border. The line exited Colorado at the top and bottom of the state, so it was good they hadn't tried to go around for long. "This is us here." He tapped a dot, which seemed to represent a circle. Cameron assumed so anyway; he'd seen the enormous monoliths around the ranch on their walks, keeping a healthy distance. The house and lab, so far as he could tell, were near the henge's middle. Well, not *exactly* in the middle. The cavern below the arch was in the precise center.

"So last time I showed you this, Cameron, it was a scattering of lines." *Lines converging on Vail,* Cameron thought but didn't say, watching Piper from the corner of his eye. "But now, see how it's fleshed out, with our new intel?"

"Where are you getting this information?" Piper had one hand on her heart. Cameron could see the way she wanted to ask about the spiderweb of lines all leading to Vail, but she was resisting, likely fearing the answer.

"I could tell you," Benjamin said, smiling, "but then I'd have to kill you. It has to do with how I can still get the Internet." He tapped the screen for emphasis. "I can't get at the websites full of cat videos for you anymore, but I do have access to a lot of well-connected nerds. People like me who've always suspected things we couldn't admit to, or who have access to information that's been kept secret. Like Area 51. Roswell. Both quite unremarkable, by the way. Roswell was about alien craft, but it was U.S. military using them — trying to recreate them anyway, and not doing very well. And Area 51 is yesterday's news. Do you know where the real action is now?"

"Don't say it, Dad."

"Area 52," Benjamin said.

Piper smiled indulgently.

"Anyway, with all these new monolith lines filled in, a pretty clear pattern is emerging. See?"

Cameron squinted at the screen. "Looks like a mess."

Benjamin zoomed out farther. "Now?"

It looked like a highway map, or maybe a flight map from the inside of an airline magazine. Everything connected to everything else. Except for Vail. That spot was special, and more rock lines seemed to move toward it than anywhere else.

"Not really."

Benjamin gave Cameron a look that said, *I have no son.* He pointed again. "It's a parallel processing network. Do you see it now?"

"Is this like seeing any three things as being Orion's belt, like the pyramids on the Giza plateau?"

"Funny you mention Giza, wiseass." Benjamin hit a key, and the screen changed to show Europe, Africa, the Middle East. There were more lines, another place more connected than anywhere else — this time in the Nile

River delta. "We're seeing the same thing there, according to my international colleagues."

"Colleagues?"

"Well-connected nut jobs." He smiled a toothy grin at Piper then took another sip of his coffee.

Benjamin clicked through screens, each showing a part of the globe centered on one highly networked hub. He read them off. "Giza, Machu Pichu, Teotihuacán, Xi'an in China. Do you want to know how many 'hubs' like this there are in total?"

"Nine?" Piper guessed.

Benjamin pointed: *one win for the lady*. "Yep. Same as the number of people still missing."

"How can you possibly be sure there are only nine people missing?" Piper asked.

"Well, we can't," Benjamin admitted. "But we do know there are nine people missing who are highly prominent, one—"

"'Prominent'?"

"Like Meyer is prominent. Not 'famous,' really, but … say … prominent thinkers? Innovators? People about whom we can, once we start investigating, clearly say, 'Ah, yes — that's why this person is special.' If I were to venture a guess—"

"Don't venture a guess, Dad." Cameron put his forehead in his palm. Benjamin had made many of his guesses in front of Cameron's friends in the past. Embarrassment always ensued.

"*If I were to venture a guess*," Benjamin repeated, "I'd say they're all representative minds of the best of what humanity has to offer."

"You think they're forming a brain trust," Cameron said, sarcastic.

Benjamin pointed at the screen. "We know they're

interested in our thoughts. What you described? The reawakening of latent extrasensory phenomena after crossing the stones? That's what I'd guess this network is for. So yes, it makes sense to me that they would be interested in people who represent 'the human mind,' say. The nine high-profile people we know are missing? There's one from each of these locations. In several cases, they actually built their own residences or structures there, as you described Meyer talking about an 'Axis Mundi.' You know that's what the Aztecs called their great temple at Tenochtitlán?"

"She does now," Cameron said.

"But in all cases, whether they were able to build their own Axis or not," Benjamin gave Cameron an eye, "they were actually *picked up* by an alien shuttle at the hub — the 'axis' — nearest them. And in a few cases," he nodded at Piper, "they had to travel quite a way to get to their pickup point. As you described Meyer's single-minded determination to reach Vail."

Piper sighed. It was impossible to tell how she was taking this. She'd seen the map already, but only in the past few days had the updates arrived to make Vail's prominence so obvious. The mess of lines had looked random before, but now they seemed much more coherent.

"Piper, you said that he didn't talk about needing to rendezvous with a ship?"

Piper shook her head. They'd been through this many times. "If anything, he seemed to want to run away from them, like everyone else."

Benjamin nodded. "I could give you my theories about that, but some people remain doubting Thomases, so I'll save it." He ticked his head toward Cameron for Piper's benefit, and her nervous veneer cracked enough to smile. "Point is, looking at these maps, it seems hard to deny a few things. For one, these sites were carefully selected. All are mystical places shrouded in lore except for, interestingly, your lovely home." He nodded at Piper, again tapping the screen. "We don't know anything special about Vail at all, probably because real estate there is too expensive for Ancient Astronaut theorists to afford land."

Piper laughed.

"Regardless," he said, "to me, this picture — lines of stones and henges — looks like a neural net." He touched a white line representing a double row of monoliths on the Colorado map. "Nerves." He touched a dot, not at Vail, representing a circle. "Node," he said, finally touching Vail.

"Brain," recited a new voice.

Cameron turned. Charlie was standing behind them.

"Quite right," Benjamin said, looking up at Charlie, knowing the newcomer had more to say.

"The spores I've been working with have been entirely dormant. But now, they're beginning to germinate."

"What does that mean?" Benjamin said.

"Ask them." Charlie nodded at Piper and Cameron then gestured toward the screen. "You ask me, the network they've been building to harvest our thoughts is finished."

He squatted in front of Piper. "So tell me, Piper, your mind is waking back up, isn't it?"

Piper nodded.

"It's about to start, isn't it?"

Cameron looked from Charlie to Benjamin, from Benjamin to Charlie. There was something here they hadn't explained. Some small detail withheld, while the past three months had ticked by, while the network of stones and nodes and brains had been stitching loose ends, inching toward completion.

"What? What's about to start?"

Cameron was asking Charlie or Benjamin, but Piper answered.

She looked up. Toward the lab's ceiling. Toward the ship hovering above.

"I can hear Meyer," she said, as if connecting pieces of a puzzle that had, until now, refused solving. "I can hear him in the ship, wanting to come home."

Chapter Forty-Three

TREVOR WAS ASLEEP, dreaming about bowling with Christopher in a non-apocalyptic world. Turns out that Christopher — in dreams anyway — liked the same kind of nachos as Trevor, like they made at the Brunswick Lanes alley, where they squirted that overly tangy sour cream that squeezed from the machine in a star. He and Christopher both had dates. Trevor's was Piper. She kept sitting on his lap between frames. Christopher's date was some blonde named Candace. She had a giant wart on her hand, and a large part of the dream seemed to center on Trevor's indecision about whether or not to point the wart out to Christopher. But he was also on his way to a 300 game, so …

"Trevor."

"Mmm."

"*Trevor.*"

"Mmm!"

His eyes came open. He rolled on the cot, annoyed at being yanked from the dream, and found himself staring up at his mother. Lila's cot was empty. Heather was on her knees at the cot's side, her hair a black bird's nest.

"What?"

"You need to tell me — what have Christopher, Dan, and Terrence been talking about, for our 'long-term plan'?"

Trevor wondered if he was still dreaming. His head felt like it weighed ten thousand pounds, and here was Mom, asking him about planning. Was she tired of being a comedian, planning a change to goal-oriented motivational speaking if the aliens ever left Earth and let the planet get back to business? *Long-term plan?* In the dark, middle-of-the-night room, her words barely made sense.

"What do you mean?"

"You know what I mean!"

His mom seemed to realize her mistake — her voice too loud and tremulous in the quiet bunker, so she looked nervously side to side and smoothed her hair with one hand, the other playing with the neckline of her nightshirt as if it needed something to do. Her eyes were too wide, missing their usual insults. Without her caustic manner, she seemed like another person, soft like a crab with no shell. Trevor felt embarrassed, as if seeing her naked.

Then, whispering a little, closer to her normal voice: "You're one of the guys. You hang out with them all the time. They have a plan, right? We've been here six months. We can't be planning to stay forever." She laughed, and it sounded off-kilter. "God, we *really* can't be planning that." Eyes darting. "When they went up that one time. When they brought back video of the big rocks around the house. They were planning something then, weren't they?"

Trevor watched his mother, unsure. Dan and Terrence were sticking to their story: they'd gone up for recon and to plant something called "sonic whistles" among the tents to drive the topsiders away — devices that Trevor had never heard of and was pretty sure didn't exist. Sonic whistles sounded like an overly convenient, artificially humane solution to the pressing need to clear space on the lawn so they could breathe below. They sounded like something people might make up to tell other folks who couldn't handle harsh realities, like how parents told children their dead pets had gone to live on a farm.

He'd told Christopher to stop bullshitting him, and Christopher had admitted they'd taken explosives. They'd only managed to plant one, and blowing it now would only hurt people and possibly enrage the alien ship that had killed Vincent.

"They were going to plant sonic whistles. To scare those people away."

"Don't bullshit me, Trevor. This is important."

"I'm not … I'm telling you the truth, Mom."

"Could you find out? Could you find out what they were really doing?"

"They weren't doing anything, M—"

She shook him by his shoulders, her mouth twisting. "Stop it! This is important!"

Her face returned to normal almost immediately, but for a moment she'd been transparent. Trevor had been worrying about his mom for a while as her habits and moods shifted and changed. This midnight encounter, with only a small, glowing night light to dispel the shadows, was only confirming the new oddity. They'd been down here too long. Trevor had found new friends and fared well, he thought, but Lila was moody and strange, Raj followed her like a servant or minion, and their mother had become … well … *this*.

"Okay, okay. They were … don't be mad."

"I won't be mad. I promise."

"Christopher says they were going to use some of Dad's stash to … well … level the house."

"His stash?"

"Some of that military stuff. Bombs, pretty much."

"Bombs?"

"Explosives? I saw a crate in there once when I was nosing around. The plastic stuff."

"*Plastic explosive?* He had plastic fucking—"

Trevor shrugged, now sitting up. "You know Dad. You saw the gas masks. And there's Uzis in there too, all sorts of stuff."

It was really no big deal. Trevor was used to certain necessities of living in the New World. Vincent was dead, Morgan Matthews's brains had stained the living room, and a bunch of people had been fried topside by the alien ships. They'd lived through a riot on the way to Vail and cleared a nest of bad guys from the house before getting inside. Things were different now.

She took Trevor by the upper arms, her face serious.

"This is very important, Trevor: how close is your sister with Christopher?"

Trevor blinked. It was the last question he would have expected. The way Heather was now, he thought she'd been about to ask for a weapon to do something stupid — in which case it would be Trevor's grim duty to rat her out to Terrence, who kept the arsenal's key. But she'd turned on a dime, now asking about her daughter's social life.

"Christopher?"

"They seem to hang out. Like the two of you do. Are they close?"

Trevor knew more about that than he should, too. As much as he didn't want to hear about his sister's sex life, it *did* seem to be part of the bro code to swap tales about girlfriends, and Lila just so happened to be both. Trevor hadn't told Christopher who he had the hots for, of course, and had instead openly pined for celebrities amid the guy talk. But he knew what Christopher and Lila had been up to behind Raj's back. It made being around Raj uncomfortable. And honestly, it had also greatly changed Trevor's opinion of Lila. She'd been nicer to Raj than ever since the botched topside mission, and they'd been together as much recently as they'd been before everything started. In Trevor's opinion, Lila should break things off with Raj, or Christopher. But she'd been playing both. And according to Christopher, she was totally into him, and they did all sorts of dirty stuff when they could find a place and a time and somehow get away with it. Lila acted differently, but of course she would, considering all she had to hide.

"I dunno. They get along."

"Do you think she could convince Christopher to do something crazy?"

According to Christopher, he'd definitely nudged *her* into some crazy stuff.

"Crazy like what?"

"Like with the explosives!"

Trevor cocked his head, not understanding.

Heather ran a hand over her hair, looked around the quiet room and especially at Lila's empty cot, then whispered to Trevor.

"Can you keep a secret?"

"Sure."

"I need your help, Trev. You're with me, right? Because you're my boy."

"Of course."

"Your sister isn't right, Trevor. She's ..." His mother sighed then tapped the side of her head with a finger. "It's not her fault. She's pregnant, so she's got the hormones. And living down here is stressing us all. Especially since

…" Her eyes trailed upward, and Trevor assumed she was imagining the ships. "Look. I have to tell you something."

"Okay."

"She thinks her baby is talking to her."

"She *what?*"

Heather nodded, her eyes serious. "She told me. Lila says she's been seeing and hearing things for almost the whole time we've been here. She says she knew about that Morgan guy before they all came. Didn't know the others were against him, of course, but she knew about him. She's told me a bunch of stuff she thinks happened with Piper and Cameron—"

"Are Piper and Cameron okay?" Trevor blurted.

"She's *crazy*, Trevor." She patted his arm, dismissing the question. "Well, that's not fair. She's … *troubled*. And she's my daughter, and I love her with all my heart. But something's wrong, Trev, and we both need to keep that in mind. Can you do that?"

"Um … sure."

"But I'm worried. Your sister seems sure that there's something wrong with this place. With where we are now. It's a 'power source' or something. But she's convinced — and I do mean *convinced* — that the baby (which she says is 'still hooked into the universal mind'; those were the words she used) is telling her to *cut off* that power source. To 'plug the hole' in some way. And I'm worried that if she has Christopher's ear, and if there are explosives, that …" She trailed off, but Trevor understood plenty.

He didn't know what to say about any of this. Lila had definitely acted moodier and more distant as her belly swelled. She was hooking up with two guys at once, for shit's sake — inside a closed ecosystem populated by seven people total. That alone seemed suicidal.

But explosives? Destroying the bunker? To Trevor, that

seemed a bit much. For one, everything was locked down. Terrence had even jury-rigged the arsenal, much like the kitchen door, so nobody was getting in without permission — a sensible precaution, given how much nerves had thinned. And second, Trevor just didn't think Lila was that far gone. She'd seemed depressed if anything. He'd found her bleak, not nuts. And while she'd admitted to hearing and imagining things, Trevor had a hell of a time believing that she could possibly think her *baby* was talking to her.

"I'm sure it'll be fine, Mom."

Heather watched Trevor for a wary second then grabbed his arm and dragged him out of the room. His feet fought for purchase, baffled at his mother's freakish strength. She'd never been large and recently had looked downright sinewy. But still, Trevor took a few uncertain seconds to gather his balance, sure that if he fell, she'd simply drag him.

They went through the living room, finding it empty. The bunker had fallen more somber since Vincent's body stayed upstairs — not because he'd been the life of the party, but because the stakes were so suddenly real.

Lila was nowhere to be seen. In with Raj or Christopher, the flip of a coin.

She dragged him through the main room, toward the area housing the dead generator. It was a somewhat concealed door, obvious only from the short end of the large room. Trevor had mostly forgotten it, seeing as nothing in there — from generator to batteries — worked. If the wind turbine and solar panels went dead now, they'd be in the dark.

She let him open the door then pulled a flashlight from a shelf and clicked it on. It wasn't burned, so someone had placed it in here after the fire. The light speared a second, smaller door at the chamber's far end that Trevor had never seen. His mother squeezed behind the generator to reach it.

Trevor did the same. The living room door closed behind them, and all the little noises — the incidental clicks of electronics, Dan's snoring, the tick of the bunker's single manual clock — fell silent. He'd never realized the door was as thick as it was, and as sound-proof — but then, with a generator that only seemed prudent.

Once through the second door, Trevor heard a new sound: a trickling, like distant water.

Heather trained the beam on the concrete floor. In the middle, a tiny pit had been chiseled with some sort of tool. At the bottom of the small funnel-shaped pit was a tiny black hole, as if the concrete excavation had finally punched all the way through. That, Trevor thought, was where the water sounds were coming from.

The flashlight clicked off. In the blackness, Heather said, "Look down."

Trevor did. Now that the lights were off, he could see a tiny and extremely dim amber glow rising from the hole.

He knelt. Listened. Then he put his eye near the hole — not against it; that felt somehow wrong — and tried to see what the glow was coming from. He caught a vague motion that might have been water before looking up.

The flashlight clicked on.

"There's something down there," she said. "And what-ever it is, Lila seems to be convinced we need to destroy it."

Trevor stood, looking down, wiping at his face. How long must it have taken to chisel a hole in solid concrete? Even working behind two thick doors, it couldn't be done in the middle of the day or you'd be seen. It would have taken nights and nights and nights of work. Work done in the quiet dark, slaving away a grain of rock at a time. The thought made him cold.

"Lila did this all by herself?"

She laughed. "Oh, no, honey. I did it."

Trevor met his mother's eyes: pits of shadow in the gloom.

"I had to. Because whatever's down there, that's what your father said we must protect."

Chapter Forty-Four

THERE WAS a knock on the door, despite the late hour.

Cameron looked up to see Benjamin with Charlie behind him. "Yes?"

"Piper here?"

"She gets tired after sunset. She's back at the house, probably asleep."

"You let her cross the lawn alone in the dark?"

Cameron shrugged. They'd ridden horses 250 miles and slept in the woods for a week. A spooky Utah ranch had nothing on Piper.

"She'll be fine."

Benjamin entered the room Cameron had co-opted as his occasional office, pulled out a wooden chair, and sat on it backward in front of Cameron. Charlie stood like a coat rack.

"Cam, for years, this was one of contemporary Earth's most paranormally active spots. Probably a place of experimentation — the way someone out there kept tormenting that poor family, what with the animal mutilations and psychic phenomena. You know there was a time they went away for five minutes and came back to find their two prize bulls locked in a cattle trailer?"

"Seems a good place for bulls."

"Not together. They'd just about torn each other apart. The door was so dented they had to pry it open, and the bulls damned near gored them sprinting out. Stuff like that happened all the time. It's a mistake to be complacent."

"Piper is—" He stopped then keyed on something else his father had said. "You don't think it's a place of experimentation anymore?"

Charlie, still standing, said, "So it's a coincidence that one of the motherships stopped exactly over our lab?"

Benjamin looked up. "Hell, Charlie, sit down. You know I hate it when you fail to get social cues."

Charlie pulled out the room's last chair and sat as if posing for an 1800s photograph.

"Until the Verdine family agreed to sell the property, we were limited in how much we could know, based mostly on anecdotal reports and the investigations of — honestly — a lot of weirdos. And that's coming from *me*."

He smiled, proving he wasn't too good for self-effacement.

"But once we were able to poke around," he went on, "we realized what we'd already sort of expected was true."

"There's a money pit here," Charlie said.

Cameron looked from one man to the other, not understanding.

"In the 1700s," Benjamin said, "some kids in Nova Scotia headed out to this little unoccupied spot in the middle of nowhere called Oak Island because they'd seen some mysterious green lights dancing around its shores. Once there, they discovered a curious indentation in the ground and began to dig, excavating what seemed to have caved in. They found a few things that were rather strange, like a mat made of coconut fiber, and I think we all know that was an odd find for Nova Scotia in the eighteenth century. But the pit itself was much more interesting: a giant layer cake, with oak planks made into platforms every ten feet. Between the platforms were flagstones, foreign to the island, just like the coconuts."

"Okay," said Cameron, unsure what any of this had to do with Utah.

"They only went down thirty feet after a lot of digging, but over the years other people got curious about the weird pit on Oak Island. People who threw a lot of money into that pit, hoping to dig deeper. Names like John Wayne and Franklin D. Roosevelt. Layering continued the deeper they dug, with these wood platforms every ten feet, down to at least two hundred feet."

"At least?"

Charlie ticked his head toward Cameron. "Nobody's made it to the bottom."

"Nobody?"

Benjamin shrugged. "They've tried and tried. Six people have died over the years. Excavations have come from the top, drilled in from the sides. They've tried to drop cameras. Nothing works."

"It keeps flooding," Charlie explained, picking up a marker from a dry-erase board and sketching a series of lines. "Someone built a rather ingenious hydraulic system under Oak Island to booby-trap what everyone assumes is some sort of a vault."

Charlie sketched a crudely oval shape to indicate the island as seen from above, drawing arrows at three points around its periphery.

"At one point, treasure hunters poured red paint down the shaft and it came out from at least three vents around the island. It's a puzzle box, and nobody knows where all of the canals and inflows are. They only know that every time someone tries to excavate, it floods and collapses."

"There are all sorts of theories as to what's down there," Benjamin said. "My favorites are crown jewels, the original works of Shakespeare, and — the granddaddy of them all — the Ark of the Covenant. I started having my doubts when, in just the past few years, more pits were discovered. Not at the 'brain' points I was showing you earlier, like Vail and Giza, but at places like Oak Island and … well … Moab, Utah, at the most haunted place in North America. Though sadly, nobody credits us with that title." Again, he smiled.

"What does this have to do with—"

"Nothing. You asked." Cameron pointed at the ceiling. "But like Charlie was saying — at least I *think* it's what he was saying; he's such a complex personality …" They both looked over at Charlie, his bug eyes staring at Benjamin from beneath what looked like an Amish haircut, his hands flat on his knees, his slacks pressed, and his shirt buttoned to the top. " … we didn't get lucky with this lab. We bought the property and built here because we assumed that when contact was made, the ships would come to places like this first. Places with 'money pits.'"

"Why?"

"To refuel, we think. Or maybe to *recharge*. Our working theory is that for short-range travel, like from Jupiter—"

Cameron laughed.

"Well, that *is* short-range. Sub-relativistic speeds, as opposed to …" Cameron looked at Charlie. "I could really go down a dozen rabbit holes. I guess I should save that bit for later."

"You could." Charlie clearly couldn't care less.

"For short-range travel, we assume they're firing on

stored hydrogen, which they may be able to skim from atmospheres or from what now seem to be possible 'hydrogen rivers' in space. But today there are motherships parked over places like Oak Island and here, with ion trails between the spheres and these old pits. We assume that means the pits have opened, but given the way ships have reacted to tampering in the past, I'm not exactly dying to walk over and see."

"This place is a gas station for them," Charlie said. "Once we figured that out, it made sense that they'd come to these places rather than their old points of contact."

"What do you mean?" Cameron asked.

Benjamin sighed then stood and turned the chair around so he could again sit with his hands atop his knees.

"Cameron, I know you never really believed and—"

"I started believing when ships came from the sky. I was wrong."

There was more, too. Cameron wasn't just *wrong*; he was *sorry. Unbelievably* sorry. Resentment had dogged him between leaving home and hearing the news from Astral. Regret and guilt had been his cancer since. He'd been able to relax a bit after completing Benjamin's errand, gathering enough information (and one helpful wife) to fill out his profile on Meyer Dempsey and, it seemed, help articulate a rather grand theory. But he hadn't said enough yet that he was sorry for all the past wrongs, and until Cameron could summon the nerve to do so, the wound would stay open.

"Then you remember what we saw. All the sites we visited."

Cameron did. Of the nine highly networked spots Benjamin had shown them on his newly complete map of stones — the nine spots where, Benjamin seemed to think, human thoughts were being collected and reported —

Cameron and Benjamin had visited eight together. Vail had been the only one missed: the sole spot about which Ancient Astronauts theorists knew nothing. There were no pyramids at Vail, no Mayan temples, no buried cities, no ancient stone megalithic structures. But Meyer, it seemed, was one of The Nine, and Vail somehow one of the sacred places.

"I remember."

"All are places where extraterrestrials have visited in the past. All places where, it stands to reason, they will contact us again. You know I've been waiting for this," Benjamin twirled his fingers in the air, presumably indicating the whole of the alien ships' occupation, "for my entire life. But the problem is that even as much as I've been waiting, there's a lot to fear."

"Fear?" Cameron knew fear well, as did everyone these days. But his father wasn't afraid of the ships or the aliens, even after what they'd done to Moscow and what Dan had said they'd done to some of the campers at Vail ... and to Vincent. That could all be a misunderstanding, Benjamin seemed to think — same for all the alien abductions in the past, slaughtered animals, reports of rectal probings. For Benjamin to speak of fear was deeper somehow — more chilling than another man's terror.

"I think we're facing a test, and I'm optimistic in spite of everything — I want you to know that. But our past, thus far, is definitely against us." Benjamin shifted, looked at Charlie, and continued. "Some of this is stated by theory, and some is new information, but it's clear that throughout history, alien visitors have contacted humanity. It's equally clear that those encounters have all ended with utter destruction. Floods. Descriptions in the *Bhagavad Gita* and other ancient texts of what sounds suspiciously like a nuclear holocaust."

Cameron's eyes flicked toward the door, toward the exit, toward where Piper had gone alone. He was being ridiculous, but he suddenly wanted her here with him after all.

"Throughout history, they've always contacted us," Benjamin said, leaning forward. "But as far as the records show, 'contact' has always been phase one."

Cameron swallowed. "What's phase two?"

Charlie answered. "*Extermination.*"

Chapter Forty-Five

THE VOICE behind Lila made her jump.

"*What are you doing?*" it hissed.

She spun and grabbed a flashlight so she wouldn't need to turn on the overheads, but halfway across the living room realized turning on the beam would give her away. She kept it off but handy, turning to face her inquisitor.

A strong hand caught Lila's wrist, another pulled the heavy flashlight from her unprotesting grip. She'd whacked the man with her big belly anyway, and braced to see if the fetus might scream from inside, yelling at her to watch where the fuck she was swinging that thing. But it didn't work that way, and she was still present-minded enough to know better.

Lila blinked in the dark, her way lit only by the small glowing night lights. She assumed it was Raj, her heartbeat ready to recede. The heavy door to the generator room had swung shut behind her mother and brother, and she doubted they'd hear her now. Lila had thought she'd managed to extricate herself from bed without waking Raj despite her wide load, but apparently not.

But it was Christopher — she could see his black goatee in the room's scant light, his olive skin several shades lighter than Raj's mahogany complexion.

"Easy, Jesus. You about brained me with this thing." He clicked on the light. Lila grabbed for it in a tangle of hands and arms, covering the lens before killing it.

"*Shh!*"

"What are we shushing for?" He looked around the dark room. "And what the hell are you doing out here with the lights off? The bathroom is that way."

Lila pointed at the generator room. "My mom and Trevor are in there."

"Why?"

Lila shook her head. It was tricky to explain. She didn't precisely think her mother was losing her mind, but if she told Christopher what Heather had told Lila, *Christopher* would think she was. Mom had told her she thought something was under the bunker — a system of curious underground canals that the builders had encountered and warned her father about but that he'd ignored — and Lila hadn't been shocked to learn that she'd been curious enough to scratch her itch by digging in concrete. The same itch had been within Lila for nearly half a year, though her source hadn't been clever enough to suggest a way to verify or deny what she felt. It sounded as if Mom had a direct line to Dad, and that wasn't fair. Lila's ... *intuition?* Was that what it was? It seemed to be filtered through her mind and preconceptions, perhaps because the baby didn't yet have a mind of its own.

That made sense. It would be crazy to assume a fetus could be logical. Believing something like that would mean she was nuts.

"They just are."

"It's all burned."

Lila snapped, still whispering, now dragging Christopher into the kitchen nook for a semblance of privacy. "I know it's burned! You did that when you invited yourself in here!"

He raised his hands, surrendering. "Okay, just saying." His eyes ticked toward the open door to Heather's bedroom, which also happened to be Lila's. "Hey. How long do you think they'll be in there?"

"Why?"

He shrugged.

"I told you. We're *over*."

"Then why did I take a shower with you the other day?"

"Because you barged in."

"And you kicked me out, right? You resisted when I—"

"Not now, Christopher."

The topic broached, he didn't want to let it go. She'd successfully deflected him for weeks, failing to deny him nearly as well when he was less conversational. Lila hated herself for it, but had to admit she rather enjoyed the way he was aroused by her changing body rather than being repulsed. Raj had put the baby in there, but seemed to be going through the motions, working around her belly when they could scrape a moment alone in the middle of the night. He was *tolerating* it. Lila supposed she was less than insistent with Christopher because he seemed to enjoy her anyway. And because she wasn't strong enough — too guilty about deeds already done — to take a stand.

"Why *not* now? It's quiet. You're up. I'm up."

"Why *are* you up?"

"Because you're up."

"I was totally quiet."

"Well," he admitted, "I know you usually get up around this time to pee. So I was, um, kind of waiting."

"You were watching Raj's door, just waiting?"

"Do you have sex with him in there? With Dan right there in the cot?"

"None of your business."

"Just sleeping together, huh. Literally?"

He was trying to wrap his hands around Lila's waist, below her bulge. When she rebuffed him, hands went higher, suspiciously near her enlarging boobs. He liked those, too.

"Get off! They could come out any minute!"

"Who?"

"My mom and Trevor. Who do you think I was talking about?"

"Dunno. Terrence? Dan?"

Lila shook her head. Christopher wasn't concerned about what was going on in the generator room at all. He was only thinking of Lila, as always. If she let him — and she had before, though it had been a terrible idea and she'd regretted it immediately, even during — he'd bend her over the table right now. Breakfast the next day, sitting with Raj and wondering if she'd left tit impressions in the butter dish, had been uncomfortable.

"Let's talk about us, Li."

"Are you kidding me?"

"No, I'm not kidding. You won't talk to me about it any other time. You say we're through, but then every time I come to you …"

He didn't need to finish the sentence. Lila could provide her own endings.

… you do it with a look of guilt on your face because that ship has already sailed. You do it because your hormones leave you wanting more than Raj is providing. You do it because you're too weak to resist. You do it because you're convinced that if you don't *do it,* I'll tell Raj

what's going on, and has been for months without you stopping it, despite the pretense that you want to.

"*Shh!*"

"I've had a long day, Lila."

"*Shh,* Christopher!"

"A long day protecting everyone here."

"I'm not going to have sex with you. I'm with *Raj*, do you hear me?"

"Hmm. And yet here we are."

"Because you were stalking me!"

"*Protecting* you."

"You're living underground, same as the rest of us."

"You didn't think that when I stepped up and took care of Morgan for you."

Lila pushed past him. She wanted to get away, without being seen. Her mother and Trevor really *could* come out any second, and Lila didn't want her mother to know she was onto her. They'd acted casual when they'd realized they'd had the same visions but different ideas of what to do. Lila knew that they had to destroy whatever was below her father's "spiritual place." But Heather, who claimed to be in communication with Dad (in dreams; how crazy was that?), said that his order was to *protect* the Axis, not harm it.

Protect it like the aliens *want to protect it?* Lila had said, keeping her voice calm, hiding her emotion.

Protect it like your father *wants it protected*, her mother corrected.

"Where are you going?" Christopher whisper-demanded, following Lila, at least catching on and keeping his voice low.

"To my room!"

"*My* room is over there."

Lila rolled her eyes, knowing he wouldn't see.

Christopher suddenly caught her arm, turned Lila around, and kissed her. It would have been a sweet kiss if it had come at an appropriate time, if she weren't scared shitless, and if his affections hadn't evoked both "lustfully desired" and "desperately unwanted" in Lila for a while now.

She pushed him away. He looked wounded.

"What?"

"You asshole. Are you really this dense?" Again, Lila pointed toward the closed generator room door. "Do you know what they're doing in there? They're conspiring. Planning against us. It was bad enough when it was just her. Just my mom. But now she has *Trevor*, too!"

"I can talk to Trevor." Christopher shrugged.

She paused. That was true. Trevor and Christopher were tight. It was usually infuriating because that gave Lila one less person (her brother) to confide in. But it could be an asset.

"That's a good idea."

Lila dragged Christopher into her room and closed the door most of the way — just ajar enough to peek through. If she saw them coming, she could still rush Christopher through the bathroom. He'd need to sneak by Terrence to get through to the living room, but that was better than being caught.

Christopher looked excited. She'd have to walk a fine line. If he came at her, Lila doubted she'd be able to resist — for about a dozen reasons, tinged with a dozen emotions.

"Talk to Trevor. Tell him that whatever my mom told him, it's wrong."

"What did he tell her?"

Lila waved it away. Time was limited, and that was

another day's discussion. "Tell him that you agree with me."

"About what?"

"Chris," she said. "Have you seen anything around here? Heard anything?"

"Like what?"

"Have you had dreams?"

He reached for her. "*Dirty* dreams."

"Not like that. Dreams of a … a pit. Something below us." Lila inhaled, held it, exhaled. Christopher followed her like a puppy when he thought she might be willing to pay him attention then grew frosty and even slightly frightening when she turned a cold shoulder. If she could keep things friendly, he'd at least listen to anything.

"Dreams that there's something here," she continued carefully, now taking Christopher's hands, "that the aliens want to keep safe." Lila sighed again, steeling her courage to convey the latest impression she'd been funneled from whatever psychic well was out there to be sampled by the life inside her. "Something that they left behind the last time they were here. Something I think they need to plug into, as the next phase of their plan."

"The *aliens?*"

"Yes, Chris." Rolling her thumbs softly over the backs of his strong hands.

"How could you possibly know their plans?"

"I just do."

He watched her for a long moment. Lila kept her eyes on his, feigning vague affection, hoping with all her heart that her mother and brother wouldn't choose this time to emerge, to approach the bedroom and break this vital moment.

"Okay," he said. "I trust you."

"Do you think if we talked to Terrence, and carefully

explained things, with you being your charming and convincing best, that he might be willing to help us?"

"I guess that depends on what we're trying to convince him to help us do."

Us. He'd said *us* and *we.* Lila exhaled a little; the ball was halfway there.

"But we'll try."

"Of course. Whatever you think is best." Christopher's hand went to her belly and rubbed it softly through her shirt. Lila leapt at his touch and felt the baby leap. "Whatever's best for *us.*"

"Good."

"What do we need to do?"

Lila told him.

Chapter Forty-Six

"CAMERON."

Cameron took his time looking up. It had been late when he'd spoken with Benjamin and Charlie the first time, and was later now. He hadn't cared for Charlie's declaration about humanity's record with extraterrestrials according to historical evidence, so he'd spent an hour after the conversation browsing the lab's records, spooling out one theory after another. It was just as crazy as he remembered it being as a kid, with plenty of fresh insanity added to the databanks since.

The evidence made him feel worse. They'd been here before, all right. They'd left people behind as prophets maybe. They'd *certainly* left trinkets — power cells at the bottom of money pits like the one at Moab and bigger, more dangerous trinkets in other money pits elsewhere, like maybe at Vail. Nobody knew exactly what had happened thousands and thousands of years ago, of course. But the ships were above now, and ashes were there in the historical record. It would be hard to sleep tonight, even with Piper by his side.

He finally heeded the voice and looked up, expecting to see his father. But the strangely quiet summons had come from Charlie instead.

"I thought you were Benjamin."

"I'm Charlie."

He gestured at a chair. "Have a seat."

Charlie sat, looking uncomfortable as usual.

"What's up?"

"Piper."

Cameron felt a moment of alarm. But nothing could be wrong; Benjamin, Charlie, and Cameron had been the only three people in the lab since dusk, and maybe just he and Charlie were here now. Charlie had been working on his enzyme reactions on the platform, not out checking on possible problems with Piper. If bad news had come over the short-range radio, Cameron would have heard it.

"What about her?"

Charlie said, "You came in to tell me something earlier, but your father got distracted. You know how he is."

Cameron laughed quietly. That had been Charlie's version of a joke. Benjamin Bannister had been born with diarrhea mouth. It was what got him into so many places he should've been barred from, but it also meant he seldom reached any point without following numerous rabbit trails first.

"Yeah. I do."

"That's why he asked if Piper was here when we came in."

Cameron waited, but apparently, a response was required before Charlie would move to the next thing. Like interfacing with a robot.

"Okay."

"But I don't think he wanted to tell you anyway. Which is maybe why he didn't."

"Sure."

"But you need to know."

"Okay. Thanks. What?" Cameron didn't care for this preamble. It was giving him time to grow nervous.

"Piper loves Meyer."

"Of … of course she does."

"So when her psychic connection strengthens, she'll want to hear what he says."

"Sure. That makes sense."

"But that means you can't trust her, Cameron."

Cameron blinked. "Why not?"

"You saw the network of magnetized stones. You can see it's basically complete. The aliens aren't like us. They don't want to just barge in because they know how humans are. They can't make contact with us until they know what cards we're holding."

"You mean until they know what we're thinking."

Charlie nodded. "It's a lot easier to play poker when you know what you're facing. Their ships are impervious, and they're in no hurry. Nowhere in the records can we see what looks like a rush. We see planning, plotting, logical thought. They come, they stake their positions, they lay their monoliths. This, with the rows, is the most developed monolithic configuration we've ever seen. In the past, they made a few points to gather what they needed to know, but humanity was simpler then. They could descend from the sky in their chariots and be seen as gods. We're not as naive now. We know what we're facing. We don't think fire is magic. They know we can fight, and they know our nature demands that we will, no matter how they might try to begin discourse. So they can't just open the window and shout hellos. They have to put their hands around our throats first then demand our attention."

Cameron nodded. This was the most he'd ever heard

Charlie speak. Charlie was brilliant but socially retarded. It was almost hypnotic to hear him in his true element.

"To me, these networks seem finished. The complexity is daunting. It means they're serious this time. They intend to act more seriously than they have in the past, and to speak to us — such as they speak, which may well be telepathic — in harsher words. But now that the network is complete, I would assume there is very little keeping this mothership overhead." He glanced upward.

"Where will it go?"

"Vail."

"Why Vail?"

"Because Vail is a brain. Like the other eight spots appear to be brains. If we understand the network at all, the brains will be where thoughts, as an average, presumably, are collected and visible to them. We can already tell something is changing. My spores are germinating. Your psychic phenomena are reawakening. And Piper can hear Meyer."

"And that's bad?"

"Your father and I are of like minds about many things, but we can only make guesses, and about some guesses we are divided. He has always been forgiving, believing that in spite of the aliens' past, this time it will be different. This time, we will make meaningful contact and share information. But I feel different. And for that reason, I believe that contact must be disrupted."

"Disrupted?"

"Piper seems to be forming a connection to Meyer. She will want to trust him, but he can't be trusted. Under different circumstances, The Nine might have been seen as gods. I would guess that instead, they will be seen as the modern *version* of gods."

"What's the modern version of gods?"

"Celebrities," Charlie said.

Cameron laughed hard at that, and the sound was too loud in the otherwise quiet lab. But Charlie's face hadn't changed or broken into a smile.

"You're serious."

Charlie nodded shortly. "They will need human corroborators. When those nine people return, which I believe they logically need to, they will be very popular with the media — the modern version of stone tablets brought down from high mountains, perhaps. But they won't be the people they once were, all of whom were already known, trusted, and liked by the population. When they return, they will be alien mouthpieces. Piper will, as I said, want to believe him, support him, just have him back. Because although we all know she's with you, she *loves* him."

Cameron considered denying, but what was the point? Everyone *did* know. They were barely even trying to keep a secret, and even slept in the same home, away from the others.

"What's this all about?" Cameron asked.

"You need to stay with her," Charlie said. "Very, very close. You probably won't be able to convince her of what I'm saying, but you can still be a counterbalance. Keep this in mind at all times, as you stick to her side like glue: for six months, humanity had cared only about finding the missing. But it is perhaps more appropriate to fear the found."

"You said something about disrupting contact."

"Contact. Then colonization. Maybe a kind of trial. Then if history shows, annihilation."

Cameron swallowed. Charlie's facade showed no fear, but his lack of fear was, in itself, terrifying. The lab was dark and silent beyond their cone of light and prophecy.

"When he returns," Charlie said, "it will logically be at

Vail. We're almost out of time, judging by the change in energy and psychic phenomena."

"So …"

"You need to go back, and be there when it happens."

"And then … ?" Cameron prompted.

His head twitched before Charlie could answer. A flick of movement had caught his eye on the monitor.

Charlie leaned in to see what Cameron was looking at. "Well, that's unexpected."

Cameron barely heard. He was out of his seat, through the office door, sprinting to beat the devil.

Chapter Forty-Seven

PIPER'S EYES OPENED.

Something had changed.

She watched the small ranch house ceiling, seeing the crack where the plaster had split, vividly recalling an emotion that never belonged to her. She remembered the night the crack had formed as if she'd witnessed it, but the sight was like an emotion. She saw both from a distance, fogged with a vague recollection's haze.

A man and a woman, not in the bed she lay in now, but in this spot. A tremor shook the ground. That wasn't unusual; the ground here, on this particular swatch of land, often trembled. The woman whose emotion she was experiencing had felt afraid the first few nights here, seeing the way lights seemed to pass the windows despite there being no roads, noticing the way, when she went to the restroom in the middle of the night, her toothbrush would invert or her hair products would seem to have subtly moved. She'd been afraid the first time she'd encountered what looked like a long, tall, gray stranger at the end of her hallway but seen nothing after she'd shouted, when her eyes had adjusted.

Piper, still in bed, looking up, felt it all.

The woman had been frightened for sure. Even her strong-and-silent rancher husband had seemed obviously shaken. But they'd adjusted. Sometimes, there were great events, like the time they'd come home to find all their cows slaughtered or the time the tractors had vanished then were found months later, buried to their steering wheels in the western field. But most of the time there were gentle tremors, lights that flitted across the sky too quickly to follow, hovering balls of lightning, green ghost lights. A person could get used to anything, and the couple who'd spent so many nights here were used to plenty.

But the night that crack had formed in the plaster, she'd been frightened plenty. There had been a sound like a passing train, close enough to be in the room. Lights had come on so brightly that the current through their filaments had popped in turn, somehow without tripping the breaker. A metal chair had skidded across the room and slammed into her husband's metal foot locker. Her metal jewelry had shot together from across the room into a clump.

Then it had ended, and she'd stared out the window, seeing a glowing light in the distance, coming from the cavern with the stone arch over its top.

Piper swung her feet over the side of the bed. She stood. She walked outside.

The air was cool despite the day's warmth, but Piper barely felt it. She slept in shorts and a tee, and was vaguely aware of gooseflesh blooming on her arms and legs.

She looked up.

The great sphere was above. An iris in the bottom opened, and even though the distance was too great and she knew it couldn't be so, she seemed to see Meyer in a transparent bubble, his arms wide like his smile. He was dressed as she remembered him most: in a suit, with a tie and dress shoes. Not a sensible way to dress for an alien abduction.

But then again, he hadn't really been abducted.

This was his power look. His in-charge look. The way he'd been dressed when she'd first met him, after he'd taken a particular interest in her clothing line, pulling it from crowdfunding consideration and moving it to the pool of candidates worth individual, one-on-one consideration. She'd entered his office and seen him like this, his smile wide and perhaps artificial, his interest in Piper a bit less than professional in a way she hadn't minded then and didn't mind now.

Did he look like a victim? Did he look like a man worth saving? A man who needed his wife to cross hundreds of miles on horseback to rescue? No. Not at all.

Meyer reached for her. The distance was, again, too far. She shouldn't be able to see him clearly but could; she definitely shouldn't be able to touch him. His arm was long; her reach was sure. She raised her hands to him as he came forward, waiting for his embrace, wanting nothing more than to be in his arms, to feel his surety, to be with his

Chapter Forty-Eight

"PIPER! PIPER, GET INSIDE!"

Cameron ran with his throat burning, wondering what he must look like. He hadn't run this fast since high school track, or with this much shameless abandon since much younger than that. His arms were wild, scissoring, cutting the air. His lungs gulped air in giant heaving breaths. His heart was thumping everywhere, too fast, fit to burst. He could feel it in his feet. In his head. And of course in his chest, rattling his ribs like an animal caged.

The ship above had moved just enough to put its titanic belly directly over the open area between ranch house and lab. Piper had come halfway, staring straight ahead, not seeming to notice or hear. The night was dark and moonless, and until the light appeared above, she'd been outside in total darkness. He'd seen her on the monitor, though, visible in the haunting green of infrared. Because of this place's reputation for attracting unwanted attention, neither the ranch house nor the cliff-bunkered lab had been built with exterior lighting. Crossing the space before dawn or after dark required a flashlight. Piper had come out with nothing, yet hadn't tripped or hesitated.

Of course now, with the light of the ship overhead, he could see her perfectly.

"PIPER, LOOK AT ME! WAKE UP! WAKE UP, DAMMIT!"

Cameron couldn't shout much more. His breath was shallow, his lungs working too fast to oxygenate his blood through efficient means. He knew the chemistry. His father had taught it to him one useless afternoon, as he'd tried explaining ways in which alien biology (since they'd clearly seeded life from their own stock) might be similar to their own. Right now, he was burning nothing but sugar. Sugar from his blood. Sugar from glycogen in his muscles. The process, ironically, happened in the absence of oxygen.

"PIPER! PI ... PER!"

She was lit from above, like a starlet standing under a spotlight. A single cone of light, shining down from up high. Light thickened into something almost tangible, seeming to become milky, churning. Her arms rose as if reaching, her head's direction not so much as registering his shouts. Liquid light wrapped and eclipsed her.

He watched her rise upward. Watched the ship's belly close.

With the bright light gone, Cameron found himself blind. There were stars above and weak lights behind, but his eyes had adjusted to the darkness, and for a terrifying moment, he was pumping forward with all his might, unable to see a thing.

His foot struck something hard. He fell. The ground's concussive force was duller than it should have been, as if it had struck everything at once. He rolled, having no idea of his orientation or what he might strike on the rebound.

Cameron finally came to rest with his back flat, one leg

slightly twisted over the other, his face throbbing and feeling somehow broken.

The dark ship above, as if to taunt him, glowed a single ring of blue around its equator.

Then it zipped out of sight, headed east with impossible speed.

Cameron lay on his back on the baked clay, heart in his ears, blood on his face, breath harsh and clawing for purchase.

Piper wasn't the only one who'd regained some of her psychic gifts.

Cameron had caught the final flicker of Piper's thoughts mingled with those of another — someone nearby, aboard the ship.

Meyer. She'd seen Meyer, calling her home.

But he'd heard *his* thoughts too. In addition to Piper's, Cameron had caught a piece of Meyer Dempsey's thoughts in that last moment … or the thoughts of whatever Meyer had become. And Cameron knew.

Charlie emerged from the lab, his feet more hurried than Cameron had ever known them.

"They took her," Cameron gasped, his breath still at a loss, "as bait."

Chapter Forty-Nine

TREVOR WAS EATING Quaker Oats from a bowl. His neck was almost sore from the vulture-like prison posture breakfast seemed to require these days. He'd surely fared better over the last months of confinement than his mother or sister, but Trevor still felt an odd *Shining* vibe. If the bunker wanted to be silent and tomblike forever and ever, every day the same — *fine*. Trevor would eat with his face too close to the bowl, scooping numb spoonfuls of gruel into his mouth like a convict in one of his father's movies, imagining himself in a black stocking cap like the one Christopher sometimes wore, his hands in black wool gloves with cutoff fingers. The gruel was Quaker Oats instead of true porridge, but what the hell. Oats froze well, and he was sick of canned shit.

For the first time, catching his mother watching him eat, Trevor wondered if he was as balanced as he believed.

"You're with me, right? Tell me you understand and are with me." Trevor shoveled oats into his maw, Heather's messy black hair barely visible in his peripheral vision.

At first, he'd eaten his oats with milk and brown sugar.

But the milk came from powder, and lately he couldn't shake the certainty that mice — mice who'd wormed through his father's ultra-secure perimeter, like maybe through the holes blown by his current best friend — had been running through the powder, even though they unfroze it in batches and stored it in sealed containers. Still, a man ate his oats plain. Like a horse.

"I understand."

"And you're with me."

Trevor hadn't slept well at all. He hadn't liked the urgent way his mother had dragged him out of bed, suddenly eager to make sides in a single-digit group. They'd all more or less been getting along. Raj had been a little bitch for a long time, but even he'd stopped complaining. They were all fine. He didn't like the idea of sides, of "being with" anyone if it meant "being against" anyone else. And this was his sister they were talking about. His *pregnant* sister, carrying Trevor's first nephew.

He hadn't liked the way his mother had apparently spent her nights chipping through concrete like a trapped animal chewing at the bars of its cage.

He hadn't liked the strange yellow light barely visible through the hole, or the sound of water.

He hadn't liked the fact that his father, who was a pretty smart guy, had okayed building atop any sort of running water. Was the underground stream new? Had the builders properly diverted it enough to not undermine the foundation? Trevor supposed it was possible. Likely even. Maybe there was water underground everywhere. That's what sump pumps were for, right?

And those were just the *new* things Trevor didn't like. The *new* things among many that kept him awake most of the night after Heather had begun snoring like the demented.

He still didn't like being here, trapped by all the people stupidly camped above, clotting their air intakes like plaque inside a hardening artery.

He still didn't like the way the spheres — ships like the one that might have taken his father — hadn't left them alone since Christopher and the others had tried blowing up the house above. It was as if they knew what was happening and meant to protect the place.

And he really, *really* didn't like the waiting. Because it seemed to Trevor that if the ships really wanted to protect the place, they could just kill off the problematic humans who'd claimed residence inside it. And it seemed that they *could* kill them any time they wanted — just blow a hole through the concrete roof with their death rays then scoop their corpses like seeds from a gourd. What were they waiting for? And what would happen when the wait — *whatever* it was for — had ended?

It was hard to believe what his mother had said, but clearly there was something under the bunker. And while he wasn't sure Lila was nuts enough to be talking to her psychic unborn baby, he did know she'd once had terrible pains and that those had stopped — as if, maybe, something had been desperately trying to get her attention, and finally had it.

"*And you're with me,*" Trevor's mother repeated.

"Fine. I guess."

"Good. Because—"

His mother, judging by black hair moving in the corner of Trevor's eye, seemed to look up, interrupting herself. He didn't want to give her the satisfaction of looking over, so he kept shoveling oats into his mouth, his eyes on the table's center.

Trevor heard Terrence, his voice tentative and wary.

"Christopher? What is that?"

Trevor looked up.

"Christopher? Why do you have that?"

Terrence was referring, apparently, to what looked like a small black tablet in Christopher's hands.

Lila was beside him, one hand on her big belly.

Heather was watching them both, while Lila's eyes, in turn, focused on her mother's.

"Christopher ..."

"I wanted to ask you about this, Terrence," Christopher said, his free hand finding Lila's waist, both of them keeping their distance. "I wanted to get your help, so I think if you just listen, you'll agree with us." The tension in Terrence and in Dan, still in the living room, was obvious, though Trevor hadn't yet figured out why. Both looked like they might be weighing odds. But Christopher and Lila were by themselves in the middle of the combined room, Christopher's thumb hovering above the tablet's surface.

"Agree with you about what, Christopher?"

"I figured if you *didn't* understand and agree, there wouldn't be another chance. So there was really no choice. This is what's best for everyone. But not everyone will agree right away." His eyes flicked toward Heather, who was still locking eyes with Lila.

"Just set it down. Just put it down, and I'll listen to your ... your *plan*. Okay?"

"We can't stay here." He was looking around the room, addressing them all. "I know this might sound kind of crazy, but ..." He looked at Lila for help.

Lila had looked self-assured while watching her mother. Now, facing everyone — including Raj, who looked wounded that she was doing whatever this was with Christopher rather than him — she seemed far less sure. Lila looked like a girl asked to sing in front of a crowd, suddenly uncertain about the voice she'd once thought so fabulous.

"Terrence," she began, seeming to find a loophole. "Remember how you felt after finding those rocks outside?"

"Surprised." Terrence removed his sunglasses and poked them into what was becoming a large, untidy afro.

"No, I mean … we could see it on the video. Or, I guess, since you were wearing the camera, maybe we could *hear* it. In your voice. Your mind kind of opened up, didn't it?"

"I don't know what you mean."

Christopher took over. "Come on, Terrence. We all saw it. You lit up like a Christmas tree. Then for days afterward you were acting like you'd intercepted the secrets of the universe. Don't pretend you didn't."

"Maybe."

"Well, I think the stones must be doing something to me. Or to …" Lila looked down, but Trevor thought he could pinpoint the second she decided not to attribute anything to her unborn baby, knowing how nuts it would sound. "To me," she repeated. "And I can kind of see some things. Or hear them, or whatever. And I know that … that …"

"You didn't even go outside, Lila." Terrence had his palm out, presumably asking for Christopher to hand over the tablet. Trevor still wasn't sure exactly what it was, but he could see the way Dan was looking, too.

"It doesn't matter. I can tell the difference between normal and … *enhanced* thoughts."

Terrence turned his outstretched hand into a pacifying, palms-forward gesture then leaned against the kitchen table.

"Okay. What do you think you know?"

Heather stood, apparently unwilling to let Lila hog the floor.

"I know it too," she said.

Terrence's eyes ticked toward Heather. So, Trevor noticed, did Christopher's. If the thing in Christopher's hand was dangerous, someone on the ball could have easily snatched it. Trevor almost wanted to. He'd thought Christopher was his friend, and yet he hadn't been told about any of this. Somehow he'd ended up shackled to his mother instead. Was it too late to change sides? Maybe he could just stand and join them, as a show of solidarity.

"This place is important to them somehow," Heather went on.

"To who?"

Heather looked up. "Them."

Terrence looked from one woman to the other. "So you've talked. You agree about something."

"Talked, yes," said Heather. "Agreed? No."

Terrence stood fully again, moving slowly. He looked again to each party in turn then held out his hand. "If you all seem to know something, we'll talk. Of course we'll talk. But we've gotta do it rationally. Hand me the controller, Christopher."

Christopher looked like he wanted to obey but shook his head. "If you don't agree with us, we'll have missed our only chance."

"What chance?"

"To destroy it."

"Chris ..."

"We can get out. There's still that one brick we left outside, by the garage. I can blow that one first. That'll create enough of a distraction to get us out without anyone stopping us or trying to get back in. Slam the door behind us. I won't trigger the rest until—"

"Christopher," said Terrence, his voice mostly steady but beginning to hitch with nerves, "tell me you didn't wire up any of the other bricks. Tell me you weren't stupid enough to try and do that by yourself."

"I saw where you stuck the spare key to the weapons closet."

"Chris …"

"And I'm not *stupid*," he said, a tad defensively. "I can stick detonators into bricks of clay."

"It's not that simple. This isn't your grandfather's C-4. It's—"

"I know they're armed." He held up the small tablet. "I did it right. We're still here, aren't we?"

"Where is it, Christopher? Where did you wire the explosives?" Both hands up now, palms out and hoping for peace. Christopher was starting to crack, and Lila had grabbed the back of a chair for stability. She looked like she might cry or pass out. Maybe both.

His eyes ticked toward Trevor and his mother. "In the generator room."

Terrence's eyes flicked toward the closed door.

"I set it right, Terrence. Blast directed straight down, just like you explained outside."

"Christopher, we're inside a concrete block. It's not like outside."

"That's why we're leaving before I blow it."

"We're not leaving," Heather said.

"We're leaving."

"We're *not* leaving." Then, unbelievably, Heather took a step forward.

Lila spoke up. "Mom, I know you think that—"

"*I don't THINK! I KNOW!*"

"You *don't* know, Mom! Just because you're having dreams of Dad doesn't mean the real Dad would—"

"Not 'would'! 'Does'! We shared things. I know goddamned well when it's him I'm talking to rather than just ... just *dreams* ... and—"

"That's such bullshit!" Lila blurted.

"Why haven't the ships broken their way in here and killed us all if you're right, Lila? If they think we're a threat—"

Lila jabbed a finger at Christopher's tablet. "We goddamned well *are* a threat!"

"And you think they don't know that? They're in my head! They're in your head! They're in *Terrence's* head, for shit's sake!" A finger jabbed at Terrence. "You saw what happened when they tried to plant just *one* little explosive outside. What happened, Li? The ship showed up and killed Vincent, that's what. Then it killed a bunch of those assholes outside to stomp its foot. But it didn't kill us, did it? And that doesn't sound like a *warning* to you? A threat that you'd make if you didn't want to hurt anyone else but needed to make a point—"

"That ship killed a whole bunch more people! And you want to do what they want? You *don't* want to destroy this thing that's so important to them, and *protect* it instead?"

"But look at *who* they killed! They got Vincent, to make a point. But not Christopher, or Terrence. They left the bunker alone, even though they have to know we're here. Why, Lila? Stop your tantrum for a fucking second, and ask yourself *why*, *why* they'd leave us alone as long as we didn't mess up their plans, and what they might do if you go and do something stupid, if ... if ..."

Heather's head cocked to the side.

"If ..."

Trevor could hear what she was hearing, too. A small noise between his mother's angry words. A tinny, canned sound, coming from one of the control room speakers.

Raj was closest. Ignoring Christopher's tablet-based threat, he looked around the rest of the group then went through the door without a word.

"Raj, get out here right now or I'll … !" Christopher stopped when Raj stuck his head back out, his face puzzled.

"It's Piper," he said. "She's outside, asking to come back in."

Chapter Fifty

Lila looked toward Raj. Christopher looked toward Lila. Terrence looked toward Christopher, and then, in the split second of distraction, kicked hard at his knee.

Christopher crumpled. Despite being the tech wizard and appearing far less impressive than Vincent, Dan, or even Christopher, Terrence must have been trained in combat because his strike was precise, hard, perfect.

Lila gasped. Christopher slid almost sideways, leg buckling, grasping at his knee, face twisting in pain. Lila saw it all. And she saw the tablet seem to leap from his hand, flat like a place setting atop a yanked-away tablecloth.

She tried to grab for it, but it had been in Christopher's other hand. She'd lost her agility to pregnancy and wasn't close. The thing struck one of the kitchen rugs on its corner, and she gasped again, somehow certain that a strike to the trigger would cause the explosives to fire. But as the tablet seemed to bounce and settle on its face, she realized that didn't make sense. Attaching the detonators and programming the trigger had been far simpler than they'd imagined. They didn't need Terrence's help for something so idiot proof.

And of course, idiots dropped things.

Lila tried to dive for the tablet, but Terrence beat her to it, stepping on the thing and pinning it to the floor. He swung back as if to hit her but seemed to reconsider striking a pregnant teenager and reached to help her up instead, still pinning the tablet.

Lila liked Terrence a lot. But stopping whatever evil stuff the aliens had in mind was important enough to risk killing them all, so instead of taking his offered hand, she punched him hard in the groin.

Terrence, unprepared, teetered with abject shock. He didn't fall but did stutter-step, sending the tablet under his foot backward, toward the living room.

Dan watched it skid out of the kitchen and leaped gracelessly over the back of the love seat, landing awkwardly in a heap. Terrence had fallen to one knee, nowhere near it.

Christopher was back on the move. Hobbling, he fell forward. His fingers grazed the tablet's brushed-metal back, but Dan's feet had landed close, and he kicked at it with the backs of his shoes, trying to knock it away from Christopher, toward his hands.

Christopher heaved, got his hand on the tablet. Dan kicked down hard, driving his rubber heel into the back of Christopher's hand.

Lila, still on her knees, could only watch. She stood in slow motion, finding herself beside her mother: the two Dempsey women reunited by turmoil. Raj was to Heather's right, still with his head stuck out of the control room like a groundhog heralding spring's arrival. He seemed torn between the screen that had so recently shocked him and the fighting outside.

Lila felt the ticking clock. Christopher had wired the bombs, placing most of the stash directly above the hole her mother had squirreled in the generator room. Lila had watched with mixed feelings. It was hard to believe that a handful of hours ago, her biggest concern hadn't been the thunderclap they were setting to destroy all her father had built — but was instead her newly implied obligation to Christopher, and what it might mean in her conflicted relationship with Raj.

For a while, Lila could only see bodies and limbs. Her heart hammered under shallow breath as time slowly unfolded. Terrence had kicked the trigger from Christopher's possession maybe twenty or thirty seconds ago, yet it felt like an eternity gone.

Dan reached. Christopher lashed out. Terrence punched Christopher hard on the side, but then Christopher took a page from Lila's book and kneed him hard in the jimmies.

The tablet skidded across the living room's glassy floor and came to rest against a pair of white-soled sneakers.

Trevor stooped and picked up the tablet. Nobody moved.

He turned the tablet over, and Lila could see that the front, made of unbreakable sapphire crystal, was undamaged. The on-screen trigger controls were still active.

Beside Lila, Heather exhaled heavily, sounding relieved that her team had the ball. She looked about to step forward when Trevor said the least likely thing anyone expected.

"Where is she?"

Heather stopped. Then, sounding out of breath despite having barely moved, she said, "Where's who, Trev?"

Trevor ignored his mother and turned to look at Raj, the tablet held firmly in his hands.

"Where is she, Raj?"

It took Raj a moment to understand. Then he blinked, looked over his shoulder, and said, "East. Looks like one of the cameras strapped to a low tree. She's talking right into the mic, which is the only reason we heard her."

"What's she saying?"

"'Let me in.'" Raj recited. He swallowed then added, "'Please.'"

"Let her in."

Raj looked helplessly at Terrence, who was still on the floor, then back up at Trevor.

"Me?"

"Let her in, Raj."

"I can't let her in."

"Do it. Now."

Raj didn't seem to know what to think, but Lila could only hear her father: Meyer Dempsey in Trevor Dempsey's words.

"I … I can't. Only Terrence can …"

Heather took another step, reaching out. Trevor turned away.

"Get back. Everyone just stay where you are."

"Trevor, honey. Why don't you give that to me?"

Trevor shook his head, looking past Raj and into the control room.

"For safekeeping, Trevor. We did it. We stopped them."

Christopher was getting to his feet. He moved to stand beside Lila, limping. The same confused, betrayed expression returned to Raj's dark features as he watched their reunion.

"Trev," said Christopher.

"Shut up."

"I need your help, buddy. We both do."

"Quiet, Christopher."

"That's right." Heather touched Trevor's arm. "Shut your fucking mouth, Christopher."

Trevor ripped his arm away and took a step back. Heather looked momentarily wounded, then hard and jaded.

"Everyone stay away from me. Give me a minute."

Distant and small, Piper's voice cut the silence. Trevor looked toward the control room, but Lila couldn't make out the words.

"We're going to get her."

"Trevor," Heather said, "the bombs."

"I've got it under control."

"Then give that to me."

"No."

Lila met her brother's dark eyes. "I told you about this. Remember? About what I was seeing and hearing?"

"And I told you I hadn't seen or heard shit."

"But you understood. You understood about what I said, about Dad and—"

"*I'm* the one who's talked to your father," Heather said, casting daggers at Lila.

"Terrence," Trevor said.

Terrence looked over.

"Open the front door."

"Can't do that, Trevor."

Trevor raised the tablet. "Do it, or I set off some fireworks."

"Careful, Trevor. You press that, and we're all—"

"Dead?" Trevor laughed. "Maybe. Maybe Lila's right, and we're supposed to stop something. Or maybe Mom's right, and we're supposed to protect it. I wouldn't know. I'm just a dumb kid who's spent half a year living in a hole — something we're clearly not going to be able to just 'go back to' after this little fight. One way or another, I think we're done here. At least some of us are." He looked up, shaking his head. "There are aliens in the sky, and they've surrounded us with big rocks. A bunch of people are camping above us, not even caring that the ships keep coming back and frying a few here and there. I don't know that I want to be in here anymore, and I *know* I want to go outside." He stared directly at Terrence. "Maybe we're already dead, and we just don't know it yet."

His finger shook above the tablet. Lila felt her breath catch, waiting.

"I'm not asking everyone to run out there. Just me. I'll go alone." Trevor moved one hand from the tablet and touched the pistol he'd taken to wearing on his hip in order to, Lila thought, look like a big shot. This time, it had worked out. Terrence and Dan, not cavalier enough to arm themselves indoors, had missed their opportunity to seize control.

"I'm tired of being down here, doing nothing," Trevor said. "*I'm going out there to get her.* I want to do some good for once."

"If I open the door," said Terrence, raising his hands, "all those people up there will come in. They'll see you walk out, and they'll swarm."

Lila flinched as Trevor's finger touched the tablet's screen once, twice, three times.

The entire bunker shook with the force of an explosion. She felt tremors climb the walls, radiate through the floors, run up her legs as if to convey news. Dust sifted down, and she felt her ears assailed, assaulted with concussive noise. Her eyes closed.

Lila was still alive when she opened them. Screaming turmoil erupted above.

Raj's attention seemed split between the group and the

control room behind him — where something terrible had happened at the home's garage end, where a single brick of directional explosive had laid buried for three months.

"There's our distraction." Trevor nodded to Terrence. "Now open the door, before time's up."

Chapter Fifty-One

Raj turned back to the surveillance screens, staring at the explosion's smoking aftermath as the door again clanged shut at the top of the spiral staircase.

He was looking for bodies, sifting feeds from the still working cameras. Trevor's temper tantrum had leveled the entire garage. And while the so-called directional explosives had been true to Terrence's description and gone into the surface structure rather than the bunker, they'd destroyed what was above.

Raj zoomed in, centering on something that seemed to be a severed leg beside a blown-open head.

Of course. The hippies kept coming, drawn by something that Lila and Heather claimed they could feel but that Raj — and everyone else; maybe it was a guy/girl thing — couldn't. So they'd filled both the ground and the house. That's why they'd smoked them out the first time, clearing the home with smoke alarms in order to sneak away. But this time they hadn't made a delicate distraction. This had been a blitzkrieg, equivalent to hitting someone's hand with a hammer to draw attention from pain in their foot. Sure, they'd look away from the kitchen when the garage blew. They'd be plenty distracted searching for gory bits and pieces of widowed wives and orphaned children.

But what Raj had taken for a leg and a head were in reality a rolled-up mat of some kind and the crumpled shade from a shattered lamp.

Lila appeared over his shoulder. She watched the second screen, following the exodus: Trevor in the lead, of course, followed at a respectful distance by Terrence and Christopher. Behind the latter was Lila's mother, surely ranting and shouting about Trevor doing wrong if Raj cranked the volume.

"Where is Piper?"

Raj pointed at one of the minimized thumbnails.

"Is that where they're headed? Toward her?"

Raj spun. He'd been angry, but hearing Lila's voice — the dismissive, by-the-way questions — made him boil.

"This was smart, Lila," he spat.

"What?"

"What the hell is wrong with you? You have a problem, something's bothering you, but instead of talking to me, you wire the fucking place with explosives. Now what are we going to do?" He pointed at the screen. "You ask me, your brother is losing his shit, and he's got the trigger tucked into his belt. We might not even have to wait for him to get stupid. He's being stupid now. The thing has a touchscreen. It's going to rub against his skin and press the wrong button, and then it'll be sayonara to us all."

Lila's face changed. For a fraction of a second, he felt sorry for her. She looked more lost than awful, confused not vindictive. Just like over the past few months she'd seemed more distant than unfaithful, even though sometimes his gut prickled with paranoid instinct. But those were his issues. He knew she'd never cheat, especially now.

"It felt like the only way."

Raj shook his head. "The only way. Great."

"Really, Raj. I don't know how to explain it, but—"

"Then don't try."

Lila seemed to consider apologizing but then wisely decided not to bother. You could say sorry for using someone's toothbrush or forgetting an appointment, sure. But attempting to blow up the house was the kind of thing most couples didn't need to face in even the most tumultuous relationships.

After Lila was silent over his shoulder for a while and he'd pinched in and out looking for bodies in the rubble, he said, "Can you disarm it?"

Raj looked up at Lila. Her lips pressed together.

"Oh, I see. You won't."

"I doubt I could if I wanted. I might blow it trying. Christopher set it up."

Christopher.

"Nice fucking mess. But that's not even the issue, is it? You don't want to disarm it."

"There's something under the bunker, Raj. Something they want. If we let them get it—"

"Save it."

There was another moment of silence. In the background, Raj could hear Dan, the only other person left in the bunker, rattling around.

Lila broke the quiet. "What are you doing?"

"Trying to figure out how many people your brother just killed."

"Oh." A pause. "How many?"

Raj didn't want to admit he hadn't found any yet. Doing so felt like a concession.

"I don't see any bodies," Lila said.

"Maybe it vaporized them."

"It didn't vaporize that end table."

Raj said nothing. Lila's hand extended in his peripheral vision. Without asking, she touched one of the thumbnails to enlarge it. A view of the lake swallowed the screen. A mass of people filled the space in front of the water. Maybe *all* the people, including those who should have been shredded in the explosion with their belongings. The explosion that by all appearances they hadn't even noticed. The group appeared almost hypnotized, staring off into the distance.

"What are they looking at?"

Raj shrugged. The screen didn't show. He only knew that they were looking upward. Probably at another kill-shuttle come to fry whomever Trevor's blast had missed.

"Dunno."

"Look. They're almost to Piper. Why isn't she coming toward the bunker?"

"Probably wants to stay by the camera. She can't know we've even noticed her out there."

They watched her for a second. Raj had turned her volume down. She wasn't saying anything new. Just repeating the same lines over and over, like a robot.

They watched the other thumbnail, showing Trevor's approach.

Raj sat back in the chair and looked up at Lila. She was standing; he was sitting. It hardly felt courteous, seeing as she was pregnant. But then again, she'd also tried to blow them all up without asking his opinion. *The father of her baby.* Talk about a lack of courtesy.

"What are we going to do next, Lila? Did you think of that? Your little coup failed. Trevor isn't stupid. He's not going to just blow the damned thing like you and your buddy were ready to." She seemed to flinch a little at the mention of "your buddy" — something Raj filed away for later consideration. "So what happens when they get Piper and come inside? They'll be able to walk right back in, by the look of it." He clicked through screens, showing empty campsite after empty campsite. The garage bomb hadn't been necessary. Everyone was at the lake, staring off into space like fools.

"So what then, Lila? Do we go back to playing house? You with your hormones and visions, your crazy mother, your homicidal brother, Piper who's been God knows where, Christopher, D—"

"Raj," she said.

Raj shrugged impatiently.

"Raj, look." Lila wasn't shouting or raising her voice. But it was filled with fear. *Deep* fear. Two words dripping in urgent terror.

Raj turned. The lake view was still maximized, but the people no longer appeared to be staring at nothing. There was the bottom of a silver sphere moving slowly overhead, big enough to block the sun.

It wasn't a shuttle. It was one of the motherships.

There was a crackling from below the control panel. It took Raj a moment to locate the source. A static-filled voice gurgled from his communicator watch — the same watch Terrence had once successfully jury-rigged to reach Cameron and Piper while they were on the road. The same blocked communication channel, apparently, that someone on the other end had finally found a way to reactivate.

" ... *trap!*" came Cameron's voice between bursts of interference. " ... Piper ... inside ... *t's a trap!*"

Chapter Fifty-Two

PIPER SEEMED TERRIFIED.

Trevor approached, struck by the change in her manner. It broke his heart. She'd left the bunker upright and strong — as buoyant as a woman could be when her mission was to find her abducted husband and save the world. People seemed to think that Piper's beauty and small size made her fragile. Or maybe it was her giant blue eyes. And because she was usually set beside the dominating Meyer Dempsey, people also thought her weak and servile. But it was not the case. In her element, Piper was capable of being a leader — even a hero, as she'd proved twice already.

But this woman was broken. Not the Piper Trevor remembered at all.

"Hey," he said.

She'd barely noticed him. Now she did. Terrence and Christopher stayed behind at enough of a distance to watch him while remaining wary of his trigger finger. Trevor could still blow the bunker as Lila and Christopher wanted or spare it for his mother (who was bringing up the rear, silent now that he'd glanced back) and Terrence. He was in a deliriously powerful position, able to cast a rather decisive final vote on the issue of "the hole" that may or may not need plugging. But he couldn't appreciate any of that now. Even with his three pursuers at the rear, unarmed so as not to antagonize him into action, he could only focus on Piper.

"Trevor?"

"Where have you been? Where did you come from?"

"Moab. Then somewhere else."

"Where else?"

She blinked. Then she blinked a few more times, looking around as if trying to clear her head. Trevor watched a confused wash of emotions splash her face. In the space of a few seconds, her demeanor changed. Where she'd seemed lost, now she seemed justifiably nervous. Where she'd seemed broken, she now seemed at panic's edge.

"They told me something," she said.

"Who?"

"*He* told me something."

"Who told you something?" Trevor asked. "Cameron?"

"No."

"Where is Cameron?"

"At the ranch."

"*We're* at the ranch. We've been here all along." Trevor looked around, scanning the trees. Where *was* Cameron? Had they walked all the way back? Had something awful happened? Had he been killed, and she'd had to make the last leg alone?

"Not this ranch."

"Which ranch."

"In Utah. In Moab."

"So you made it to Moab? And you did whatever you needed to do?"

"He told me something," she repeated.

"Someone at the lab?"

Piper shook her head, as if unable to remember. The struggle for recall, painted on her pretty features, looked frustrating.

"You, Trevor," she said, blinking harder. "And Lila. Where is Lila?"

"She's in the bunker." He reached for Piper, but she flinched back. "What about us?"

"You're his bloodline."

"Whose?"

"Your father's. And those before him. I'm supposed to … I'm supposed to …"

There was a shout in the distance, coming from behind. Trevor turned at the same time as Christopher, Terrence, and Heather. Lila was running as best she could with her large bouncing stomach, one hand to her abdomen, with Raj close behind, seemingly trying to hold her back. Lila kept shaking him away, pushing him, surging forward. Shouting for Trevor.

"It's a trap! It's a trap! They sent her here as bait! Get back to the—"

There was a tremendous humming from the sky, stopping her. Trevor looked up and saw an enormous alien mothership blur into place overhead. The movement was almost instant. One moment it wasn't there, and the next it was, not braking so much as stopping on a dime, exactly as the shuttle had moved in Terrence's video. Christopher had said it crossed the horizon in less than a second. Trevor hadn't believed it. But seeing the mothership move, he believed it now.

The humming grew. And grew. And *grew*. A physical

presence against Trevor's eardrums. Between him and the ranch, between him and the ship, Trevor watched as the other five clamped their hands to their ears.

There was a crack like lighting, and a beam of light lanced straight down from the bottom of the ship. It struck the remains of Meyer's house, detonating it into splinters and debris. From somewhere far off, beyond the oppressive hum, Trevor heard screaming.

There was no fire or smoke. The home had been smashed as if by a giant hammer. They were slightly up a hill, and Trevor could see the way the enormous beam had punched not just through the home, but through the bunker's top. And then, as if to prove a point, the bunker itself seemed to detonate in a shower of stone. The air grew hot, and a wave almost shoved Trevor to the ground.

The others swayed on their feet as the wave passed. The sound dialed down, moving from the roar of terrible feedback to the electric hum of overhead power lines. Every few seconds, something seemed to crackle, the beam sparking with thin trails of branched lightning.

Trevor followed the line down to the destroyed bunker, counting bodies around him, seeing that Dan was missing, now gone forever.

He looked up at the ship.

"What's it doing?" he asked, now finding himself able to hear.

Behind him, Piper said, "Docking."

Chapter Fifty-Three

PIPER WATCHED the ship slowly lower its enormous belly closer to the ground, feeling a strange mixture of hope and abject terror. There was so much she understood, and so much she couldn't fathom at all.

In front of her, Trevor pulled a small tablet from the back of his pants, where he'd apparently stowed it for safe-keeping, and ran his fingers over its surface, frenzied, breath leaving his lungs as if in flight. The four others behind him (absent the late Vincent and now Dan — where had Dan gone while she was away?) surged forward as Trevor worked, whatever restraint they'd been showing now gone. Piper couldn't make sense of the melee. Terrence, Heather, and Raj seemed to be on one side, but Lila and Christopher seemed to be on the opposite side, actively batting the others away so Trevor could do his work.

"Don't!" Heather shouted.

She reached. Christopher extended an arm and planted an undignified palm in Heather's face, mashing her lips against her gums. She elbowed Christopher aside while Terrence reached and was elbowed in the throat — accidentally, it seemed — by Lila.

Trevor yanked free, darting a few steps toward Piper before managing to mash his finger onto the screen's big red button.

Nothing happened beyond a line of red text in a black bar: an error message in any system.

"The fucking bunker is gone, Trevor!" Terrence shouted, his cool entirely gone. "You can't blow something up when it's *fucking gone!*"

A blur of motion wrapped them from front to back. Piper couldn't tell what had happened until she turned to see several large, spherical shuttles nestled between the trees. She couldn't help but look up. They must have descended from above. They were too big to squeeze between the trees, and would knock them over if they were forced to herd the humans forward.

"What now?" Trevor asked.

Lila nodded toward the waiting mothership. "I think we're supposed to go to it. To the ship."

"No." Christopher shook his head. "No fucking way."

Trevor walked to Christopher then slapped him companionably on the arm. He managed a small smile despite the situation, punctuated by the descending mother sphere's steady electrical hum, and pointed at the shuttles that had descended at their rear.

"You can stay here, I'm sure, but I don't think they'll like it if you do." Trevor walked past Christopher, taking the lead beside his sister, as Lila fell into step beside him.

Bloodline.

Piper didn't recall much from her trip here — or *anything*, really. On one level of her mind, she only remembered falling asleep in Utah then having an extremely vivid dream. There was a break at that point, in the way dreams sometimes splice from one place to another with nothing in between, and next she'd been aware only of the tree and the camera concealed there, along with the desperate need to get inside.

Or, maybe, to make sure Trevor and Lila *weren't* inside.

Because yes, there did seem to be another layer to her thoughts, the more she considered it. Piper assumed from context that her trip must have been made inside the newly arrived mothership. That in itself should have scared her, but it made sense. Of course Meyer was aboard. Of course he'd want to come home. And of course, given Meyer's intense drive to reach this place during the exodus (not to mention his drive to build it in the first place), it made sense in retrospect that this plot of land had turned out to be special. There was something sacred below this mountain — very far down, hidden for an untold length of time — that Meyer wanted. That the aliens wanted. Necessary to end the first phase.

But beneath her (lack of) factual knowledge and suppositions, Piper recalled something further down. Something that felt like collective consciousness. Something that even now felt like a gossamer thread connecting her mind to Lila, and Lila's mind to the new life growing inside her. Connecting them all. But most of all, that thread ran between Lila and Trevor. Between the children and their mother as well, yes, because they were linked by blood.

And to their father.

Get the children out.

Because just as the children had their descendants, Meyer had his.

Duly connected to its source — to the network Benjamin had shown her and Cameron what felt like a thousand years ago — the mothership continued to descend. Beneath it, the blue column of light sparked and hummed. The aggregate thoughts of humanity flowing into the nexus. Into the ship. The ship itself "plugging the hole" as she'd sensed Lila thinking even from a distance — not with debris to destroy it, but like a plug in a socket.

She comprehended without understanding.

She knew that Meyer was aboard but didn't believe she'd seen him or spoken to him or been near him.

She knew that Lila and Trevor mattered. That Meyer mattered. That the other eight human cogs, simultaneously docking at their own nexuses around the world, mattered.

They've been here before.

And something else Benjamin thought, though Piper had no way to know it, other than through intuition and three months' worth of cobbled discussions:

And if we fail, they will be here again.

Piper saw a field filled with fossils. Fossils from the new age, again somehow cast in stone, as it always had been before.

Enormous protrusions emerged from the sphere, like legs from the thorax of an enormous insect. The blue column of energy buoyed the craft as legs descended, finally making tentative contact with the ground. The ship sighed its weight onto them, depressing the turf. Then the ship settled its lowest point into the bunker's indentation, atop the home's shattered foundation, the blue glow now only visible as a halo from beneath.

"Contact," Piper whispered.

Trevor and Lila were ahead of her. Christopher, Raj, and Terrence were behind. Piper looked down when she felt a hand slide into hers, then up at Heather's terrified face.

Piper couldn't help but feel some of Heather's fear. Somehow, she seemed to know that the last time this loop had unfurled, it had all gone wrong — and the time before that, and the time before that.

She stared forward as a door appeared in the ship's belly. Compared to the stadium-sized breadth, the door was insignificant, the curved surface into which it was cut appearing almost flat.

A human shape appeared in the doorway, backlit and visible only in silhouette.

The being came forward, descending an extending ramp. Behind it, more human shapes appeared. The latter were larger than the first. Taller. Broader. A gaggle of gods standing behind a single ordinary man.

Piper stepped forward, moving between Lila and Trevor. She took his hand in hers. His human hand in her human hand, skin to skin.

Behind her, Heather said, "That's not him. That's not the Meyer I know."

But it was the Meyer that *Piper* knew, sure as anything.

She looked up at him. He was waiting for her to speak first — that familiar handsome, cocksure smile on his face. But still Piper couldn't help thinking of the ship that had destroyed Moscow, the footage of menacing spheres on the news, the destruction of the bunker, the story she'd heard about Vincent and the people who'd died with him, burned alive.

The ship's very presence was a menace. The air smelled like fear and death.

"Are they here to wipe us out?" Piper whispered, fear returning despite her relief.

"No," Meyer said, still wearing his maddening smile.

Behind him, the enormous mothership idled and hummed. The large, human-shaped silhouettes waited in the doorway. There were pops and crackles as the ship harvested thoughts from below. Gathering information. Watching them all.

"They're here to *save* us."

Piper wanted very much to believe him.

But she didn't.

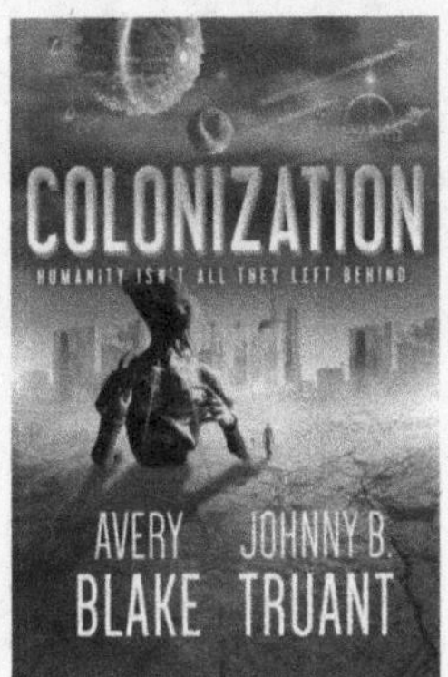

Humanity isn't all they left behind...

Two years later, the world lives in fragile peace. But a clandestine search has begun ... and a clock has started ticking.

Get Colonization today!

A Quick Favor...

If you enjoyed this book, please take a moment to write a short review on your favorite online bookstore so other readers can enjoy it, too.

Thanks so much!
Johnny and Avery

About the Authors

Avery Blake doesn't want you to know where she lives, or what she does. She travels the world, moving from place to place quickly to ensure she can't be tracked. It's safer that way.

When she's not looking over her shoulder, you can find her in the corner of a cafe, facing the exit, typing as fast as she can.

~

Johnny B. Truant is co-owner of the Sterling & Stone Story Studio, an IP powerhouse focusing on books and adaptations for film and television. It's the best job in the world, and he spends his days creating cool stuff with partners Sean Platt and David W. Wright, as well as more than 20 gifted storytellers.

Johnny is the bestselling author of over 100 books under various pen names, including the Fat Vampire and Invasion series. On the nonfiction side, he's also co-author of the indie publishing mainstay Write. Publish. Repeat. and co-host of the weekly Story Studio Podcast.

Originally from Ohio, Johnny and his family now live in Austin, Texas, where he's finally surrounded by creative types as weird as he is.

The Hidden

The Saved

The Next Evolution

Transition

Convergence

Evolution

Stand-Alone Novels

Analog Heart

Family Royale

Ruthless Positivity

Vicarious Joe

Robot Proletariat Series

En3my

Robot Proletariat

The Infinite Loop

The Hard Reset

Cascade Failure

Reboot

The Invasion Series

Longshot

Invasion

Contact

Colonization

Annihilation

Judgment

Extinction

Resurrection

The Tomorrow Gene Series

Null Identity

The Tomorrow Gene

The Tomorrow Clone

The Eden Experiment

Stand Alone Novels

Pretty Killer

Pattern Black

Burnout

The Target
The Island
Devil May Care